Praise for
ROBERT DUGONI'S
Novels

DAMAGE CONTROL

"Dugoni's second thriller features a dynamite heroine."
—TheMysteryReader.com

"A thrilling reading spree, filled with suspenseful twists
and turns."
—FreshFiction.com

"A highly entertaining suspense thriller that grabs you on
page one and doesn't let go until the end...enjoyable and
highly readable with a fantastic heroine, a dash of para-
normal, a smidgen of romance, and lots of thrills and sur-
prises...Highly recommended!"
—TheRomanceReadersConnection.com

"An emotional journey ripe with the promise of danger."
—WantzUponATime.com

more...

THE JURY MASTER

"John Grisham, move over...a riveting tale of murder, treachery, and skullduggery at the highest levels."

—*Seattle Times*

"Smart and savvy...Combining an astonishingly good plot, perfectly drawn characters, and intensely sharp writing, Robert Dugoni has put the thrills back into the genre."

—Nelson DeMille

"As fast-paced and arguably more extensive than anything Grisham has written in the past few years."

—*Tampa Tribune*

"A thriller of the first order, delivered in high-octane prose...a winner."

—John Lescroart

"Reminiscent of the early John Grisham and should easily find its way onto the bestsellers lists."

—*Library Journal*

"Looking for a distinctive new voice? Robert Dugoni's debut won't soon be forgotten. *The Jury Master* is a confident, complex, expansive thriller—part legal, part political, but always relentlessly paced and exciting."

—Stephen White, *New York Times* bestselling author of *Missing Persons*

"A rapid-fire fictional debut...The action keeps coming."

—*Booklist*

"An exhilarating thriller about heroes who won't take 'no' for an answer—from the government or anyone else. This novel will make you wish you were brave. I could not put it down."

—Tess Gerritsen, *New York Times* bestselling author of *Body Double*

"A writer to watch." —*Kirkus Reviews*

"An exhilarating ride...interesting...a great cast of characters who are sure to capture your interest. Be sure to add this one to your reading list...highly recommended."

—Bestsellersworld.com

"An unusual and gripping thriller." —BookLoons.com

"The finest legal thriller I have read in years. I became immersed in Dugoni's story from page one and quickly grew to care about the characters and what happened to them. The ending had me gasping for air."

—Michael Palmer, *New York Times* bestselling author of *Society*

"Dugoni keeps *The Jury Master* moving quickly...in one book, he can create enough memorable characters and action scenes to fill three. You can't ask for much more than that." —BookReporter.com

"All of Dugoni's characters have a fresh and believable edge, and there is plenty of action in far-flung settings."

—*Publishers Weekly*

ALSO BY ROBERT DUGONI

The Jury Master
The Cyanide Canary

DAMAGE CONTROL

Robert Dugoni

GRAND CENTRAL
PUBLISHING

NEW YORK   BOSTON

This book is a work of fiction. Names, characters, places,
and incidents are the product of the author's imagination
or are used fictitiously. Any resemblance to actual events, locales,
or persons, living or dead, is coincidental.

Grand Central Publishing
Hachette Book Group USA
237 Park Avenue
New York, NY 10017
Visit our Web site at www.HachetteBookGroupUSA.com

Grand Central Publishing is a division of
Hachette Book Group USA, Inc.

The Grand Central Publishing name and logo is a trademark of
Hachette Book Group USA, Inc.

Printed in the United States of America

Originally published in hardcover by Hachette Book Group USA
First Mass Market Edition: February 2008

10 9 8 7 6 5 4 3 2

*For my mother, Patty Dugoni, one of the
thousands of breast cancer victims living today.*

*And for my cousin, Lynn Dugoni,
one who is not.*

＄

Every little girl knows about love.
It is only her capacity to suffer
because of it that increases.
—Françoise Sagan

No man can climb out beyond the
limitations of his own character.
—John Morley

＄

DAMAGE CONTROL

1

〜

Redmond, Washington

Dr. Frank Pilgrim adjusted the flexible lamp clipped to the edge of his cluttered metal desk, but the additional illumination did not keep the typewritten words on the page from blurring. He set his wire-framed glasses above his bushy gray eyebrows and pinched the bridge of his nose. His eyes had reached their limit; they could no longer take the strain of a night reading small print.

Pilgrim glanced across the room, the details a blur. It wasn't too long ago he could watch the television screen atop the military-green filing cabinets without glasses. Now he could barely make out the cabinets, even with prescription help. His cataracts were getting worse. It didn't matter. With all the reality-TV crap being broadcast, he had long since relegated the television to background noise. It kept him company at night. He liked to listen to the Mariner baseball games, though the team continued to disappoint him. At seventy-eight, he didn't have many years left to experience a World Series in Seattle.

The telephone on his desk rang at precisely ten p.m., as it had every night for the past forty-eight years. "I'm just finishing up," he said, speaking into the old-fashioned handset. He rocked in his chair, bumping against floor-to-ceiling shelving cluttered with a lifetime of books and knickknacks from his and his wife's trips around the world. Their next stop would be China in the summer. "Just a couple more minutes and I'll be done, dear."

His wife told him to be careful walking to his car, reminding him that he was an old man with a cane and an artificial hip and no longer the starting wingback at the U-Dub. "I'm as young as you are, beautiful," he said. "And as long as I still feel like I'm eighteen, I intend to act that way."

He told her he loved her and hung up, looking out through the wood-shuttered window of his ground-floor office. His fifteen-year-old BMW sat parked in its customary spot beneath the flood-lights' tapered orange glow. When he'd opened his practice, the lot had been surrounded by cedar and dogwood trees, but that was a good many years ago, when getting to Redmond required taking a ferry from Seattle across Lake Washington. With the construction of the 520 and I-90 bridges, the population on the east side of the lake had exploded. Office complexes and high-rise condominiums now shadowed his medical building.

Pilgrim rolled back his chair, closed the file, and carried it to the cabinet, pulling open the drawer to the file he'd angled as a marker and sliding it back in place. Then, as was also his routine—rain or shine—he slipped on his raincoat and hat that he used to think made him look like Humphrey Bogart in *Casablanca,* and reached to shut off the television. He hesitated at the lead news story.

"Robert Meyers was at the Washington State Convention and Trade Center in downtown Seattle today to give the keynote address at a conference on global warming."

Pilgrim turned up the volume and watched the charismatic young senator enter the convention center, shaking hands with some of the attendees.

"Meyers took the opportunity to continue his attacks on the current Republican administration's record on the environment."

The broadcast cut to a shot of Meyers standing at a podium behind a throng of microphones. "This is an issue whose time has come," he told the audience. "The people of the Pacific Northwest know this as well as any in the United States. The current administration's continued disregard for the environment is a further demonstration that it is out of touch with issues that will affect the future generations of this great country."

The story ended, and Pilgrim switched off the television. Curious, he raised his glasses back onto the perch above his eyebrows and used his finger to trace the faded letters on the white cards on the front of the file drawers. His daughter remained determined to modernize the practice, which was now hers, but to him the computer screens, hard drives, and printers throughout the rest of the office made it look like the control room of a spaceship. Not so in the sanctity of his four walls. All he needed were cabinets and the twenty-six letters of the alphabet— a filing system that had worked just fine before Bill Gates and computers. His daughter had relented, but only after he agreed to separate his active from his inactive files. In exchange, she promised not to ship any of his files to storage. His cabinets would leave his office with his body.

He stepped to the cabinet containing his closed files and slid open the third drawer down, straining to read the faded ink on the raised tabs. He pulled the file from the crowded drawer and raised the next in sequence to mark its place, then walked to his desk. Sitting, he heard the familiar sound of the bells indicating the front door had opened. At this time of night, he locked the front door, though the janitor had a key, and Emily occasionally came back to do paperwork after putting her two children to bed. She had her father's gene for long hours.

Pilgrim stood and pulled open his office door. "Emily, is that you?" The well-dressed man in the dark suit and raincoat stood like a giant amid the miniature chairs and tables. More curious than concerned, Pilgrim asked, "Can I help you?"

"Dr. Frank Pilgrim?"

"Yes. How did you get in?"

The man closed the outer door, locking it. "I brought a key."

"Where did you get a key?"

The man approached. He did not answer.

"What is it you want?" Pilgrim asked. "I have no money here, or anything that would even remotely be considered a narcotic."

The man reached into the pocket of his raincoat, pulled out a syringe, and removed the stopper at the end of the needle. "That's okay, Dr. Pilgrim. I've brought my own."

Pilgrim's eyes narrowed. He balled his fists. "My daughter is here. She's…she's in the office right over there." He called out. "Emily! Emily, there's a man here. Call the police."

The intruder stepped forward, displaying no concern. Pilgrim stumbled into his office and closed the door, but the man caught the edge and pushed it open, knocking Pilgrim backward. He closed the door behind him. Pilgrim scrambled for the telephone, but his momentum abruptly stopped, and he felt himself being pulled back by his collar. Instinctively, he turned. The man grabbed him by the throat and jabbed the hypodermic needle into Pilgrim's chest, depressing the plunger. A burning sensation spread quickly across Pilgrim's shoulders and down his arms and legs. Pain gripped him, constricting the flow of air to his lungs. He righted himself, then fell backward into the filing cabinet, shoving closed the drawer. The images blurred, distorted and unrecognizable. He lurched for the telephone and managed to grasp the receiver, but the strength in his legs dissolved and he collapsed across the desk, sliding to the floor, his arms pulling forty-eight years of clutter on top of him.

2

Seattle, Washington

HER KNUCKLES FELT thick and swollen, and her skin was as chilled as if she were working outside in a numbing-cold rain. Dana Hill fumbled with the button of her silk blouse and missed the hole. The button slipped from her grasp. She flexed her fingers and noticed the tremors. She could not steady her hand. She chastised herself, grabbed the stubborn button again, adjusted her blouse, and pushed the bead through the slit. Then she worked her way down the row and tucked the shirttail into her wool skirt. Sweat trickled from beneath her arms—the radiologist had advised that the aluminum in deodorant could interfere with the images.

She sat in one of the chairs and pulled a binder from her briefcase, flipping it open to her presentation. She read three sentences, made a note in the margin, then closed the binder and set it on an adjacent chair, and considered the room. The pastel colors and floral wallpaper contrasted sharply with the vinyl table in the center. The sheet of white paper covering it always made her feel like a slab of meat being weighed at the butcher shop. A colored diagram of the female body hung on the wall, the fallopian tubes a bright red, the ovaries blue, the uterus green. She considered her watch. How long had she been kept waiting? At Strong & Thurmond, she billed her clients in six-minute increments; few would tolerate being kept waiting. Every fifteen minutes was a .25 on Dana's billing sheet, which translated into $62.50, based on her $250-an-hour billing rate. The numbers caused her to reconsider the statistics she'd read in the articles from the Internet. Who said too much information was a good thing? Did she need to know that one of every seven women in the United States develops breast cancer, that a new case is diagnosed every three minutes, or that a woman dies of the disease every twelve minutes?

One every twelve minutes. A .20 on her time sheet.

Her cell phone beeped, mercifully interrupting her train of thought. She retrieved it from her briefcase and noted that she had missed a call from her brother, James. She was not surprised; she'd read that twins could have an almost innate sense about each other. Her brother always seemed to know when she was troubled. Sadly, she had either not inherited the same gene or had never managed to cultivate it. She returned his call.

He answered on the first ring. "Dana? How come you didn't answer your phone?"

"I've had the ringer off."

"*You* had the ringer turned off?" His voice rose with incredulity.

"Very funny. I'm at the doctor's."

"I know; your secretary told me. Is everything okay?"

"Everything is fine," she said, trying to sound convincing. "Just annual checkup stuff."

He didn't buy it. "You don't sound fine. You sound anxious."

She debated what to tell him and decided on the truth. "I found a small lump in my breast in the shower the other morning. I'm just here to have it checked out. I'm sure it's nothing."

"What did the doctor say?"

She noted the alarm in his voice. "I don't know; I'm waiting to talk with the radiologist." She sat in the chair. "I'm sure I'm fine." Seeking to change the subject, she asked, "Why did you call?"

He sighed, then asked, "Why don't you ever listen to your messages?"

"Because it takes too long. Do you know how many messages I get? It's quicker to just call back. Did you call to gloat again about how much more you love teaching the law than practicing it?"

He didn't answer her.

"James, that was a joke."

"I know . . . Listen, this can wait. I'll call you later."

"It's fine. I'm just sitting here waiting for the doctor. You know how that goes. I could be here until tomorrow. Is anything wrong?"

Again he paused. "I have a problem. I'm not sure how to handle it."

"What about?"

"It's complicated. I'd rather not talk to you about it over the phone. Can we have lunch? I could meet you downtown."

She shut her eyes. It seemed she never had time. She

rubbed her forehead, feeling the onset of a headache. "I can't today. I have to give a presentation this afternoon. What about tonight? Grant is picking up Molly. I could meet you after work."

"I can't tonight," he said. "I have a late class and forty legal briefs on the Erie Doctrine and federal jurisdiction to read."

"So teaching isn't all peaches and cream after all?"

"What about tomorrow?" he asked.

"You're not sick, are you?"

"No, nothing like that."

"I don't have my calendar with me. Call Linda and make sure I'm free."

The door to the room pushed open. A tall woman wearing a white smock over a beige shirt and blue cotton pants stepped in holding two X-rays. "James, I have to go. The doctor just walked in."

He rushed the next sentence. "Okay, but call and tell me what the doctor says."

"I've got to go."

"Dana?"

"I'll call you. I'll call you." She disconnected and shoved the phone into her briefcase. "Sorry about that."

"Not a problem. I'm Dr. Bridgett Neal. I'm sorry to have kept you waiting." Dr. Neal's white smock seemed a size too large. It dangled to her knees and hung from her shoulders as if she'd borrowed it from a big sister. "The mammogram went all right?" Neal wore no jewelry or discernible makeup. She had dark hair with a curl and fair skin. Dana guessed Irish, maybe Scandinavian.

"As well as having my breast flattened like a pancake can go." Dana mustered a smile. Her conversation with

James had distracted her. Now anxiety seeped back into her joints, making her restless.

Neal smiled. "I tell my husband every man should have a similar experience with their testicles to appreciate it fully."

Dana chuckled. "And you haven't had any volunteers?"

"Imagine that." Neal flipped on the light box and snapped three X-rays in place. "We've located the lump." She pointed the end of a red-capped pen at a subfusc gray dot the size of a pea. "When was your last exam? I didn't find any notation in your file."

"About a year ago. I asked my doctor to have the files sent over."

Neal sat on a rolling stool and adjusted the height. "I have them. I'd like to talk with you about the incident in high school." She reviewed notes Dana assumed had been made by the nurse during their earlier conversation. "You indicated there was no mammogram taken?"

"I don't think so. Dr. Watkins described it as hard tissue that became inflamed when I had my period."

Neal grimaced. "It's too bad they didn't do a mammogram, but they didn't always do them back then. It would have been a useful baseline to compare with these images." She pointed back at the mammogram. "How old was your mother when she had her mastectomy?"

"My age—thirty-four." Dana's stomach flipped. She brushed strands of hair from her face, pulling it back off her forehead and readjusting the clip, then she wrapped her arms across her chest. She wished she'd brought a sweater. Why did they always keep these rooms so cold?

Neal put down the pen. "Lumps are not uncommon in younger women. They can come and go with your menstrual cycle."

"I'm on the pill."

Neal picked the pen back up. "Lumps are still not uncommon. How long have you been on the pill?"

"Since my daughter was born, almost three years . . . and four years before that. I've wanted to stop, but my husband refuses to wear a condom."

Neal finished making a note, and slipped the pen into the front pocket of her white coat. She stood. "Will you open your blouse for me?"

"Again?" Something was wrong.

Neal looked calm. "I'd like to feel the nodule."

Dana sat on the edge of the examination table. The buttons were decidedly easier to undo. She unclasped her bra and raised her right arm over her head. Neal probed with her fingers, looking past Dana at the diagram on the wall. "Do you have any pain in that area?"

"No."

Neal wrote some additional notes in the chart. Dana reclasped her bra. "Hold on." Neal looked up. "As long as you're here, I'd like to do a fine-needle aspiration."

The words hit Dana like a blow to the chest. "What? Why?"

Neal pointed to the X-rays. "The bump you found appears to have an irregular edge, and its hard."

"Oh, shit," Dana said.

Neal raised a hand to calm her. "That doesn't mean it's cancerous."

"Then why the aspiration?"

"Without another mammogram to compare it to, I don't know how long it's been there or if it's changed shape. A fine-needle aspiration allows me to have some tissue examined under the microscope."

Anger began to replace Dana's fear. Her mother had lost a breast thirty years ago, and it seemed nothing had changed. "How long will it take? I have an important presentation to give today." She thought it sounded like an excuse.

"Just a few minutes. It will save you the trouble of having to come back. I can give you the results over the telephone. If it's fluid, we'll know immediately. If it is a mass, I'll obtain some cells and send it down to the lab. Depending on how backed up they are, they should have the results in a few days. The alternative is to schedule you for a biopsy in the surgery clinic downstairs."

Dana sat again. Neal opened and closed drawers, removing a needle and syringe. Dana said, "You know, when I was seventeen, I never thought anything about it. I remember being embarrassed because my mom was freaking out in front of the doctor. Now I know exactly how she felt. I'm most concerned about my daughter."

Neal snapped on latex gloves. "How old is your daughter?"

"Three. I read that breast cancer can be genetic."

"Let's take it one step at a time. We'll do the aspiration today, and I'll give you some written information to take home to read. I'll call you with the results as soon as I get them. In the interim, try to find something else to focus on."

Dana nodded, though she was unable to think of anything at that moment.

3

∽

DANA TOOK A detour off the elevator to avoid the northwest corner of the floor and slipped into her office, closing the door behind her. Her desk overflowed with legal treatises, partnership agreements, and share-holder resolutions for a multitude of Strong & Thurmond's corporate clients. Marvin Crocket continued to push her to the limit, trying to force her to cry uncle and quit, or just fail. She wouldn't give him the satisfaction. She'd never quit anything in her life. She wasn't about to start now.

She set her briefcase beside her desk and rubbed at the stinging sensation where the needle had pierced her breast.

The floor vibrated. The door to her office burst open.

"I see you've arrived." Crocket stepped in. At five foot seven and 250 pounds, with a nearly bald head, Crocket resembled a bowling ball. He didn't walk the halls so much as he rolled through them, causing an unmistakable tremor—a silent alarm to the associates who toiled for him that Crocket was out of his cage. In his late fifties, he was a psychologist's dream, a walking series of complexes: short, bald, and fat. Crocket, however, was no joke. He masked his weight well beneath designer clothes and staggering success. The managing partner of Strong & Thurmond's business department, Crocket was a relentless worker, billing over 2,800 hours each year, and a rainmaker who had amassed a book of business that exceeded $6 million in annual legal fees. He kept Dana and twelve other associates busy, going through them like a chain smoker does a pack of cigarettes, tossing aside the burned butts. He would be particularly unpleasant today because he had invited a potential client to Dana's presentation and was intent on adding the client to his book of business.

"I want to review your presentation," he said.

Dana reached across her desk and handed him a binder. Thank God Linda had made the copies. Crocket took the binder as if it might bite, sat in a chair, and flipped through it quickly. Apparently unable to think of anything negative, he snapped it shut. "Don Burnside will be there."

Crocket had been courting Burnside like a post-pubescent teen. "I know. You told me."

"And the Feldman incorporation papers must be filed today."

"I filed them yesterday," she said.

"The Iverson IPO is in three weeks."

He was meeting with the client on Monday. "You'll have all the necessary paperwork on your desk by noon today."

Crocket's dislike for Dana was basic. After Molly's birth, she had opted for a three-day work week and put being a mother before her career, which, according to Crocket, meant she shouldn't have a career. The other firm shareholders had also not been pleased, though for a different reason. Dana had been a rising star amid Strong & Thurmond's 225 associates, the kind of lawyer whom law firms love to market to clients: a good-looking capable female who knew when and how to schmooze clients and when to bust balls.

Getting nowhere, Crocket said, "I was looking for you this morning."

"I had a doctor's appointment this morning."

"You're not pregnant again, are you?"

She wondered if the term "sexual discrimination" even entered the man's thoughts. "No, not yet, but you'll be the first to know."

Crocket crossed a leg with difficulty. "What kind of doctor's appointment?"

You asked for it.

"Actually, I've been having some irregular bleeding, Marvin, spotting. I decided to have it checked out."

Crocket's face flushed, and he stood with a grunt. "I'll see you at five sharp in the conference room."

Dana closed the door behind him and sat at her desk. She wanted to both laugh and cry. Her to-do list had grown to three pages. Crying would make her feel better. She looked to the bookshelves, focused on a framed picture of Molly, and was suddenly overwhelmed by the thought that she could possibly leave her little girl. For six years, Dana had ingratiated herself to Strong & Thurmond's twenty-five shareholders, working long hours and weekends to chalk up substantial billable hours and to drum up business. She had thought being a partner at one of Seattle's top law firms was what she wanted. But Molly's birth had changed her perspective, and she'd agonized over what to do. Grant had offered little support, saying they'd suffer financially if she cut back, especially with the new house and higher monthly mortgage payment. But she'd felt too much guilt over leaving Molly in day care every day of the week and then having to work on the weekends. She was cheating her daughter. She was cheating herself. She had asked to be removed from the partnership track. Marvin Crocket was the black hole to which the firm had condemned her.

Her telephone rang. She hit the speaker button. "Your husband is on the phone," Linda said.

"Thanks, Linda. Put him through." She left him on the speaker. "Hi, Grant."

"I've been trying to reach you all morning," he said, confirming that he had not remembered her doctor's appointment. "Listen, I can tell already this deposition in Everett is going to take longer than I expected. The witness is giving me bullshit answers and brought a stack of exhibits two feet high. I won't be back in time to pick up Molly. You'll have to get her."

Dana felt the floor fall out from beneath her. "No, Grant. I told you, I have my presentation today."

"Call Maria or your mother."

"I can't. When you said you wanted to pick up Molly, I canceled Maria. My mother has bridge this afternoon."

"I don't know what to tell you, babe."

"I don't know what to tell you, either. You agreed to do it. We scheduled this a week ago." They had actually coordinated their Palm Pilots.

"Can't someone else do the presentation?"

She suppressed her anger. "It's my presentation. I worked my ass off, and Crocket is just waiting for me to screw it up. Why can't you cut the deposition short and resume it another day?"

He sounded aghast. "No way. This is the Nelson case. The defense lawyer is a complete prick; I don't want him thinking he's doing me any favors. Besides, there *are* no other days available. We're in expert depositions right up to trial. I have to finish this guy today."

"Dammit, Grant, couldn't you give me any notice?"

"Don't blame me, Dana. I'm up to my ass in alligators here. How important can a practice group meeting be? Just reschedule the damn thing."

"There are thirty people involved, and Crocket is bringing a potential client. I can't go into his office to reschedule; he already has me under a microscope, you know that."

"Look, I can't fight that battle for you. You're a big girl. Handle Crocket or quit complaining."

"How about if I just quit?" It was her trump card. Without her income, which was higher than his, he couldn't afford the lease on the BMW or the house in Madison Park.

"My break is over. Do what you have to do."

He hung up.

4

❧

DANA STOOD BENEATH the covered patio with the mail clenched between her teeth, a bag of groceries balanced on a knee, and the dry cleaning stretching the tendons of her fingers. With her free hand, she continued to rummage through the pens and paper clips at the bottom of her briefcase in search of her house keys. Water seeped between the butted ends of the plastic corrugated canopy overhead and dripped on her shoulder. Molly stood beside her, crying. Grant had promised her an ice cream after day care, something Dana did not allow before dinner. Dana kept a foot wedged in the dog door, struggling to keep Max, their eighty-pound golden retriever, at bay. She heard the telephone ringing inside the kitchen.

She found the keys, inserted the correct one in the lock, and turned the handle. Molly shoved the door. "Molly, don't push," Dana mumbled, but it was too late. Max wedged his nose in the crack and bulled the door open, bounding out, knocking Molly over. The bag of groceries toppled from Dana's knee. A carton of eggs hit the ground with a crack. Two red apples rolled across the kitchen floor. Dana stepped in, spitting the mail on the table. She stepped around the carton of eggs, kneed Max in the chest to keep him off her, and hung the dry cleaning on the swinging door to the formal dining room. Then she stepped back outside and picked up Molly, carrying her into the house and sitting her on the kitchen counter. Tears streamed down the little girl's cheeks; she'd scraped her knee just below her blue dress. Behind them, Max licked at the egg yolk as if he hadn't been fed in a week. Dana's cellular phone rang— Grant calling from his cell phone. She answered it while continuing to wipe Molly's tears and hug her.

"Dana? Where were you? I just called the house. What's wrong with her?"

"She wants an ice cream. She says her daddy promised her one."

"Oh God, don't start with me about that again. Ice cream isn't going to kill her."

"Dammit, Max." The dog had pulled a package of hamburger meat from the grocery bag. "Hold on." She dragged Max outside by the collar and shut the door and the dog door. He pawed and barked to get back in. She picked up her phone. "Where are you, Grant?"

"Jesus, someone is in a foul mood."

"Where are you?"

"I'm just leaving my office."

"Your office?" She looked at her watch. "What happened to the deposition in Everett?"

"Most of his documents were bullshit. I finished his ass by three. It gave me time to get back to the office and do trial prep. This Nelson case is killing me." Dana heard voices in the background. "Listen, don't count on me for dinner. Softball tonight. I'm late. I'll call you later."

"Grant?" But he was gone. Dana closed her phone and picked up Molly, burying her face in her daughter's hair. Outside, it had begun to rain again.

THE SOUND OF the electric garage door prompted Dana to look up from the black binder to the ornate clock on the mantel above the fireplace. Eleven-twenty. She lay in bed, fighting to keep her eyes open. When she'd told Crocket of her conflict, he had ranted and raved for thirty minutes about commitment, teamwork, and priorities. Then he'd sent out a memorandum notifying the practice group that the presentation had been changed to the following morning. When Linda had seen the memo, she'd walked into Dana's office and told her that Don Burnside from Corrugate Industries had called with an unexpected conflict just minutes before Dana went into Crocket's office. Crocket had already rescheduled the presentation.

Dana heard Grant come through the kitchen door. Max was whining, his tail whacking against the wood cabinets with a dull thud. The dog had not been run in weeks, not since the Nelson case exploded and Grant quit his morning jog. Grant had insisted they buy Max from a breeder for those rare occasions when he went bird hunting with his fraternity brothers in eastern Washington, but he had never bothered to train the dog. Max had yet to retrieve anything. He usually shredded the newspaper on the front lawn. Dana felt a perverse sense of satisfaction at the sound of condiments rattling in the refrigerator door—Grant searching for something to eat. The groceries she had picked up were staples. She hadn't done a full shop in weeks. She and Molly had eaten hamburgers and milk shakes. She'd made a patty for Grant, then fed it to Max.

Max's paws pounded the stairs, and his nails clicked and clacked on the hardwood floor leading to the master bedroom. He nudged open the door and stormed in, tongue hanging out the side of his mouth, tail ecstatic to announce his master's arrival. Yippee. Grant stepped in wearing a Maxwell, Levitt & Truman pin-striped softball shirt, sweatpants, and a baseball hat. He smelled of beer and cigarette smoke.

"Wasn't sure you were still awake. All the lights are off downstairs." He sat on the couch beneath the bay window and kicked off a rubber cleat. It landed under the cherrywood desk. The second shoe followed it.

"Where have you been?" she asked.

"Softball," he said matter-of-factly. He removed his socks and rubbed his feet. "And I know what you're thinking; I can tell by your tone. 'If he had time for softball, why couldn't he pick up Molly?' Because the deposition ended, and I had fires burning back at the office. I had to bust ass just to make it to the game and didn't get there until the second inning. Bergman had given up four runs before I got there. We barely pulled it out."

"Hurray for our team." She refocused on her presentation.

He threw his socks on the floor. "Come on, Dana. Knock it off."

"What time did the game end?"

He stood. "Don't cross-examine me. I've been busting my ass for a month. This is the first chance I've had to blow off steam in weeks."

That wasn't true, but she wasn't about to debate it. "I'm not cross-examining you. It was a simple question. It's called dialogue."

He walked across the Persian area rug, pulling the softball jersey over his head. "I have 'dialogue' all day long. I *fight* all day long. I don't need it at home." At forty, he remained in excellent physical condition. When not preparing for trial he ran and lifted weights at the Washington Athletic Club downtown. Dana tried not to dwell on it. She had been unable to lose the extra five pregnancy pounds and didn't have time to even think about working out. "I went out for pizza and beer after the game." He turned his back to her and walked toward the antique dresser. "Jesus, you'd think I do this every night."

"No, the other nights you have a client dinner or a late meeting, or you head to the driving range."

He put his wallet, change, and watch in the leather case atop his dresser. "We've been through this," he said, his tone tired. "If I want to make partner, I have to bring in clients, and I can't do that Monday through Friday, nine to five. Bergman is on my ass about increasing my business. Profits are down. They let three shareholders go this year. I don't think you want me looking for a job, unless you plan on working full-time again."

"I know you work hard, and I don't like being put in a position of being the house bitch—"

"Then don't."

She clenched her teeth. "You could have called." She regretted saying it the moment the words left her mouth.

He seized them like a lifeline to diffuse the situation and avoid the real issue. "You're right. I should have called. I'm sorry. This Nelson case has me all screwed up. I'm tied up in knots." The subject had changed. "I'm going to take a shower. Care to join me?"

She thought she might scream. He stood naked. It had become the extent of their foreplay, and she wondered how it had come to this. The physical chemistry that had drawn them together in law school had been so powerful the first time they made love, she'd thought she would explode. What with the daily stress of teachers peppering her with complex questions, the omnipresent anxiety of final exams, and the fierce competition to get the best grades and best jobs, Grant had become her life preserver. They hadn't made love. They'd released their built-up tension in an evening of fierce and prolonged passion. But things had changed after he failed the bar exam, and they got worse when he didn't make partner at his first firm. He came to resent her. His failure illustrated what they both knew but never spoke aloud. She had received better grades and gotten the better job. She made more money. His ego couldn't stand it. Making love now amounted to his climbing on top of her and climbing off.

"I have work to do," she said, "and I have to get up early."

"Fine." He stormed to the bathroom. "Do your work." He stopped at the door. "You're in a mood."

"I'm in a mood? You haven't even asked me about my day." She regretted throwing him another lifeline.

"Is that what this is about? I forgot to ask about your day?" He sat naked on the bed, apparently not yet willing to give up. "You know I've been preoccupied. If I win this Nelson case, Bill Nelson will transfer Nelson Construction's entire book of business to the firm. This is a hundred-and-fifty-million-dollar breach-of-contract case,

Dana. It will make headlines all over the country. Bergman made it clear if I win this, my place at the firm will be secure." She'd heard it before, about a thousand times. "So how was your day?"

"I had my mammogram this morning."

"Oh yeah. How'd it go?"

"They're going to call me," she said, no longer interested in providing details.

"You don't know? So what are you so worked up about? Wait for the results and go from there." He pushed a strand of hair from her face and kissed her on the lips. His hand caressed her thigh. She wanted to forget about Dr. Neal, Marvin Crocket, and the damn presentation. She wanted to be lost in pleasure again. But she had also come to realize she no longer wanted Grant to bring her there.

"I'm going to take that shower," he said and left the room.

A moment later, she heard the water and closed the binder. She set it on the nightstand, reached up, and turned off the light. Then she rolled over, pulling the covers around her.

5

JAMES HILL'S LUCK ran out. His euphoria over finding a parking space within two blocks of his Green Lake home dissipated with the first drops of water splattering on his windshield and hitting the roof and hood with dull pings. The weatherman had predicted an evening thunderstorm. Normally, you could throw darts and come up with a more accurate five-day forecast. Damned if this wasn't one of the few times he'd gotten it right. It was Murphy's Law. If James had remembered his umbrella or found a spot directly in front of his home, it would have no doubt been clear skies. But street parking in his neighborhood was tough to come by. Four miles from downtown Seattle, Green Lake had become a trendy residential district.

No chance to wait it out. The raindrops were starting to fall frequently. He stepped from the car and hurried around behind, popping the hatchback to gather his students' briefs, balancing them in a stack. His leather briefcase felt like it had an anvil in it. Thunder rumbled across a blue-black sky, and a strong wind ruffled the pages of the top brief and brought the smell of the cherry blossoms. He closed the hatch and started up the sidewalk. Pink petals sprinkled it like a wedding aisle. The windows of his neighbor's Craftsman cottages reflected blue flashes of light. James envied their time watching mindless television. He wouldn't have that luxury. He'd had one of those nonstop days—three classes, a faculty meeting, and two hours of office time that his students had used to the last minute.

The thought hit him like a drop of water—Dana. She hadn't called him back. At one point during the day he'd picked up the telephone but became distracted, then forgot. He hoped her silence didn't mean bad news. Though she had tried to disguise it, he'd heard the anxiety in her voice. They had been old enough to remember their mother's mastectomy and subsequent treatment that had left her weak and thin. James regretted mentioning his own problem, but he was at a crossroads. There was no one else he trusted, and he sensed things coming to a head quickly.

The rain peppered him. He quickened his pace past a couple bundled in rain gear, out walking their dog. He turned right down Latona Avenue. The rain, as if sensing that he was nearing shelter, took one last shot at him. His students would wonder if he'd used their briefs to clean up a spill. He climbed the steps to the front porch. His home had a driveway and detached garage, but both were presently clogged with the building materials for his remodeling project and the remnants of his furnishings from the ten-room house on Capitol Hill that he'd sold when he quit the law. On nights like this, he longed for a garage to park in. He rearranged the stack of briefs, retrieved his

key, and unlocked the door, stumbling into the entryway.
The legal briefs spilled across the hall table, and several
slid onto the floor, where he dropped his briefcase. He
removed his glasses, spotted with rain, placed them atop
the pile on the table, and found his cell phone, punching
in Dana's number. He hung his leather coat on the staircase banister as her phone rang, and started down the hall
when she answered. She sounded half asleep.

"Dana, I'm sorry to call so late; I meant to call earlier,
but I got tied up. How was your mammogram? Is everything okay?"

"They took tests today." Her voice faded. "I'll call you
tomorrow."

"I can't hear you."

"Tomorrow."

He stepped into the living room at the back of the
house. "Are we still having lunch? Your secretary said
you were free. Dana?" She didn't answer. The light from
the back porch filtered into the room through the French
doors that opened to a patio garden. It shaded everything
black and gray, like an old movie. "Dana?"

"I'll call you." Her voice was a faint whisper.

"All right. Sorry to call so late. I love you."

"I love you, too, James."

Thunder rumbled across the sky, and the rain pecked
at the shingled roof like the beaks of dozens of birds. He
pulled the chain to the lamp on the end table, bringing
forth a tapered beige light. The room looked off-balance
and unfamiliar, things out of place, books on the floor,
pillows strewn from the couch. The floor creaked behind
him. He turned and caught a glimpse of the long hair and
thin face. "Who—"

The object swept across his vision, striking with a sudden sharp pain. His body spun as if on a swivel. Blood splattered the African tribal masks on the wall, their hollow eyes bearing witness. He stumbled backward into the couch. His legs buckled. The second blow knocked him forward like a felled tree, his face impacting hard against the wood-planked floor. Then the sky opened—pellets of water beating on the roof and the glass panes of the French doors. And the blows cascaded down upon him.

6

❧

IT WAS GOING well. Hell, it was going great. She felt the high one feels on a good run, her body moving in effortless rhythm. Her words flowed with confidence. Her hand gestures offered just the right amount of emphasis. The faces around the marble table looked on attentively. Most people took notes. All ignored the pastries and the smell of freshly roasted coffee. Ordinarily, associates despised the mundane drudgery of practice group seminars because they could not bill the time to a client. Seminars represented a lost chunk of their day that the partners didn't consider toward yearly bonuses and compensation.

Marvin Crocket sat at the head of the table next to Don Burnside, the president of Corrugate Industries. Burnside smiled, giving Dana his undivided attention. A good-looking, distinguished man with flags of gray at the temples, Burnside had made a point to introduce himself to her before the presentation. When she excused herself to pour a glass of water, she knew he would find an excuse to continue their conversation. She saw it in the sparkle of his eyes, the toothy smile, and the extra moment he had clasped her hand. Dana had played her part, smiling warmly while maintaining a professional demeanor. Now she was dazzling him with her mind. Crocket would invite her to lunch and add another client to his considerable stable. It was all he cared about. For a few hours, all would be forgiven.

The door to the conference room crept open. As the person entering came within Dana's peripheral vision, she recognized Linda. She lost her train of thought. The words stopped flowing, and her voice became indecisive. She had yet to use a notecard, and now she had no idea where she was in her presentation. She paused and looked up at Crocket and Burnside with a pained smile. "Excuse me for a moment."

Burnside reacted like a man dancing with a beautiful woman when the music abruptly stopped. Crocket looked like he'd bitten into something distasteful but covered it by clearing his throat and trying to sound casual. "We've been going about forty-five minutes. Now would be a good time for a short break."

Dana ushered Linda to the reception area as the attendees reached for the Danishes and filled their mugs with coffee. They stepped around a mahogany table of neatly arranged magazines to a large potted palm in the corner of the room.

"I'm really sorry," Linda said before Dana had time to chastise her. She clearly looked uncomfortable.

Dana suppressed her anger. Staff was underappreciated when things went well and abused when things went wrong. "What is it?" she asked, exasperated.

"Your husband is on the phone."

Tension burst across the back of Dana's neck. She spoke from between clenched teeth. "Tell him I'm in a meeting and will call him later."

"I did. He insisted that I get you."

Out of the corner of her eye, Dana saw Crocket lumbering toward them, gaining momentum like a ball pushed downhill. "What the hell is going on? Can we move this forward?"

"I'm afraid I have to take a call, Marvin."

"Now? You have to take it now? Who the blazes is it?" He looked and sounded apoplectic.

"My husband," she said reluctantly.

Crocket rolled his eyes and pulled at the taut sleeve of his cuffed shirt to view the face of his Rolex. "Bad timing. This is very bad timing." He stormed away.

Dana started for the telephone in the small alcove off the conference room. Linda said, "He told me he wanted to speak with you in your office, in private."

Dana nearly growled. She stormed around the corner. It likely had to do with Molly—the school had called and Molly was sick and had to be picked up. Or Grant needed a clean shirt or an errand or some other goddamn thing he couldn't or wouldn't do for himself.

She slammed her office door and snatched the receiver, knocking the telephone off the desk. The cord dangled over the side. "What the hell is it? I am in the middle of a meeting, and Crocket is about to explode."

"Dana, I'm sorry. I know you're in your seminar."

"Was, Grant. I *was* in my seminar. Now I'm standing here talking to you while Crocket makes notes in my file about why the shareholders should fire me. Is that what you want, because—"

"Dana, I have bad news. I think you should sit down."

"No, I'm not going to—" She caught herself. The tone of his voice was not demanding. It was not confrontational. He sounded passive, almost timid. A tremor had caused his voice to flutter. *I think you should sit down.* Her heart pounded with a jolt of adrenaline. Fear. "What's wrong? It's not Molly."

"No, Molly's fine." He paused.

"What is it?"

"It's your brother."

"James?"

"I'm afraid it's bad, Dana. It's very bad. The police caught me in the driveway. I'm still at home."

"Home? What are the police doing at our house?" She felt like she'd walked into the middle of a conversation. "Grant?"

"Your brother is dead. He was murdered last night."

7

DETECTIVE MICHAEL LOGAN sipped a cherry-flavored Slurpee and carried a half-eaten foot-long hot dog topped with onions and relish. The top step sagged. Logan stepped off it, then reapplied his weight. The ends of the board lifted to catch the heads of the raised nails. Dry rot was prevalent in the older Northwest homes. The constant damp never gave things a chance to dry out. Wood wasn't intended to last forever. The whole staircase would have to be ripped out and replaced, which was likely the reason for the lumber and construction materials in the driveway.

Neighbors had gathered along the sidewalk, standing alongside television crews behind the police barricade. The reporters held microphones, rehearsing their stories for when the morning news anchor went live to the scene of what appeared to be a homicide in Green Lake. Murders in suburbia were always big news.

A uniformed officer stood just inside the doorway of

the home, holding a clipboard. Logan exchanged his Slurpee for a pen and signed his name to the log. It recorded the crime scene detail—who came in and out of the home. The list included the uniformed officers first on the scene; Henry Rodriguez, the evidence technician; Carole Nuchitelli, from the medical examiner's office; the crime scene technicians who would remove the body; the crime scene photographer; and the forensics team. Logan took back his Slurpee and bit into the hot dog, working the flow of relish into his mouth as he stepped into the entry. Papers lay scattered on the floor next to a well-worn briefcase, the large kind that lawyers favored. The papers had apparently toppled from a stack on the table. A black leather jacket hung on a banister. Logan walked down the hall to a room at the back of the house, where the crime scene detail moved in a rehearsed dance around the victim—a man, judging from the khaki pants and brown loafers sticking out from behind the couch.

"Oh, God," Logan said, stepping farther into the room.

Carole Nuchitelli looked up at him. "Welcome to the party." She fitted the right hand of the victim with a plastic bag. She'd already tagged the ankle and placed the contents of the man's pockets in Zip-loc bags next to her on the floor. Blood had puddled and rolled with the sag in the dark wood and matted the man's hair a deep burgundy. His head was fractured and swollen. Nuchitelli pointed with a latex-gloved finger. "Nice breakfast. Don't get any of that crap on my victim."

"Lunch. I've been up since five; it's noon for me," Logan said, studying the scene.

"And you chose that?"

He crumpled what was left of his hot dog in the plastic

wrap and shoved it in his coat pocket, no longer hungry. "You know me, Nooch. I have to eat six times a day just to keep the weight on."

"Poor baby. Why couldn't I get a metabolism like that?"

Nuchitelli stood, and they stepped back to give the crime scene photographer room. Logan noted nothing wrong with her metabolism. At nearly six feet, with strawberry-blond hair that reached the middle of her back, and the legs of a college volleyball player, the King County medical examiner was a sharp contrast to the brutally ugly crime scenes where she and Logan met.

"Bad one," he said.

"Aren't they all?"

"Scale of one to ten."

Nuchitelli considered the body and sighed. "Beatings are always the worst. With gunshots and knife wounds, it can be pretty clean. But beatings..." She paused. "It's the savagery. It's the thought that someone stood here and administered each blow. It's sick. I'd give it an eight."

"How many blows you estimate?"

"More than ten. Twelve to thirteen."

"Fear or rage," he said.

Nuchitelli nodded. "We haven't been out here much." She was referring to Green Lake. "Can't remember the last time. But it didn't take you long to find the fast food."

Logan had been reassigned to the North Precinct six months earlier. Normally, he worked with a partner, but his was in New Jersey for a son's wedding. The North Precinct wasn't as busy as the South Precinct. Logan had been transferred when he was promoted to homicide, after working eight years with the robbery and sexual assault units.

He shrugged. "All I had time for."

"You're breaking my heart."

"Breaking it? Hell, I've been trying for three years to capture it."

Nuchitelli smiled and shook her head. "Right. Talk about taking work home with you."

Their flirtation was innocent. Logan wasn't looking to complicate his life by dating a professional acquaintance. He just liked to make Nooch smile. Smiles were rare for the men and women working homicides.

"Besides, you're too old for me," she said.

"Easy. I hit forty last week, and I'm sensitive about it."

"You're not sensitive about anything."

"Ouch again."

She considered him. "Forty? You don't look that old."

"Are you trying to be nice or mean?"

"I meant it as a compliment. I would have guessed thirty-five. You'd probably look even younger if you didn't put that crap in your system. You must have the metabolism of a jackrabbit." She picked up a plastic bag and handed the object to Logan.

He weighed it in his hand. "Marble. Solid. Probably six pounds."

"Definitely the murder weapon."

The statue was carved with the face of an African tribal warrior. It had no flat surfaces. Pulling a print would be impossible. Logan considered the rest of the room. Blood-splattered wooden masks and tapestries hung on the walls. On a table below them, stone carvings of elephants, lions, zebras, and giraffes had toppled over. They, too, were spotted with blood. Logan took out a handkerchief and picked up a marble statue similar to the one in his hand. It had the carved face of a female. A matched set.

"Get pictures of this wall, Jerry," he instructed the photographer before turning back to Nuchitelli. "So what do we know?"

She took another breath and let out a burst of air like a broken steam pipe. "The initial blow appears to be across the face, but the majority were administered to the back of the head. Given the savagery of the beating, I'd say someone came here with the intent to kill and surprised him in the dark."

"Good guess," he said. "But I don't think so."

She shrugged. "Okay, Sherlock, go ahead, give me your best shot."

Logan always professed to be able to figure out a crime scene in five minutes. "The perp didn't come here intending to kill him. The victim surprised him, and he panicked. That's why the perp hit him so many times. It was fear." He walked back into the hallway, toward the front door. Nuchitelli followed. He pointed at the stack of papers. "He comes home, drops that stack of papers on the table, and puts down his briefcase. That tells me he didn't hear anything until he got back there, and since the killer didn't just run out the back door, either he didn't hear the victim come home or he wasn't in that back room." He pointed to a room next to the back room, then stuck his head in. The dresser drawers were open, clothes strewn from them and from the closet. Books had been toppled from a bookcase. "He was likely in here."

"Maybe he was lying in wait," Nuchitelli suggested.

"Maybe, except then he would have likely brought his own weapon." Logan walked back to the body. "He came up from behind. The victim turned and got hit while standing, which explains the blood on those masks six feet up the wall." Logan pointed. "Was that light on?"

"Far as I know," she said.

Another voice shouted from the back of the room, one of the technicians. "The lamp was on. Only light on in the house."

"Why wouldn't the victim pick up the papers from the floor?" Nuchitelli pointed back down the hallway.

Logan turned. "What's the estimated time of death?"

"Based on the body temperature, between ten-thirty and midnight to one in the morning. Give or take."

Logan thought for a moment. "Okay. He gets home late, tired after a long day. He's hungry, so he heads for the kitchen. Or maybe he had to pee, but I don't think so if the perp was in the bedroom, because that would have given him time to get out."

"Maybe the perp was upstairs," Nuchitelli said.

"Then the victim likely would have heard him. No. I think the perp was definitely in the bedroom." Logan turned in the doorway, facing the room with all the activity. He rocked as if walking down the hallway. "So he drops the papers on the table, and some fall. He puts his glasses on top, hangs his coat on the banister, and walks down the hall to get something to eat."

"Why would he take off his glasses?"

"I don't know." Logan thought but didn't come up with a plausible explanation. "Anyway, when he does get here, it's dark, so he reaches and turns on the light. He hears something behind him, turns partway, and bam! He's hit. The force of the blow pushes him against the table, knocking those pieces over, and he pinballs against the couch." Logan mimicked the motion of the initial blow and fell to his knees, careful to avoid the marked evidence. "The second blow catches him in the back of the head."

From his knees, Logan noticed the object sticking out from beneath the black leather couch. He called over one of the technicians and asked for a plastic bag. The man pulled one from a bunch clipped at his belt and handed it to Logan. Logan reached beneath the couch and pulled out a cell phone. It was on. He stood and slipped the phone into the bag. Through the plastic, he pressed a button that pulled up the last phone numbers dialed and received. "Huh. Guess I'm wrong. He might have been going to the kitchen, but the reason he didn't pick up those papers or clean off his glasses was because he was on the phone."

"How do you know it's his phone?"

"Because I'm a pessimist, and I just can't believe the killer would be so kind as to leave behind his phone for us to use to convict him. Time of death was eleven-ten," he said, turning the phone so Nuchitelli could see it. "Give or take." He wrote the number in a notebook and handed the telephone to the technician. "We'll want a log of every number he called. Start with the past twenty-four hours." He turned back to Nuchitelli. "What do we know about the victim?"

Nuchitelli shook her head. "You know me, Logan; this job is hard enough without making it more personal."

"How'd we hear about it?"

"Neighbor phoned it in. Someone is next door calming her. She's pretty upset." Nuchitelli pointed to a doorway with no door. "Rodriguez is in the kitchen."

Logan walked into the kitchen. A short Hispanic man stood observing an evidence technician attempting to lift fingerprints off the inside and exterior knobs of a back door. Head of the forensics laboratory for Seattle's police districts, and fastidious to the point of neurosis, Rodriguez stressed over the slightest detail. In a career that often involved micromillimeters and particulates of evidence, he was well suited for his job.

Rodriguez pointed at Logan's shoes, aghast. "Slipcovers. Why won't you ever put them on?"

"Sorry, Henry, I don't carry them around with me in the car. Anything useful?"

Rodriguez shook his head, annoyed. "Always something useful. Just have to find it. This place is loaded with fingerprints. Whether they belong to any of the killers, I don't know."

"Killers? As in more than one?"

"I'd say two. Outside the door you'll find two different shoe prints in the garden soil. From the depth of the prints, I'd say they took off running down the back steps and jumped. Two distinct imprints; one looks to be a tennis shoe, I'd guess a size eight. The other is a boot. Bigger. Size twelve. Given the imprint, that person was heavier. "

"Could one of them be the victim's?"

"I doubt it. They're fresh." Rodriguez pointed in the direction of the victim. "He has no mud on his shoes, and he's wearing loafers, a ten and a half. But we'll cast the impressions and compare them with other shoes we find in the house."

"What else do you know about him?"

"Not my area, Logan."

"Humor me. Nooch says you told her a neighbor called it in."

"Apparently, the guy was a law professor at Seattle U. The neighbor knocked on his door this morning to get coffee. When he didn't answer, she figured he'd forgotten. She got down the block and saw his car and thought that maybe he was in the shower or something. So she came back and knocked louder. When he still didn't answer, she thought it odd and went to get a key he gave her."

"Key? She a girlfriend?"

"Not unless it's a *Harold and Maude* type thing," Rodriguez said.

"A what?"

"*Harold and Maude*—you know, the movie. It's a cult classic. A twenty-year-old kid falls for an eighty-year-old woman."

"I think I'll pass. I just ate."

"Whatever. Apparently, the victim and the neighbor exchanged keys in case one got locked out—a neighbor thing. She said she opened the door, stepped inside calling his name, and saw his legs on the floor. She thought maybe he'd fainted until she got close enough to see the blood." Rodriguez paused, considering the body. "Heard they've reached the guy's sister."

Logan sighed. "I don't envy her."

8

DANA GRIPPED THE edge of the desk, holding on.

"His neighbor found him. She called the police."

"No," she said. "I talked to him yesterday." Her body started to shake. "I did. We were going to have lunch. I had to cancel—"

"—Dana. Dana?"

"Yesterday. I talked to him last night." Her legs gave way. She collapsed into the chair, dropping the telephone to the floor.

"Dana? Dana, are you there? Dana?"

A hollow ringing echoed in her ears. Her office swirled about her, unfamiliar. The walls collapsed inward, shrinking like a visual effect, sucking the air from the room. She couldn't breathe. She felt the floor vibrate, and with that came a harsh reality. The door to her office burst open. Crocket stepped in, berating her. "Do you think we can get on with the meeting? This is reflecting very poorly on the entire business..."

She looked at the phone dangling by its cord.

James is dead.

Crocket's needling voice jabbed at her, and she hated him more at that moment than she ever had. She hated him because Marvin Crocket represented reality. This was not a nightmare. She would not awake. This was real. The pain gripping her chest exploded from her like a shock wave from the center of a blast. In a burst of fury she shot from the chair, flipping the desk as if it were a balsa-wood fake. Clutter and computer equipment slid off its face, crashing to the floor with a resounding thud.

Hours after she had rushed from her office in a daze of grief and a fog of disbelief and despair, Dana sat staring at fluorescent light reflecting off the waxed linoleum in the basement of Harborview Medical Center in Seattle. Next to her sat a female police officer. Despite the harsh reality of the stark white hallway, a part of her still clung to the faint hope that James was not dead—that it was all some horrible error, some egregious mistake to be rectified with profuse apologies. But she had been through this denial before, sitting on the same bench outside the King County medical examiner's office, waiting to identify her father's body.

There was no mistake. This was real. Her brother was dead.

"Ms. Hill?"

She looked up. There stood a well-dressed man in a tailored blue suit, white shirt, and diamond-patterned tie. He looked like a lawyer. "I'm Detective Michael Logan," he said.

She didn't bother to stand.

"I'm very sorry for your loss. Would you like to get a cup of coffee, something to drink?"

She estimated him to be six feet, with broad shoulders and a young face, freckles sprinkled across his nose and cheeks. His red hair had a light curl and was damp, presumably from the rain. "Do you know anything more?" she asked.

He sat beside her on the bench. "Not for certain. We believe your brother returned home at approximately eleven o'clock last night and walked in during a burglary. He may have been on the telephone, talking to you."

Dana dropped her hand from her mouth. "Me?"

"That's the last number on his phone. He called you at eleven-ten."

She lowered her eyes to the floor, remembering. She had been stressed and anxious after the doctor's appointment and Crocket's tirade. She'd been fighting with Grant, then rolled over, exhausted. James's call woke her. "Yes," she said.

"You remember the call?" Logan asked.

She nodded. "You mean he was on the phone with me…" Tears streamed down her cheeks with the knowledge that her brother's final act had been to call and find out if she was okay and tell her that he loved her.

Detective Logan gave her a moment to compose herself. "Do you recall what you and your brother talked about?"

She took a deep breath. "He had called me earlier in the day. I'd forgotten to call him back. He was just checking on me." She remembered their conversation. "He said he had a problem."

"What kind of problem?"

She shook her head. "He didn't say." She thought a moment. "We were going to have lunch today."

"Did he say anything else?"

"No. He was just...he didn't want to talk about it on the phone." She looked at Logan. "He said he didn't want to talk about it over the phone."

"And you have no idea what he was referring to?"

"No. James never had problems."

"Never?" She heard skepticism in the detective's voice.

"No," she repeated.

"So if he called you and wanted to talk in person, it was probably something important."

"I don't know," she said, tired. "I guess so."

"Could it have been the kind of problem that would lead to something like this?"

"What do you mean?"

"I'm sorry to have to ask, Ms. Hill, but was your brother into anything—drugs, gambling, anything that might have put him in a situation where someone would have wanted to kill him?"

"You said it was a burglary—that James walked in on a burglary."

"I did. I'm just following up on what you've told me, that your brother called and said he had a problem."

She shook her head. "No." She hesitated before becoming more definitive. "No. James didn't do drugs. He was a vegetarian; he was a fanatic about what he put into his body. And I never knew him to gamble except maybe the college basketball pool at work. My brother was a good man, Detective. Everybody liked James. I never met anyone who didn't like him." Her voice became edgy with frustration and anger. "This just doesn't make any sense. None of it makes any sense."

Logan nodded. "Senseless acts of violence are difficult to understand and even more difficult to accept, I'm afraid. We have officers taking statements from your brother's neighbors to determine if anyone saw anything suspicious or out of the ordinary—strangers walking around, a car that appeared out of place. The technicians found fingerprints in the house and shoe prints outside the back door. We'll check to determine if there have been recent burglaries in the area. We'll do our best to find out what happened and see if we can make some sense of it."

"Ms. Hill?" Dana turned to a different voice. A man wearing blue hospital scrubs and a white smock stood in the hallway. "We're ready for you now." Dana stood. The man looked past her, down the hallway. "Is there anyone here with you?"

"No," she said softly. "I'm alone."

Logan stood from the bench. "I'll go in with you."

THE HILL FAMILY home in Medina was a five-bedroom house on an acre of well-manicured lawn, hedges, rhododendrons, and tulips. The backyard sloped gently from a pool to the edge of Lake Washington. Dana parked in front of the three-car garage to the left of the home, where the car could not be seen from the house. She sat undetected and wished she could remain there forever. She couldn't, of course. Nor could she break down in hysterics or collapse from the pain and agony that felt like someone was standing on her chest. She had a job to do. She had to deliver bad news again. That was her job in life, delivering bad news. She had been the one to tell her mother when her father died. James had been out of town. She had told them both the story that her father's law partner implored her to tell—that her father collapsed during a racquetball game at the Washington Athletic Club and died on the way to the hospital. That her father had been at his secretary's condominium drinking his lunch and lying on top of her when he died was deemed irrelevant, a fact that would only serve to hurt her mother.

The image of her brother's battered and distorted face haunted her, and she knew it would continue to do so for many years. The doctors had done their best to clean him up. She tried not to consider what he'd looked like before they did. His face was swollen and bruised, a strange maroon and purple color. His eyes were thin slits, as if he were peeking out from a deep sleep. His face was so foreign to her that Dana had hoped that it wasn't her brother after all, though that hope had been fleeting.

"I need to see his hand," she said.

"Which one?" the medical examiner asked.

"His left."

She walked around the tray table to the left side. On the pinky finger, at the tip, was the odd-shaped mole, the same mole she bore on the same finger of her left hand. It looked like Saturn, a planet with a ring around it. As kids, she and James would swear secrecy by pushing those two moles together. It was James's mole. It was her mole. It was their mole.

No mistake. "It's James," she said.

Somewhere down the street, the McMillans' beagle barked the mournful wail of an old, tired dog. Dana remembered when he was a puppy. What would she tell her mother this time to temper the bad news? What would lessen the pain of a mother's loss of a child? What else to say but "Mom, James is dead. Someone killed him. I don't know why, and why doesn't matter. He's dead."

"Oh, God." Dana covered her mouth. Tears streamed down her cheeks. She felt herself coming unglued again and gripped the steering wheel, her body racked with sobs.

Then the infrastructure collapsed, and she cried long, sorrowful heaves.

MORNING PASSED. The blanket of gray gave way to a blue sky with rolling white clouds. A chill remained—spring fighting the lingering winter. Dana stepped along the stone path amid the lambent shadows from the pine and dogwood trees swaying in a light breeze. She passed the Dutch door to the pantry off the kitchen. It had been the only door she and James had ever used growing up. But this was no longer her home, and it hadn't been for some time. It would send the wrong message to use it now.

A part of her wished her mother wasn't home, but where else would she be? Her mother had never worked. Not a day in her life. There was no need with a husband earning hundreds of thousands of dollars a year and who had left her a sizable estate—if not acquaintances. Following his death, her mother maintained few of their friends or hobbies. The law partners and wives who had been such good acquaintances when James Hill, Sr., was making rain for the firm—silent conspirators to his years of infidelity—suddenly disappeared. She canceled the family membership at the Overlake Golf & Country Club, not interested in pulling a golf cart around the course alone, and sold the cabin cruiser. She kept the speedboat, not for herself but for what she hoped would be many grandchildren. Most days she stayed at home knitting, doing needlepoint, and watching the soaps and talk shows.

Dana stepped beneath the peaked pediment supported on two white pillars, and took a moment to control her emotions. Then she raised the horse-head door knocker and rapped three times. After a moment the door pulled open. Her mother stood wearing yellow rubber gloves and holding a blackened sponge that smelled of a powerful chemical. She broke into an uncertain smile. "Dana. What a pleasant surprise. Why didn't you use the side door? Don't you still have your key?"

They touched cheeks, her mother careful to avoid getting any of the black grease on Dana's suit. Voices from the television talked in the background. If Dana's disheveled appearance and swollen eyes were apparent, her mother did not remark on them. But then the Hills had never been a family to confront the obvious, her father's twenty-year fling with his secretary being the obvious example.

Dana followed her mother through the formal dining room into the kitchen. Sliding glass doors overlooked the backyard. A spray of water from the pool sweep whipped through the air like a snake.

"I wish you had called." Her mother put the sponge in the sink, removed the rubber gloves, and used the back of her arm to push aside a strand of hair that had uncurled from the bun on the back of her head. The oven door hung open, the stove burners in the sink. The room smelled of ammonia and badly burned toast. "I'm just cleaning the oven."

"It's a self-cleaning oven, Mom," Dana said. She walked to the sliding glass door and opened it. A breeze fluttered the curtains. "You need air in here."

"Are you out on business?" Medina was across Lake Washington, just five miles east of downtown Seattle and accessible by either of the two bridges, though her mother always made it sound like an arduous trek. "How's Molly? How's my sweet little angel?" Her mother was flustered, her routine disrupted.

"Molly's fine."

Her mother pulled open the refrigerator. "Let me fix you something. How about a glass of lemonade? I have turkey. Or I could defrost some chicken. I think I may have—"

"—Mom."

Her mother paused.

"I'm not out here by accident. Come sit down."

Her mother closed the refrigerator. "What is it? What's wrong?"

She walked cautiously to the round kitchen table; a vase filled with fresh-cut roses from the yard was in the center. She pulled out a chair and sat on the edge of the seat.

"I have bad news," Dana said, and she knew from her mother's expression that she had heard the same echo Dana had heard from five years earlier.

"You're not sick; are you? Molly's not sick."

"No, Mom. Molly's not sick," she said. "It's James." The words caught in Dana's throat. Tears streamed down her cheeks. "He's gone. James is gone."

Her mother's brow furrowed. Her eyes watered. "Gone?" she asked, the realization registering as it only could in a mother who had just lost a child. Her body collapsed under the weight of her agony.

"He's dead, Mom. James is dead," Dana said, and she knew she would hear the echo of those words as well for many years.

9

⌒

T HE DOGWOOD SHADED the kitchen a parlor gray
as the sun dipped below the top of the foliage. Dana
stood at the slate kitchen counter filling a teakettle with
water and staring out into the backyard. The patio furniture had rust along the legs of the table and chairs. They
would need to be cleaned, the seat cushions removed
from storage, the white pop-up tents erected. There would
be another gathering at the Hill home on the shores of
Lake Washington. An Irish Catholic wake. Break out the
liquor.

The adrenaline that had fueled her through the initial trauma and given her the strength to identify James's
body, to tell her mother, and to call the appropriate relatives and friends had given way to a dull lassitude. Some
friends and relatives had already heard the news. They
wanted to talk to her about it and ask her questions,
but she had no answers for them and no desire to try to
explain. Some offered to come to the house. She politely

declined. Reporters called. She told them the family had
no comment. Then she unplugged the telephone.

Her mother lay in her bedroom upstairs, behind the
closed door at the end of the hall. She had collapsed in the
kitchen, toppling from the edge of her chair, and would
have crashed to the floor had Dana not caught her. Jack
Porter, for years the Hill family doctor, did not hesitate
when Dana called him. He came to the house and gave
Kathy Hill something to calm her nerves and to lower her
blood pressure.

The hot water from the faucet overflowed the top of the
teakettle, stinging Dana's hand. She turned it off, drained
water from the top of the kettle, and turned instinctively to
where the stove had once been but where now was a tiled
counter. Her mother had remodeled the kitchen after her
husband died, along with the three bathrooms. The stove,
a restaurant-size range with eight burners and a grill big
enough to cook for an army, was now located in a center island below a hood from which hung pots and pans.
Dana had never understood why her mother had waited
to remodel until she was alone in the house. Now Dana
thought she understood perfectly. It was the same reason
her mother had persisted in cleaning a self-cleaning oven:
She needed things to do.

Dana put the kettle on the front burner. It ignited with
a small pop and brought the faint odor of gas. Blue-yellow
fingers lapped at its copper bottom until Dana adjusted
the flame. She heard the sound of car tires turning into the
driveway, and stepped to the Dutch door. The blue BMW
rolled to a stop next to her Explorer. Grant emerged carrying Molly, who was eating a chocolate ice cream cone,
remnants smeared on her face and down the front of her

blue dress. Dana looked at her watch; Molly would never eat her dinner. She shook her head. It suddenly seemed so unimportant.

She opened the door and walked outside. Upon seeing her, Molly ran forward, smiling brightly, the chocolate around her lips giving her a clownish appearance. "Mommy."

The site of her little girl brought Dana to tears. She crouched and hugged her. When she pulled away, Molly asked, "Why are you crying, Mommy?"

Dana wiped her tears. "Mommy's sad, honey."

"Don't be sad." Molly held up the melting cone. "Do you want a taste?"

Dana took a small taste.

"Is that my little girl? Is that my Molly?" Kathy Hill came through the Dutch door wearing a white bathrobe and slippers, her hair flowing down her back. Makeup did not hide her puffy red eyes.

"Mom, Dr. Porter told you to stay in bed."

Her mother walked past Dana and took Molly in her arms. "Is that my baby? Hello, my angel."

"I got an ice cream, Grandma."

"Yes, angel, I see that." Kathy closed her eyes, cradling the little girl.

"Hi, Kathy," Grant said.

Kathy did not look up. "Hello, Grant."

"I'm very sorry about James."

"Thank you." Kathy swept up Molly in her arms. "Come on, angel, let's go upstairs and read some books."

"Grandma's sad."

"Yes, angel. Grandma's very sad," she said, carrying Molly back through the Dutch door.

Dana stepped forward, burying her face against Grant's

starched white shirt, crying on his chest. He caressed the back of her head as the events of the day cascaded down on her like broken glass, leaving tiny, painful cuts. After a minute she stepped back and wiped her tears. She'd left a smudge of mascara on his shirt. "Thanks for bringing her out here." Her voice was thick and husky.

"I'd keep her with me if I could."

Dana cleared her throat, pulled a wad of tissue from her back pocket, and blew her nose. "It's okay. I want her here with me. She's good therapy for Mom."

Grant looked up at the dormer window on the second level. "How's she doing?"

"As well as can be expected. You could go up and talk with her."

Grant looked away from the window. "Probably not a good idea. I never seem to be able to say the right thing. You know she has issues with me. Have the police told you anything more?"

She shook her head and closed her eyes. "They beat him to death, Grant."

"Jesus."

"For what?" she asked, feeling the anger burn. "James didn't have anything. He'd given everything away after he quit practicing law. Why would they rob *him*? Why not come here?" She extended her arms. "This is where the money is."

"People here have walls and gates, Dana. They have security systems."

"They killed him for nothing, Grant. They killed my brother for nothing."

"And the police have no idea who it was, no leads of any kind?"

"No," she said, shaking her head. "They have fingerprints and shoe prints but nothing confirmed yet." She sighed. "I'd like you to stay, Grant."

He stepped forward and held her again. He smelled of Armani cologne. It reminded her of law school and those moments when he had been there for her. But that was before the pressures of billable hours and making partner and finding and keeping clients had changed him. It was before ten years of getting up every morning and going to work to fight with someone had made him confrontational and cynical of people and their motives. It was before his own failures had made him resent her success. Sensitive to this, she rarely discussed her own career and instead focused on encouraging him, even after the second law firm had let him go. But after Molly's birth, there wasn't enough time in the day to be a wife, a cook, the family chauffeur, errand girl, lawyer, mommy, and to pacify a grown man's ego. Grant responded by working more and finding excuses to stay out late.

He spoke with his chin resting on the top of her head. "Your family needs you to be strong." His hands pressed her shoulder blades, but she felt no warmth. His voice contained no comfort. The wool of his suit jacket itched her cheek. "You're strong. If anyone can get through this, it's you."

"It's too much," she said, crying again. "It hurts, Grant. God, it hurts to lose him."

He held her, and for a moment she thought he might stay. But then his hands slipped from her back. "You know I start the Nelson trial in Chicago on Monday, and the rest of this week is just out of control. Hell broke loose today. They filed thirteen motions in limine and a forty-five-page trial brief. I can't do anything less."

"Couldn't Bergman handle the trial?"

He pulled back with a look of incredulity. "This is my chance. Bergman is giving me Nelson Industries on a silver platter. When I win, I'll put another thirty million dollars in the shareholders' pockets—the biggest contingency award in the history of the firm. I'll be a superstar. It's my tenure. Nelson Industries will be a guaranteed three-million-dollar client in my column. I'll be—*we'll* be set for life. We can get a house on the lake, a boat, everything we've wanted."

At the moment she didn't want anything. She no longer wanted him. The law had not changed him. It had just defined who he was all along. She studied the moss that had worked its way through the mortar of the stone walkway, undermining its integrity, and thought of her marriage. Removing the moss would not be easy.

10

❧

Espn's SportsCenter filled the cramped motel room with animated chatter. Two sportscasters sat behind a miniature studio desk, narrating the day's highlights. Laurence King turned the volume up high, but the newscasters' voices still did not drown out the sound of the woman through the paper-thin wall.

"More, honey. Yes. Yes. Yes, baby."

The photograph of Mount Ranier on the wall thumped rhythmically. The lamp shade on the wood-veneer nightstand vibrated. Had it not been bolted down, it likely would have slid off. The woman was being well paid to moan, but at the moment King didn't want to hear it.

"Oh, you're big. You're so big. You just fill me up, baby."

King pounded his fist on the wall. "Shut the fuck up." The grunting and groaning continued, uninterrupted. King paced the worn brown carpet, alternately rubbing at the coarse dark stubble of his chin and biting at his thumbnail, perpetually stained with grease and dirt from his work as a day laborer for a construction company. The room held the smell of body odor and moldy wood.

"Fifteen thousand." Marshall Cole paced an area near the bathroom, stepping around and over fast-food bags, a grease-stained pizza box, beer bottles, and articles of clothing he continued to discard—first his shoes and socks, then his shirt. He stood naked to the waist, his blue jeans hanging from narrow hips, holes worn in the knees. They had buried his other clothes in a dirt field behind the motel, digging the hole deep enough to prevent stray dogs from unearthing them, searching for the scent of blood.

"Fifteen thousand." Cole compulsively tugged at the bill of his Seattle Mariners baseball cap, alternately pulling it low on his forehead and pushing it onto the crown of his head. "You tell him we want fifteen thousand. I didn't sign up to kill nobody, Larry. No fucking way." He pointed to King. "It was supposed to be a burglary. That's what you said. You said the man told you it was a burglary. Empty. The fucking place was supposed to be empty, man."

"Shut up," King shouted at the wall, growing more angry.

"Nobody said nothing about killing anyone. I ain't no killer. They'll kill me for this. They'll kill us both."

King turned from the wall and took a step toward Cole. "Shut up." He'd had enough whining from the little prick. "Shut the fuck up. Don't tell me what to do. Don't fucking tell me what to do."

Cole stepped back, no match for King, who stood six foot two and weighed 255 pounds. Cole was rail-thin, with a washboard stomach that displayed protruding ribs. He had a nervous stomach and irritable bowel syndrome, which caused him to spend more time in the bathroom than a janitor and prevented him from keeping anything in long enough to put on weight. With full lips, green eyes, and sandy-blond hair that hung past his shoulders, Cole would have been called pretty if he'd been born a woman.

"Fifteen thousand," Cole muttered under his breath. "Enough money to get out of here. Maybe go to Canada. They don't extradite from Canada, do they? Shit!" He threw the cap on the floor and tugged at his hair. "I had to do it. He saw me. He looked right at me."

"Just take it easy." King walked to the window and eased back the heavy curtain. The Emerald Inn sat like a boil on a dog's butt. King hadn't chosen it for the ambience. He'd chosen it because the rooms were off an outdoor landing that offered a clear view of the dirt and gravel parking lot out front. The same four cars remained. More would arrive after last call at the Four Aces Bar, half a mile down the road. King checked his watch and turned from the window. "I'll get the fifteen grand, and we'll get out of here. Nobody's going to know anything."

"Something's wrong." Cole stood and paced again. "Something ain't right. I can feel these things. I told you, I can feel them."

"I'll handle it," King growled.

Someone knocked on the door.

Cole's head snapped as if on a string, his eyes wide as those of a spooked horse. King put a finger to his lips and quietly pressed an eye to the peephole. No way the man could have parked the car in the lot, then walked up the two flights of stairs and down the landing without King hearing him. Fuck, the landing shook each time someone passed the door. And yet somehow the man had done just that. He stood on the landing, his face distorted in the round hole, the pointed nose bulbous and hooked at the tip, with his black wraparound sunglasses bulging like the depthless eyes of a hawk. King stepped back and pointed to the interior door that led to the adjacent room.

Cole shoved the cap back on his head and quickly gathered his clothes. He grabbed a 9mm automatic from the top of the television, dropped a tennis shoe on the floor, and kicked it ahead of him as he hurried through the doorway, closing the door behind him.

King stuffed a Falcon 9mm in the front of his jeans and pulled his shirt closed, then rethought it and pulled it open. Show of force. Let the man know he meant business. He removed the security latch, pulled open the door, and stepped back. The man entered and closed the door without uttering a word. He wore a brown leather jacket, straight-leg blue jeans, and black boots. In his right hand he carried a green garbage bag. He dropped it on the carpet. King knew the man was military of some kind: army or marines. King had done four years in the army. He understood military. He could spot it from across a fucking room. This guy wasn't just a grunt, though. He carried himself different. He was likely one of those Special Forces types—a Ranger or SEAL or some damn thing. Whatever he was, the guy gave King the creeps. He never smiled. Never changed expressions. Just stared with that blank expression, King's distorted image reflecting back at him in those ever-present sunglasses. King wished he'd never spoken to the man at the bar. He wished he'd just turned down the drinks and walked away. But five thousand bucks for a simple burglary had been too good to pass up, and King needed the money to pay his ex-wife child support or his ass was going back to county. Besides, what was done was done. There was no sense crying over it.

King stood at the foot of the bed closest to the bathroom with his hands on his hips and his shirt pulled back to display the butt of the Falcon against his hairy stomach. "We have a problem. The place wasn't empty. You said it would be empty."

The man put his hands in his jacket pockets. "It was."

"*Was* for about twenty minutes. Then the fucking guy came home and walked right into the room."

"So I read." The man was obviously referring to the article in the metro section of the *Seattle Times*. His fucking face was like a damn statue. "Unfortunate."

"Unfortunate? Unfortunate, my ass. You didn't say anything about killing anybody."

"No, I didn't."

In the background, the sportscasters continued to discuss the baseball highlights from games played earlier that day.

"And we didn't sign on for killing nobody. We ain't killers. That's not what we was paid for," King said.

"Did you get the items?"

"Maybe we did. Maybe we didn't. What we need to talk about is what we were paid to do and what we weren't paid to do. The place was supposed to be empty. That's what you told us."

"Did you get the items?"

"Are you deaf?" The man did not answer. He just kept staring the fucking stare that sent a chill through King. He fought against it, but his eyes shifted to the pillow on the unmade bed. The man walked to the head of the bed, rolled back the pillow, and picked up the manila envelope. He opened it, studying its contents.

"Oh, God," the woman next door yelled. "Harder, baby. Harder. You just about there, sugar."

"We want more money," King said. "Fifteen thousand."

"Bring it, sugar. Harder. Bring it harder."

The man rummaged through the envelope. "You did not get all the items."

King laughed. "Are you shitting me, man? The guy came home! Shit, you're lucky we got that much stuff. Cole was in the goddamn bedroom when the guy walked in. So, fuck yeah, that's all, and fuck if I care. Fifteen thousand. We need to go somewhere for a while and let this die down."

The man shoved the envelope inside his jacket, returning his hands to his pockets. "I didn't ask you to kill anyone," he said matter-of-factly. "It was not your assignment."

"Now, honey. Now. Come on. Come on, sugar."

King was stunned. "You are a piece of fucking work. My assignment? This ain't the military, shithead, I don't take orders from nobody no more." He pointed at the envelope for emphasis. "We got what we could, nearly everything. We did more than our assignment. We did a hell of a lot more. We didn't sign on for killing nobody."

"You don't want to go back to jail, is that it?"

"Fuck no, I don't want to go back. I go back, I go back forever. I ain't going back, and not for killing nobody. They'll kill us for that."

"No," the man said. "They won't."

King shook his head. "News flash, Einstein. This here is a capital murder state. They'll kill us. They'll say we murdered him during the commission of a felony, and we'll get the juice in the arm, and lights out, Martha."

The bullet ripped through the leather jacket without

making a sound. King fell backward. The woman next door moaned.

"Yes. Oh, yes. Yes. Yes."

The man removed the gun from his pocket and stood over King's body. Blood oozed from the dime-size hole in his forehead. He pulled a watch from the envelope and dropped it onto the carpet next to King's body. Then he opened the green plastic garbage bag and scattered blood-stained clothes about the room. Finished, he checked the door handle to the adjacent room and determined it to be locked. He stepped back and planted the heel of his black boot just above the lock. The cheap wood crashed inward, the force driving the doorknob through the Sheetrock on the other side. Two shots rang out from inside the room, causing the man to duck behind the doorjamb. He waited a beat, then swung the gun around the frame, his gaze sweeping the room.

Cole sat with his feet dangling out the bathroom window. He fired another wild shot over his shoulder, dropped his shoes and clothes out the window, and jumped. The man hurried to the window. Cole rolled off the roof of a car onto the ground, looked up, and fired another shot before limping across the highway and disappearing into the darkness.

The man turned from the window and hurried back across the motel, stepping over King and pulling open the door. The man who had been receiving sexual accolades from the woman in the room next door stood on the landing, barefoot, shirt open, struggling to zip his fly. His unfastened belt buckle dangled below a large, hairless belly.

The gunman aimed head high. The man froze, hands

on his zipper, eyes wide. The color rushed from his face, leaving him a jaundiced yellow from the dull glow of the landing lights. The gunman smiled, raised a finger to his lips, and shook his head slowly. Then he turned and walked toward the staircase at the end of the landing.

11

⁓

THE EIGHT CONCRETE stairs shook with each step. The handrail rattled in his grip. The motel was classic construction from the 1970s, when the building industry was booming and you couldn't throw a hammer without hitting someone who claimed to be a framer. A two-story box with a flat tar-and-gravel roof, the building had been tagged with gang graffiti; the aluminum-framed windows were rusted and pitted, and the decking peeled and worn. At the top of the landing, Logan checked the intersection between the iron railing and the stucco wall. The large black bolt had wiggled free, creating a hole that allowed water intrusion. Probably dry rot. The handrail wouldn't support a man's weight leaning against it.

The rooms were located off the landing, a staircase at each end. Room 8 wasn't difficult to find—it was the only room with the door open and an armed police officer standing guard. Logan nodded to the officer and scribbled his name on the log before stepping in. Carole Nuchitelli knelt near a body, a man lying faceup on a shag carpet the color of a thick glass of Nestlé Quik.

"You keep following me, Nooch, and people will think we're dating."

Nuchitelli looked up with seeming disinterest. "I've been here an hour. I think you're stalking me."

The room held the stench of soiled carpet and death. Logan looked down at the corpse. The man's bowels had released. His eyes were open, his face pale and devoid of any emotion. But for the dime-size hole in his head, the man looked frozen. A dark halo around the back of his head indicated that the carpet had absorbed much of the blood. "Looks like a twenty-two," Logan said.

"Falcon nine-millimeter," Nooch said.

Logan pointed to the bullet wound in the forehead. "I'm not talking about the gun in his pants. I'm talking about the hole in his head. Looks like a twenty-two."

She shrugged. "Or a nine-millimeter."

"Or a nine-millimeter," Logan agreed. He turned and studied the doorway. "What do you estimate the distance to be?" he asked, pacing it off.

"Eight to ten feet."

"Eight feet," he confirmed. He wiped sleep from his eyes. "Heck of a shot."

Nuchitelli shrugged, unimpressed. "Not that far."

"Not if you have time to aim."

She stopped what she was doing, sat back, and smiled up at him. "All right, go ahead. You know you want to."

Logan pointed at the butt of the Falcon. "That tells me the guy didn't even see it coming. He was shot in the forehead so he was obviously facing his killer, but, he didn't even have the chance to reach for his weapon."

"Maybe the guy surprised him."

Logan nodded. "Oh, I'm sure he did, but not the way you're thinking." He pointed to the front door. "No forced entry. So either he had a key or he was already in the room. Do we have an ID?"

"You know I like them anonymous, Logan. What are you doing out here, anyway?"

"Murphy called. Said he had something for me."

She pointed at the doorway to the adjacent room and rolled her eyes. "He's in there."

"I think he just likes getting my ass out of bed for kicks."

"You may be right."

As Logan started for the other room, he noticed a wad of bills on the floor, partially hidden by the body, as well as bloodied clothes. "His?" he asked, referring to the corpse.

Nuchitelli nodded. "In his right-front pants pocket."

"Whose clothes?"

She shrugged. "Don't know. His I guess."

Logan walked toward the door that separated Room 8 from Room 7.

The door frame between the two rooms had been splintered. This was a forced entry. Maybe the killer *had* surprised him. Patrick Murphy stood with his partner, Debra Hallock, and a swarm of people inside the room. Murphy and Hallock worked out of the South Precinct. Murphy was a stereotype: Irish and looked it, with fair skin, ruddy cheeks, and freckles, and was proud to profess his heritage to anyone and everyone. Thin blue veins traversed a bulbous nose that revealed a penchant for happy hours.

Murphy grinned. "Look what the cat dragged out late at night." He parted his thinning hair in the middle to try to effect greater coverage. Signs of his age rolled over the waist of his pants.

"I hope you have a good reason for getting my ass out of bed, Murph." Logan offered his hand to Murphy while acknowledging Hallock. "Hey, Deb."

"Shit. I have to give you something to do in between rescuing cats from trees and playing with your pecker," Murphy said.

"Firemen rescue cats. And I've told you, it's the Irish, not the Scottish, who play with their peckers." He looked at Hallock. "Sorry, Deb."

She raised thin eyebrows on a not unattractive but unmemorable face, as if to say, "What else is new?"

"So, what the hell am I doing here?"

Murphy answered, "You had a murder in Green Lake last night—guy named James Hill?"

Logan nodded. "Yeah."

"Come here." Murphy led Logan back into the room with the corpse. Several pieces of evidence had already been bagged in plastic evidence bags and placed on the bed. "We found this near the body." He handed Logan a bag with a watch. "Read the inscription on the back."

Logan turned it over and held it up to the single bulb in the overhead light fixture.

To James Jr., Esquire
6-22-90
Congratulations
Dad

"We checked it out," Hallock said. "Your James Hill was a junior."

Logan considered the watch, then the corpse. "So who's the stiff?"

"Laurence King," Murphy said, grinning.

Not sure Murphy was serious, Logan asked, "You mean like the talk-show guy on TV?"

"That's *Larry* King," Hallock said.

"Career shithead," Murphy offered. "Spent most of his formative and adult years behind bars mostly for burglaries. Held up a gas station seven years ago and did six at Walla Walla before parole. Been out about a year. Two-strike loser. His probation officer says he's been working construction and keeping his nose clean. Guess not."

Logan looked down at Laurence King's feet. He wore work boots, the kind that would make a size-twelve imprint like the one in the mud outside James Hill's back door. "Not a murderer, though?"

Hallock shook her head. "Not until last night, apparently."

"So the blood on those clothes could be James Hill's?" Logan mused.

Murphy shrugged. "Could be, but why would they be covered in dirt?"

Logan thought about it. "Send one of the boys outside to look for a hole in the ground."

"A hole in the ground? You think King buried them?" Murphy sounded skeptical. He shook his head. "Then why the fuck would he dig them back up?"

Logan reconsidered the watch and the cash.

Hallock directed an officer to search around the outside of the building for a hole. "You think the other guy set King up and left us this stuff so we would think King killed Hill?"

"I don't know. Make sure we get an imprint of King's shoes," Logan said. "Don't suppose we have any witnesses?"

"The guy at the front desk is doing a 'see no, hear no, speak no' routine at the moment, but he's just being a tough guy," Murphy said. "He'll talk when I tell him he's gonna have a patrol car parked up his ass from here to eternity and he can kiss his customers good-bye."

"Anybody else that was here took off," Hallock added. "The guy at the desk said King and another guy came in about midnight yesterday and rented Room Eight."

"Did he give a description of the second guy?" Logan asked.

Hallock looked at her notes. "Nothing to rival Hemingway. Five-six to five-eight. Slight build, long hair."

Logan reached down and picked up a pair of jeans, considering the waist. Then he looked at Laurence King. "These would never fit him," he said. "Could be our guy."

"Guy at the desk said King came back in about six o'clock and asked to rent Room Seven as well."

"Did he say why?" Logan asked.

Hallock shook her head. "This place gets a lot of business. The prostitutes hang out near the bars down the street. The guy says he assumed King and his pal were getting a couple of visitors for the evening and didn't want to 'tag-team them' in the same room. His words, not mine."

"You want my two cents?" Murphy said. "King and his pal have a dispute over the money, and the guy shoots him. Bang." He pointed at King and imitated the kick of a handgun with his hand. "Then the guy spooks and leaves behind some of the money and the watch and the bloody clothes to make us think King is the guy who killed and robbed James Hill."

Logan considered the theory. "I don't know a lot of guys on the run to leave behind a wad of cash—or clothes that could implicate him in the murder."

"Shit, we ain't talking about a fucking Ph.D. Ten bucks says he's a loser like King. Only now he's running scared because he killed someone and he ain't thinking straight."

"Detective?"

All three detectives turned. One of the technicians stood between the two beds, near the headboards. When they approached, she pointed with a pen, indicating a bullet hole near a framed photograph of Mount Ranier. The hole was partially camouflaged by the mosaic pattern of the wallpaper. The technician pointed to a second dime-size hole several feet away. The bullet had nicked the edge of the picture frame before embedding in the wallboard. Judging by the size of the hole, it, too, had been either a 9mm slug or a .22.

Logan pointed to King. "He never got the Falcon out of his pants, and the guy who shot him had to be standing near the front door. Not even a blind man could have missed this badly. Right, Nooch?"

Nuchitelli looked up. "Not even a blind man," she said.

"Shit, you should be a detective," Murphy added.

"Please, not with the money my parents spent on my education."

Logan suppressed a laugh, turned to consider the trajectory that would have been necessary for the bullets to embed in the wall, and deduced the shots had to come from the adjacent room.

"King's pal was in there," Hallock said, noting his gaze. "That's why they got the second room; he was supposed to be King's backup."

"So whoever shot King then likely kicked in the door to go after him," Logan said.

"What are you saying?" Murphy asked.

Logan walked back into the adjoining room, Hallock and Murphy in tow. "I'm saying I think King's pal was inside this room and is either a terrible aim or was just firing at random, panicked." He faced the damaged door frame, stepped back, and bumped up against the bathroom doorjamb. Turning around, he noticed an open window, walked in, and leaned over the tub to look out the window on a dirt lot, careful not to touch the sill. It was a long fall, but not too long if someone was shooting at you. He walked back into the room where King's body lay. Nuchitelli stood and removed her gloves. Two men were preparing to put the body in a yellow body bag and zip it closed.

"Dust that ledge for prints and send them over along with prints from the victim. I want to have them compared with any prints found in James Hill's house." Logan turned to Murphy and Hallock. "I'm meeting Hill's sister at his house tomorrow. We were going to go over items that might have been stolen. That doesn't appear to be too urgent anymore." Logan looked at his watch and let out a tired sigh. Morning would come too early. "I'll ask her about the watch and if her brother would have much cash in the house. If anything else is missing we'll get out a list to the local pawn shops."

"Shit, like that will do any fucking good with those

thieves." Murphy grinned. "We solved your murder, Logan. Even bagged him for you."

Logan stared at Laurence King's body, now encased in the yellow bag, and sucked in air through the small gap between his two front teeth. He didn't think so.

12

❧

D ANA COUNTED THE panels on the front door of her
brother's home. Twenty-four: four panels across, and
the six panels down. Twenty-four. Simple math. No matter
how many different ways she considered it, the end result
was always the same. She wondered why her brother had
painted the door red—a sharp contrast to the pale green siding, which stood out even more now, like a bloody reminder
of what had happened inside.

She couldn't recall having ever truly considered the
exterior of James's home. Her brother had often invited
her to dinner or to stop by after work or on the weekend,
but she rarely did and never stayed long. She was always
late picking up Molly from day care, or getting the dry
cleaning, or heading home to cook dinner, or trying to
finish a rush project Marvin Crocket had sprung on her.
James had never complained. He'd never made her feel
guilty.

"Maybe next week," he'd always say.

But next week never worked. Now next week would never come. And that wasn't going to change either, no matter how many ways she tried to consider it.

She felt herself slipping again into the dark gray vortex of despair and dug in her heels to stop the momentum. Now was not her time to grieve. She needed to get through the details. She retreated from the mist to the shelter beneath the pediment and leaned against the clapboard siding, physically and emotionally spent. She had rushed from the funeral parlor after choosing a simple forest-green casket for her brother's body. Her next task was gathering his personal papers from his home and determining for the detective what had been stolen. She checked her watch and the tree-lined street. With no sign of the detective, she closed her eyes, seeking a respite, but instead recalled the reception following her father's funeral. The catered leftovers had been wrapped in clear plastic, the tables and chairs folded and stacked, the guests and relatives gone. Dana and James had sat in the den, James staring at the blue and yellow flames in the brick fireplace.

"I'm leaving the practice of law," he'd said without looking at her. "I haven't been happy for some time." He sipped a beer from a red plastic cup and sat back, looking up at the painting of a three-masted schooner above the fireplace. "I wouldn't do anything about it with Dad alive; I was too worried about what he would think. Practicing law was the only part of my life he ever took an interest in."

She did not take her brother seriously, believing his emotions to be the product of their father's unexpected death, a jolting reminder of their own mortality, and that time was the most precious of all commodities. "Take a couple of months, James. Now is not the time to be making life-altering decisions. You've been through a lot these past four days. You're not seeing things clearly."

"This is not a spur-of-the-moment decision." He sat forward, speaking with greater urgency. "I've been *thinking* about it for a long time. I don't have a life. I'm at the office sixty hours a week, and when I'm not there, I'm still there—managing my cases, considering trial strategy, dreading what fires will ignite to ruin my weekend. Look at me." He pulled his hair. "I'm thirty-two years old and I'm losing my hair. What's left of it is turning gray. I'm not married. Hell, I don't even have a steady girlfriend."

"You're up for partner next year."

"That's what *really* scares me. Half the shareholders at the firm are divorced. They make four hundred thousand dollars a year, but their mortgages and child support are killing them." James picked up his beer and sat back, shaking his head. "I'm not going to die at my desk like Dad."

A part of her wanted to tell him that work had not killed their father, far from it, but as angry as she was at her father, telling her brother the truth would only be cruel. Boys put their fathers on pedestals and considered them heroes. Girls had the unfortunate experience of growing up and getting their hearts broken by men. They knew their fathers' flaws and weaknesses. They knew they weren't heroes, often far from it.

"Don't use Dad as an example; he was a workaholic," she said.

"I've felt this way since the first week of law school."

Dana raised her eyebrows. "Really?" She had also questioned her own decision to go to law school—one she made more to spite her father than to appease him. He hadn't thought she had what it took to be a lawyer.

"The next thing I knew, I was sitting behind my desk at Dillon and Block, three doors down from Dad in the anti-trust department." James laughed again. "I hadn't even taken a class on anti-trust. Dad would hand me a file and go on and on about this and that, and I would just sit there looking concerned, nodding, throwing in a few 'sons of bitches' and 'goddammits.'"

They both laughed.

James drank from his beer. "At least you had the good sense to work someplace else."

"I was defiant."

"Well, so am I. Better late than never. I'm getting out."

"What would you do?" She hoped her brother would provide them both an answer.

"Teach."

She laughed, then caught herself when she realized he was serious.

James cradled the plastic cup in his hands, flexing it. "A friend called to tell me that Seattle U has a position to teach legal research and writing and trial advocacy."

"You're serious. You've looked into this."

He nodded. "I forwarded my grades and references last week. If all goes well, next fall I could be trading my suits and Ferragamos for khakis and loafers."

She stared at the coffee table, filled with a sense of loss unrelated to the death of their father.

"Come with me," James said, perhaps sensing her despair. "Let's celebrate Dad's death by getting lives."

She took a sip of wine. "Right. What would Grant think?"

"Who cares? This isn't about Grant. It's about you."

"He's my husband, James."

"Don't remind me." He raised both hands. "Sorry."

She knew her family did not care for Grant, but it was not a topic of discussion. Grant was her husband. "Our mortgage is more than we can afford on both our salaries. We owe a hundred thousand in student loans between us, and our car payments are more than some people's house payments."

"Sell it all." James leaned forward, elbows on his knees, his blue eyes sparkling. "That's what I'm doing. Sell the cars and the house. With the equity in the house, I can pay almost all cash for something smaller."

She laughed out loud. "With the equity in our house, we might be able to afford dinner and a nice bottle of wine."

"You'd be free."

She didn't even know what that meant. "We've talked about children."

He sat back. His tone changed. "Really?"

She nodded. "We've been married five years, and I'm not getting any younger."

"Are you getting along better?"

"We're trying. It's just the strain of work. It'll change once we have children. It will give us a new perspective."

But it had been her brother who gained the new perspective. James sold his home on Capitol Hill, sold his Mercedes, and gave his suits and most of his ties and dress shirts to Goodwill. He dropped his membership at the Washington Athletic Club, stopped dining at expensive restaurants, and rarely spent the $150 greens fees for a round of golf at the private clubs. He liked to joke that he had to quit his high-paying job in order to save money.

"I'm very sorry, I'm late."

Dana opened her eyes. Detective Michael Logan stood at the bottom of the steps with rain dripping from his umbrella. "I could lie and blame it on traffic, but the truth is I overslept. I got a call in the middle of the night, a murder out in Rainier Valley. It turns out it's connected with your brother."

She felt her anxiety rise. "My brother?"

Logan looked up at the sky. "Let's step inside, out of the rain." The yellow police tape was still wedged between the door and the jamb. "Do you have a key?"

"No," she said, embarrassed.

Logan nodded. "The neighbor has one. I'll be just a second."

She watched him jog across the lawn to the next house and return moments later with the key. Logan removed the strip of police tape, unlocked the door, and pushed it open, but Dana paused at the threshold.

"We can do this later," Logan said. "Given what I learned last night, it's not as urgent."

Dana faced forward, eyes focused down the hallway, recalling the first time she stepped to the edge of the high dive on the floating pier at Madison Park and tried to convince herself to step off. It wasn't courage that had caused her to take the step. It was the fear of looking afraid.

"Thank you, Detective. I appreciate your thoughtfulness, but there's no reason to wait. It has to be done, and I'll be the person who will have to do it."

"I wasn't thinking of your brother's belongings," Logan said. "I was thinking of you." The comment surprised her. She turned. He looked down at her with bloodshot green eyes. "I mean perhaps another time—when someone can be here with you," he said.

Dana shook her head. Then she turned back to the threshold, and stepped across.

Legal briefs were strewn across the table. Several had slipped onto the floor next to James's leather briefcase. She walked down the hallway, struck with the same odd feeling as when she went into the house across the street from Ford's Theatre, where Abraham Lincoln had died after being shot. Everything seemed like a prop abandoned on a stage after the final act. Time stood still, a horrible moment forever frozen. A dark stain colored the hardwood floor. Dana turned and covered her mouth.

"Are you all right?" Logan asked.

She took a moment to regain her composure, relying on the part of her that would always be a lawyer—the need to get answers to her questions. "You said a murder in Rainier Valley might have something to do with my brother?"

Logan reached into his pocket and handed her a plastic bag. "The responding detectives think they found your brother's watch."

Dana turned it over and read the inscription, nodding. "My father gave us each one when we graduated from law school." She showed the detective her wrist. "Do they have the man who took this?"

Logan shook his head. "He's dead. Someone shot him."

"Who is he? Why would he kill my brother?"

"The man's name was Laurence King. He was pretty much a career criminal, a thief whose crimes were escalating in violence. He was paroled three months ago."

She closed her eyes and shook her head. Her anger spiked. A released convict. "I know you said my brother was killed during a robbery, Detective, but I'm having a hard time accepting that. Look around; he didn't own anything of value."

Logan nodded as if he'd heard the rationalization before. "You'd be surprised. I've seen people get killed over a five-dollar dispute. We're still trying to get all the information we can, but what we know is that King was a two-strike felon. He had a lot to lose if he got caught. He also hung out with a man named Marshall Cole, another petty thief. We think Cole might have been the person who killed your brother."

"Why?"

"We found bloody clothing at the motel along with your brother's watch. The clothes are too small to have been King's. Based on a physical description from the motel attendant and Cole's police file they likely belonged to Cole."

"Do you think this man Cole also killed King?"

"We don't know yet. We're trying to find him. The motel is known to do a brisk business with the local prostitutes. King could have been killed during a random dispute and Cole took off, not wanting to be a part of it. Do you know whether your brother kept large amounts of cash, either on him or in the home?"

"My brother? Not that I'm aware of. Why?"

"In addition to your brother's watch, King had upward of fifteen hundred dollars on him."

She shook her head. "I guess it's possible, but I doubt James would keep that much money here, and he certainly wouldn't carry it on him."

"What about jewelry or things King could have hocked to get that kind of money?"

She surveyed the room. "My brother sold or gave away

most of his possessions when he quit practicing law. He never owned much jewelry. The watch and his class ring were the only things I knew of."

They walked through the rooms, Logan making an inventory of possessions. The thieves had not taken the television or stereo, both of which were relics by modern standards, nor had they taken the laptop. They'd also left his collection of compact discs and a checkbook Dana found in the dresser in the bedroom. Even Logan thought that was odd.

After an hour together, they again stood in the back room. Logan flipped his notebook closed. "Okay. I'll give you some privacy to collect your brother's personal things. You have my business card. If you think of anything or notice anything that seems out of the ordinary, let me know. I'll keep you informed if I learn anything new."

Dana thanked him and watched him walk down the hallway, leaving her alone, a stranger in her brother's home.

SHE STARTED WITH the rooms at the back of the house and worked toward the front door and her escape. She felt uncomfortable in the house, the hollow, lifeless eyes of the African tribal masks staring at her, wondering why she hadn't spent time there when her brother was alive. She wasn't sure what to do with them or the African tapestries and sculptures. She knew that James had brought them back after a six-week safari from which he returned thin, tan, vegetarian, and in better spirits than she could recall. His hair had grown from the corporate downtown cut to curls that lapped over the collar of his shirt, and he had exchanged contact lenses for wire-rimmed glasses.

Still, she didn't want the masks staring at her, a constant reminder of the tragedy they had witnessed. She decided she would call the Seattle Art Museum and ask if they had interest in the pieces or knew of another museum that might. The rest of the kitchen and the living room, with the exception of the larger furniture, fit in one box. James had taken on a somewhat monastic lifestyle. She assumed he ate most of his meals at the school.

She moved down the hall to the bedroom, knowing this would be the most difficult room in the house. Books and framed photographs filled the built-in shelves and overflowed onto the hardwood floor. An entire shelf was devoted to historical biographies of Civil War commanders. Another shelf held the classics: Hemingway, Fitzgerald, Faulkner, and Twain. She picked up a multipane picture frame and sat on the edge of the bed. Each panel held a photograph of James with Molly—Molly in a backpack, at a museum, at the zoo with her face painted.

Dana cradled the frame to her chest, sick with the thought of how she would explain to a little girl that her uncle was gone and never coming back. Her shoulders shook uncontrollably. Sobs of pain escaped her throat. She let herself cry, a prolonged five-minute burst before she could pull herself together and open her eyes. When she did, a stocky blond man stood in the doorway.

"Jesus." She stood, dropping the picture frame. The glass shattered on the hardwood floor.

"I'm sorry. I didn't think anyone was here." He was neatly dressed in a navy blue suit of good quality, a button-down shirt, and a tie.

Dana wiped the tears from her cheeks, embarrassed and angered by the intrusion. "Can I help you?"

His face was angular, with strong features, his eyes unnaturally dark, a coal black. He pulled a wallet from his jacket and showed her a badge. "I'm Detective Daniel Holmes, Ms. . . ."

"Hill. Dana Hill. Are you working with Detective Logan?"

He nodded and slipped the wallet back inside his jacket. "Mike is handling the murder. I'm focusing more on the burglary—items that could have been stolen. I'm sure he mentioned getting out a list to the local pawnshops. Tell me, were you married to the decedent?"

"Married? Oh . . . no," Dana said. "Hill is my maiden name. James was my brother."

"I see. Well, I'm very sorry for your loss."

"I already spoke with Detective Logan this morning, and we put a list together," she said. "But I'm not sure I'll be of much assistance. My brother didn't have much besides his watch, and I don't really know what else is missing."

"So you've found nothing of interest?"

"Of interest?"

The detective pointed to two boxes outside the door. "Have you found anything that thieves would ordinarily take but left behind? Sometimes we can learn as much from what's left as what's taken. For instance, if they took only the electronic equipment—televisions and stereos—but left behind jewelry or artwork, we could better pinpoint the pawnshops they might target."

"They don't appear to have been interested in the electronics. As I said, Detective Logan has the list."

The man nodded. There was an uncomfortable pause. "Well, I won't delay you further. I apologize again about startling you."

Dana followed him to the front door, closing it behind him. Then she turned the deadbolt.

Back in the bedroom, she knelt to pick up the pieces of glass embedded in the throw rug that covered the area beneath her brother's bed. She ran her hands over the threads, feeling carefully for the smaller pieces, noticing a glint of light reflecting near the headboard, a small prism of colors. She stretched out her arm, feeling blindly for the object, and pulled it out.

"Oh, my," she said, sitting back to consider it.

13

T HE FOLLOWING MONDAY, Dana sat clasping her
    mother's hand in the front pew of St. James Cathe-
dral in downtown Seattle. Molly sat between her and
Grant. James's casket had been wheeled down the center
aisle and draped with a white vestment. Incense perme-
ated the darkened cathedral, puffs of smoke rising from
the censer as the priest swung it, the three gold chains
clinking rhythmically. The arched stained-glass windows
emitted minimal light, the colored panes muted by the
persistent gray skies. The candles on the altar flickered in
an unfelt breeze, stirring with the movement of the large
crowd that had gathered in the pews behind them.

The priest returned to the altar. Adorned in green and
white robes, he spoke with a thick Polish accent that made
him difficult to understand. Dana listened to the service
without hearing. The weekend had passed in a slow roll,
though Dana had remained in constant motion—allowing
the details to take up the minutes, the minutes becoming

hours, the hours becoming days. She slept and ate little, thought a lot about the past, and avoided thinking about the future. The present was difficult enough. She had been so completely absorbed by preparing James's wake, funeral, and the reception to follow that she had forgotten about her biopsy. Then she checked her messages at work—a lawyer's habit—and the sound of Dr. Neal's voice brought back her anxiety. But the doctor had only called to advise that her lab results were not yet ready.

The priest invited the attendees to sit, then looked down from the altar to Dana. This was her cue. When they met to discuss the funeral, the priest had asked her for details about her brother's life. Dana had started to compile a list, then stopped. She did not want her brother to be remembered as an afterthought—to have his eulogy given by someone who had never known him in life. Hard as it would be, she would deliver her brother's eulogy. When the priest expressed concern about whether she would be emotionally capable, she dismissed him. "I'll get through it," she said, "for my brother."

She released her mother's hand and made her way to the lectern, hearing stifled sobs. When she adjusted the microphone, it emitted a sharp whistle. She unfolded her brother's eulogy and cleared her throat. She had struggled with the words, with how to sum up thirty-four years of her brother's life in minutes. The clichés would not save her. This was not a celebration of life—the funeral of an old man. Nor had James been freed of the pain of a terminal illness or the victim of a tragic accident. Her brother had been murdered. Beaten to death in cold blood. Two men had taken his life and put an end to his existence. Stomped on him like a bug. The fact that her brother had just started to live the life he wanted only made it more painful. James had the guts to do what she did not: face the unknown, to hell with everyone else's expectations. He set out to do what he wanted with his life only to have a couple of two-time losers steal it from him. At least that was what the police continued to maintain. They said James had been killed during the commission of a robbery. They said it happened all the time. They said it happened over drugs, over parking spaces, and over amounts insufficient to buy a value meal at a fast-food restaurant. It just didn't happen as often to people living in middle- and upper-class white suburban neighborhoods.

And that was what bothered her.

Her legal training mandated that she try to make sense of what had happened, to question the facts and make them fit into a coherent theory. But she had yet to piece together the facts of her brother's death. She had yet to come up with a coherent story, and in law, if the story wasn't coherent, facts were missing or someone was lying. Foremost among those questions was why would Laurence King and Marshall Cole, two-strike felons, target her brother? If they were to risk a return to jail, possibly for life, why wouldn't they choose a wealthier home?

As she stood at the elevated podium Dana's stomach burned, causing her to grit her teeth. The pain came amid her sorrow and with her realization that Laurence King and Marshall Cole had not taken just her brother's life. They had taken a big part of her life and her mother's and Molly's. They had stolen from every person in that church. It made her angry. It made her damned angry. So when she opened her mouth to deliver the eulogy, Dana had already decided that the best way to honor her brother would not be to live in the past. It would not be to sit around feeling sorry for herself. Remembering would not purge her anger. It would not answer her questions. No. The best way to honor her brother was for Dana to find out why he was dead.

She looked out over the dark clothing and somber expressions, her gaze drifting from the collage of familiar and unfamiliar faces until it came to rest on a face in the second-to-last pew on her left. Detective Michael Logan.

DANA WALKED TOWARD the kitchen, the destination giving her a look of purpose, though inside she felt adrift. Around her, the alcohol flowed and the food was served buffet-style, twice what was probably needed, though she hadn't been about to argue with her mother. Every few steps, someone would step forward to offer condolences, to express sorrow, or to tell her how much everyone had enjoyed her eulogy. She smiled, thanked the people for coming, and continued on.

The kitchen was her refuge, a place to catch her breath and compose herself. She took a minute, then walked out onto the patio. A line of guests snaked through the buffet line, filling china plates with cold cuts, steaming lasagna, poached salmon, salads, and bread rolls. The weather had cooperated. Patches of blue emerged from the gray cloud layer. Dana walked around the pool to where Grant stood talking to a partner at Dillon & Block, her father's former firm. The limbs of the tree that still cradled her and James's tree fort shaded Grant's face but did not temper his voice. She heard him exhorting the facts of the Nelson case and the large dollar figure at issue. Grant never passed up an opportunity to brag. Molly sat on a folding chair next to Maria, her babysitter, looking like a porcelain doll, dressed in a dark blue dress with a white lace collar, Mary Jane shoes, and white ankle socks.

Dana stepped to Grant's side and heard the partner at Dillon & Block ask, "Wasn't Bill Nelson indicted on a money-laundering charge?"

Grant bristled. "The charges were dropped. The proponent of the charge—the one pushing the district attorney—was one of Nelson's top competitors."

The attorney furrowed his brow. "I thought there was more to it than that; that there were allegations of insurance fraud."

Grant shook his head, defiant. "All fabricated. All baseless."

Dana had started to interrupt when she felt a hand on her arm. "Dana?" She turned. The look on her face must have betrayed her inability to pull the balding man's name from the catalog in her brain. Before she could embarrass herself, however, he bailed her out. "It's Brian. Brian Griffin, from down the street."

Her mind visualized hair on the top of his head, shaved the neatly trimmed beard, and removed the round wire-rimmed glasses. "Brian, of course," she said, ashamed to have forgotten the name of someone she and James had played with nearly every day of their young lives.

Griffin smiled and rubbed the top of his head. "I guess I've changed a bit since I was thirteen."

"N- no," she faltered. "Well, yes, I guess we all have."

"Not you. You look the same."

"I don't. I'm sorry, Brian." She gave him a hug. "I just didn't recognize you." She touched his beard. "I like it. It looks good on you."

He smiled wanly, and his eyes watered. "I'm so sorry about James. I'm so damn sorry."

"Thank you for coming."

"I'll miss him. I felt like I just got him back. Everybody at the school is in a state of shock."

She stepped back and realized that Griffin stood with a group from Seattle University. "You're a law professor?" she asked.

"I teach tax," he said.

"It was you who convinced James to teach."

Griffin nodded. "It didn't take much convincing."

"James mentioned a friend but not by name."

"James and I touched base at an estate planning seminar, and he sounded interested. When the opening for a trial advocacy teacher came up, I called him. James was a wonderful teacher, just a natural. The students loved him. It's why so many of them wanted to be here. I hope it's all right."

"Of course," she said, looking at the young men and women standing nearby. "It's wonderful you brought them."

"You can't teach experience in the trenches, trying cases, but James was sure good at sharing it." Griffin looked around at the pool, reminiscing. "God, I was in this backyard every day of the summer for so many years. I don't think I've been here in twenty years. Where does the time go?" Again, his eyes watered. "Well...I don't want to keep you. Today is not the day to catch up on old times. Perhaps we could get together?"

"I'd like that," Dana said. "Thank you for coming."

As she turned toward Grant, she noticed several of the young female students. Pending crow's-feet remained laugh lines around their eyes; their hips were narrow and firm, without the stubborn pregnancy pounds. "Brian?" she called. Griffin stepped back from the group. "There is something."

"Sure, Dana, anything. Anything at all."

"It's just that James seemed to have a whole new life." Her voice sounded forced even to her. "Do you know if James was seeing anyone?"

"I don't know for certain. Your brother kept some things close to the vest, and that was one of them. Every so often he would slip and intimate that he was dating someone, but it was never anything concrete, and I didn't think it was my business to pry. I figured he'd tell me when he told me, you know?"

Would there be anyone who might know?"

Griffin touched her arm. "Dana. Your brother loved you more than anyone in the world, with the possible exception of that little girl sitting in that chair over there. If you didn't know, I am fairly certain no one does."

She nodded: That was true. "What about any problems? Did James mention if he was having any sort of problem recently?"

Griffin shook his head. "I can't think of anything. He helped me a tremendous amount when I went through my divorce; I'm afraid I unburdened myself on him more than I should have, but . . . no. I can't ever recall him saying he had a problem."

"Thanks again, Brian. I'll call you to have lunch," Dana said.

When she turned, Grant had finished off his Scotch and soda and was wiping his mouth with a napkin. The partner from Dillon & Block had left. He nodded toward Griffin. "Who's that?"

"A friend. We grew up together."

"Needs a new sport coat." He handed her the glass and an empty dish. "I have to get to the airport. My flight leaves in two hours. I'll be staying at the Marriott in downtown Chicago. The telephone number is on the refrigerator, if you need to call, but I'll be in court most of the time, so I'll have my phone turned off. Leave me messages at the front desk. I'll pick them up at the end of the day. I'm sorry about the timing. Wish me luck?"

"Good luck," she said.

He pecked her on the lips. "I'll call when I can. You're sure you're going to be okay?"

She nodded. He squeezed her shoulders. Then he walked out the lattice gate at the back of the yard, and she watched it swing closed behind him.

DANA WIPED DOWN the kitchen counter and rinsed the sponge under the tap. The counter and the kitchen stove were spotless. The caterers and the rental company had removed the furniture and food. After four days of turmoil, there was suddenly nothing more to do. She put the sponge in the sink and remembered the same moment following her father's reception. The friends and family had gone back to their everyday lives, leaving her and James and their mother to cope with their loss. Their lives had been changed forever.

She turned off the lights and made her way up the stairs, hearing the faint melody of her mother's voice, an Irish ballad, she supposed.

Little girl, little girl, don't cry, little girl.
'Cause I'm coming in the morning to get you.
And you'll smile and we'll play and together start a day,
And we'll all be happy in the morning.

At the top step, Dana peered through the gap between
the door and the wall of what had been her bedroom. The
pink lamp shade cast a rose-colored glow across the canopied bed, where her mother sat against the headboard,
Molly in her lap, a book opened on the flowered sheets.
Molly's head drooped, and her eyes fluttered with each
soft stroke of the bristled brush as it pulled through her
hair. Her mother had remodeled every room in the house
except Dana's and James's. Children's books filled a bookcase. Stuffed animals overflowed an antique steamer trunk.
It remained a perfect room for a little girl, though growing up, Dana had resisted the pink lace around the canopy.
She had wanted to hang out with James and his friends.
It had been much more fun to play their games. When
she'd graduated from college and told her father she, too,
wanted to attend law school, he'd looked at her as if she
had been struck insane.

"Why would you want to do that?" he demanded.

"To be a lawyer," she replied sarcastically.

"The law is a jealous mistress," he warned, though it
apparently had not been enough to satisfy him.

Dana closed her eyes and recalled sitting on the bed,
staring at the pictures of Snow White, counting every
bed, every pickax, every bowl on the table to ensure there
were seven, one for each dwarf. She felt the soft bristles
touch her scalp and glide through her hair, the strokes in
rhythm with her mother's cadence, until she had heard the

sound of the car in the driveway. She recalled her father's footsteps ascending the staircase. In her mind, she raised her eyes and saw him standing on the top stair, looking into the room, though not crossing the threshold.

Her mother would continue to brush. "Do you want me to make you something to eat?" she would ask, not looking at him.

"I ate at the office."

"Did you get everything finished?"

"Not everything."

"James waited up for you."

"I'll tuck him in," he'd say, and his footsteps would soften down the hall.

Then her mother would place the brush on the night-stand, close the book, and cover Dana with blankets, tuck-ing them under her chin and bending to kiss her on each cheek, the nose, the forehead, and finally, the lips.

"Why are you crying?" Dana would ask, feeling the moisture on her mother's cheeks.

"Because I love you so very much," her mother would whisper.

"Why are you crying, Mom?"

Dana opened her eyes. Molly stared at her from the bed. Dana wiped her cheeks as she entered the room. Her mother continued to stroke the little girl's hair. Dana bent down and kissed Molly on each cheek, the nose, the fore-head, and finally, the lips. "Because I love you so very much," she whispered.

14

〜

THE FLOOR OUTSIDE her office vibrated. Dana reached for the phone on her desk and placed it to her ear, but the door did not burst open. She hung up, wondering how long it would be before Marvin Crocket regained his nerve. Her first day back at work, their paths had crossed that morning in the hallway, and Crocket had considered her warily, likely recalling that the last time they crossed paths, she had hurled a standard-size office desk at him. According to Linda, Crocket had burst from the office that day like a bull running the streets of Pamplona and didn't stop until he reached the office of Gary Thurmond, ranting and raving for fifteen minutes, an expletive-filled diatribe on Dana's mental instability and lack of professional conduct. Crocket had concluded with a request for Dana's head on a platter. Barring that, he sought her immediate expulsion. Thurmond, a sixty-five-year-old warhorse who had known and respected James Hill, Sr., in the courtroom and on the golf course, didn't agree. The morning of her return, her nameplate remained affixed to the wall outside her office door, and a bouquet of flowers had been arranged on her desk.

The floor shook again. Dana snatched up the telephone a split second before Crocket burst in. "We have to get the proposal to Corrugated Indus—"

She looked up at him with feigned indignity, then returned to her imaginary conversation, leaving him to fidget. When he did not immediately leave, she rested the phone on her shoulder and held her hands as wide apart as she could to indicate her conversation would be lengthy. Frowning, Crocket mimed in response that he wanted an immediate call. He left without closing her door. Dana waited a beat before hanging up. Linda peered in from the hallway. "Is there anything you need?"

Dana shook her head. "No, thank you, Linda. I'm fine. Could you shut my door?"

Linda stepped in and closed the door behind her. In her twenties, she had fire-red hair, multiple earrings in her right earlobe, a nose ring, and a tattoo on her back. She didn't exactly project the corporate-law-firm image that Strong & Thurmond sought to foster in Washington's competitive market for elite corporate clients, but Linda had been discreet. She had interviewed in a conservative blue suit with her hair pulled back in a tight bun and had retained the vestiges of that appearance throughout her ninety-day trial period. When she emerged some of the shareholders wanted to fire her, but she had proved an excellent secretary. Any ostensible reason for her termination would have been a thinly veiled excuse subject to a wrongful-termination lawsuit. Instead, they sent her from lawyer to lawyer, each papering her employment file with some inane complaint. Eventually, she came to rest in the cubicle just outside Dana's office, and over the past two years, they had developed a kinship as outlaws.

"I'm glad you're back," Linda said.

"I'm glad to have you here, too."

"Crocket has been asking to review your files and your time sheets. He's looking for things. I saw a memorandum regarding the practice group presentation. He hit you pretty hard."

At the moment it all seemed unimportant. "Thanks for looking out for me, but don't get yourself in any trouble, Linda. Just give him what he wants. I'm not worried about Crocket. He can attack me, but he can't attack my work. That's what pisses him off." She winked. "But I don't think I need to tell you that."

Linda laughed. "Maybe you should get a nose ring."

"I'd like to give him a nose ring. Would you hold my calls? I'm going to be taking care of some personal matters."

Dana opened the box on the floor that contained James's personal papers. Over the next hour, she sorted through his credit card and bank records. The estate was not inconsequential, but because he had sold most of his possessions, it was not complicated. He had $183,000 in a retirement fund and another $78,000 in stocks. His Green Lake home had an assessed value of $425,000. He had an additional $62,000 in cash from the sale of his Capitol Hill home invested in mutual funds. He also had a $1 million life insurance policy with Molly his beneficiary. Dana had contacted the insurance company; who advised her that they would be conducting an investigation, apparently to determine whether her brother could have beaten himself to death, suicide not being a covered event. Brian

Griffin had told her that he'd drafted a will and a trust for James, but Dana did not find copies of either. She had made an appointment to see Griffin later in the week.

James had done most of his banking online. His password was written on the inside of his file, M-O-L-L-Y. Dana accessed the website for his credit card and scrolled through the entries. A careful review did not reveal what she was looking for. She then logged on to his banking site and reviewed his statements for the previous nine months but again did not find any large withdrawals or checks. About to log off, she noticed a check entry to a company called Montgomery Real Estate for $695 and considered it of interest since, to her knowledge, her brother did not own any real estate besides his home. Scrolling back through the records, she noted the same entry the previous month and the four months prior to that as well. She wrote the name of the company on a legal pad as her direct line rang, indicating an in-firm call. She checked the extension before answering.

"I know you didn't want to be bothered," Linda said, "but a Dr. Bridgett Neal is on the telephone for you. She said it was important."

15

~

ROBERT MEYERS EMERGED from beneath the apple-red wing of the Meyers International floatplane and stepped down onto the deck before turning and offering his hand to his wife. Elizabeth Meyers stepped out, resplendent in a royal blue St. John's pantsuit. Meyers smoothed his tie and adjusted his blazer as the couple strode up the wooden pier hand in hand. His father, the former two-term governor of the state of Washington, had taught him that life was about making entrances and exits.

"Nobody remembers what happens in between," he would say.

It was the reason Meyers had opted for the floatplane. Today he intended to make an entrance. The weather had certainly cooperated, providing a glorious sky, and sunshine reflected in the windows of Seattle's downtown skyscrapers to the immediate south. Days like these had earned Seattle its nickname, the Emerald City.

As the couple reached the end of the dock, the group standing across Fairview Avenue in the courtyard of Seattle's Fred Hutchison Cancer Research Center raised their hands to shade their eyes from the glare off Lake Union. Behind them stood a magnificent seven-story glass and brick structure, a red ribbon and bow draped across the front entrance. Fast becoming one of the best cancer centers in the world, the medical complex had sprung up along the shores of Lake Union along with a host of medical and biotech companies fueled by pioneers of the dotcom craze in the 1990s, particularly Microsoft billionaire Paul Allen. Glimmering brick and glass buildings were fast replacing the one-story industrial buildings that had surrounded Lake Union for fifty years.

When Meyers and his wife approached, water sprouted from the rock fountain centerpiece in the courtyard, and the crowd broke into spontaneous applause. Meyers dropped his head like an embarrassed schoolboy bringing his girlfriend home to meet his parents. Everyone knew the ostensible purpose for the event—Meyers had come to dedicate the addition that would bear his father's name, Robert Samuel Meyers III. But by appearing in the sparkling sunshine with his beach-boy-blond hair blowing in a gentle breeze, Meyers had still managed to give the event a spontaneous feel, another skill his father had taught.

For four generations, the Meyers family had personified the American dream in Seattle. Meyers's great-grandfather had emigrated to the Pacific Northwest from Sweden with little more than pocket change and taken a job as a logger for Weyerhauser, the lumber giant. His son founded Meyers Construction and built it into the largest developer of homes in the Pacific Northwest; he had also used his financial resources to become active in civic affairs, becoming Seattle's mayor. His son graduated from the University of Washington with engineering and architecture degrees and transformed Meyers Construction from a builder of homes to a leader in the construction of Seattle's skyline. During the economic boom of the 1980s, Meyers Construction cranes and banners flew atop nearly every high-rise being built. Meyers III's political success also reached greater heights. When he became governor, he passed the company on to his son, making Robert Samuel Meyers IV the chief executive of the largest construction company in Washington state. Then the recession hit and the cranes stopped building. It was a recipe for disaster, but Meyers had the foresight to divest the family fortune, founding Meyers International, a venture capital company that invested heavily in the high-tech and bio-tech craze sweeping across the Pacific Northwest. The deals turned the family's millions into billions. Armed with a family name that appeased Seattle's blue blood, and a reputation as an entrepreneur that appealed to the young, Meyers was uniquely situated to take the family's political ambitions still higher. At thirty-six, he successfully campaigned for a seat in the United States Senate, where he employed the same youthful vitality, work ethic, and vision to carve his name on the national political scene. When one Washington, D.C., publication referred to his Senate campaign as "a return to Camelot," other national publications pounced on the theme, and the American public became wistful, thinking of the possibility. Meyers became the poster boy for the next generation, much like John F. Kennedy had been for his.

Meyers stepped to a podium adorned with multiple microphones. Cameras whirled and clicked, and film crews jostled for a shot of Meyers with the fountain and the glass facade in the background. Meyers draped both hands over the top of the podium, relaxed in the spotlight and content to give them that shot. He addressed Bill Donovan, the correspondent for ABC's affiliate in Seattle. "Bill, you better put on some suntan lotion. You're liable to get burned standing out here in this bright sunshine."

Donovan rubbed the top of his balding head. "It's not the suntan I'm worried about."

The crowd laughed. Meyers liked to remark that politics were in his family's genes. "A person does not choose politics," his father had been fond of saying. "Politics choose the person."

Meyers pulled his hands back and straightened. "Thank you all for being here today. My family and our friends suffered through the illness that befell my father and appreciated your caring support. Although my father's illness will help to heighten public awareness in the battle against cancer, his death taught us we still have a long way to go. His battle was both valiant and courageous, and when it was over, it was a sad time for our family. But through that sadness, this addition to this incredible center has risen. Elizabeth and I are proud to dedicate the Robert Samuel Meyers wing of the Fred Hutchison Cancer Research Center. Let it serve as a declaration that our fight against cancer did not end with my father's death. It began."

The crowd applauded.

"Cancer took my father too young, but with funding for centers such as this, we can find a cure. And we will.

People say we are winning the battle to treat cancer. I say that is the wrong battle. I say we need to eradicate the disease."

Again the crowd applauded.

Meyers brushed his hair from a face that maintained much of its boyish charm. "As most of you know, my father was a religious man like John F. Kennedy and he too believed in the verse from Luke quoted by our former president: 'To whom much is given, much is expected.' My great-grandfather came to this country a poor immigrant. But he came with a dream—the kind of dream many Americans once had. He dreamed of a better life—for himself, for his family, and for the generations to follow. He realized that dream through hard work in a country that believed it could be the best in the world. My grandfather and my father were blessed with that same work ethic and that same desire to serve others, particularly the people of this great state that has for too long been ignored on the national political scene."

The applause grew, the anticipation building.

"The issue is service, stewardship, and vision. The future should not scare the next generation of Americans. The future should excite them, as it once excited the generations that came before us." The anticipation reached a crescendo. "America needs fresh ideas to solve old problems. America needs leaders who see the future of America, not its past." His comment was a not so subtle reference to the age of the Republican Party's leading presidential candidate, New York governor William Andrews. "I see that future as clearly as I see that range of mountains in the distance. And like those mountains, the future is closer than it appears. The future is now."

A roar erupted. The crowd cheered wildly. Signs emerged from seemingly nowhere as Meyers shouted, "Today I am proud to announce that I am a candidate for the Democratic nomination for president of the United States."

He raised his wife's hand overhead and soaked in the adoration, allowing the photographers to snap their front-page pictures. It was the perfect way to whet the public's appetite without infringing upon the speech he would give Saturday evening at a gala to officially kick off his campaign and fund-raising. Meyers stepped from the podium, and an aide handed him an oversize pair of scissors. Meyers stepped to the front doors and cut the ribbon across the entrance to a building that would stand for his father's legacy. Then Robert Meyers took his wife's hand and together they walked inside to see the future.

16

◆

D ANA LOOKED DOWN upon the crowd gathered in the courtyard. She recognized the man at the podium; everyone in Seattle knew Senator Robert Meyers and deduced from the red ribbon and bronze letters across the front of the brick structure that Meyers had donated a substantial sum of money to the Research Center.

"Ms. Hill?"

Dana turned from the window. A nurse beckoned. Dana followed her to a patient consultation room, where the woman took her vitals before departing. This time Dr. Bridgett Neal did not keep her waiting. A minute after the nurse left, Neal stepped in. "I hope you didn't get stuck in the traffic out there."

"It wasn't too bad." Dana did her best to sound casual but felt her heart thumping.

Neal opened a file. "I'm very sorry it took this long. I don't like to keep patients waiting for their results, but because the biopsy section was small, the pathologist chose not to do a frozen section, which would have provided an immediate diagnosis." Neal put on a pair of glasses. "He chose to do a more thorough assessment, and it takes several days to process permanent sections of tissue for examination in greater detail. The distinction between benign and cancerous cells can be subtle. Dr. Kapela wanted your results reviewed by a second pathologist."

"I'm sensing this is not good news," Dana said.

"They've both concluded that the cells are malignant. I'm sorry."

Dana felt a lump in her throat. Her eyes watered, but she took a deep breath and exhaled, and though she fought against it, tears rolled down her cheeks. Neal handed her a tissue.

"The good news is that you detected it very early, and it is not considered an aggressive cancer. We have a number of different options available to us."

Dana swallowed her anger. She refused to become hysterical or to panic. She would not begin the "why me" lamentations. She would not be one of the statistics, one of the women who died every twelve minutes—a .20 on somebody's goddamn time sheet. She was just thirty-four. She had a daughter to raise. She asked the question dutifully, feeling the need to maintain professional composure and demeanor in front of another female professional. "What are those options?"

"You can have a mastectomy, in which case—"

"No." She thought of her mother.

Dr. Neal nodded. "And I don't recommend a mastectomy in your case. I recommend what is referred to as BCT, breast-conserving treatment."

"It sounds like a pleasant acronym for a not so pleasant procedure."

"Basically, we remove the lump, along with some normal tissue surrounding it, for further examination. It would be combined with level-one axillary dissection, which is removal of a pad of tissue and lymph nodes under your arm, followed by radiation therapy."

Dana rubbed her forehead and took another deep breath, exhaling. She forced a smile. "I don't suppose there's a door number three with a trip to an exotic island, is there?"

Dr. Neal shook her head, her smile equally tight-lipped. "I'm afraid not." She let Dana absorb the information for a few moments.

Dana tried to calm herself and think of questions. "Why pull the lymph nodes if we don't know whether it has spread?"

"Good question. My consultation with other doctors indicates it would be prudent because of your family history—your mother's breast cancer. And it can also be done in a single operation."

"When would you want to do it?"

"As soon as possible. How much time do you need to get other things organized?"

Dana laughed to herself. "Six months wouldn't help me get things organized. My brother died last week. Things are in a state of turmoil and likely to remain that way for a while."

"I'm so sorry. Was it sudden?"

"He was murdered."

"Dear God." Neal paused. "He was the man on the news, wasn't he? Oh, Dana, I'm so sorry. I didn't put it together. That was your brother."

Dana nodded. "You don't expect these things to happen to you. They always happen to other people, don't they? My father used to say bad news came in threes. For my sake, I hope not." She regrouped. "Where do we start?"

"I'd like you to meet with the surgeon I'm recommending for the lumpectomy, as well as the radiation oncologist and therapist who will monitor your radiation treatments. They can help relieve some of your anxiety. I can also put you in touch with organizations of women who have gone through what you will be experiencing. They can tell you what to expect. You won't be going through this alone."

"How long will I be out of work?"

"The surgery itself is done with a local anesthetic. If all goes well, you'll be released the same day. We can schedule it for a Friday afternoon so you'll have the weekend to recover. The length and dosage of your radiation treatment will be decided by your radiation oncologist, but it is usually five days a week for five to six weeks, though the actual treatment in your circumstance should take just a few minutes each day. There's a very good facility not far from your office. They could schedule you late in the afternoon."

Dana wrapped her arms across her body, suddenly cold. "Could I have the lumpectomy without the radiation?"

"You could. But I wouldn't recommend it. The procedure is contemplative of all three treatments for maximum effectiveness. And that is what we're seeking here. Over ninety percent of women who find and treat their breast cancer early are cancer-free at five years."

Five years? Five years was nothing. Molly would be just eight years old, still a baby. Who would take her to school and pick her up? Who would tell her all of the things she needed to know? Leaving her alone with Grant would...Dana dismissed the thought before she could finish it.

Dr. Neal sat forward, hands folded. "There are more than two million breast cancer survivors living in the United States."

"How many aren't?" Dana asked, already regretting it.

Dr. Neal sat back. "Forty-four thousand last year."

17

A S SHE DROVE FROM the medical facility, Dana could not dismiss the thought. She was going to die. *Malignant. Cancer. Malignant. Cancer.* The words ran through her mind as if on a continuous reel. As brave as she had been in Dr. Neal's office, she was crumbling under the onslaught of her relentless mind. She had cancer, and no matter how Dr. Neal dressed it up with smiling office personnel, pastel colors, and optimistic statistics, she could not deny that breast cancer remained a killer. Dana looked up at the billowing white clouds. As a girl, she used to believe angels lived on those clouds, and beyond them were the gates to heaven. She wanted to believe James was up there, sensing she needed him, as he always had in life. She wanted to ask him to help her. She wanted to ask God to help her. But she had fallen out of touch with her faith. Before James's funeral, she couldn't remember the last time she had set foot in a church or had a heart-to-heart discussion with God.

There are no atheists in foxholes, her father had also liked to say.

Could she ask for divine intervention? Would it make her a hypocrite? God was benevolent, wasn't He? She was no longer certain.

She made a left on Fifth Avenue and followed it to Olive, driving in the direction of her office, her body on autopilot. "I could use some help down here," she said to the clouds.

She pulled the car to the curb and sobbed, her shoulders shaking. It was too much for one person. She picked up her cell phone and rummaged through her legal pad, looking for the number she had copied from the piece of paper on the refrigerator. She punched in the number. When the hotel receptionist answered, she asked to be connected to Grant Brown's room. It rang once.

A woman answered.

Flustered, Dana hung up. She checked the number and reentered it. When the receptionist answered, she specified that she wanted Grant Brown's room. "I don't want the suite that the law firm is using. I want his room, his private room."

"There's just one room under that name," the woman said.

Dana froze.

"Would you like me to connect you?"

Dana couldn't speak, the back of her throat dry. "Check if there is a room reserved under the name Maxwell, Levitt and Truman," she said, her voice barely above a whisper. "It's my husband's law firm."

After a moment the woman replied, "Nothing under that name. Would you like me to connect you to his room?"

"Yes," she said, and she closed her eyes as the phone

rang. The same woman answered. Dana gathered herself. "Is Grant in?"

A pause. "Um... he's not here. He's in court. Can I leave him a message?"

"No," Dana said. "You can't."

She disconnected, gripping the phone. Tears of sorrow now mixed with tears of frustration and anger. She threw the phone on the passenger seat and slapped at the steering wheel. "Stupid. Stupid. So goddamn stupid."

The late nights, the softball games and pizza that Grant never invited her or Molly to attend. Grant coming home smelling like smoke and beer. It had all started at the same time, when the firm hired the twenty-six-year-old Demi Moore look-alike with the perky breasts and tight butt.

Bad news always comes in threes, she heard her father say, and she hated him for it.

SHE SAT FEELING numb, letting the day pass, not caring. Her cell phone rang. The caller ID indicated it was the law firm. She took a chance, thinking it was more likely to be Linda than Crocket.

"Are you coming back today?" Linda asked. "Crocket is looking for you."

Dana exhaled, frustrated. "Yeah. I'm on my way back. I'll be there in five minutes."

"Are you okay?"

She didn't immediately answer. She stared out the windshield at the clouds floating overhead, thinking again of her brother. Finally, she said, "I'm fine," disconnected, and put the phone down on the legal pad. When she did, she noticed the name she'd written while going through

James's financial records. She picked up the phone and dialed 411. "Montgomery Real Estate," she told the operator. "It's a business."

A moment later, she pulled from the curb, continued down Fifth Avenue, and turned right on James Street. At the bottom of the hill, just before the pergola at the corner of First Street, she found a parking place and pulled to the curb, taking a moment to check her appearance in the rearview mirror. Mascara shaded her eyes. Her nose was rose red. She fished in the glove compartment for her makeup bag and did her best to clean herself up. Then she stepped from the car, put two quarters in the meter, and walked across a cobblestone courtyard lined with tourists waiting for a guide to take them on the underground tour. After a turn-of-the-century fire destroyed much of the city, Pioneer Square, a district of redbrick buildings home to bars, restaurants, art galleries, and many of Seattle's downtrodden and homeless, was built atop the rubble, including buildings that had not been destroyed. An entrepreneur had turned it into a business.

A bronze plaque on the side of the building declared the old Pioneer Building an historical landmark. Dana didn't bother to read it. She climbed up the marble steps and pulled open the door into a lobby of mahogany paneling that looked like the entrance to an old hotel. A directory mounted on the wall indicated Montgomery Real Estate was a tenant on the third floor, Suite 326. She stepped into an old-fashioned elevator and closed the cage door. The elevator jerked and ascended. An open atrium rose six stories to a glass-reinforced roof. Vines from potted plants hung from the ceiling and the wood railings of the upper floors.

Dana found Suite 326 and stepped into a small lobby. A black woman with elaborately manicured nails greeted her at the counter. Three minutes later, a woman dressed like a cruise-ship director in white slacks, red blouse, and blue blazer introduced herself as Bernadette Georges. Georges led Dana to an office with two brick walls and a window that opened to allow in fresh air and the sounds of cars, birds, and voices. Dana declined a cup of coffee and sat across the desk. A computer screen on the credenza traced geometric images.

"I apologize for not calling," Dana said. "I was in the neighborhood and decided to just drop in. I've been handling my brother's papers, and I'm curious about the monthly checks he was writing to your company."

Georges said the intrusion was not a problem. She told Dana she was sorry for her loss. "Your brother was renting a cabin just outside Rosyln, about a mile from the downtown area. Are you familiar with it?"

"I've visited, I haven't spent any time there," Dana said. It was a small mining town about an hour and a half east of Seattle, in the Wenatchee National Forest.

"Finding it can be a challenge—the cabin, not Rosyln," Georges said. "Developers are finding Rosyln and the surrounding area rather quickly, I'm afraid."

"How did my brother find it?"

"I found it for him. Your brother wanted something within driving distance but still rustic and remote. We looked into cabins on the San Juan Islands and on the Olympic Peninsula, but he didn't want to take a ferry. This seemed to suit his needs. I take it your brother was the outdoor type?"

Not that Dana knew. With their father working most

weekends and spending his off hours with his secretary, he hadn't exactly fostered a love for the great outdoors. Her mother's idea of hiking was walking through Nordstrom. "What's up there?"

"Hiking and fishing—the Yakima River runs through the back of the property—and horseback riding. People swim in the reservoir nearby. It's remote, though a new development is going in nearby with golf courses. Mostly, there's peace and quiet. It's beautiful country."

"The records indicate my brother was up there every month."

"Your brother rented the cabin for about five . . . no . . ." Georges turned and checked her computer. "Six months. He picked up the key here whenever he wanted to use the cabin."

"How often was that?"

"I can't say for sure. He rented it for the entire month, so I was more lenient about allowing him to keep the key, though he didn't seem intent on doing so."

"Why do you say that?"

Georges smiled. "I liked your brother; he struck me as honest. I told him he could keep the key, but he said he was absentminded and would lose it."

That was also not in keeping with the James Dana knew. She was scattered. Her brother had incredible organizational skills. It was another gene he'd gotten that she had not.

"How often are you aware that he did use the cabin?"

"Sometimes he would pick up the key three, four times a month. Sometimes not at all."

"Did he say why he didn't just rent the cabin when he needed it?"

Georges shrugged. "We discussed that. The owner was interested in selling, but your brother said he wasn't prepared to buy. He just wanted the flexibility of being able to go spur-of-the-moment. He said he was busy and didn't want to be tied to a schedule. There was no routine to when he used the cabin, as far as I could tell. Sometimes he'd call to pick up the key at three in the afternoon on a weekday, and I would find it in an envelope under the front door the next morning. He was never there longer than twenty-four hours, that I know; he never even took an entire weekend."

"Did he always come here to pick up and deliver the key himself?"

"Every time."

"Did you ever see him with anyone?"

Georges shook her head. "No. He was alone."

"Did he ever say anything to lead you to believe he took someone with him to the cabin?"

Georges again shook her head.

"Did he say he was visiting someone, that he knew someone who lived up there?"

Another shake of the head. "I'm sorry. I wish I could be of more help."

Dana nodded. Unable to think of anything else, she considered her watch. "Thank you. I appreciate your time."

Georges stood to walk her out. "I'm very sorry about your brother. When I read the article in the paper, I was shocked. He was such a good man. I liked him very much. He seemed to be a kind person."

"He was," Dana said.

At the door, Georges said, "It was upsetting when the police came."

Dana stopped. "The police came here?"

"Yes."

"What did they want?"

"The detective said there had been a murder and they were conducting an investigation. He asked for the key and directions to the cabin."

"When was this?"

"The day after your brother was killed."

Dana felt herself becoming angry. Logan had given her no indication that he knew of a cabin or that he had searched it. "Did he say why they wanted to go to the cabin?"

"No, just that it was part of their investigation."

"Did he ask for anything else? Did he ask you any questions?"

"No. He said they wanted to look through the cabin. That was it. He still has the key, though. I keep forgetting to call and get it back."

"Don't worry," Dana said. "I'll get it back for you."

18

⟿

DANA DIALED THE telephone number in the elevator, and it rang as she pushed through the glass doors and stepped from the lobby. She navigated her high-heeled shoes across the cobblestone courtyard to a bronze bust of Chief Seattle and an Eskimo totem pole.

He answered the phone with a single word. "Logan."

"Why the hell didn't you tell me about the cabin?"

"Excuse me?"

"The cabin, Detective. Why didn't you tell me about the cabin my brother was renting near Rosyln?"

"Who is this?"

"It's Dana Hill."

Logan paused. "I don't know what you're talking about, Ms. Hill. What cabin?"

She paced the cobblestones, her heels turning on the uneven, rounded surfaces. "I just came from Montgomery Real Estate. The woman there told me a detective came to her office and asked for the key to my brother's cabin as part of a murder investigation."

"What?"

Dana began to sense that Logan's confusion was legitimate. "She said a detective came to her office, asked about the cabin, and wanted directions and a key. I assume that was you."

"I've never heard of Montgomery Real Estate, and I don't know anything about a cabin. Why don't you start over and tell me what you're talking about."

Dana looked up through the leaves. An airplane had left a trail in the cloudless blue sky. She could tell from Logan's tone that he was genuinely perplexed. She went back through the story, starting with finding her brother's payments to Montgomery Real Estate.

"Where are you now?"

"Outside the building in Pioneer Square," she said, providing him with the address.

"Wait there. Do not let that woman leave."

THE PERPLEXED LOOK on Bernadette Georges's face had graduated from confusion, when Dana reentered the office, to concern when she introduced Logan.

"You sure," Logan said, "this man identified himself as a police detective?"

Georges nodded. "Yes, I checked my day timer after you left," she said to Dana. "I wrote down his name. Detective Daniel Holmes."

"Can you describe him? What was he wearing?" Logan asked.

"He was about your size but heavier. Muscular. Sandy-blond hair, narrow face. Dark suit. He was very well dressed, like you."

"Did he show you a badge?"

"Yes, a silver badge, just like yours."

Logan turned to Dana. "And you think this is the same man you say came to your brother's house the morning I met you there?"

"It sounds like him. He said he was focusing on the burglary—that you were focusing on the murder, and he was focusing on the burglary and local pawnshops. Is that not the case?"

Logan didn't respond. He turned his attention back to Georges. "Anything else you can remember about him or what he said?"

Georges smiled, nervous. "He had a gun?"

"Do you know that, or are you guessing?"

"My husband has handguns. I could tell by the way his suit jacket hung." Georges made a fist and placed it inside the lining. "He definitely had on a shoulder holster."

Logan handed her a business card. "If you think of anything else, you can reach me at that number."

Logan and Dana took the elevator to the lobby. "Why didn't you tell me about the man who came to your brother's home?" Logan asked.

"I thought you knew," Dana said. "Who is he?"

Logan shook his head. "I have no idea."

As they stepped outside, they heard someone calling to them. Georges was descending the staircase awkwardly holding the banister for balance. She was out of breath when she reached them. "There was something. I don't know if it means anything, but I just remembered it, sitting at my desk. His eyes."

"His eyes?" Logan asked.

"Yes. I remembered thinking that they were...well, dark for a man with his hair color and complexion."

"Brown?" Logan asked, not sounding impressed.

"Black," Dana said, remembering.

Georges nodded to her. "Yes, black. He had the darkest eyes I've ever seen."

THEY DROVE EAST on Interstate 90, Logan talking on the telephone with his office. He was upset and didn't try to hide it. It gave Dana a moment to consider him. She had pegged Logan as fastidious, from his neat appearance and well-made suits. From her years working around lawyers and shopping for Grant, she knew quality. Logan's shirts were starched. He wore black cuff links, and his tie was well chosen and tightly knotted. Inside the car, she detected a hint of cologne. Logan's green 1963 Austin Healey was equally well kept. The exterior looked to have been freshly polished. The cherry-red leather interior and walnut dashboard glistened. There was not a scrap of paper on the floor. A gumshoe, Michael Logan was not. But he also did not appear prissy. When he had removed his jacket before getting into the car, Dana noticed he had the broad shoulders and the taut chest of someone who worked out regularly. When they shook hands, she felt calluses. The back of his arm pressed his shirtsleeve tight.

Logan disconnected the call and shifted his weight to clip the telephone into a holder on his belt.

"Anything?" Dana asked.

He shook his head. "There's a Detective Dan Holmes.

But he works out of another precinct. They're trying to reach him."

"What would he be doing on my brother's investigation?"

"I have no idea, but the answer better be 'nothing.'" Logan turned down the volume on the radio. "If you don't mind me saying so, your brother seemed to keep quite a few secrets."

Dana bristled at the statement. "What does that mean?"

"It means you said you'd never even been to his house before, and now you find out he rented a cabin you didn't know about. Yet the two of you were supposed to have been close."

"We *were* close." She sounded defensive even to herself. "How do you know that?"

Logan calmed. "The next-door neighbor."

"You asked her about me?"

"I asked her about your brother. She offered the information about your family. She likes to talk."

"My brother and I were close. We're twins." Again, she sounded defensive.

"Look, I'm not saying you weren't, but if you were, why wouldn't you have known about the cabin? Did your brother keep things from you?"

Dana looked out the window at the Cascade foothills. With intermittent logging, the hills resembled a patchwork quilt, some of the squares bald, some with new-growth timber, others still pristine. A thin cloud layer had settled atop the peaks. Those she could see remained powdered with winter snow.

"My brother hit midlife crisis a little early. After our father died, he quit practicing law, sold his house, and changed his lifestyle. When we both worked downtown, it was hard enough to arrange our schedules just to have lunch. After he left the law, it became even more difficult. Talking on the phone with friends and relatives is a luxury you try to avoid when you're expected to bill every six minutes of your day. Between work and a family, I didn't have a lot of time. I'm not surprised there are parts of his life I didn't know about, and I regret that now more than ever. I saw James when he came to pick up Molly, and even that was brief."

"Molly?"

"My daughter. Molly was the one thing James didn't change. Once or twice a month, he'd take her for a day. They were very close."

Logan backed off. "How old is your daughter?"

"Three."

He smiled. "Must be a great age."

"We survived the terrible twos, barely. Do you have children?"

Logan shook his head. "No. I'm not married."

Dana glanced at Logan's left hand on the steering wheel. She thought she had remembered seeing a gold wedding band when she met him at the house, but the finger was bare.

The sports car climbed the Snoqualmie Pass, the terrain becoming more rugged. Waterfalls of melting snow cascaded down the sheer rock face where the highway had been cut through. Around them, a sea of green pines spread out lush and thick as far as the eye could see. Rivers flowed along side the road with men in waders flyfishing for steelhead. Most people thought Big Foot was a myth, but people who lived in the Pacific Northwest knew places remained where such a creature could exist and never come in contact with humans, if it so chose.

Logan loosened his tie and undid the top button on his shirt. "What's our landmark?"

"Cle Elum. It's another hour." She leaned across the seat to look at the odometer. The needle was pushing 90 mph, though she hadn't felt it from the ride. "But at this speed, forty-five minutes."

Logan slowed. "I'm sorry. Bad habit. Am I making you nervous?"

"No. I'm surprised how smooth the drive is."

Logan smiled. "British engineering. What's after Cle Elum?"

Dana pulled out the piece of paper. "Rosyln's about ten minutes off the highway. We drive through town and follow the signs for the cemetery. Then we look for a white boulder along the side of the road."

He looked at her in disbelief. "You're kidding, right? Cemeteries and boulders are our landmarks?"

Dana shrugged. "I just wrote down what she told me."

"Then I guess I better slow down; we don't want to miss any rocks."

She smiled at the comment.

"There it is."

Dana startled and looked out the window. "What?"

He pointed to her face. "A smile."

She felt herself blush. "I haven't had a lot to smile about lately."

"I'm certain you haven't, which was why I was hoping to get one from you."

She looked over and smiled again.

"Two, wow."

"I owe you a couple of thank-yous while we're at it," she said.

"For what?"

"That day at the coroner, to identify my brother's body, and the day at my brother's house. You didn't have to go in with me, but you did. I appreciate it."

He nodded. "Those aren't things someone should have to do alone."

"No," she said, thinking of Grant. "They aren't."

TEN MINUTES AFTER exiting the highway, they drove through the center of Rosyln. A wide street lined with brick, stone, and clapboard one-story buildings, it looked just like Georges had described it —an old western mining town. A black slate monument paid tribute to the miners who had worked and died there.

"Why does that place seem familiar to me?" Logan pointed to a mural of a moose painted on the stucco of a building.

"Georges said they used the facade of the town to film the television show *Northern Exposure*," Dana said.

He shrugged. "Maybe that's it."

Just outside of town, she pointed at a small green street sign with the word "cemetery" and an arrow pointing to the left. They turned and drove up a small incline past two-story A-frame homes. At the top of the incline she saw tombstones in a sloped plot of land surrounded by a wrought-iron fence.

"Now the road—"

The car dropped and bottomed out. The pavement ended. Dirt and gravel crunched beneath the tires and pinged the underside.

"—ends," she finished.

Logan slowed as the cloud of dust kicked up around the polished paint. "You didn't tell me about this," he grimaced.

Georges had warned her that the Forest Service maintained the dirt road but might not have groomed it after the winter. As smoothly as the sports car had floated along the highway, it was not made for the potholes and gravel. Dana felt like every organ in her body was being rearranged as the car pitched and listed.

"Now we look for the boulder?" Logan asked.

"And there it is." She pointed, a smug smile on her face.

The boulder had indeed been painted white. From an overhead log entry gate hung a weathered sign, the letters hand-carved and faded from what appeared to have been a rich red color at one time. WILBUR RANCH.

Logan descended a steep driveway, stopped the Austin Healey near the covered porch of a rustic log cabin and got out. When Dana opened her car door, she was surprised to find Logan offering her a hand. "I'll never complain about the potholes in Seattle again. I think I blew out three discs," he said. He looked down at her heeled shoes. "Are you going to be all right in those?"

"I'll be fine." She released his hand, took a step, and stumbled into him.

Logan caught her about the waist. "Whoa."

She regained her balance. "Sorry about that."

Barbed wire and weathered split-rail fences, some in need of repair, divided the property into multiple pastures. Horses or cattle had probably done the mowing when the property was used regularly, but now the log cabin sat amid a sea of tall grass with trace patches of brown. The dirt drive continued past a weathered barn and livery stables with dilapidated wooden hay wagons on rusting spoke wheels. Horseshoes and metal spikes hung from the beams. The property looked like something from a ghost town.

Dana smelled the scent of pine on the breeze. "It's beautiful," she said.

Logan swiped a finger across the car hood, leaving a streak in the thin dust. "It's secluded." He took her arm and helped her up three wooden steps—logs split in half—to a porch. "You should have an easier go of it up here." He picked out a chunk of the mortar from between the logs. "Needs a lot of work, and there's not a lot of amenities." He pointed to an old-fashioned hand pump in the yard. "No running water or electricity. Was your brother handy?"

She laughed. "My brother? James needed directions to change a lightbulb."

"Well, if he was looking to get lost, this is a pretty good place to do it." He unlocked the front door with the spare key Georges had provided, and stepped aside.

Dana stepped into a kitchen, wincing at the aroma. "Smells like someone got carried away with the lemon Pledge."

Logan stepped in behind her. A stack of wood was piled against the back wall near a wood-burning stove. On the other wall was a deep washbasin with no faucet and an old-fashioned icebox. A table draped with a red-and-white-checked tablecloth and two chairs were positioned beneath a four-pane window that looked out on the valley of tall grass. An arrangement of flowers in a wine bottle had wilted.

They walked through the kitchen into the main room, which had a beamed ceiling with a bearskin rug and pine floors. Two crushed brown leather chairs and an equally worn couch faced a river-rock fireplace. Stones stuck out from the mortar to form a mantel. On it someone had placed vintage copper pieces—a teakettle, pot and spoon, and two oil-burning lamps. Dana examined the spines of several books: Mark Twain's *Tom Sawyer* and *Huckleberry Finn*, Charles Dickens's *A Tale of Two Cities,* Ernest Hemingway's *The Sun Also Rises,* F. Scott Fitzgerald's *The Great Gatsby.* "These were James's," Dana said.

Logan continued through a doorway to the left of the fireplace. Dana followed him into a bedroom. The fireplace extended through the wall. "Central heating," Logan said.

A bed frame made from stout tree limbs stripped of their bark faced the fireplace. A goose-down comforter covered the mattress, with a hand-knitted quilt folded at the foot of the bed.

"Your brother was a romantic," Logan said. Then his cell phone rang, and he excused himself and stepped out of the room to answer it.

Dana walked around the bed to an unfinished pinewood nightstand and opened and closed the drawers. They were empty. She opened the closet door and found an extra blanket and pillow on the shelf. Wire hangers hung on the bar. She turned back to the bed, dropped to a knee, and pulled up the comforter. When she sat up, Logan stood in the doorway looking down at her.

"Whatever it is you're looking for, you're not going to find it. Whoever was here wiped this place down clean."

She stood. "What do you mean?"

He held up a plastic bag that appeared empty, then held

it to the light from the window. "Magnetic powder. There's trace amounts throughout the cabin. It's an iron base compound used to lift fingerprints. That smell in here? That's ammonia. It's a base in the cleaner used to wipe away the powder. My guess is that Detective Daniel Holmes, whoever he is, dusted this place for fingerprints, then wiped it clean. The only fingerprints in here now are probably yours and mine. Care to talk about it over dinner?"

19

〜

T HE ALL-PURPOSE store in town sold staples like soap, toothpaste, and toilet paper. The window displayed the same kind of antiques as on the mantel in the cabin. Logan hoped the man behind the counter might recognize James Hill from the photograph Dana carried in her wallet. He didn't. After leaving the store, they walked along a wood-plank sidewalk. It felt like being on the back lot of a Hollywood movie studio—the mining town re-created to attract tourists. In their business attire, Dana and Logan looked out of place. She felt a noticeable drop in the temperature and crossed her arms against the cold.

"You want my jacket?" Logan asked.

She declined. He pushed open the glass door to a café. A string of bells alerted the entire clientele to look up from their plates. A woman behind the counter motioned for them to take a table near the window. It provided a view of the street, which included a hitching post for horses. After a moment the hum of voices again mixed

with the ting and clatter of plates and silverware and
food sizzling on the grill. Dana smelled bacon. It made
her mouth water. The woman behind the counter handed
them each a single-page handwritten menu before departing with a promise to return with two cups of coffee.
While they waited, Dana called home to confirm that
her mother would pick up Molly from day care. As five
o'clock approached, and an hour-and-a-half drive ahead
of them, she'd never get back in time. Next she checked
her messages at work. Grant had called. She thought it
interesting that he would leave her a message at work
rather than call her cell phone. He did his best to diffuse
the fact that a woman had answered the telephone in his
room, explaining that "the stupid receptionist" had given
Dana the firm's "war room." It was another lie. When
Grant started making excuses, Dana knew he was lying.
She dialed the number for the hotel as the waitress arrived
with their coffees.

This time Grant answered. "Dana. Hey. They said you
called earlier. Why didn't you leave a message?"

"I didn't want to bother you." She noted his use of "they"
instead of "she."

"You should have left a message. The team is floating
from room to room here. We have documents spread out
everywhere."

She closed her eyes and visualized the lie punching
another hole in her paper heart. When Dana was a young
girl, her grandmother had once used a paper heart to show
her how each lie and hurtful word punched a hole, leaving
less and less of the heart. Dana wondered how much heart
she had left. "How was court?" she asked.

It seemed to catch Grant off guard. He sounded relieved

to change the subject. "We have them on the run. The judge granted nearly all our motions in limine and denied most of theirs. We took a couple on the chin, but we delivered a lot more blows than we absorbed."

"Any talk of settlement?"

"Not anymore. Our demand is off the table. Fuck 'em. I gave them the chance to die gracefully. Now they're going to have to pay. Listen, I have to run. The team is having dinner. We'll be working late, so don't call. I'll call you if I get a chance."

"Right," she said. "I'll talk to you then."

"Aren't you going to wish me luck?"

"I don't think you'll need it," she said. "I have no doubt you're going to get lucky." She disconnected and put the phone down on the table, looking out the window at the alpenglow coloring the mountaintops red and orange. Nearing dusk, the town took on a dull brown appearance.

"Everything okay?"

"What?"

Logan spoke from behind the porcelain cup, casually reviewing the menu. He glanced up at her. "With your daughter. Is everything okay? Do you need to get home?"

"No. Everything is fine, Detective."

"Mike." He put down the cup and the menu. "I'm Detective Logan by day. After hours, I'm Mike. You'll make me feel old."

Dana turned off her phone and put it in her purse. She picked up her menu as the waitress came back to take their order. "How you folks doin'?" She wore tight blue jeans, a colorful glass bead necklace, and a sleeveless blouse revealing surprisingly muscular arms for a woman who appeared to be in her mid-fifties.

"Just fine," Logan said.

The waitress looked back at the counter to see if any dinners had come up from the grill. "What can I getcha?"

Dana turned the menu back and forth, in search of something appealing. "What do you recommend?"

"Fried chicken is the best you'll find," the woman said with noticeable pride. "It comes with garlic potatoes, side salad, and bread roll."

Dana grimaced. "Do you have something low-calorie?"

The waitress thought for a moment, then said, "I could fix you up a nice salad."

Dana nodded. "That will be fine. Could you bring the oil and vinegar on the side?"

The woman looked to Logan, who said, "Well, I'm not about to pass up the best fried chicken in Washington. Do the mashed potatoes come with butter?"

The waitress smiled. "They can."

He handed her his menu. "Is that apple pie I smell?"

"Fresh-baked. You have a good nose."

"Is that also the best around?"

"I'd like to believe so, but I am biased."

"We'll take two slices after dinner."

"Not for me," Dana said quickly.

Logan winked at the waitress. "Just bring the slices. They won't go to waste." He patted his stomach. "Or maybe they will."

The waitress laughed. "Coming right up."

When the woman left the table, Dana said, "You charmed her."

His eyebrows arched. "This appears to be a one-horse town, and judging by your brother's cabinets at his home and cabin, he wasn't much on shopping or cooking. I'm hoping he stopped to eat here. Let me have his photograph again." Dana handed him the photograph of James holding Molly on his shoulders. Logan put it on the table. "So why do you think your brother would come all the way out here, Ms. Hill?"

"Dana," she said. "Since it's after hours."

"Dana. Pretty name."

"Thank you." She found herself more pleased by the compliment than she should have been. "It was my grandmother's name."

"So, Dana, why do you think your brother would choose a cabin way out here?"

"Privacy, I guess."

"Didn't he live alone?"

Dana stirred her cup of coffee and lifted the mug to her lips with both hands, blowing at the surface. After a sip, she set it back down on the table. "You know he did."

"Was your brother gay?"

"No."

"So do you know who the woman was?" Dana looked up at him. "I don't know a lot of guys who would go to the trouble to drive two hours for a romantic interlude by themselves. The flowers on the table, the books on the shelves...usually, when someone goes to this much trouble for privacy, there's someone else involved."

"No," she said, "I don't know who it was."

"But you knew he was seeing someone."

Dana shook her head and picked up her coffee. "No. I don't know that, but I suspect he was."

Logan took a sip of coffee. "Another secret your brother was keeping?"

Dana put down the mug, opened her purse, and handed

Logan what she had found beneath her brother's bed. Logan held the earring up to the light. Multiple diamonds surrounded a large blue stone, and below it hung a teardrop-shaped diamond. Both were so large that Dana had initially thought it was costume jewelry, something James had bought for Molly, who liked to play dress-up. Upon closer inspection, however, she grew convinced the earring was real. "I found it under my brother's bed," she said.

"Just one?"

She nodded. "I couldn't find the match."

"That's what you were looking for under the bed in the cabin?"

"I figured it couldn't hurt to look."

Logan's eyes widened. "Your brother must have been serious."

"I don't think he bought it. I went through his financial records—that's how I found Montgomery Real Estate—but I didn't find any transactions for jewelry stores or for large withdrawals. If he bought the earrings recently, it would have been a significant withdrawal."

"So someone could have forgotten it?"

"Possibly."

"But you don't think so."

"It's an earring, and an expensive one. I don't know a lot of women who would forget an earring, especially just one."

"Maybe the person was in a hurry, couldn't find it, and was going to get it later."

"Maybe."

"But you had no idea that your brother was seeing anyone."

"None."

"What about other family members, friends?"

"His closest colleague at the school didn't know, and the neighbor never saw anyone. I asked when I returned her key."

Logan sat back. "And you planned on telling me this when?"

She shrugged, gripping the mug of coffee as if warming her hands. "I'm sorry. I should have told you."

Logan thought for a moment. "There are a lot of hotels and motels closer to your brother's home, if he was looking for privacy. It seems to me your brother was looking for something more; he wanted atmosphere and seclusion. He cared."

"Maybe it's somebody who lives here," she suggested.

"Then he wouldn't have needed the cabin." Logan put an arm along the back of the booth. "Unless the woman was married."

Dana felt a twinge in her stomach and picked up a spoon to twirl her coffee. The waitress returned with Dana's salad and Logan's fried chicken. The potatoes were steaming with butter. Logan closed his hand around the earring and spoke to the waitress. "You didn't lie. This looks great."

He had a boyish charm about him. Dana had to admit the chicken looked good, particularly in comparison with her plain salad.

"Are you Fae?" Logan asked the waitress, referring to the name of the diner.

"Fae's my mother." The woman refilled Logan's cup. "I named the diner after her, since most of the recipes are hers. My name is Bonnie. Where're you folks from?"

"Seattle," Logan said.

"Well, you make a sharp couple, if you don't mind me saying so."

Dana laughed. "We're not a couple."

The stream of coffee stopped in midpour. "I'm sorry. There I go jumping to conclusions. You just have that look to you."

Logan picked up the photograph from the table. "Actually, I'm a police officer. I was wondering if you might be able to help me." Logan held up the picture. Bonnie took it, putting the pot on the table. "Have you ever seen this man before?" Logan asked.

Bonnie studied the picture, her eyes shifting between it and Dana.

"He's my brother," Dana said. "He may have had a beard and a little longer hair."

"I can see the resemblance," she said. "Is he missing or something? Are you trying to find him?"

Dana looked at Logan, who nodded for her to go ahead. She looked up at Bonnie. "He's dead."

"Dead? You mean he was killed?"

"I'm afraid so."

"We're trying to retrace his steps," Logan said. "He used to rent a cabin out past the cemetery."

"The Wilbur Ranch? I'd heard someone was there. The place hasn't been lived in for years."

"That's the one," Logan said.

Bonnie looked at the picture again, studying it. She nodded, almost imperceptibly at first, then with growing confidence. "Yeah. Yeah, I think I do remember him. Did he wear glasses?" She made a circle in front of her eye. "Oval-shaped, like a writer or something. Wire-rimmed."

"Yes," Dana said.

"Yeah. He came in once or twice that I can remember. Nice guy. Polite. Good-looking. His hair *was* longer."

Logan smiled up at her. "I thought you might remember him. You strike me as the type of person who has a good memory for faces. Did he ever come in with anyone?"

Bonnie handed the picture back and put a finger to her lips. After a moment she said, "No. Can't say he did, although I guess someone could have been waiting in the car. He used to come in and order food to go. We talked a bit once while he waited. Nothing particular, just 'how you doing' and stuff like that. Like I said. Nice guy. Do you think the person killed him?"

Logan looked across the table at Dana. "That's what we're trying to find out."

20

〜

MARSHALL COLE RECLINED against the pillows, legs spread, hands gripping the sheets. The woman's head bobbed rhythmically between his knees. At the foot of the bed, the television glowed blue in the dark motel room. Cole groaned, but it was more from frustration than from pleasure. Since the incident in the motel, with Larry King getting shot and all, Cole had been unable to relax, unable to stop looking over his shoulder, unable to close his eyes without seeing the man with the black sunglasses, unable even to enjoy a good blow job.

The woman sat up to catch her breath and massaged the muscles in her jaw. She grabbed his erection with her hand and roughly stroked him as she reached down the side of the bed to retrieve her longneck Budweiser. "You think it's gonna happen anytime this century, Marshall?" She took a pull off the beer, and a stream rolled down her neck between pert breasts.

Unable to see the television, Cole grabbed her head and

lowered her back onto his erection, trying to concentrate. The beer had not dulled the throbbing pain in his ankle from the fall out of the bathroom window or helped him forget the haunting image of the man. He reached for his bottle on the nightstand and finished it while listening to the newscast. The goddamned weatherman was blathering on about the forecast for the rest of the country. Who gave a shit? How many people in Washington really cared that it was 85 degrees in Los Angeles or balmy in Hawaii? Talk about rubbing everybody's noses in it. Cole figured they could cut the forecast by two to three minutes and give the extra time to sports, which always came last and was always jammed for time. If he owned the station, he'd put sports first. Hell, it was the only part of the news that wasn't bad news.

"Come," the woman said with aggravation. "Come, Marshall, come. I can't go all night." Cole lowered her head back in place.

When the weatherman finished, Cole opened his eyes, but the station had cut back to the two newscasters, a man and a woman behind a desk having a fucking yukfest. Cole closed his eyes. Another news story—what they called a "filler" before the sports. Blah, blah, blah. What Cole cared about was whether the Mariners were still three games back of the Angels in the American League West. The boys had won six straight, and Cole wanted to know if the streak had reached seven. The Mariners were about the only thing he cared about in Washington. Rained too fucking much. He was going back to southeast Idaho, where it was dry, even in the winter, when it snowed.

Cole started to drift off, the alcohol making him sleepy,

hearing intermittent bits of the news story. He concentrated on his groin. If he timed it right, he could come just before the sports. He heard cheering and opened his eyes, fearing he'd fallen asleep, but it was just some dumbass in a suit mingling his way through a crowd. About to close his eyes again, he suddenly saw the face. Then the woman's head bobbed up, blocking the television. Cole sat bolt upright and forced her head to the base of his shaft. A chill ran through him. "Son of a bitch," he whispered.

The woman grunted. Cole ignored her. Then she bit him.

"Shit."

Cole grabbed her by the hair and threw her off the bed, scrambling forward, holding his dick in his hands. The face on the television was gone; he was looking at the news anchor's big head.

The woman got up from the floor, slapping at him with both hands. "Goddammit, Marshall. Fuck you. You're an asshole. What is wrong with you? You can beat your own self off."

Cole held her away with one arm, bending her wrist backward as he changed channels to search the other broadcasts. The newscast on Channel 5 went to the sports desk for a quick teaser. Then it went to a commercial.

21

~

"I SWEAR TO GOD, he's going to explode." Linda sounded both concerned and amused as she reported to Dana on Marvin Crocket the following morning. "I just hope he doesn't have a heart attack and need mouth-to-mouth, because if that's the case, somebody better call the coroner."

For Dana to have been AWOL an entire afternoon and now tardy the following morning was, to Crocket, open insubordination. Given that he wanted to fire her, it was also ironic that his biggest fear was undoubtedly that she was out interviewing with other law firms and scheming to steal his clients. "Tell him you can't reach me. Tell him I have my cell phone turned off." Dana smiled, thinking about the reaction that would get. Then she ended the call and did turn off her phone.

She stepped from the car and crossed Harrison Street in a drizzling rain, pushing through the heavy doors of the stucco building near Seattle's city center. Drills buzzed like a horde of mosquitoes, and she detected a faint metallic odor that reminded her of the dentist's office. Three Korean men sat hunched at cubicles, deft fingers working drill bits and blue flames over fine pieces of jewelry. Dana approached an unfinished wooden counter nicked and charred by cigarette butts and pen and pencil markings. She asked the woman behind the counter if she could speak with Kim, uncertain despite years of patronage whether Kim was the Korean owner's first or last name. Everyone, it seemed, just called him Kim. Kim had been her mother's wholesale jeweler and had set Dana's engagement ring and wedding band. Each anniversary, she returned to have him add a single small diamond. Over the years he had also worked on earrings, bracelets, and a watch, repairing clasps or adding brackets.

"Mrs. Dana." Kim walked to the counter through a string of beads hanging over a doorway. He wore the same outfit each time she came—black polyester pants and a white shortsleeved shirt with a pen clipped to the breast pocket. The cloth above the pocket was marked with blue ink dashes. Though Kim had to be in his sixties, he had an ageless round face free of wrinkles. His eyes were magnified behind black-framed glasses from which extended an antenna-like wire to a magnifying glass he could lower over his left lens.

"Is it time already?" Kim turned to a calendar on the wall. "Nine diamonds?"

"No, not yet." *Probably not ever,* she thought. "We have another four months to survive."

Kim smiled, choosing to interpret her comment as a joke. "You survive," he said with confidence. He raised his hands and shook them. "Three years, I have many women coming to have their wedding rings made into earrings. After three years, not so many. You solid."

"I have a favor to ask." She reached into her purse. "I found a piece of jewelry, and I think it might be expensive. I was hoping you could tell me about it."

Kim flipped the magnifying glass on the end of the wire into place, staring out at her like a cartoon character with one enormous black eye. Dana placed the earring in his callused hand, and he rolled it along his fingertips, then bounced it lightly in his palm as if he could weigh the stones by feel. He held the earring by the clasp and considered it like a very small fish. Finally, he turned on a high-wattage lamp and examined it under a bright white light.

"Very expensive. Blue stone is tanzanite. Rare. The diamonds are very high quality, and the setting is unique."

"How much would something like this cost?"

Kim looked up, propping his elbows on the counter while continuing to hold the earring underneath the light. The intensity of his concentration indicated he was adding and multiplying figures in his head. "For two?" He spoke out loud but for his own benefit. "Possibly fifty, fifty-five thousand. Maybe more."

Dana had expected the price to be high, but the number still surprised her. "That much?"

"At least." He stood up. "You see here, design is trademarked. Make more valuable."

"Trademarked?"

"Only one. So price could be much higher if you have two."

"I've never heard of jewelry being trademarked."

"Oh, yes." Kim nodded decisively. "I have my own trademark." He took a pad of scratch paper near a telephone and pulled the pen from his pocket, clicking it once and scribbling what looked like a "K" within a circle. "Many pieces my own design. You wearing one of them." He slipped the pen back into his pocket without clicking it, leaving another blue ink mark on his shirt. He handed Dana the earring and a small magnifying eyepiece. "On back you see marking. That is trademark."

Dana flipped over the earring and examined a small etching that, when magnified, appeared to be two "W"s interlocked by the center "V." She knew from patent work for her business clients that there were governmental offices for the registration of trademarks. "Is there a place where the jeweler registers his trademark, Kim? Where would I go to determine the name of the artist with this trademark?"

Kim smiled. "You would come here. Lucky you." He laughed. "Wait one moment." He stepped away from the counter, disappearing again through the beaded doorway.

Behind her, Dana heard the sound of a drill and instinctively ran her tongue along the fillings of her teeth. Kim reemerged with a well-worn magazine, set it on the counter, and flipped through torn and dog-eared pages. He used an index finger blackened and scarred with tiny burn marks to scan the pages. When he found the interlocked "W"s, he traced it to a page number, then fanned the pages of the magazine. After another moment, he closed it.

"William Welles," he said.

"That's the jeweler?" Dana asked.

Kim nodded. "That is the designer."

"William Welles," she said, as if trying it out. Her decision to talk with Kim had not been such a long shot after all. "I'd like to find him. How would I do that?"

Kim nodded and slipped the top magazine to the side, beginning the process anew with a second magazine. Dana searched through her purse for a pen, but Kim reached for the pen in his pocket and handed it to her without looking up from the magazine. She tore off a piece of paper from the scratch pad on the counter. "If he has a telephone number, perhaps I can call before I go by."

Kim shook his head. "You might call him today, but you not going to drive by. Not unless your car float."

22

⌒

THE SOUND OF a car door slamming caused Marshall Cole to sit upright in the chair. The television chirped at him like a bird at the first light of day. He peeked through the thick curtain pulled across the hotel window and squinted at the bright stream of sunlight. He'd fallen asleep, or likely passed out. During the night, he'd gotten up and used the gap in the curtain as a portal to the parking lot, watching intently for any sign of the blond man with the dark sunglasses. It was him. Cole was sure of it. Damn sure. Shit, how could he forget? He saw the face in his dreams every night—a fucking nightmare.

King had said he thought the man was Special Forces or some shit like that, but now Cole was thinking maybe the guy was more like Secret Service or, worse, a mercenary. Those dudes were the real badasses; the law didn't mean shit to them, and they were just as well trained in all the covert shit as the Special Forces guys. They just didn't live by any rules. They made their own. It explained how the man could appear at the hotel like a fucking ghost. He'd probably been one of those tunnel rats in the jungles of Vietnam or a sniper killing all the fucking towel-heads in Iraq. And now he was intent on killing Cole. Shit. Larry King had gotten them into a whole nest of trouble. The fuckhead. Whatever was going on, whoever the dude James Hill had been, this was bad shit. They'd killed King, and they would kill Cole. They could do it, too, people in the military. They could kill people. Make them disappear, wipe out birth records, anything that said the person ever even existed. Hell, they could make your own mother and father forget you. They had drugs to do that. Cole had seen it once on an *X Files* episode.

Cole turned from the window and felt a sharp pain in his neck. He rubbed it vigorously. Longneck bottles lay scattered about the carpet. One, partly full, lay on its side near a wet spot. Cole had indeed passed out. Shit. He pulled back the curtain again. The glare of the sun reflected off the windshields of the cars in the lot. Had the same cars been parked there last night? Which ones? He couldn't remember. He had kept track of the cars for hours, afraid the man would pull another Houdini, but then he'd passed out. Now everything was a blur.

He patted his stomach, did not feel the butt of the automatic, and fumbled along the sides of the chair until realizing the gun was in his other hand. He stood. He was losing it, starting to panic. He picked up the bottle and drank the warm remnants in two swallows. When he burped, a burning sensation filled the back of his throat. He needed some food to calm his stomach. It felt like he'd swallowed red-hot coals. Taking a shit would be like shooting flames out his ass. He shoved the automatic in his pants and walked to the bed. Andrea Bright lay facedown on top of the covers, naked, mouth open, snoring. Her left eyeball rolled back and forth beneath the lid. Her name was what people called an irony, since she wasn't bright by any stretch of the imagination. She was dumb as a stump. But she did give a good blow job, not that Cole could appreciate it under the circumstances. He slapped her on her ass. It brought her head off the pillow.

"Huh? What?" She brushed strands of thin brown hair from her face.

"Get up. Time to go."

She put her head back down. "Too tired."

He slapped her again, harder. The flesh of his hand cracked like a whip. "Get up, goddammit."

She sat up with her arms and legs flailing and threw a pillow at him. "Fuck you."

Cole shut off the television, gathered his brown leather jacket, and pulled a wad of cash from a pocket. He unfolded it and counted the bills on the cheap laminate dresser. He still had more than eleven hundred, close to twelve hundred. The hotels had been inexpensive. He'd been careful how much they spent.

"Where are we going?" The woman slipped on a pair of blue jeans without any underwear and sucked in her stomach to snap the button.

Someone rapped three times on the door. Cole pulled the automatic, flipped off the safety, and damn near started shooting through the hollow door. He raised one finger to tell Bright to keep quiet. She rolled her eyes and flipped him the bird. He carefully pulled back the curtain. A diminutive Mexican woman stood beside a pushcart loaded with toilet paper and towels.

"Don't need anything," Cole said, angry. The woman had frightened the shit out of him.

The woman spoke through the door: "You want fresh towels?"

Bright laughed and flopped on her back on the bed, pulling up her knees like it was a real riot fest.

"No!" Cole yelled. "Don't need anything."

"When you want me to clean the room?"

"I don't give a shit, Señorita. Go get a taco or something. Not now."

The woman frowned and pushed the cart down the concrete walkway. Cole waited until he heard the same three rhythmic knocks, followed by the same series of questions.

Bright pulled a T-shirt over her head and struggled to find the armholes, still laughing. "What? You think the maid is gonna shoot you, James Bond?"

"Fuck you. I said get dressed."

She sat on the bed, pulling on white pumps. "Where are we going, anyway?"

"Idaho." Cole slipped on his jacket.

"Fuck that. Bunch of redneck hicks in Idaho."

"You want to stay, stay." Cole held out his hand. "Give me the keys to the car."

"It's my car, Marshall."

And therein was Cole's dilemma. He would have liked to dump Bright and save himself the expenses and aggravation, seeing as how he couldn't even enjoy a blow job, but he needed the car, and Bright was vengeful enough to call the police if he took it. "Then get your ass in the car." He shoved her toward the door. "Move."

Bright bent down and picked up her underwear and bra, holding them in a ball while retrieving her jean jacket from the chair. She pulled open the hotel door. "You're an ass."

23

∽

LOGAN SAT AT his desk sipping coffee and picking at a blueberry scone while he reviewed the lab tests on the clothes found in the Emerald Inn motel room. The lab concluded that the dirt and soil could be found almost anywhere in the state of Washington. Big help. Logan could tell them exactly where to find the dirt. It had once been in the hole in the ground at the rear of the motel. Logan was also correct that the blood on the clothes belonged to James Hill. With the advent of DNA testing, there was no doubt. The forensic team had also lifted hair fibers from the clothes that did not match either the DNA testing for James Hill or Laurence King. There were no DNA tests on file for Marshall Cole, but based on the sizes, the clothes were surely his. Of more interest to Logan was the ballistics test. The bullet that had killed Laurence King was a .22-caliber slug. The bullets pulled from the hotel wall were fired from a 9mm handgun. The technicians calculated that the bullets embedded in the wall had been shot from the adjacent room. It left one logical conclusion. Logan had been right again. Someone other than Marshall Cole had shot Laurence King. Cole was likely in the other room as King's backup, but spooked when King got shot, and fled, firing shots at random to slow down his pursuer before he jumped out the bathroom window.

The telephone rang. Logan answered while continuing to consider the ballistics test.

"Mike? It's Dana."

Logan smiled at the sound of her voice. The rest of their dinner at Fae's in Rosyln had been pleasant. She had finally relented and shared his fried chicken, and he didn't even have to tempt her with the apple pie. She ate an entire slice. They sat for over an hour, drinking coffee, and she didn't seem in any particular hurry to get home. As the sun set, he had considered her in the fading light through the window, and it did nothing to change his initial perception. Dana Hill was a beautiful woman, and for the first time in a long time, Logan did not feel guilty for thinking it or for having taken off his wedding ring. He had felt something for her the moment he saw her, a feeling he had not felt in years. Whether she had any feelings for him was difficult to tell. Dana Hill was guarded. When she smiled, her blue eyes sparkled, but it was a brief flash that faded quickly, as if sadness inside her dulled the color. Logan knew that kind of sadness, the kind that had grayed the world and his life for so long. Dana Hill had asked him a lot of questions about himself and his career, but she had avoided asking him anything too personal. She'd also avoided discussing her personal life or her husband, another sign her marriage was not going well. No man who loved his wife would have allowed her to identify her brother's body or clean out his house alone. And though he had tried not to eavesdrop, Logan had heard a distance in her voice when she spoke to her husband on the telephone. It sounded like a business conversation. Logan suspected he knew why.

I have no doubt you're going to get lucky. You didn't need to be a detective to figure out that Dana Hill was giving her husband a not so subtle warning that she knew what he was up to. Then she had turned off her phone, apparently uninterested in talking with him further.

It didn't matter. Dana Hill was the sister of a murder victim, a crime Logan had been charged with solving. She was also a married woman with a three-year-old daughter.

Logan cupped his ear. "I'm having trouble hearing you. There's a lot of background noise."

"I'm at Sea-Tac."

"The airport? Where are you going?"

"I'm taking a trip. My flight is about to leave."

"Good for you. Are you taking Molly?"

"No." He heard a hesitation in her voice. "I think I might have found a lead on the earring. I won't know until I get there."

Logan dropped his feet from the corner of his desk and stood up from his chair. "Dana, hold on. I just spoke with personnel; there is no one who even remotely resembles the man you and Bernadette Georges described. Daniel Holmes is bald and five foot seven. He is not the detective who came to your brother's house or to the real estate office. They couldn't trace the number on the business card, and the address was a fake. Whoever he is, judging by the condition of the cabin, he knows what he's doing or has access to people who do. That means he also likely killed King and that makes him very dangerous, Dana."

"Tell me, Detective, do you still think two petty thieves killed my brother?"

"What I thought isn't important. I needed evidence, you know that."

"And do you have it?"

"We got back the lab tests on the clothes from the motel. The blood on them matches your brother's. They belonged to Cole. He and King buried them behind the motel, and there is no plausible reason why they would have dug them back up. If we accept that premise, then the same person who shot King and left the watch also dug up the clothes. That means he probably also sent Cole and King to your brother's house. It was a setup. He knew when your brother would get home, and he knew they would kill him because of their criminal history. Now he's covering his tracks, and that could include finding an expensive earring. Why else would he go back to your brother's house unless he's looking for something? If I'm right, you're the next logical choice of people who could have it. You were cleaning out his house."

"The earrings are trademarked. There's not another pair like them in the world. If I can find the man who designed them, he might have billing records that can tell us who he designed them for."

He heard a voice in the background, advising passengers that the plane was boarding. "Dana, don't get on the plane."

"I have to go. I have to do this."

"No. You don't. Whatever guilt you're feeling about your brother being killed, you can't change what happened. This was a premeditated, well-thought-out murder."

"They're closing the gate. I have to go."

"Whoever owns those earrings would also know who designed them."

"Which is why I can't waste time. This is the only direct flight of the day."

"Then the person who killed King may be on it."

"I have to go."

"Tell me where you're going?" He could call the local police. "Dana? Don't get on that plane." He persisted more urgently. "The killer is an excellent shot." He looked at his watch. "Take a later flight. I'll go with you."

"I can't waste time. I'll call you," she said, and he heard the phone disconnect.

"Dammit." He slammed down the phone. When it immediately rang, he snatched it from the cradle. "Dana?"

Patrick Murphy greeted him with a profanity. "Shit. I should have known I'd find you at your desk while I'm out here humping on one of your cases."

Logan wasn't in the mood. "If you're humping one of my cases, I'm in serious trouble."

"Shit. You should be so lucky. We got a lead on your friend Marshall Cole. Apparently, he's got a girlfriend in Auburn who lives in a mobile home park. He visits when he needs to get his rocks off."

"You got an address?"

"Do farts smell?"

24

~

MARSHALL COLE CHECKED the rearview mirror. He saw nothing out of the ordinary and hadn't since they left the motel room. He would have known, too. He'd checked the mirror every ten seconds—seemed like it, anyway. He was driving southeast on Highway 82. Though he couldn't remember the last time he'd been home, he hadn't forgotten the way. He'd fill up the tank in Yakima, which was just about the last big city of consequence for a bazillion miles, then beeline it to Highway 84 through the northeast corner of Oregon. From there it was a straight shot across Idaho to the southeast corner of the state near the Wyoming and Utah borders. There he'd jump on Highway 30, and that two-lane road would take him all the way to Grace, a town that, when he'd left, didn't warrant anything more than a four-foot-tall sign on a post stuck in the ground, and likely still didn't. Cole had hoped he'd seen that sign for the last time in his rearview mirror. Now he wouldn't relax until he was taking the same turnoff for home.

At the moment, however, he had more pressing needs. The fuel tank was running low, and he needed to take a monster shit. Most mornings he was like clockwork—first thing out of bed. And he didn't need any cup of coffee to get the machinery working. But the damn cleaning lady knocking at the door had thrown him off his rhythm, and he couldn't go before they left the hotel. He grimaced and adjusted in his seat; the pain in his gut had become a cramp just above his belt buckle.

Cole had wanted to leave Washington right after he saw the man's face on the newscast, but he had already finished ten beers by then, and he didn't see well at night. He had some type of psychosis, or stigmatism, or some damn thing that the optometrist at Costco had said made everything blurry. At night, headlights and streetlamps stretched like taffy, making it damn near impossible to focus on the road. And he didn't want to risk getting pulled over. Once they logged him into the computer, he was a goner. They'd take his ass to jail, and the next thing he'd know, someone would be coming for him with official-looking paperwork, and he'd be on a bus to nowhere— gone without a trace. Never even existed. Never born.

Andrea Bright slept with her head propped back against the headrest, eyes closed, mouth open. The interior of the car smelled like beer and feet. Her white pumps stank. He had half a mind to throw them out the window. He continued to turn the dial through the radio stations, stopping when he heard a disc jockey giving what sounded like the news, but it was just some jackass reporting again on the weather.

"Rain, asshole. How much more do we need to know?"

How the fuck was he going to follow the Mariners from

Grace? None of his brothers had cable last time he was there, and he doubted the local paper had gotten much better since he left. High school sports were about all it covered, as if anyone really gave a shit how many touchdowns Johnny scored at the big homecoming game.

In the distance, he saw a bright orange and blue Union 76 ball. It came not a minute too soon. The cramping in his stomach had become epidemic. "Thank the fucking Lord and praise Jesus," he said.

He took the exit, waited at a stop sign for traffic to clear, then punched the gas across the intersection. The orange ball must have triggered something inside him, like that Pavlov dog thing, because now that his mind was set on taking a dump, all systems were go, and there wasn't going to be a long countdown to blastoff. He pulled up to the pumps beneath the overhang and backhanded Bright in the throat. "Wake up."

She choked as if she'd swallowed a fly and sat up coughing. "What?" she asked, annoyed.

He pulled the wad of bills from the leather jacket on the seat and handed her a twenty. "Fill it up and buy us something to eat. I got to go."

Bright looked around. "I don't want to eat at some fucking convenience store. Why don't you spend some of that money you got wadded up in your pocket and get us a restaurant for once? How'd you get that much money, anyways?"

"You don't need to know none of that. This is just a snack. Get me a milk. My stomach is killing me."

"Yeah, that cleaning lady really scared the shit out of you, huh?"

He shoved her into the door and dropped the bill in her lap. He didn't have time to fuck around. "Just do it."

Bright crumpled the bill and pushed open the car door, then slammed it closed. "Asshole."

Cole followed her across the blacktop to the small grocery store. She flung open the glass door at him, and he swatted at the back of her head, missing. The clerk looked like a teenager going through puberty. The hair sticking out from beneath his blue uniform cap was as orange as the Union 76 sign, and his face was pocked with acne. A peach-fuzz mustache grew above his upper lip.

"Bathroom?" Cole asked.

"Around back on the side." The kid reached under the counter and handed Cole a key attached to a huge piece of wood. "People forget to bring the key back," he explained.

Cole stepped around Bright and grabbed a newspaper from the rack as he hurried out the glass doors. "She'll pay for it," he said. "And get another six-pack of Bud."

Bright flipped Cole the bird, then leaned against the counter, feeling nauseated. The kid had his cap pulled low on his head, but it didn't hide the fact that he was staring at her breasts, particularly at her nipples, which the air-conditioning had caused to protrude through her T-shirt. She busted him when he looked up at her, and he quickly diverted his eyes.

"Uh, what pump?" he asked, his stare now fixed on the computerized keypad beneath his fingers. His cheeks had become damn near the color of his hair.

"It's the only car out there."

His eyes sneaked another peek. "There's three pumps: regular, unleaded, and supreme. You want unleaded, regular, or supreme?"

"That depends on who's pumping." Bright leaned across

the counter. "I give nothing less than supreme, but I don't always get it. Are you going to be doing the pumping, or am I?"

The kid flashed red as a traffic light. Bright was enjoying this. "It's self-serve."

"Too bad. You look like you could do some supreme pumping." She did a hip thrust and handed him the twenty.

"How much do you want?"

She stuck the tip of her finger to her mouth. "Fill it up," she said, then inserted the finger to the last knuckle.

The boy swallowed hard. "I'll hold the money until you're finished," he stammered.

She walked about the store grabbing a six-pack of beer, a box of doughnuts, a bag of potato chips, and a liter of Coke, and left them on the counter. "Fetch me a pack of Marlboros, too," she said. She walked to the door, smiled at the thought, then turned back around and raised her shirt, exposing her breasts. "Nice and cool in here," she said, fanning her chest. "Feels good."

COLE HURRIED INTO the bathroom stall. He didn't bother taking the time to put down a seat cover. He sat flipping through the newspaper. "Bullshit, bullshit, and bullshit."

He still didn't know if the Mariners had won or lost. After the blond man's face flashed on the television screen, he'd been too unnerved to do anything but pace the room. It had taken four more beers just to settle down. He might have only finished the tenth grade, but Cole had known something wasn't right about the guy from the start. He had a sense about those kinds of things that made the hairs on his neck tingle. Not that King would ever listen to him. King had said Cole was a dumb shit and that he was the brains of the operation. Yeah? Well, who was the dumb shit now, Larry? King had been a bad influence from the get-go. Bad luck was all the luck King ever had. Everything he touched went wrong. A big talker and a born loser. Well, the son of a bitch was dead, and Cole was still alive. King was going into a hole in the ground, and Cole was going home. *Who's the brains now, Larry? Who was the loser now?*

"Fuckhead," Cole said out loud.

King had refused to believe that he and Cole had been a couple of pigeons. Cole had known it. He'd told King that's exactly what they were. Pigeons. The man wasn't supposed to be home. Bull-fucking-shit. When Cole heard the front door open, he'd been standing in the bedroom and dropped the shit he'd been told to get. He had hoped the man would just go up the stairs. But he hadn't. He'd walked right down the hall, right past where Cole was hiding behind the bedroom door, and right into the room where Larry had been—the one with all the fucking masks on the wall staring at them. Cole was going to just hit the guy in the head and knock him out from behind, but then the fucking guy turned around and looked right at him. Fuck. He looked right at him, like his eyes were memorizing Cole's face. Cole had no choice but to kill him, and now he was convinced that was exactly what the guy who'd hired them had wanted. He'd wanted James Hill dead, whoever he was, and now he wanted King and Cole dead, too.

Cole's only chance now was to get far away, to a place where most people knew him and his family and would let him know if the man came looking for him. In the meantime, he'd have his dad get him work at one of the phosphate companies in Soda Springs, and he'd race dirt bikes on the weekends, which was what he should have done in the first place. If the police ever did catch up to him, he could pin the blame on King, say he had nothing to do with no robbery and didn't know nothing about killing nobody. He'd say King had boasted about a robbery and about killing a guy, and that was that. But that was for later. The police weren't his concern at the moment. His concern was the fucking ghost.

He found the sports section, dropped the rest of the paper on the tile floor, and read the headlines. The Mariners had lost. The Angels had won. They were four back. "Fuck it," he said. Things weren't looking good.

BRIGHT PUMPED UNLEADED into the Nova, watching the meter spin faster than a slot machine at one of the tribal casinos. She knew her car would take more than fifteen dollars in gas, especially with the Arabs bumping up the price for the summer, like they always did. And the food on the counter cost more than five. Hell, the beer alone was at least that much. Shithead Cole would just have to fork over more money. He could afford it. She'd seen the wad of bills he kept tucked in his jacket pocket. Cole thought she was a dumb shit and a good lay, and not in that order, but she was smarter than he knew. She had a lot of Marshall Coles, and she got what she could from each. Besides, she needed a good lay every once in a while, too, and Cole wasn't bad in that department, and she liked it a hell of a lot better when he had cash.

She heard the bells ring, tires crossing the rubber hoses stretched across the concrete floor. She looked over her shoulder at a navy blue Ford continuing to the far end of the station and stopping near a telephone booth. A man stepped out, dressed in a brown leather jacket, jeans, and cowboy boots. He paused and gave Bright a look and smile. Damn, he was cute. Bright stood straight and brushed a strand of hair from her face, smiling back at him. Then she turned her back and bent over to remove the nozzle from the gas tank, moving her hips forward and back to give him a good look at what was still her finest attribute. But when she straightened and turned to put the nozzle back in the pump, the man was gone. She looked across the parking lot but did not see him walking to the convenience store. He'd probably gone to use the bathroom. Too bad for him. In the morning it smelled like something had crawled up Cole's ass and died.

THE DAMN PITCHING was killing them. The bullpen had given up eight runs in two games. They already had a team earned-run average of more than five runs a game and had fallen way behind the Angels. Shit, the Athletics were breathing down their necks for second place, and the Mariners sure as shit didn't have the offensive firepower to hold them off. Play-offs already looked like a long shot. And they could forget the damn wild card, which Cole thought was for losers anyway. With Boston just trying to keep pace with the Yankees, one of them would get the wild card. Cole had seen it coming. He'd said it in the off-season, when the Mariners were busy signing a bunch of free-agent hitters. Pitching. Where the fuck is the pitching? Good pitching beat good hitting every time. The Yankees, Red Sox, and Angels had it. The Mariners didn't. They never learned.

"Dumb shits."

Cole heard the door to the bathroom swing open. He shook the newspaper to let the person know the stall on the left was occupied. Last thing he needed was some guy yanking open the door and getting a glimpse of his johnson. He heard water running in the sink, then the towel roll thumped twice. Cole went back to the article, but he'd lost his place. He heard the sound of a fly unzipping and looked underneath the stall. The toes of the two cowboy boots faced toward the wall where the urinal was mounted. Cole snorted a laugh. The guy was probably some neat freak, washing his hands first. The world had all kinds.

The urinal flushed. Cole watched the cowboy boots disappear. A moment later, he heard the water in the sink again, followed by two more whumps of the towel rack. Unbelievable. He waited a beat, not wanting to be interrupted again, but didn't see light stream in, as it had when the man opened the door. The guy was starting to annoy him. Cole looked at the box scores. The Red Sox had won for the third night in a row and were now only two back of the Yankees. The Mariners were going to have another lousy sesaon, and all because they'd forgotten the number one rule of the game. Pitching.

Cole lowered the paper when he still hadn't heard the door to the bathroom open or seen any light. This was getting fucking weird. He looked up, thinking the guy might be some pervert trying to sneak a peek over the top of the stall, but no one peered down at him. Then he saw the cowboy boots outside his stall.

"It's taken," he said loudly, not trying to hide his annoyance. The door to the stall next to him opened and closed, the lock sliding shut. "Jesus," he said loud enough to be heard, no longer caring. "Make up your damn mind."

He looked under the stall to satisfy himself that the cowboy boots were on the tile and facing forward. The man had seriously thrown off Cole's rhythm. He knew he wasn't finished. He needed a good uninterrupted fifteen minutes in the morning to give his bowels a full opportunity to purge. He focused again on the article, reading about how the Mariners had blown an opportunity in the fifth inning, getting nothing after loading the bases with no outs. He lifted his head at a noise coming from the other stall, one he couldn't identify. It sounded almost like mice eating wood chips, or the sound that a tiny blade might make sawing through a piece of wood. He put his ear against the metal stall. The industrial-sized toilet paper dispenser fell from the wall and crashed to the tile, leaving a baseball-sized hole in the metal frame separating the stalls.

Cole nearly fell off the toilet getting out of the way. "Hey, asshole. I'm about to kick your fucking ass." He leaned forward and peered through the hole. "Did you hear me?" he shouted. Then, "Oh shit."

BRIGHT STOOD WITH her back to the counter, staring out at the gas pumps. She was no longer interested in being the young boy's wet dream. The gas pump had shut off at $16.68, and she'd topped it off at $16.75.

She turned to the boy. "What time is it?"

"What time do you want it to be?"

She shook her head and looked at him with revulsion. "Time?"

"Eleven-forty-five."

Cole was such a jerk. She had another six minutes to wait and he would make her wait every one of them. He could never cut it short. He always had to take fifteen minutes, just to give himself enough time to read about the damn Mariners. He was an asshole, and he drank too much and treated her like shit whether he was drunk or sober. He had no job except for occasional laborer's work on a construction site, which was why he bothered hanging out with that loser Laurence King. Then he stayed out all night drinking and spending what money he made, showing up at her house whenever he felt like a blow job. Now he was paranoid, convinced of some government conspiracy fantasy King had probably dreamed up. She wasn't surprised someone had shot King. He was an even bigger asshole than Cole. But she sure as shit knew the government wouldn't go to the trouble of doing it. It was probably some lowlife King had pissed off or who he owed money.

The more pressing matter was what the fuck was she going to do in bumfuck Idaho. And with Cole's relatives? Please. He and his brothers would probably take turns screwing her, or worse, do her together. That was just what she needed. Christ, what had she gotten herself into?

She looked out at the Nova. Cole's leather jacket was draped over the backseat. He hadn't taken it with him. The money was in the pocket. The keys were in the ignition. She smiled and turned to the clerk. "What's the total?"

"Twenty-four thirty-five."

"Make it twenty even." She slid the grocery bag toward her. "For five bucks, I'll give you another peek, a quick feel, and you can get a hard-on under that orange smock."

25

∽

DANA DISEMBARKED FROM the United Airlines 747 into the open-air terminal of Kahului Airport on Maui. She stopped to search her purse, then proceeded from the gate, stopping again to adjust the heel of her shoe. A short distance later she paused to admire the landscape and smell the fragrant flowers and tropical plants on the warm breeze. Each time she watched the people who passed, looking for any indication that someone was following her. The man who had come to her brother's house was not on the plane. She had walked throughout it to check. She also had not seen him in the airport. If there was anyone else following her, she couldn't tell. She rented a car just outside baggage claim and caught a courtesy shuttle to the rental car lot.

She had arrived in Maui during the heat of the day, gaining three hours with the time change. The sun burned a bright white, and she estimated the temperature at perhaps 90 degrees. Twenty minutes later, she stepped from the sanctity of an air-conditioned bus and walked to her rental car, a bright orange Jeep. If someone was following her it would have to begin here. She'd been to the island before and knew that Maui had a two-lane road, one lane in each direction. Sunglasses adorned, she pulled from the rental lot and deliberately drove the wrong direction for several minutes, then made an abrupt U-turn. No car behind her made the same maneuver. She followed the road around the island, the Pacific Ocean to her left, dark-skinned kids sitting on surfboards without a care in the world but to catch the perfect wave. The woman at the car rental counter had smiled when Dana asked for directions to Lahaina. "It is a small island. If you don't find it the first time, just go around again."

Dana found it the first time. She turned off the main road, pulled to the side, and stopped. The three cars behind her on the highway continued past the turn. She drove toward the water and turned right on Front Street. It led past a school and a park with an enormous banyan tree. The tree's roots and branches spread out like the tentacles of a huge octopus, creating an umbrella beneath which artists set up booths to sell jewelry, beaded necklaces, and paintings.

Front Street went through the center of Lahaina—mostly single-story buildings. The sidewalks bustled with tourists in shorts, sandals, and tank tops. Dana turned down an alley to a pay parking lot and found a spot. She took a moment to straighten her appearance. Her hair had wilted in the heat, and the wind had wreaked its own havoc. She pulled it back into a ponytail, fixed her makeup, and adjusted her blouse and slacks.

She got out of the car and walked along Front Street.

Most of the stores were Hawaii's version of five-and-dimes, selling tourist knickknacks, bamboo beach mats, and T-shirts. Jimmy Buffett music blared from a second-floor restaurant and bar. Diners sat on a balcony eating a late lunch or getting an early start on happy hour. Toward the north end of town, the number of tourists thinned, and the quality of the merchandise in the stores improved. Art galleries and fine jewelry stores replaced the five-and-dimes. Dana considered the jewelry in several store windows. She decided against the discount wholesalers and searched instead for stores off the beaten tourist path. Walking down an alley, she came to a tiled inner court-yard with palm trees and a fountain. A tanned man in a gray polyester blazer and open-collared shirt stood outside a storefront that displayed glass sculptures—dolphins and whales, a colorful glass bowl. Stepping closer, Dana saw jewelry, including several of the ocean-blue stones like the one in her pocket. As she approached, the guard nodded, pulled open the door, and welcomed her inside to air-conditioned relief.

She removed her sunglasses and let her eyes adjust to the subtle lighting. A glass counter contained blue gems and diamonds.

"The stone is tanzanite." The woman behind the counter greeted her with a British accent.

"They're beautiful," Dana said. "My favorite."

"They are many people's favorite, though they continue to be somewhat of a secret in the United States. Where are you from?"

"Seattle. My husband and I were on the islands about ten years ago." Dana subtly placed her left hand on the counter to display her adorned diamond ring.

The woman used a key to unlock the display case and took out one of the larger blue stones. She placed it on the counter. "There is only one producing mine left in the world. The others flooded several years ago, and the African miners will no longer go down the shafts because of superstition. We import these from Grand Cayman."

Dana pulled the earring from her pocket and placed it on the counter. "Actually, I'm hoping to match my earring. I'm afraid I lost the other and have given up any hope of ever finding it. It makes me sick; it was a wedding present from my husband. He had it crafted here on the island. We've returned for our ten-year anniversary, and I'd like to surprise him . . . and me."

The woman smiled. "May I?" she asked, her interest at a peak. She held the earring up to the natural light, admiring its beauty.

"I believe the artist's initials are on the back," Dana said. "William Welles."

The woman shifted her gaze to Dana, as if uncertain she had heard correctly. She rolled the earring in her palm and looked at the back of the clasp. Astonished, she asked, "How long have you had this?"

Dana tried to remain casual. "As I said, for about ten years."

"That's about the time he stopped designing jewelry," the woman said, speaking almost to herself.

"Stopped designing?" Dana grew concerned. Ten years was a long time. William Welles could have died or moved from the island. She hadn't thought of that.

The woman nodded. "Yes. William Welles no longer designs jewelry."

"But he's still alive?" Dana asked.

"Oh, yes." The woman sighed. "He strays into town infrequently." She paused, obviously searching for the proper accolades. "William Welles is an artist. Most of the sculptures you see here in town are his work. He is a genius, if eccentric." She refocused her attention on the earring. "I don't know him to have crafted a piece of jewelry in quite some time. You have a real piece here."

"Half a piece, I'm afraid . . . unless I might find him?"

"We can craft the piece here," the woman offered. "My husband designs jewelry."

"I'd prefer to have Mr. Welles craft it, for reasons I'm sure you can understand—though I'd certainly be willing to purchase the stones through your store." Dana hoped that would appease the woman. "Do you know how I might find him?"

"I'm told he lives on the northwest coast, off the Kahekili Highway, on a ridge overlooking the ocean, but it can be difficult to find. He does not accept visitors."

"Could you tell me how to get there?"

The woman shook her head. "I'm afraid I don't know the way."

Dana sighed. She sensed the woman was being reticent because she wanted to get the business for herself. "That's very disappointing. I was hoping to match the earring with a bracelet and necklace."

"Of the same design?"

"Of the same design and quality," Dana assured her.

The woman's face pinched. Her eyebrows pulled together, and her nostrils flared as if she were on William Welles's scent at that very instant.

26

‿

"S HIT, NICE BROAD. She leaves him sitting on the toilet. That's cold."

Patrick Murphy spoke as Logan approached. Multiple patrol cars, unmarked vehicles, and an ambulance were parked to the side of the convenience store. Two men from the Yakima County coroner's office lingered outside the door to the bathroom, kicking at the gravel. The two Yakima detectives who initially responded had run Cole through the computer and learned that he was wanted in Seattle on one and possibly two murder charges. That set off bells and whistles until they reached Murphy and Logan. Logan requested that the detectives maintain the crime scene until he arrived, and they obliged him.

Logan detected the distinct odor of whiskey on Murphy's breath. He pointed to the convenience store, where he had just spoken with a kid who'd been working behind the counter when Cole and his girlfriend walked in. "The kid says they came into the store, Cole asked for the key to the bathroom, and she picked up some snacks. Then she apparently flashed her boobs at him before going out to pump the gas."

"Excuse me?" Murphy said.

Logan nodded. "That's what he said."

Murphy grinned. "Shit. I told you she was a nice broad."

"After she pumped the gas, she went back inside but didn't have enough money to pay for the gas and the groceries. The kid said she and Cole didn't look to be getting along, and she seemed to get impatient waiting for him. Then she offered to flash the kid again for a discount."

"What was his response?"

"She walked out with the groceries."

"Good boy." Murphy smiled. "Opportunities like that don't come along but once in a lifetime. Did she have a nice set of ta-tas?"

"We didn't get that far, Murph. I didn't think it was germane to the investigation."

"Shit. It might increase police interest. You put out an APB for a pair of 36Ds, and you'll have every patrol car in the state looking for her."

Logan nodded. "You might be right about that."

"What about the shooter? Kid have any information?"

Logan shook his head, frowning. "Thought he saw another car drive in while the girlfriend was pumping gas but couldn't be sure. My guess is he was watching her. Said he thought she was driving a Nova, blue or tan. I had Yakima put out an APB on a blue or tan Nova."

"With one nice set of headlights," Murphy added.

"What about her home?"

"I got guys camped there, but no sign of her, and probably not for a while. She might be hiding; Cole doesn't come off as the kind of guy to take being left on the crapper real well."

"Yeah, well, that's not her worry anymore."

"The kid couldn't ID anyone else going into the bathroom? What, was he in the back pullin' on his puddin'?"

"Like I said, he has a vague recollection of hearing the bell go off, but he's pretty much immune to the sound. My guess is he was fixated on Bright. We're lucky he caught a glimpse of the car."

"He was spanking his monkey, was what he was doing," Murphy said. He nodded to the bathroom around the side. "You been inside yet?"

"Not yet."

"It's a real treat, let me tell you—a corpse sitting on the crapper with his pants around his ankles."

"Can't wait," Logan said.

He followed Murphy. The two detectives from Yakima waited with Deb Hallock and a uniformed officer who had apparently come with Murphy. Logan thanked the detectives for waiting, then he and Murphy walked toward the door.

"Didn't even get a chance to wipe his ass," the uniformed officer said to Murphy as they stepped into the bathroom. "That's cold."

Murphy stopped at the door. "What? Did you look, Turketti?"

The officer stammered, "No—no, I didn't look."

Too late. Murphy frowned and shook his head. "You sick son of a bitch. I always had my doubts about you."

Flustered, the officer turned a deep shade of red. "I didn't look. There's no paper in the toilet."

"Shit. You are sick, Turk."

"I didn't look," the officer pleaded.

Logan stepped inside the bathroom. The floor tiles were one-inch squares, the kind that came on twelve-by-twelve netted sheets. It was cheap and could be easily installed and easily replaced if an individual tile broke. The wall and counter tile were pumpkin orange. Logan pulled on latex gloves and swung open the stall door by the top edge. Marshall Cole sat pitched off kilter, like a passed-out drunk. The bullet had hit him in the right eye, which was now a gaping hole. Otherwise, Cole looked like there wasn't a scratch on him. It reminded Logan of a crow he'd shot with a pellet gun as a kid. The pellet had struck the bird in the eye, and it had fallen from the sky like a stone. But for the empty eye socket, the bird had looked like it could fly away. But the bird never got off the ground again, and Marshall Cole wasn't getting off the toilet.

Blood had dripped down the wall and formed a puddle flowing with the grout lines, partially absorbed by an open newspaper. At the side of the toilet was an industrial-size roll of toilet paper still in its plastic case. A hole in the wall separating the stalls indicated where the toilet roll had once hung. There was a handgun on the toilet tank.

Logan stepped back and opened the door of the second stall. The dispenser was also on the floor. The toilet bowl was clean. He stepped back to the first stall and bent down to check the pockets of Cole's jeans, covering his mouth with a handkerchief.

"Shit. What're you going to do, give the guy a blow job, Logan?"

Logan spoke through his handkerchief. "I've told you—it's the Irish, not the Scottish, who give blow jobs." He stood.

"You remember the stash King had on him? I wanted to see if Cole was carrying a similar amount." He wasn't. Cole's pockets were empty except for some pocket change. Logan bet when they found the woman, they would find a wad of cash. If she had left Cole at a gas station, there had to be a good reason. Either they really weren't getting along or she'd seen an opportunity and taken it.

Murphy turned to the young officer, who stood waiting. "Turketti, quit staring at the guy's dick and find out the estimate on the time of death." He turned back to Logan. "Might help us to figure out how far the woman's got."

Logan nodded. "The kid at the counter says she and Cole came in about eleven-thirty. She left fifteen minutes after that. He got curious after she took off without Cole but said he wasn't anxious to tell Cole his girlfriend left him for a box of doughnuts and six-pack of beer. He let another half hour go by, then decided to find out what Cole did with the key. Said the door was unlocked, and when he pushed it open, he could see Cole's boots. He thought maybe he'd passed out. Then he saw the blood." Logan looked at his watch. "She's long gone. Best bet is to sit on her home."

"And the kid didn't hear a shot?" Murphy asked. "It would have echoed like a bass drum in here."

Logan examined the bullet wound. "Twenty-two or nine-millimeter, and the killer probably used a silencer. Remember? Nobody at the motel heard anything, either." He stepped out of the stall.

Logan pulled open the door of the adjacent stall again. He walked in, sat on the toilet, and looked through the hole where the dispenser used to be. He made the shape of a gun with his hand and stuck his finger in the hole. "Bang," he said softly.

"No offense, Logan," Murphy said, looking into the stall, "but I've had very few images of you, and this one isn't the most flattering."

Logan chuckled. "What was he doing?"

"Shit. Taking a crap and enjoying the sports page. That's a man's God-given right."

"I don't mean Cole. I mean the killer. What was the killer doing in here?" Logan stood up. "He could have walked in, shot him, and walked back out. Why go to all this trouble?"

Murphy shrugged. "Cole was armed. If he took a couple of shots at the guy in the motel, like we think, the guy would have known it. Maybe he was concerned Cole was waiting for him on the other side of the stall door."

"Maybe," Logan said. He braced an arm against the back wall of the stall, reached over Cole, and picked up the gun—a nine-millimeter automatic, a candy-store popgun that could be purchased anywhere. He wrapped it in his handkerchief and walked out. He told the two Yakima detectives he was finished.

Outside, he handed the gun to Murphy. "You'll want to have the lab run a ballistics test and compare it with the bullets pulled from the motel wall where we found King."

Murphy looked back at the door to the bathroom. "Shit. Who is this guy?" he asked, and for the first time that Logan could remember, the profanity meant something.

"I don't know, Murph. I don't know."

27

THE WOMAN HAD REFERRED to it as a narrow road, but that was a matter of perspective. The Kahekili Highway that wound its way along Maui's northwest coast was in many locations barely wide enough for one car and had no guardrails along the steep embankment above a deep gulch. Dana drove until the state route signs ended and the highway became a county road, which meant dirt. She slowed to fifteen miles an hour but still had to brake around some of the blind turns. The road was littered with rocks from the cliffs above it. None were big enough to block the road, but they were plenty big to knock her out if one hit her in the head. She wished she'd rented a car with a roof. She set her speedometer just before mile marker 16 and found the landmark that the husband of the woman in the jewelry store had provided, a boulder near the road called the Bellstone, because if struck in the correct location with another rock or stone, it emitted a bell-like sound. At mile 8.3, the car was perched on the

side of a cliff, and she seriously reconsidered her decision
to find William Welles. At mile marker 14.6, she entered
Kahakaloa, a small isolated village that the man had said
was home to no more than a hundred people. Then the
road again wound up the hill with frequent potholes and
depressions that caused the Jeep to bounce and dip.

The store clerk had become extremely accommodat-
ing upon hearing Dana's plans to adorn the earrings with
a necklace and bracelet. She'd telephoned her husband,
who had appeared in the store in under twenty minutes,
apparently also convinced that tens of thousands of dollars might be at stake if Dana could find William Welles.
The husband told Dana that Welles had been a preeminent designer of jewelry whose name had spread quickly.
The fact that he was a recluse and extremely selective of
his clients only heightened the interest in, and the value
of, his work. Welles could have capitalized on his success by attaching his name to a line of commercial jewelry, but he'd designed only individual pieces and would
go months, sometimes years, before agreeing to design
another. Then, just as suddenly and inexplicably, he had
stopped designing jewelry altogether and began making
metal sculptures.

Around another turn, Dana saw the roadside snack
stand, another of the few landmarks the store owner could
provide her. She slowed and again checked the mileage.
The owner had described the road to Welles's home as
nothing more than a dirt path approximately two miles
beyond the stand. He couldn't be more specific because he
had never met anyone who had actually visited Welles's
home, but said that if Dana reached an intersection and
started seeing highway signs for State Route 30, she had

gone too far. She checked the rearview mirror and slowed the Jeep to a crawl; the only thing about the road that gave her comfort was there was no way anyone could be following without her knowing it. She surveyed the dense, overgrown brush alongside the road. The store owner had also said Welles infrequently came into town to drink at a local bar but went absent for months, perhaps while artistically inspired. If Welles was in the midst of an artistic hiatus, an entire jungle could have grown up to obscure the road.

Dana spotted what appeared to be an opening just beyond a large chunk of lava rock. She stopped the jeep, jumped out quickly, and looked to be sure she wasn't about to drive off a cliff. The scrub grabbed and snagged her pants as she pushed through and found an even narrower dirt road. Returning to the Jeep, she drove slowly into the foliage. Branches scraped the sides of the Jeep like brushes in a car wash, and the chassis pitched at awkward angles caused by two deep ruts in the road. If she got stuck, she'd never get out. She leaned forward, slowing, and was about to stop when the scrub suddenly cleared and she drove into a round clearing, a turnabout. In the center was a freestanding metal sculpture she estimated to be perhaps fifteen feet tall—a rusting idol of metal strips welded on a thick stone base like an ancient ruin abandoned from a long-extinct civilization. It seemed at first sight to have no form, but as Dana stepped from the Jeep and circled it, the metal strips appeared to melt together, though she could not quite determine the shape in detail.

She turned her attention from the sculpture and considered her surroundings. An ocean breeze laden with the smell of salt rippled through the brush and the scraggy branches overhead. She saw a stone wall she had not immediately noticed, partially hidden by a lush tropical vine with budding red flowers. Stepping alongside it, she came to a rusted iron gate—the entrance to an arched tunnel in the hillside that narrowed to a small circle of light no larger in diameter than a basketball. She looked around, hoping for another entrance, but saw none. If there was a house somewhere, it was, unfortunately, at the end of the narrowing tube of light. With trepidation, she pulled at the gate. It did not swing freely. With effort, the hinges groaned, and she opened the gate just wide enough for her to slip through.

The inside of the tunnel was damp and smelled of decomposing plants. A trickle of water echoed in the tube and, although she fought against it, she thought of bats and snakes. Goose bumps lined her arms. She could handle just about anything but bats and snakes. She stepped forward, stooping slightly, though she sensed the tunnel was tall enough that she could have stood straight. She kept her hands at her sides, unable to bring herself to touch the walls or look overhead, concentrating only on the circle of light. With each step, it expanded in diameter, giving her comfort that she was making progress. She estimated that the tunnel was thirty yards, the circle becoming as large as the entrance into which she had stepped—the narrowing, like the sculpture in the clearing, some sort of optical illusion.

She raised her hand to deflect the focused glare as she neared the end of the tube. When she did, she saw a stucco structure as if she were staring through the lens of a telescope. She stepped from the tunnel and felt as though she had walked onto the canvas of a painting. The jungle had come to an end. So had the lava rock. The rounded struc-

ture before her was built on the edge of a cliff, floating
between the crystal-blue waters of the Pacific Ocean and
an endless horizon, anchored in a manner hidden from
the eye.

A deep, guttural sound broke the tranquility, and a
brick-red Doberman inched its way out of the brush, ears
pinned back, teeth bared.

And mean dogs. Snakes and bats and mean dogs.

With nowhere to go but the tunnel, a thirty-yard sprint
to the gate that the dog would surely win, Dana had little
choice but to stand her ground. "Easy, boy. Easy, now,"
she whispered.

The dog inched forward, head down, growling. Her
limited experience with dogs amounted to the neighbor's
basset hound and her own untamed golden retriever. She
knew the most important thing was not to panic, that dogs
could sense fear. Easier said than done.

"Easy, boy. Nobody means any harm here." She looked
around. There was no safe haven. No weapon miracu-
lously appeared, as in the movies.

The dog crept closer, then stopped, front legs spread.
Dana struggled to control her breathing. She kept her
voice soft and reassuring. Slowly, she raised the back of
her hand from her side, trying not to shake or curl her fingers into her palm. The dog eyed it suspiciously, then padded forward and stretched out its neck. Dana fought every
instinct to pull it back. She felt the cool wet of its nose
touch her skin. It sniffed at her hand.

"Nice doggy. That's a good boy." Continuing her slow,
deliberate movements, she reached under the dog's snout
and gently scratched its jaw and neck. The dog looked up
at her. Its ears relaxed. Then its tongue slipped from its

mouth and it stood panting. Dana worked her hand to the top of its head and behind its ears to the scruff of its neck. As she scratched more vigorously, the animal stepped closer, leaning against her with its head turned away, offering its backside.

"Is your master home?" The dog perked its unclipped ears and looked back at her. "Can I knock on the door?" Hoping the truce would continue, she stepped forward to an unassuming arched door at the bottom of four stone steps and raised a dull iron knocker, rapping three hollow knocks. The dog stood at her side, looking up at her. When no one answered, she reached again, but the knocker pulled from her grasp and the door flew open. Dana gasped.

28

∿

THE KILLER HAD toyed with Marshall Cole.

Logan reached that conclusion as he stood in the gas station bathroom. Reconsidering everything about the crime scene as he drove back to Seattle with the radio off did not change that conclusion. He used the silence to figure out what had bothered him about the crime scene, and the dilemma that Cole's death presented. Both men who had robbed and killed James Hill were now dead. Neither would provide Logan any answers as to why they had killed Hill, or who had put them up to it, and he was convinced someone had.

Logan was also convinced that the same person who killed Marshall Cole had killed Laurence King as well, which wasn't a large leap in logic, given the evidence. There were too many similarities. In each instance, the killer had used a .22-caliber gun that no one heard, fired by a someone no one saw. Both Cole and King were dead before either had time to react. Each shot was accurate and lethal. One bullet.

Their killer was no run-of-the-mill bookie or drug dealer whom King or Cole had pissed off. Nobody at the Emerald Inn or at the gas station had seen or heard anything, though Cole's girlfriend was still a possibility. Whoever the killer was, he or she had managed to get into the hotel room and the gas station bathroom undetected.

And yet the killer had still toyed with Marshall Cole.

There were other possible conclusions. The killer could have been being cautious, as Murphy had suggested, but that led to the same conclusion: He knew Cole was armed. And the person who would have known that was the person Cole had shot at with the 9mm at the Emerald Inn Motel.

But Logan didn't think the killer was being cautious. Cole had placed the gun on the back of the toilet and sat reading the sports page—a man's God-given right, as Murphy had said. That meant Cole wasn't concerned that he'd been followed. He wasn't worried that the person who walked into the bathroom and sat in the stall next to him was his killer. He was content to catch up on the latest scores, to read about his favorite sports teams. That meant two things. Cole had no idea he'd been followed—the killer was that good, and Cole hadn't given the killer any indication that he was concerned. If that were also true, then the killer, who *had* followed Cole, knew Cole was a sitting duck, and could have just walked into the bathroom, yanked open the stall door, and shot Cole in the head. But he hadn't. It also didn't appear the killer had tortured or tormented Cole. He had just toyed with him like a cat does with a mouse, let him live long enough to think he might survive. Then he had killed him.

The killer's motivation had not been robbery; he had not taken money or wallets or jewelry. And it was not out of concern that Cole had been going to the police. He'd been running, apparently to Idaho, where he had relatives. He got on the road sometime early that morning, and a couple hours into the drive, he needed a bathroom, the car needed gas, and the woman had a change of heart. The fact that the killer went to considerable trouble to hunt down and kill a man clearly on the run meant he had been determined to kill Cole from the start. If not for money, then because Cole knew something; something the killer considered a danger, something related to the burglary at James Hill's flat. It explained Cole's bloody clothes being dug up, and Hill's watch being left in plain sight at the motel. The killer wanted it known that Cole and King had killed James Hill, but he did not want anyone to know who had hired them to rob the house in the first place. Those thoughts floated in Michael Logan's head along with another. In his experience, the only plausible reason why the killer had toyed with Marshall Cole was because the person gained some pleasure from it. And people who enjoyed killing usually kept on killing.

29

~

DANA STUMBLED BACKWARD. The bottom step hit the back of her calf, and she nearly fell over but managed to regain her balance. A man in a metal hood stood in the doorway, a flame emanating from a spear held in his gloved hand.

"Freud!" The voice echoed hollow, like a shout into a metal drum. Then the blue flame extinguished with a pop, and the gloved hand flipped the lid of the welder's hood to reveal the sweat-stained face and salt-and-pepper beard of a dark-skinned man. He disregarded Dana, focusing his glare on the dog. "No visitors when I am working, Freud. No visitors."

The dog sauntered past him, unrepentant at the apparent breakdown in the security system. The man eyed the dog, then turned his attention to Dana. "Who are you?" He spoke with an English accent, his voice deep and full.

"Dana Hill," she said, uncertain what to add.

William Welles's face knitted. He seemed to consider

her intently. Dana was certain from his annoyed expression that he would slam shut the door. But he took a breath, and his features softened, as did his tone. "Well...Freud seems to regard you with interest." Saying nothing more, he turned and walked back inside his home, leaving the front door open for Dana to follow.

Each room resembled an igloo. The ceilings were concave, with thick wood beams riveted to posts by square black bolts and metal plates that shaped the walls like the skeletal structure inside an animal. There appeared to be no order to the home—pieces of furniture arranged amid sheets of metal, piles of metal strips, and sculptures. And yet, in some mystical manner, the rooms appeared to blend together, unrestricted by wooden studs and Sheetrocked walls. The large wings of a sculpted eagle framed an entryway that led to a sitting area with bench seats and pillows. It flowed to a table with chairs, which flowed to a workshop at the back of the home. The jewelry store owner had told Dana that Welles's genius was no two people saw precisely the same image in his work. As with his sculptures, Welles had put together his home with just the bare essentials, preferring to allow the imagination to fill in the empty spaces. Or perhaps he didn't care. Perhaps anything beyond the essentials was unimportant to him.

Welles removed the welder's hood and gloves and placed them on a thick wooden table. He hung his apron on a wall peg. As he peeled off his armored suit, he revealed himself to be a gnome of a man, much like his home—short and round. Not over five feet tall, he had a rim of hair encircling his head like a monk. It continued down his neck, disappearing below the collar of his sweat-stained white T-shirt. He had large ears and deep-set eyes that looked out from beneath thick eyebrows. The salt-and-pepper beard covered much of his face. Welles shuffled about the floor as if trying to keep his feet from slipping out of oversize slippers. His arms and legs seemed too short even for his small body, though he had no difficulty lifting a large black kettle. He filled it from a crude piece of galvanized pipe protruding through the stucco wall and placed it on a burner of a cast-iron potbellied stove that vented through a pipe to the roof. Then he bent to unlatch a door and shoved two pieces of wood into the fire, stoking the flames by stepping three times on a billow in the floor.

On a nearby table lay an elaborate scattering of metal strips. Welles had apparently been assembling them when Dana interrupted him. The sculpture looked to Dana like some sort of bridge spanning jagged metal—perhaps meant to signify rocks or waves. She studied the piece for a moment, then closed her eyes. She saw the image of a bridge, though she did not get the feeling that it was suspended over water. There was something disturbing about it, but further concentration revealed nothing more. She opened her eyes, concluding that the sculpture was a work in progress, perhaps a scale-size model of a piece to be constructed and too early in the process for the imagination to complete.

Welles readied two porcelain cups while waiting for the water in the kettle to boil, content not to speak or to ask her more questions about the purpose of her visit. Dana turned toward a picture window that faced the ocean—drawn to it, as to the light at the end of the tunnel in his yard. As she approached, she had the uneasy desire to continue right through it and step into the blue sky. She had to close her eyes to fight the feeling of vertigo.

Thwack.

The sound startled her. She turned to see a meat cleaver embedded in the wooden block and a lemon split in half.

"Lemon?" Welles's voice remained deep but gentle. He peered at her over the bottom half of bifocal glasses.

"Excuse me?"

"Do you take lemon in your tea?" he asked with the politeness of a British gentleman.

"Yes, thank you." She walked back toward him. "Your home is amazing. The view is beautiful. Did you design it?"

"One bag or two?" Welles looked up at her. "Your tea. One bag or two?"

"One," Dana said.

"Cream?"

"No, thank you."

He shook his head and spoke as if to himself. "I shall never understand you Americans and your tea." To her, he gestured with his hand. "Please, be comfortable."

Dana sat on the edge of a bench seat covered in thick blankets. When the kettle on the stove hummed like the whistle of a steam engine, Welles slipped his hand inside the welding glove and lifted the kettle from the stove, deftly pouring the two cups. He added a slice of lemon to each, placed the cups on saucers, and put two cubes of sugar in his own cup, hesitated, then dropped a cube in the other. He walked to where Dana sat and handed her the cup. "Tea without sugar is simply not civilized," he said.

She noticed that his hands were meaty paws and stumpy fingers twice the diameter of her own. She wondered how such hands could have created jewelry so delicate and fragile, so beautiful. Welles shuffled away from her into the living portion of the structure. When she realized he was not coming back, Dana stood and followed. She found him sitting in a rocking chair with his back to the view. He stared at the floor and sipped from the edge of the cup. She sat on a stool across from him and noticed that the scattered furniture had actually been arranged to accommodate an intimate conversation. She sipped her tea, a blend she was certain she had never tasted. Sweet, it had a hint of licorice that the lemon slice did not completely conceal.

"It's very good. Thank you."

"You are most welcome."

"May I ask the brand?"

"My own." Welles took another sip.

Dana looked at the sculptures in the room. Each was unique and intriguing in its own way, and some were more easily identifiable than others—an eagle in flight, two whales side by side, a school of fish.

"I don't get many visitors. I have a rum cake."

"I'm not hungry, but thank you. I'm sorry to disturb your work."

"You have come a long way to disturb my work. A cup of tea is the least that I can offer."

"From Seattle, Washington, actually."

"Hmm."

She cleared her throat. "And the tea is more than enough. I do apologize for dropping in unannounced."

"My dear lady, do not keep apologizing and thanking me. If I did not want you here, I assure you, you would not be here." Welles said the words without anger or threat;

rather, like the hint of licorice in the tea, with a subtlety
that suggested he had somehow been expecting her. He
put his cup on a barrel near the chair and scratched an
itch on the top of his head. A tabby cat appeared from
under a pile of blankets. Welles eased it onto his lap. After
a moment Dana heard it purring under the gentle strokes
of his hand.

"I received your name from a jewelry store in Lahaina
familiar with your designs."

"And are you familiar with my designs?" He asked the
question without looking up from the cat.

Dana placed her cup and saucer on a nearby barrel and
pulled the earring from her pocket. She handed it to him.
"I believe this is one of your designs."

In the time it took Welles to adjust the bifocals on the
tip of his nose, he had taken the earring and handed it
back to her. "Yes."

Dana played a hunch. "Would you duplicate it?"

"Never." Welles picked up his cup of tea from the barrel and again sipped from the edge.

"Because you won't or because you can't."

"Neither and both."

"I'm sorry, I don't understand."

"No, you do not." He made a face and seemed to chastise himself. "Now it is my turn to apologize." He took a
deep breath. "Once it is created, it is created. I have no
interest in re-creating what I have already created. Nor
can I."

"So it's one of a kind?"

"If that pleases you. It pleases some that my work is one
of a kind. It makes it more valuable —to them, not to me,
I assure you."

Dana nodded. "Is that why you no longer design jewelry. Because others were selling it for a profit?"

"I have no knowledge or interest in whether others are selling my pieces or at what prices."

"Can I ask, then, why you no longer design jewelry?"

Welles took a deep breath and continued stroking the cat. "What I design, I design for the person to whom it will belong. A sculpture—be it a piece of jewelry or a piece of metal—cannot exist on its own. Like each of us, it exists within a particular environment, shaped and molded by that environment. Only then can it be fully appreciated. You could never appreciate my work unless I were to create it for you. Then you would feel its inner beauty as strongly as some see its exterior beauty."

"Is that why the sculpture out front sits rusting? Because it hasn't found a place?"

Welles nodded. "Without the right place, even the most beautiful things are left to rust. Most people don't see what I sculpt because they are too busy or have simply chosen to no longer look below the surface to see what beauty lies inside."

"People can be superficial," she said.

"No. People can be blind." Welles returned to his tea. "To survive, as we all must, I was required to sell my work. I never intended others to make a living from me." He allowed a small grin to crease his lips. "Though it is ironic."

"What is?"

"When they sell my work, they do so to extract a profit. Yet in reality, the piece becomes worthless. It has lost its existence and thus its beauty." He set the teacup back on the barrel. "What brings you all the way from Seattle, Washington, Ms. Hill?"

She held up the earring. "I found this; it doesn't belong to me, though you already know that."

"Yes," Welles said. "Though it could."

"What do you mean?"

The tabby had left his lap. Dana found it at her feet, rubbing against her leg. She picked it up and held it, petting it gently until it again purred.

"Your heart is heavy. You have lost your sense of existence. Animals sense these things. Freud sensed it, which is why you sit here now." He nodded to the cat. "Leonardo does as well. You are in need of comfort. What burdens your heart and makes it heavy?"

For reasons she did not know, Dana felt tears well in her eyes. When she spoke, she was filled with a warm but uneasy feeling not unlike the one she'd had as a young girl in the church confessional—relieved to be unburdening her sins, uneasy about the impending consequences. "My brother was killed a week ago. Someone murdered him. I found the earring in his home."

"Your brother's death provides you a reason to express the sorrow you feel within, but you have been filled with that sorrow for many years. Something else burdens your heart, makes you unhappy. You have kept those tears on the inside. Now you are drowning in them and will continue to do so until you do what you know you must."

Dana thought of Grant and her marriage. "My brother was not married, Mr. Welles—"

"William, please. It does bring satisfaction to an old man to have a woman as beautiful as you call me by my first name."

She smiled.

"As does your smile bring joy to another who appreciates it, and who appreciates you."

She thought of Michael Logan and his comment about her smile as they drove to Roslyn. "I'm unaware that my brother had a girlfriend. I'm hoping that if I can find out who this belongs to, I might be able to find out who killed him. My brother had no enemies. He was not a wealthy man. He was a teacher. He was quiet and humble, a good man. Now he's dead. There was no reason for anyone to kill him. I'd like to know why someone did."

Welles remained silent, his eyes closed. Dana could hear the low hum of the wind off the ocean through an open crevice somewhere in the structure. Above her, one of the ceiling fans began to turn in the breeze. Metal bars pulled and tugged on one another, causing the ceiling fan in the kitchen to turn as well. Then the billow near the furnace rose and fell in a slow inhale and exhale, stoking the fire.

"Jealousy."

Welles said the word so softly that Dana was uncertain he had spoken. "Excuse me?"

"You asked why one man kills another. Jealousy."

"I asked why my brother was dead."

Welles nodded. "It is the same question."

Dana stared at the little man, puzzled and intrigued by him. "Do you know who killed my brother?"

Welles shook his head. "No. Only why."

"And you think it was because of…jealousy?" She leaned forward. The cat leaped from her lap. "Do you keep records of who purchases your pieces? Records of who you create them for?"

He shook his head. "I have no interest in records." He offered his lap back to the displaced cat.

"What about bills of sale, records for income tax purposes?"

Welles grinned. "I keep no records of any kind. Never have. As for your American taxes..." He shrugged and gave an impish grin.

Dana's adrenaline dissipated, and with it, her hope. She sat back, suddenly exhausted from the long flight and the anxiety-riddled drive. She had come a long way, as Welles had said. Unfortunately, it had been for nothing. She looked out the window behind Welles and saw that the light was fading. She had no desire to drive back down the narrow, treacherous road at night.

She finished the last of the tea, placed the cup on the barrel and stood. "I've taken up enough of your time. I am sorry to have disturbed your sculpting. Thank you for the tea."

Welles stood. "You truly must stop apologizing. The comfort of a beautiful woman is to be treasured." He winked. "Like sugar in tea."

She laughed lightly and took his hand. "Thank you, William."

She started across the room, then stopped with a peculiar thought. "You said that you created your pieces with a specific individual in mind, and yet you said this earring could belong to me. How can that be so?"

"Because the person for whom I created it is very much like you. She loved what you loved and is unhappy for the reasons you are unhappy."

Dana stepped closer, the realization making her light-headed. "You remember her, don't you?" she said softly.

"Oh, yes," Welles said. "I do remember her."

AN HOUR LATER, Welles walked Dana to the door, accompanied by Freud. The cat, Leonardo, had retreated beneath the blankets. "Freud will see you safely back to your car," Welles said.

Dana nodded and stepped outside. The air had chilled. She wrapped her arms around her. The drive back would be cold. She felt the need to make contact with Welles and bent down to kiss him lightly on the cheek. When she did, Welles placed a hand on the back of her arm and handed her a small brown sack.

"Tea," he whispered. "Drink it every day with sugar until it is gone." Then he lowered his eyes, stepped back, and softly closed the wooden door, leaving Freud to escort her back to the Jeep.

30

⚘

THE DRIVE DOWN the mountain in the fading light had required all of her powers of concentration. When Dana returned the rental car at the airport, she failed to recognize the woman behind the counter as the same attendant who had greeted her that afternoon until the woman expressed surprise that Dana was leaving so soon. Uncertain how much time she would need on the island, Dana had purchased a one-way ticket. Now she thought it was a mistake. She wanted nothing more than to get off the island, but the woman behind the Hawaiian Airlines ticket counter simply shook her head: The flights out that evening were sold out, most overbooked.

"It's an emergency," Dana pleaded. "It's imperative that I get home tonight."

The ticket agent suggested she buy a ticket on a morning flight, then wait to go standby if a spot opened on a flight that evening. The chances were not good, but it was the best the agent could offer. Dana bought a ticket; then, no longer feeling safe, decided it was better to remain in a public place than a hotel room. She sat in the Hawaiian Premier Club, sipping a vodka and orange juice while listening to a computerized voice call out the numbers of flights departing and arriving. Her attempts to reach Michael Logan at work were unsuccessful.

Sitting by a plate-glass window, Dana watched a plane taxi in the fading daylight and thought of the odd little man who lived on the mountain and what he had told her. The feeling that Welles had somehow expected her grew stronger, as did her feeling that Freud had allowed her to walk through the tunnel because it was inevitable she would do so. But how could Welles have known? It was impossible. And yet... She removed the earring from her pocket, rolling it in the palm of her hand. She had been mesmerized by its beauty—guilty of what Welles had found so distasteful that he had stopped designing jewelry. She had focused on its monetary value. Now she saw the earring differently, and it brought a profound melancholy. Welles had chosen the blue stone not for its beauty but because it reflected the sadness radiating from a young woman's eyes. The diamond drop beneath it represented one of many tears that woman had and would shed—a woman, Welles had said, who was much like Dana.

"Why design it at all?" Dana had asked. "Why create a piece that represents sorrow and pain?"

"Because to not create it would have made me just as blind. To see the world and those who live in it is to see the good as well as the evil. We cannot see beauty if we do not see what is ugly. We cannot feel joy if we do not feel pain. We cannot smile if we do not cry."

The earring's owner had turned to James Hill for comfort. How else could it have found its way into his home? Dana closed her eyes to the enormity of the implication. Her rational side—the side she cultivated as a lawyer—tried to dispute Welles's recollection of the young woman. Yet each time she tried to convince herself he was mistaken, she knew he wasn't. The pieces of the puzzle suddenly slipped into place, and the picture they created explained James's guarded protection of his personal life—the remote cabin in Roslyn, and why Laurence King and Marshall Cole would rob the home of a man who had already sold everything he owned. King and Cole had not chosen James Hill. James Hill had been chosen for them.

Jealousy. A motive as old as history.

And Dana had the only piece of evidence to prove who had killed her brother.

But you're not the only one who knows who it belongs to or who designed it.

The realization of her mistake came abruptly. Blinded by her desire to know who had killed her brother, she had not thought through her actions. Now the blindfold had lifted, and the light brought a sense of trepidation. She had used a credit card to purchase her airline ticket and to rent her car. No one had to follow her to know where she was going. All they had to do was consider her actions to know she had the earring. Why else would she have flown to Maui, the home of a man who had designed it ten years earlier? Why else but to find out if Welles still recalled the earring's owner?

She grabbed her purse, ran from the club, and hurried down the corridor toward the airport entrance. The woman behind the car rental-counter looked wide-eyed when Dana stepped up to the counter.

"I need a car," she said, pulling out her wallet.

～

AFTER THE SAME routine, Dana was speeding along
the highway. She contemplated calling the Maui police,
but what would she tell them? What evidence did she
have that William Welles was in danger? What questions
would that provoke about her being on the island and asking his whereabouts? She began to climb the switchbacks.
With the sun having set below the ocean's horizon, the
temperature continued to drop as she gained altitude. Her
hands felt numb gripping the steering wheel. The ascent
up the narrow road was more difficult to navigate under
the cloak of night. Darkness made everything look foreign. The lava rock formed shadowed lumps and bumps
in the Jeep's cone-shaped lights. She looked for her mark-
ers and tried to gauge her distance carefully. Her only solace was that at night she would see headlights of any cars
approaching.

As she drove through Kahakaloa, she tried not to rush,
tried not to panic. It would do her and Welles no good if
she drove herself off a cliff. She searched for the Bellstone
but sensed she'd gone too far. She knew it when she arrived
at the intersection of the road with State Route 30.

"Dammit. " She made a U-turn and headed back.

31

~

THE GLASS WINDOW of William Welles's helmet reflected the pinpoint blue flame at the tip of the welding rod in a bright white light. He soldered the joint with precision, a surgeon sewing a thin white line. The ceiling fans spun freely. The furnace burned a white-hot fire. When he had attached the strip of metal, he turned the knob on the pipe, shutting off the flow of gas feeding the flame. It extinguished with a small pop. He flipped up the welding mask, then removed it and wiped the perspiration from his brow on the back of his sleeve. He stepped back to consider his piece, seeing mostly flaws, as always. And yet he knew it was finished. He had no more time to devote to it.

He placed the welder's gun on the wooden table and removed his gloves. Freud sat in the corner of the room, head resting between his front paws. Leonardo had curled into a ball on the pile of blankets. Welles bent to open the door of the stove and inserted two pieces of dry wood. "There is no reason to hide," he said.

The blond man stepped into the room from the shadows of the doorway. The flames reflected shades of orange and red in his eyes and flickered shadows across his face. Freud did not stir.

"We have been expecting you." Welles reached for the kettle on the stove.

"You've been expecting me?" A smile creased the man's lips.

"Yes." Welles filled the kettle with water and placed it on the back burner. He looked up at the man. "Someone like you."

The man looked around. "Then why are you so unprepared?"

Welles shuffled to the shelf and reached for the tea. "Unprepared? To the contrary, we are quite prepared. One's destiny is one's destiny, should one choose to accept it. I have chosen to accept mine and have for some time."

The man looked at Welles with curiosity. "And what is your destiny?"

Welles raised the knife from the butcher block and whacked a slice of lemon, the knife embedding in the wood with a thud. He did not answer.

"The woman was here," the man said. "Did she show you the earring?"

Welles dropped a slice of lemon in the cup and pinched a spoonful of tea, the last of the bag, into a small strainer. "I said I knew that you would come. I did not say I had any interest in speaking with you. Why do you delay that which we both know you will do?"

The man removed the gun from the pocket of his jacket.

"This piece is yours." Welles gestured to the sculpture on the table.

The man considered it. "A gift? And I brought nothing to carry it in."

Welles smiled. "You will carry it with you. And in *your* hour, you will see it clearly, for it is your destiny, and it will bring a pain unlike any that man could inflict in death. Yours shall be an eternal pain."

The man snickered. "Aren't you a strange bird," he said, and pulled the trigger.

Freud rose slowly from his bed and walked to where his master lay bleeding. He licked at Welles's perspiring face, then whimpered and lay down beside him, curling into a ball.

The man stepped forward. There was no reason to check for a pulse. One shot was all he ever needed. He considered the metal sculpture and its lack of shape or form. "Art to some, junk to others," he said. Then the metal strips seemed to move, blending together like molten metal. The kettle on the stove whistled, distracting him. When he looked back at the sculpture, he saw a bridge. Though he could make out no human form, in his mind he saw himself standing on it, suspended over what at first appeared to be water but, he realized quickly, was something altogether different. The jagged pieces of metal were not the gently lapping waves of the ocean. They were not waves at all. The bridge traversed a valley of fire, the flames wicking up to burn his flesh and to torment him.

Then the bridge collapsed.

32

~

DANA DROVE SO slowly, she was certain a car would come around one of the switchbacks at any moment and rear-end her, pushing her off the cliff. She knew she had again missed the road to William Welles's home when she saw the village below her. Growing more frustrated, and feeling she was running out of time, she backtracked again, one eye on her rearview mirror, one eye searching the edge of the road. This time she saw the boulder, though it looked different at night. She squeezed the Jeep down the narrowing passage. When she neared the clearing, she turned off the headlights and plunged the car into total darkness. She shut off the engine and allowed the car to coast forward beneath the sculpture, which now stood like a darkened monolith.

She stepped quietly from the car, leaving the door open, hearing only the wind. The gate to the tunnel was open. She couldn't recall whether she had shut it but thought she had. This time there was no comforting light to pull her through the cylindrical tube. She took a deep breath, gathered her courage, and walked into the darkness, brushing her hand against the edge of the concrete tunnel for balance despite her own revulsion. As she neared the end, the darkness shaded a navy blue, and she emerged to a sky pocked with stars. Freud did not emerge from the shadows to greet her. At the bottom of the stairs, the wooden door was open a crack. It made her stomach flutter. Despite the cool temperature, she felt herself perspiring. She pushed open the door, the room sweeping into view. She saw no sign of Leonardo or Freud, and their absence made her heart pound still faster. The stucco walls in the sitting room reflected the flickering light of two candles. The ceiling fan turned slowly. She walked into the kitchen. The wall became a burnt orange from the glow of the stove. She smelled the faint odor of lemon and licorice. The cleaver was embedded in the woodblock, a lemon split in half near a full cup of tea. Dana put her hand on the mug. It was cold to the touch. The sculpture on the counter, the one Welles had been working on earlier, appeared to have collapsed. She heard a dog whimper and stepped around the counter.

Freud looked up at her from beneath sad eyes and whimpered again. Near him lay Leonardo, neither far from the body. Dana felt pain grip her chest. She brought a hand to her mouth, stifling her sobs as she knelt down and touched William Welles on the cheek. But for the hole in his head, he appeared to be asleep, even the hint of a smile on his lips. She took out her cell phone, then stopped herself. What would she say? Why was she at Welles's home, all the way from Seattle, flying on a one-way ticket?

She dropped her phone back in her purse, stood, and

removed the meat cleaver from the block, starting back across the room toward the door. Halfway across she stopped and looked back at Freud and Leonardo.

"I did this," she said. "I brought this here." She walked back, picked up Leonardo, and gently grabbed Freud by his collar. "Come on." He resisted. "Come on, boy," she said. The dog rose and padded forward at her side. He stopped at the door to look back at his master, then shifted his gaze and looked up at her as if to ask what would become of them.

"I'm sorry," Dana said. "I'm sorry I brought this to you."

She closed the door behind them and continued to coax Freud forward, her senses now on full alert. At the tunnel, Freud hesitated. It gave Dana pause, but it was the only way back to her Jeep. "Come on, Freud," she whispered. "We can do this."

The dog turned his head to look behind them. Then he started to growl, low and deep in his chest. Dana looked over her shoulder but saw nothing. The dog looked at her as if telling her to run. Then he pulled from her grasp and rushed into the foliage barking and snarling.

Dana clutched Leonardo to her chest and ran into the tube, struggling in her leather shoes, feeling them sliding on the slick surface. A couple of times she felt herself nudge the wall and corrected her angle. Running blind, she had to fight her instinct to stop, feeling that she was about to hit something impenetrable. Her breathing became more rapid. The sensation that someone was chasing her drove her forward, Leonardo bouncing against her. She burst from the tunnel as if emerging from deep water, gasping as she rushed across the clearing. She dropped Leonardo onto the backseat, hoping he would not jump out. Then she opened the driver's door and pulled herself in using the steering wheel. Her hands shook so violently, she had trouble finding the teeth of the ignition. She forced herself to concentrate, inserted the key, and started the engine. Then she threw the Jeep into drive and made a circle around the sculpture. As she passed the tunnel, a shadow burst from the darkness and leaped for the back of the Jeep, making it in one bounding leap.

Freud.

WHEN THE STATE road signs indicated she was off the county road, Dana felt a wave of relief. She had been certain that a car would appear behind her, bumping her on the decline until she lost control. She punched the accelerator, speeding along the highway until she saw a gas station. She pulled off and asked the attendant for a phone book.

"What you looking for, lady?" the man said with a Hawaiian accent.

"I need a kennel," she said. "I have to go out of town unexpectedly, and I need someone to watch my animals until I can make it back."

The man told her he knew of a kennel not far from the airport. They found it together in the phone book. Dana called and asked the woman not to close before she arrived. The woman told her it was not a problem, the kennel was behind her home. Twenty minutes later, Dana pulled up to a piece of property with two cars parked on the lawn beneath swaying palm trees. Lush tropical foliage obscured a mostly cinder-block house. The woman who came to the door assured her Leonardo and Freud would be well taken care of. The kennel behind the woman's home had a large fenced area where Freud could get exercise. Still, Dana couldn't shake the feeling she was putting him into a prison.

"I don't know for certain when I'll be back to get them," she said, handing the woman a credit card.

The woman smiled to reassure her. "No problem. They'll be here."

Dana hugged Leonardo and heard him purr against her face. She handed him to the woman and knelt down and cradled Freud's face in her hands. He looked at her with sad eyes, the skin above them furrowed.

"Don't worry, boy," she said. "I'll be back to get you. I won't forget you, Freud." She rubbed his head and pulled it close to hers, feeling the warmth of the dog's face against her own, and kissed his head. Then she stood and started for the Jeep, fighting the urge to look back.

Dana drove from the kennel and stopped at a pay phone in the parking lot of a fast-food restaurant. She called the police and told them William Welles was dead. Then she hung up and drove back to the airport. Once inside the terminal, she made her way to the gate. The ticket agent advised her that they had taken no standby passengers on the earlier flights. The last flight from the island to Seattle was a red-eye, leaving at midnight. They would call standby passengers when the plane was about to depart.

Dana took a seat in the terminal, waiting and watching the people around her. An hour later, the passengers boarded the plane, and she began to mentally prepare herself for a long night in the airport.

Then the ticket agent looked over and gestured her to the counter. "Must be your lucky day," he said. "You got the last seat."

33

❧

THE PASSENGERS STUMBLED from the plane, exhausted, trudging up the gate like herded cattle at the end of a roundup. Dana took her time getting off the plane, in order to watch the people around her depart. The woman in front of her, dressed in shorts, tank top, and flip-flops, crossed her arms as she stepped from the plane and encountered the nearly forty-degree drop in temperature. As Dana ascended the ramp two well-built men stood at the top, dressed in official-looking blue slacks and white short-sleeve shirts. Next to them stood a less muscular man in the same outfit but wearing a blue polyester sport coat. He held a walkie-talkie. Dana's anxiety increased when he looked at her, then spoke into the radio.

She dropped her purse, spilling its contents, including her in-flight dinner—a wrapped ham sandwich with a mustard pack and a half-eaten Snickers bar. As she bent down, she slipped the earring from her pocket as she retrieved her things. Then she stood and walked forward.

At the top of the ramp, the man in the sport coat stepped forward. "Dana Hill?"

"Yes," she said.

"Would you mind coming with us, please?"

"Coming with you? Who are you?"

"Airport security," he said, showing her identification.

She smiled, trying to sound casual. "What do you want with me?"

"Is that your only luggage?" The man pointed to the small carry-on bag hanging from her shoulder.

"Yes."

"Will you come with us, please?"

"Would you tell me what this is about?" she asked, more forcefully.

The man in the blue jacket remained polite but decidedly firm. "Please." He motioned with an arm.

She looked at the other two agents and got the distinct impression that the choice was not hers. If she started ranting and raving about being a lawyer, it would only draw more attention and suspicion. "Fine," she said. She followed the two guards through the terminal, the fluorescent lights making it as bright as day. She felt a cold sweat on her forehead. They led her to an unmarked door. The man in the blue blazer opened it for her and she stepped inside a room with white walls, a wooden table, and two chairs. She sat with legs crossed, still trying to appear calm. She felt her pulse beneath her armpits.

"Could you explain to me what this is about?" she asked again.

The man rubbed a finger over a mustache a shade darker than his salt-and-pepper hair. "May I look inside your bag?"

Dana shrugged and slipped it from her shoulder, handing it to him. He opened it and searched the contents. Then he asked, "And your purse?"

She handed it to him. He pulled out her flight itinerary and driver's license. Then he pulled out the half-eaten Snickers. "Breakfast of champions," Dana said, smiling.

The man returned a polite smile then left the room with her driver's license, itinerary, and the brown bag of tea that William Welles had given her. She looked up at a camera mounted to the ceiling in the corner of the room. She never should have called the police in Maui. She should have waited until she was back on the mainland. Could the news of Welles's death have spread so quickly that the couple in the jewelry store had called the police and told them of the woman from Seattle who was inquiring about where Welles lived?

The door on the opposite side of the room reopened, and a younger man wearing a better-quality suit walked in carrying her license, itinerary, the brown bag, and a notebook. He had a more professional demeanor. "Sorry to keep you waiting, Ms. Hill."

"That's all right, but I would like to get home. It was a long flight, and it will be an early morning."

"I'll try not to keep you long. I'm Agent Donald Hollas with the DEA." He pulled out a chair and sat across from her. "You traveled to Maui and back today?"

She chuckled, almost relieved. "Is that what this is about? Do you think I'm some sort of drug courier?" When he didn't respond, she answered his question. "Yes, I traveled to Maui."

"For just one day?"

"Yes, for just one day."

He looked up from his notepad. "Why?"

"I had business there." She said it nonchalantly.

Hollas nodded. "What type of business?"

"I'm a lawyer," she said, thinking quickly. "My firm has clients with business interests in the islands. I was looking into the potential legal and tax ramifications for a client purchasing one of those interests."

Hollas sat back in his chair. "What firm do you work for?"

"Strong and Thurmond. May I?" She reached into her purse, popped open a card carrier, and handed him a business card.

"And what was the name of the company with the business interests?"

"I can't tell you that."

Hollas looked up from the card. "And why not?"

"The matter is confidential. The acquisition of the competing company will not be voluntary."

"Hostile?"

Dana smiled. "Yes."

"Can you tell me what they do?"

"No."

A thin smile creased his lips. "Also confidential?"

She shook her head. "I have no idea what it is they do, exactly. They are a subsidiary of a subsidiary, and I think that may just be the first layer. That's why I was there. The documentation alone to name the proper entity will be a pile high. But I have no idea what the subsidiary does. I'm an associate at the firm, Agent Hollas. I'm afraid that means I get the grunt work."

"This business took just one day?"

"It's really all I could spare. I anticipate several late nights as it is. There will be long telephone conversations and, if the takeover is successful, more trips to complete the matter."

Hollas sat back, tapping the itinerary on the table. "And yet you purchased a one-way ticket. Why would you do that if you were intending to return today?"

Dana had not thought it through, but she had always been good on her feet. "I had no idea how long the business would take. I was fortunate to get done what I needed to do today. My husband is also a lawyer. He's in a three-week trial in Chicago. As I said, this trip was unexpected. We have a three-year-old daughter. I don't like to leave her when my husband is also gone."

Hollas slid her itinerary across the table. "My kids are four and five. I know the feeling." He held up the brown bag, opened it, and brought it to his nose.

"It's tea."

Hollas shook the bag and removed a pinch of the dried leaves. "So it is." He stood and handed it to her. "I apologize for delaying you. Thank you for your cooperation."

Dana took the brown bag and put it in her purse. "So, I'm free to go?" she asked, trying to make light of the situation.

Hollas nodded. "Free to go." He reached for the Snickers bar. "I can throw that out for you."

"No." Dana caught herself. "I mean...I haven't eaten since lunch, and I doubt there will be much open this time of night."

Hollas handed it back to her. "Okay."

OUTSIDE THE ROOM, Dana wanted to break into a gallop but resisted the urge. Despite her best efforts, she could not fight her spreading sense of paranoia, certain now that she was being watched. The janitor pushing a wheeled garbage can through the terminal diverted his eyes when she looked at him. The skycap in the rolling cart smiled and nodded as he passed. The man on the telephone watched, then turned to speak into the receiver. Halfway down the corridor, she saw the universal sign for a women's bathroom. Feeling light-headed and short of breath, she turned into the blue-tiled room and rushed into a stall, locking the door. She leaned against the wall, struggling to catch her breath, waiting for her heart to stop racing. An overhead vent in the ceiling tiles blew cold air at her.

Thump-ack.

Dana started.

Thump-ack.

The sound came from her right—someone shoving open the stall doors, making his or her way down the row.

Thump-ack.

She sat on the toilet and braced her feet against the inside of the door.

Thump-ack.

The stall door next to her shoved open. She felt pressure against her feet. The lock of her door rattled. Dana caught her breath. "It's in use."

She heard a squeaking sound. A yellow bucket rolled beneath the stall door.

It's just the janitor. She waited a beat, then slid the lock on the door and exited quickly. The janitor's apology trailed her out of the room.

She hurried through the terminal to a down escalator,

looking back up as she went. At the bottom, the airport
train that would take her to baggage claim and the parking
garage had already arrived, its doors open. She hurried off
the escalator and stepped inside as the sliding glass doors
closed. To her right, she saw a man do the same, entering
one door down, a suitcase in hand. He stood holding the
handrail. At the first stop, no additional passengers stepped
onto the train. The man did not get off. As the train started
again, Dana moved toward the doors. A moment later,
when the train stopped, she stepped off quickly, following the signs to baggage claim. She looked behind her.
The man in the suit followed, luggage rolling behind him.
She ascended another escalator, then a flight of stairs to
the enclosed catwalk, and walked across the road to the
parking structure. Behind her, the man ascended the escalator, his head coming into view first, then his body. In the
garage, she paid her parking fee at one of the machines.
The man walked across the catwalk. She took her ticket
and walked to the elevator, one eye watching the lights
above the six elevators in the bank, the other watching as
the man stopped to pay his parking fee. She heard a car
door close, an engine start, and the squeal of tires on the
slick pavement. The elevator bell on the left rang. The man
at the ticket machine bent to retrieve his ticket. The elevator doors slid open. No one got off. Dana stepped inside
and hit the button for the third floor. When the door didn't
immediately close, she pressed the close button repeatedly,
then stepped back, relieved, as the doors slid together.

A hand knifed between them, slapping the rubberized
edge.

34

THE ELEVATOR SHUDDERED, the doors stubborn and at first unwilling to concede to the hand. Then they split and pulled apart. The man from the train smiled a sheepish grin and stepped on.

"Sorry. I've been a step late all day," he said. The doors closed. He pulled down the knot of his tie and unbuttoned the top button of his shirt.

Dana looked at the panel of illuminated lights. He had not pushed a button for an exit floor.

"Cold," he said, turning toward her. "I'd hoped that we'd left winter behind, but I guess we have a few more months to go."

She nodded, wishing she'd kept the canister of mace in her handbag, but that was not possible after September 11 and all the security precautions at airports. The elevator descended to the third floor. When the doors opened, the man looked up at the illuminated three. Then he stepped back and motioned for Dana to go ahead of him. She stepped out, forgot for a moment where she had parked, then remembered writing the row letter on her flight itinerary. She pulled it from her purse and walked down an aisle of columns marked "E." Behind her, she heard the wheels of the man's suitcase rolling on the pavement. It sounded like the low hum of a small engine. She continued down the row, the sound of the rolling suitcase fading, and with it, her immediate anxiety. As she approached the Explorer, she fumbled through her purse for her keys and hit the button for the automatic lock. When she reached the driver's side, she pulled the door handle. It remained locked. She hit the button again. The car did not chirp. She pressed the button again. Nothing happened. Puzzled, she used the key to manually unlock the door and pulled it open. The alarm did not sound. She took a quick look over her shoulder, saw no one, and climbed behind the wheel, throwing her bag on the passenger seat. She shut the door and locked it, then sat back against the leather seat and closed her eyes, telling herself to relax. She would drive to her mother's house and call Logan. She exhaled, sat forward, put the key in the ignition, and turned the key.

The engine whimpered like a beaten dog. Then it died.

She pumped the gas pedal and tried again. The engine groaned. She pumped the gas pedal repeatedly, her father's voice admonishing her from the recesses of her mind. *Don't flood the engine. Don't flood the engine.*

She turned the key again and again, urging the engine to kick over. Each time it failed. Then there was only the clicking of a dead battery.

"No. Goddammit!" She slapped the steering wheel, threw herself back against the seat, and saw the man standing outside the window of her car.

35

⌐∽⌐

THE MAN RAISED his arms as if under arrest, a pained expression on his face. Dana reached into the glove compartment and pulled out the canister of mace.

"I'm sorry." He spoke through the glass. "I didn't mean to startle you again. I heard your car struggling." Dana tried to appear in control but fought a bile taste in her mouth, as if her stomach were close to emptying its contents on the floorboards. "It sounds like a dead battery. I have jumper cables. Would you like a jump?"

She scanned the parking lot, a strange yellow-orange from the encapsulated lights. She saw no one. She had her cell phone in her purse but knew that at this hour, road service could take an hour or longer. She could call the police and tell them...tell them what? That a man was asking her if she needed assistance jump-starting her car?

He waited patiently. His eyes were bloodshot and tired.

He's trying to help. Your imagination is making you

paranoid. The events of the day have worn you thin. You have a dead battery. He's just being kind.

Maybe. She kept the Mace in her hand and opened the car door.

"I understand if you're nervous." The man reached into his back pocket, pulled out his wallet, and removed a business card. "My name is Fred Jeffries. I'm an attorney, though I wouldn't want you to hold that against me." He smiled. "Here's my card."

Dana recognized the business as a large insurance defense firm with a downtown office. She knew several lawyers there. She wanted to laugh but could not bring herself to do so.

"I don't mean to keep startling you," Jeffries said, continuing to flog himself.

"You just surprised me," she said. "I'm wound a bit tight tonight."

"I don't blame you." She could see, with his suit jacket off, that Jeffries had a belly. He looked anything but menacing. "I have a wife and two teenage daughters who I wish were a bit more careful. In this day and age, you can't be too cautious; you really don't know who you can trust." He rolled his eyes and shook his head. "Listen to me. I'm probably scaring you even more."

"No. I'm fine now."

He turned his attention to her car. "Mind if I give it a try? It sounds like you have a dead battery."

Dana stepped back to allow Jeffries to squeeze between the door and the adjacent car. He lifted a leg up into the cab and held the steering wheel to climb into the driver's seat, sitting at the edge to reach the pedals.

"I tried not to flood it," Dana said, trying to sound knowledgeable.

He waved her off. "Forget flooding it. These all have electric ignitions and fuel injection. Don't need to even hit the gas pedal." He turned the key. The engine clicked. "That's a battery, all right." He shut off the key and sat back, his hands apart as he examined the dash. "Here's your problem." Dana leaned inside, and Jeffries sat back to show her. "You left the lights on."

Dana felt like an idiot. "They encourage you to drive with your lights on now." She shook her head. "I was in a hurry this morning, getting to the airport."

"It happens all the time." Jeffries climbed down from the seat. "Actually, that's good news. It means there's nothing wrong with the battery. It's just drained, but it should hold a charge. I have jumper cables. Road service can take hours this time of the night. I know. I've been through this." He pointed. "I'm parked just a couple of stalls down this same row."

"I'd really appreciate it."

He looked around the front of her car. "You lucked out. You have an open space in front of you. Let me pull my car around. We'll have you out of here in no time."

Dana reached inside the car for her travel bag and pulled out her cell phone, suddenly curious to see if Grant had called. She watched Fred Jeffries hurry down the aisle and disappear from view as he lowered himself into his car. A moment later, she heard an engine and watched a blue BMW back from a stall and drive around the end of the aisle. Linda had left her three messages: In the last, Marvin Crocket demanded she call him. Jeffries drove up the aisle one over and pulled into the stall in front of the

Explorer. Dana directed him with hand signals until his bumper was just inches from a waist-high concrete barrier separating the row of cars. He bounced out of his car, now fully enveloped in his knight-in-shining-armor role. He left the engine of the BMW running and waved to indicate that everything was going to be okay. Then he opened the trunk and reappeared carrying black and red jumper cables.

"Do you think they'll reach?" Dana asked. She listened to the final message, her mother confirming she had picked up Molly. There was no call from Grant. She contemplated calling his hotel room again, just to unnerve him.

Jeffries squeezed through a small gap between the concrete barrier and a concrete pillar. "We'll make it work. Hopefully, our batteries are on the same side," he said, as if talking about kidneys.

Dana shut off her phone and put it back in her travel bag. She had no doubt this was not the first time Fred Jeffries had played the Good Samaritan. "I really have to thank you for doing this."

Jeffries dismissed it. He stood at the front of her car, rolling up his shirtsleeves. "The latch for the hood should be on the left, under the dash." He pointed to the cab of her car.

Dana reached inside and pulled the knob under the dash toward her, hearing the hood pop open. "I hope you'll let me take you to lunch," she said, emerging. "You've been so kind."

"I'm always interested in going to lunch, though I wouldn't allow you to pay. I just like the company of nice people, especially after days like today." Jeffries opened the hood of the Explorer. He studied the battery for a moment. "You wouldn't happen to have a flashlight, would you?"

"I'm afraid not."

He stood on his toes. "These things are pretty standard. Red is positive. Black is negative." He continued studying the battery. "Huh. You seem to have an extra cable. Never seen that before."

"Is it going to be a problem?"

Jeffries shook his head. "Shouldn't. It's probably a ground of some sort. They're all overloaded with power locks and windows and air-conditioning. Can't even find the spark plugs anymore. The main thing is you want to get a good set on the connection. Your battery looks almost new; we should have you out of here in a minute." He connected the jumper cables to both batteries, then brushed his hands. "You might have to get in my car and rev the engine a bit. You don't want to floor it, but sometimes you have to give it some juice."

The concrete barrier gave her little room. She walked through the gap and stood on the other side. Jeffries climbed into the seat and held up two crossed fingers. The battery kicked and whined, but the engine did not start. Jeffries leaned out the side of her car. "Okay, rev the engine a bit," he said, indicating the BMW.

She nodded, walking behind the concrete pillar as Jeffries turned the key. She heard the engine whine, gain momentum, and kick over with a deafening roar.

36

∽

S HE LAY ON her back, staring up at the roof of a car.
A woman leaned over her, talking. Dana's head felt
like it was splitting down the middle. When she tried to sit
up, the woman put a hand firmly on her chest. Dana felt
something over her mouth and nose and tried to remove it.
The woman grabbed her hand. "You're in an ambulance.
We're transporting you to the hospital. Do you feel pain
anywhere? What about your chest? Are you having trouble breathing?"

She was wearing a mask. She felt the cool flow of oxygen. Though she heard the woman speaking, her mind was
not assimilating the information. She recalled hearing a loud
roar and feeling a rush of energy, as if she were being pushed
from behind by a huge wave. It had knocked her forward,
swept her up, and dropped her violently to the concrete.

"That cement barrier and pillar took most of the force,"
the woman said. Dana reached up and felt a bandage
across her forehead. "You struck your head pretty good.

I'm afraid we couldn't find your shoes." Dana looked down at her bare feet. She had gauze wrapped around her lower legs. The synapses in her brain continued to trigger memories. She recalled being facedown, feeling the cold concrete against her cheek, shards of metal and crystals of glass raining from the sky amid a deafening cacophony of bells, beeps, and whistles in the airport garage. There had been sirens.

The paramedic pulled open Dana's eyelids and shone a bright light in her eyes. "I'm checking the dilation of your pupils." The powerful light blinded her. "Are you having any blurred vision?"

Dana's neck felt stiff and sore. She remembered the man, the Good Samaritan. Fred Jeffries. "The man in the car," she mumbled through the mask.

The paramedic shook her head. "Are you having any trouble breathing, any discomfort in your chest?"

Dana put her head back against the pillows. "The man in the car," she said again, her voice muffled.

"Just try to relax," the woman said.

Tears rolled from the corners of Dana's eyes, diverted by the plastic cinched tightly to her face. The ambulance slowed and turned. Out the back window, Dana saw a sign for the emergency entrance to Highline Community Hospital in Burien. The ambulance stopped beneath a covered entry. The back doors were flung open. Two paramedics pulled the stretcher out the back, revealing a gunmetal-gray sky. "My bag?" Dana asked, panicked.

The female paramedic reached into the ambulance and handed it to her. "It's right here. Nobody was going to take that from you. You had a death grip on it when we arrived."

⤙⤚

Mᴀɪᴄʜᴀᴇʟ ʟᴏɢᴀɴ ʜᴜʀʀɪᴇᴅ down the hall, nearly jogging. During their short telephone conversation, Dana had said only that there had been an explosion and she was in the hospital. She did not want to call her mother. Would Logan come? From the tone of her voice, Logan sensed there was something more, something Dana was not going to tell him over the telephone. Two minutes after hanging up, he pulled on a pair of jeans and a sweatshirt and threw his leather jacket into the Austin Healey.

When he reached the door to her hospital room, he knocked twice before pushing it open. She sat upright in the bed with a piece of gauze across her forehead. Though she looked battered and bruised, she was in better shape than his mind had conjured on the drive to the hospital. A nurse stood taking her temperature and blood pressure. Dana smiled when she saw him. Logan let out a sigh of relief. Then he turned to give her and the nurse a moment of privacy. After the nurse left the room, he walked to the bed.

Dana spoke as he approached. "I need you to get me out of here."

Logan shook his head. "I spoke to the nurses. They want to keep you at least overnight. They're monitoring you for a concussion and possible internal bleeding."

She threw back the sheet and started to lower her legs over the side of the bed. She had bandages on her shins. "I can't stay overnight. I need to get home."

He put a hand on her shoulder. "Take it easy. I sent a police car to watch the house, just as you asked. Now tell me what happened."

She shook her head. "Someone blew up my car."

"I know," he said. "I called the SeaTac Police Department on the drive over here and spoke to the detective who responded." The detective had told Logan they'd descended on the place like an army unit, concerned that the explosion was some sort of terrorist attack. The initial indications were that someone had used C4 and a device set to detonate when Dana's car engine started. "Whoever set it up was a pro," the detective had said. "He wasn't messing around."

"Then you know that you have to get me out of here," Dana said.

"Do you know who did it?"

"Get me out of here," she said. "We have a lot to talk about."

The tone of her voice told Logan she *needed* to leave, that she did not feel safe. "I can put police officers outside your door."

She got out of the bed and walked toward the bathroom. Her hospital gown splayed open, and she reached behind to pull it together. She removed her bag from a closet in the room and emptied the contents on the bathroom counter. "Come in here," she said.

She stood at the sink, holding the half-eaten Snickers bar. It looked to have melted. She peeled away the remainder of the paper and rinsed the gooey mess under the faucet. As the chocolate and caramel fell away, Logan saw the earring. She looked up at him. "This is important. More important than we realized. I'll tell you everything. But first I want to take you someplace."

"Where?"

She shook her head. "I have to show you."

Logan nodded. "All right, I'll see what I can do," he said, and walked from the room.

~⌒~

TWENTY MINUTES LATER, he pulled the Austin Healey to the curb and got out to open the passenger door. A nurse stood next to Dana, who sat in a wheelchair beneath a darkening gray sky that had all the indicators of an impending heavy rain. The wheelchair was a small concession to hospital protocol. Logan had to sign a consent form acknowledging that he was taking Dana against the doctor's protestations.

Dana grimaced as she lowered herself into the car and bent her legs into the cramped front seat. Her clothes were ripped, torn, and stained. The nurse handed Logan a bag with pain medication from the hospital pharmacy. Then he walked to the driver's side and started the engine.

"What time is it?" she asked. Her watch had stopped.

"A bit after nine."

Dana took out her cell phone. "I need to call my mother and tell her to keep Molly home today. I'm sure she has anyway."

"Where to?" Logan asked.

"Montlake."

"Can I ask why?"

"I have something to show you. Don't drive directly there. Take a couple of detours."

Logan decided not to debate the matter with her further. In the wake of Marshall Cole's murder, he knew things were not as they seemed. He had no reason to doubt she knew why. He made several detours and took back streets off the freeway. He saw no indication that they were being followed. When they reached Montlake, he followed her directions, made a right onto Interlaken, and crossed over a one-lane bridge.

"It's the colonial on the left, the last house before the arboretum. Drive down the driveway," she said.

He pulled down a steep driveway to a white colonial with hunter-green shutters.

"There's a side yard just past the house. Park under the carport. The car won't be seen from the street, and there's an exit out the back."

Logan drove beneath a white trellised carport and followed the driveway to the back of the property. He parked in front of a freestanding garage. Unlike the house, the garage needed a coat of paint. One of the panes of glass in the door had been broken. Dana exited the car with some difficulty, not waiting for Logan to assist her. She grimaced and held her ribs.

Logan came around the side. "Are you okay?"

She took a breath, grimaced again, and walked to a wooden gate. She waited for Logan to reach over and unlatch it. The backyard was an expansive green lawn surrounded by dogwood and maple trees. Behind the property fence, the Washington Park Arboretum offered a green canopy. In the corner of the yard, a hot tub sat beneath a redwood gazebo. Logan followed Dana to a side door and took the keys from her. Before opening the door he checked around the frame for any indication of wires that could lead to a detonator. Finding none, he opened it, and followed her inside. If the disarray inside the house surprised her, Dana did not reveal it. He sensed from their brief conversation at the hospital that she had expected it and had prepared herself. This trip had been for his benefit.

Logan followed her from room to room, stepping around her possessions, strewn books and pictures and emptied drawers. She showed little emotion. He followed her upstairs. When they reached what he presumed to be her bedroom, she stood at the windows, looking out at the trees, their branches seeming to gently envelop the room.

"I used to love to sit here with Molly and look out this window," she said. He noted that she had used the past tense. "It made me feel like being a kid in a tree house again, you know? Did you ever have a tree house growing up?" When he didn't immediately respond, she turned and looked at him.

"Not growing up, no," he said.

She turned back to the window. "James and I asked our father to help us build one. He hired a contractor instead. It had a trapdoor and a rope ladder. Nicest one in the neighborhood. My father never skimped. I used to like to go there and sit and think. I guess I still do."

"Are you all right?" he asked.

She continued to gaze out the window. "I found out why my brother is dead." She turned and handed him the earring. "The markings on the back are the artist's initials. It's a trademark. Reputable jewelers won't copy it. The artist's name is William Welles. He lives on Maui."

"That's where you went?" he asked, rolling over the earring to see what appeared to be two interlocking "W"s.

"The earring is one of a kind. I thought if he had records, he could tell us who he made it for."

"Did he?"

"No," she said. Then she looked up at him. "But he remembered her."

37

Elizabeth Meyers sat on the bench seat in a corner of the family kitchen. One of three in the compound, this kitchen was closest to their living quarters on the second floor. It was also rarely used. Her husband preferred to eat either at restaurants or at his desk. Though there was a stocked refrigerator, Elizabeth rarely opened it. There was no need. She had a staff to do those things. When she wanted something to eat or drink, she asked for it, and it materialized. If she said, "I'd like a Coke," someone brought her one. "Make it a root beer," and someone changed it. "A tuna sandwich. A steak." Anything she wanted, she got. The staff was never far away.

She pulled her bathrobe around her and sipped a cup of chamomile tea. Carmen Dupree, a rail-thin black woman with a shock of gray hair, stood humming and peeling a green apple. Carmen had worked for the Meyers family for the better part of thirty years because she could bake an apple pie that Robert Meyers III could not live without. As Carmen liked to tell the story—and she told it often—her pie had taken first place at a county fair in Seattle the year Robert Meyers was stumping the state, in search of the black vote for his run at governor. Meyers had been an honorary judge at the fair and insisted on a photo with the winner. Carmen wasn't dumb. She knew Meyers was more interested in a photo opportunity with a poor, dark-skinned black woman from slave roots, but she also knew that once he ate her apple pie, he would be hooked—everyone was, especially men. It was never enough to keep them around full-time, but, as with sex, they always returned for it.

Robert Meyers was no different. He sought out the recipe, even offered to buy it. No fool, Carmen refused to let it part her lips. When Meyers was elected governor, he sought her out again, this time dangling a job as bait. It was another photo opportunity, and Carmen was once again a prop. She didn't care. She said she liked to imagine what her mother and grandmother would say, knowing that a Dupree was working for one of the wealthiest families in all of Washington. Then she would chuckle and answer her own question. "Probably that the size of the house only meant there was more house to clean."

Carmen popped a slice of the apple into her mouth and savored it with her eyes closed, as if letting it melt. Concluding that it met with her approval, she continued cutting razor-thin pieces, letting them fall into the center of the second of two freshly made pie crusts. The first pie baked in one of the three ovens. Carmen spoke to Elizabeth as she peeled the skin from another apple. "It's a shame to waste the skin. That's where you find the nutrients. But it can be bitter, and that takes away from the flavor of the cinnamon. And cinnamon"—she looked over at Elizabeth—"is what makes an apple pie, apple pie."

Elizabeth smiled in reply.

Carmen cut the last of the slices onto the mound in the uncooked pie crust, then put down the knife. She checked the clock on the wall, wiped a spot on her forehead with the back of her hand, and walked to the ovens, turning on the light to study the pie through the window. She gently eased open the door as if worried she'd wake what was inside. "Golden brown. Not a bit darker, or the crust can crumble on you," she said.

She donned two oven mitts and gently removed the pie. The hidden ingredients passed down through generations of Dupree pie makers overwhelmed the room with the aroma of vanilla, cinnamon, and baked apples. She placed the pie on the counter and smiled down at it as if it were a newborn baby. The pie was as much art as delicacy. The crust crisscrossed in a perfect grid pattern. Baked apple oozed to the surface through the squares.

"Would you like a slice of pie, Mrs. Meyers? Need to let it cool a spell, but it will be ready in no time."

Elizabeth looked up from her cup of tea. No matter how many times she asked, Carmen refused to call her Elizabeth. Her husband had made a point that first names were not appropriate, and the staff abided by it. "No, thank you, Carmen. It does smell wonderful, though."

"You need to keep up your strength, Mrs. Meyers." Carmen leaned over the pie. "It's going to be a busy year for you and Mr. Meyers. Busy, indeed."

"Well said, Carmen."

Elizabeth dropped her cup. It shattered on the tiled floor, tea splattering.

Robert Meyers stood in the doorway, cinching tight a silk bathrobe. Carmen calmly walked to a closet in the servants' pantry and retrieved a broom, dustpan, and mop, sweeping up the shards of porcelain. "Don't cut your feet, now, Mrs. Meyers. You just stay put."

"I've been telling Mrs. Meyers she needs to eat better, but she doesn't seem to want to listen to me." Meyers shuffled across the white-tiled floor in bedroom slippers, careful to avoid the tea casualty. "I can get an entire company to move with just a word, but I can't get my own wife to eat. What do you think about that?"

Carmen used a white towel to wipe up the tea that had spattered the side of the bench seat. "I wouldn't know nothing about that, Mr. Meyers. I ain't never had a problem eatin', or getting my men to eat."

Meyers went over to where his wife sat and stroked her hair. "I awoke to find you missing. I was worried. Having trouble sleeping again?"

Elizabeth nodded.

"Well, it's probably the tea. You know caffeine keeps you awake. You should be drinking warm milk. Isn't that right, Carmen?"

"Chamomile tea don't have but a bit of caffeine, Mr. Meyers, and I wouldn't know about not sleeping, neither." Carmen wrung the wet rag over a sink and ran it under hot water. "I've never had trouble sleeping, and I drink a cup of tea or more every night. Tea soothes the body."

Meyers continued to stroke his wife's hair.

"Can't speak for the soul," Carmen added quietly.

"What's that?" Meyers asked, turning toward her.

"Oh, nothing, Mr. Meyers, just mumbling to myself as I do."

Meyers walked to the counter, broke off a piece of the pie crust, and nibbled on it. "So, what were you two ladies discussing at this late hour?"

Carmen ran the towel under the water, wrung it out again, and walked back to finish wiping down the table and floor. "Woman talk, Mr. Meyers; nothing that would interest a man."

Meyers turned from the pie and leaned against the granite counter, his hands in the pockets of his bathrobe. "Well, that makes me all the more interested. It sounds like something secretive and exciting."

Carmen shook her head. She had her back to him as she finished wiping down the table. "Nothing secretive or exciting about it. Just this and that."

"Hmm. Well, I think I'll have a slice of pie, even if Mrs. Meyers won't join me. Do you think it's cooled enough?"

"It could cool some more."

"Just the same, I think I'll have my slice, now that I'm awake. Cut me a piece, won't you?"

Carmen left the wet rag on the table and wiped her hands dry on the light blue apron around her waist. She walked to the counter and picked out a sharp nine-inch knife from a wooden block. Meyers remained stationed at the counter. She looked up at him, knife in hand. "Excuse me, Mr. Meyers, but if you're fixin' to have a piece of pie, you'll need to let me cut it."

Meyers moved to his left, allowing Carmen just enough room to step past. She cut through the outer crust of the pie slowly, careful not to break the rest of the grid and risk caving in the entire pie. As she moved her hand to make the second cut, Meyers reached out and took her wrist. Elizabeth looked up from the table.

"You have to give a man a bigger slice of pie than that." Meyers moved Carmen's hand to the right. "You never want to cheat a man out of something he has become accustomed to having."

Carmen's focus remained on the pie. She waited patiently until Meyers released her wrist. When he did, she looked up at him. "My mother said you always give a man what he deserves. Just what he deserves," she said. Then she lowered the knife, and her gaze, and cut the slice of pie exactly where she had intended.

38

HE WANTED A gift for his young wife," Dana said. Logan sat on the edge of the bed, waiting patiently for her to tell him what she knew. She had trouble finding the words. She finally said, "He was a wealthy businessman from a prominent Seattle family." Then she looked back out the window and recalled Welles calmly seated with his head down, like an old man asleep in a chair.

She had walked back toward him. "You remember her, don't you?"

"Yes," he'd said. "I remember her."

Dana sat, her heart thumping wildly in her chest. "Will you tell me her name?"

Welles had raised his eyes. "Elizabeth Meyers."

Disbelieving, she'd asked, "Robert Meyers's wife? Senator Meyers's wife?"

Welles had shrugged, his face a blank mask. "I wouldn't know."

"But you said—"

"I know what I said. Who he is now is of no concern to me." He had rocked rhythmically in his wooden chair, stroking Leonardo's back. *"He wanted an anniversary gift. He wanted to surprise her. But as I said, I do not create anything without meeting the person who is to wear it. He did not understand at first, and I did not expect him to. But he relented. I spent an afternoon with her. A charming woman, like yourself, but one filled with great sadness. Ultimately, he was quite pleased by the design. He believed the tanzanite brought out the blue of his wife's eyes."*

Dana looked again at Logan. "Six years ago, the man who paid for those earrings became a United States senator. A week ago, he announced his candidacy for president of the United States." She said the words without emotion. When Logan did not immediately respond, she said the name for him. "William Welles made the earring for Robert Meyers's wife, Elizabeth."

"Dana . . ."

She raised her hand to stop him. "I had the entire flight home to consider it. It explains why Laurence King is dead. It explains why he chose to rob a man who had given away almost everything he had of value. It explains why Daniel Holmes—or whoever the man is—came to my brother's house and why he went to the cabin. He's looking for the earring. They know that she misplaced it and that it can be traced to her and her only. They must have been watching her closely."

"Is it possible that there is more than one pair? That this is a copy?"

She shook her head. "Not with that engraving on back. It's one of a kind."

"And you think Robert Meyers sent King and Cole to get the earnings?"

"I think he's ultimately behind it, yes."

"Maybe she sent them."

She shook her head. "It was Meyers."

"That remains an awfully big leap, Dana."

"Find Marshall Cole and ask him."

Logan hesitated. "Marshall Cole is dead. We found him in a gas station bathroom in Yakima. He was apparently driving back to Idaho, where he had relatives."

She shook her head in frustration. "It fits. We both know it fits."

Logan ran a hand across his chin. "It might explain some things, but to allege that Robert Meyers had your brother killed because he was having an affair with his wife will require a lot more evidence than an earring."

"I know that. . . ." Her voice trailed away.

Logan ran a hand through his hair. "Let's start over. Tell me what happened in Maui."

Dana agreed, because she knew how Logan felt—the only thing that would convince him would be the reality of what had happened, the facts that neither could discount. She recounted her trip to the island, her efforts to find William Welles, and the substance of their conversation. It wasn't hard to do. She kept replaying their meeting and conversation over and over again in her head.

"He said the blue stone reflected the color of her eyes and her beauty, the diamond below it, a teardrop. He said it was one of many she had and will continue to shed."

"What about?"

"I don't know for sure," she said. Then, "But Welles said to look within myself to understand the earring."

She turned and looked out the window, not wanting to see Logan's face when she continued, embarrassed. "I have a bad marriage. It's been bad for some time. I've just refused to accept it. Now I don't have a choice." She looked at him. "My husband is cheating on me. He probably has before. I've shed more than a few tears over my marriage. I imagine I'll shed more."

Logan waited a moment, and she let him process the information. "And you think that Elizabeth Meyers also has a bad marriage, that it's the reason Welles designed the earring as he did?"

"I suspect it is."

Logan rubbed the stubble on his chin, thinking it through, not dismissing her but still puzzled. "How would this guy Welles know that about you?"

"I don't know," she said. "You had to be there. You had to have met him. He knew. Somehow he knew."

Logan cleared his throat. "Assuming you're correct, why wouldn't Meyers confront his wife—tell her that she had to stop seeing your brother? Why wouldn't he just keep her under lock and key? With the security entourage he employs, it certainly would be possible. Why kill your brother and put everything at risk, everything he's worked to achieve?"

"Why?" Dana had also considered this on the flight home. "Why did Jack Kennedy sleep with Marilyn Monroe in the White House? Why would Bill Clinton sneak out of the Arkansas governor's mansion with his wife asleep in bed beside him? Why would he risk getting caught having sex in the Oval Office? Why would Richard Nixon, a landslide winner in every poll, order the break-in to the Democratic headquarters?" There were other questions she could ask, like why would men at Enron and Arthur

Andersen and dozens of other companies around the world do the things they did. "Men in power think they're omnipotent. They think they're beyond reach, that the rules governing the rest of society don't apply to them, because normally, they don't. They do what they want because no one has ever told them they can't. Maybe that's what my brother was going to tell me. Maybe Elizabeth Meyers was the problem he wanted to talk to me about."

"But to have your brother killed. To risk—"

"If word got out that his wife was having an affair, it wouldn't rock just Meyers's marriage, it would rock his entire world. It would shatter the image that he and his political advisers have so carefully cultivated to get him where he wants to go. The return to Camelot is a sham. It's a house of cards, and if you pull this card, the house crumbles. He knows that."

Logan paced, mentally switching gears to homicide cop. "Will this guy in Maui give a statement? Will he identify the earring and say who he designed it for?"

Dana shook her head. A tear escaped the corner of her eye and rolled down her cheek. Several others followed. "I used a credit card to buy my ticket. You were right. I was the next logical choice. Someone followed me to the island and killed him." It pained her to imagine someone taking William Welles's life. He was a gentle man. Too good for this world, he had created his own.

Logan took a deep breath and rubbed the back of his head. "That's a problem," he said, leaving unspoken what they were both thinking. If Dana was correct, there were only two people in the world who could identify the earring's owner. One was dead, and the other likely wouldn't dare.

39

~~~

BRIAN GRIFFIN STOOD from his desk with a look of alarm when Dana walked into his office on the fourth floor of the Seattle University School of Law. His expression and first question told her that a warm shower and change of clothes had not concealed how she looked.

"Dana. What happened?"

Griffin's concern also didn't begin to describe how awful she felt. She didn't know what it felt like to be run over by a truck, but she couldn't imagine it was much worse than how she felt at the moment. The burning sensation from the cut in her forehead had become a dull, pounding headache that two aspirin didn't dent. She felt dizzy. Her forearms and shins stung from the cuts and burns, and she was having difficulty taking anything more than shallow breaths; the pain in her side was at times excruciating.

Logan stepped into the office from the hallway, and Dana introduced him. "This is my colleague Michael Logan. I asked him to give me a ride."

"Let me get you a place to sit," Griffin said, turning his attention to Logan and starting to remove a stack of papers from the second of two chairs near the door.

Logan waved it off. "Don't trouble yourself. I'd prefer to stand."

Griffin closed the door behind them, making the cramped office feel even smaller. It was half the size of an associate's office at Strong & Thurmond. Dana had never been to her brother's office. She had been expecting the halls of academia, with rich dark wood and Tiffany lamps, but the law school was a newly constructed redbrick-and-steel-beam building with a lot of glass to allow for natural light. The interior was a modern design, with light wood and carpeted hallways well lit by overhead skylights. Griffin's desk was a horseshoe shape; the office had wall-to-ceiling built-in shelves stuffed with law books and knickknacks. The wall where diplomas and professional certificates traditionally hung in law offices held framed photographs of Griffin and an attractive redhead who Dana assumed was his former wife.

"What happened?" Griffin stepped back to allow Dana to sit in one of the two chairs.

"I was in a car accident."

Griffin moved to the inside of the horseshoe to make room for Logan. The office windows, which overlooked a courtyard, were at his back. "Are you all right?"

"My car was totaled, but I'm okay." She looked to Logan, hoping to further explain his presence. "The doctors have advised me against driving for a few days. The medication can make me drowsy. But you know me, Brian. I'm a workaholic. Have to keep up the billable hours."

Griffin shook his head, disbelieving. "My God, when did this happen?"

"Just yesterday," she said, wanting to avoid details. "Really, I look worse than I feel. The entire thing was my fault."

"Molly wasn't in the car with you, was she?"

"No, thank God; it was just me."

Griffin shook his head. "You really didn't need this now. Is there anything I can do for you?"

The only person Dana suspected would know more about her brother was Brian Griffin. She knew what it was like to spend ten to twelve hours a day with colleagues. After a while, you got to know some as well as a spouse. She suspected Griffin and her brother had spent a lot of time together. Her brother's office was just three doors down.

The reason for her visit was a story that had run on the front page of the metro section of the *Seattle Times* perhaps six months earlier. Dana remembered the article only because she'd seen the name of the law school, and she paid closer attention to things connected to James. The article itself had been bland. She hadn't given it a second thought until she sat for six hours on the plane back from Hawaii, mulling over how James could have come in contact with the senator's wife. She was able to find the story on the Internet and print a copy for Logan.

Griffin reached into his pocket and pulled out a red bandana, cleaning the lenses of his glasses as he spoke. "Did you want to discuss James's estate now?"

"Actually, I'm hoping you can help me with something else. I was going to call. I'm sorry for the intrusion."

"Not at all. What is it?"

"Well, the law firm is sponsoring a seminar on women in the law here in Seattle, and I'm on the committee," she said, trying to sound convincing. "And I recalled an article in the *Seattle Times* a while back that Elizabeth Meyers spoke here at the law school."

Griffin nodded. "It was a bit of a coup for the school. She doesn't make public appearances very often."

"That's what I understood. So I was hoping to find out how the law school got her to come."

The cell phone clipped to Logan's belt rang. He removed it and stood. "I'll take this outside." He answered as he stepped into the hallway, closing the door.

Dana turned back to Griffin. He had a smile on his face, and for an instant she thought he was about to ask her what she really wanted to know. She tried to cover it with another question. "Am I missing something?"

"I'm sorry, I didn't mean to..." Griffin chuckled, finished polishing his glasses, and put the wire frames back around his ears. "When I think of James, I just naturally think of you being there. Sometimes I forget you weren't a part of everything we did. You don't remember her, do you?"

"Remember who?"

"Elizabeth Meyers. Elizabeth *Adams*."

Dana shook her head. The names rang no bells.

"She was in James's and my freshman dorm."

Dana and James had chosen different dorms, believing that going to the same school was close enough for twins.

"You remember? James brought her home to your house for Thanksgiving, freshman year. Actually, he invited her and her roommate. Don't you remember that?"

As Griffin spoke, Dana's mind peeled back the years

until she saw the auburn-haired girl with the bright blue eyes and perfect smile in the family kitchen. With finals a week after the holiday, some students who lived out of the area didn't have time to get home and instead spent the holiday with friends. "She looks a bit different now, with her hair darkened and the nose job," Griffin said, adding, "I don't know why she would do that, or why she always wears sunglasses. I guess it's the Jackie O thing."

Elizabeth Adams was tall, with long legs and a thin waist. She had walked into the kitchen, confident and sure of herself, and asked to help with the dinner, immediately ingratiating herself to Kathy Hill. The two of them had spent hours talking while James sat on a stool at the counter, slobbering like a big dog waiting for a bone. When it came time for dinner, Dana intentionally sat between them. Her mother had made her move.

Griffin leaned back, twirling an unfolded paper clip between his thumb and index finger. "She lived right across the hallway from us freshman year. I kept pushing your brother to ask her out, but he said he didn't want to spoil their friendship. He said he was afraid that if it didn't work out, he'd have to live next door to her the rest of the year. Truth was, she intimidated him. Hell, she intimidated all of us. I think he convinced himself that being friends with her was better than being her ex-boyfriend." He stopped twirling the paper clip and looked up at the photographs on the wall. "I married my college sweetheart, and hindsight tells me there is some truth to that. By the time James mustered the courage to ask her out, Elizabeth was no longer a well-kept secret within the freshman class. Every guy on campus either knew her or wanted to know her, including Robert Meyers." Griffin put down the paper clip. "At least your brother didn't lose out to a beer-swilling fraternity slob. Not too many people can claim they lost the love of their life to a future president."

Dana felt tongue-tied. Obligated to say something, she said, "No, not too many people can claim that."

"After Meyers and Elizabeth got involved, she was never around. Then we heard she dropped out and went with him to Harvard and got married the following year."

"How did you get her to speak here?"

"It was a program for female law students. James and I were part of the committee. At one of the meetings, he looked across the table at me and said, 'What about Elizabeth Adams?' I thought he was kidding, but everyone else thought it was a great idea. They got him to do what took me twenty years of trying."

"So James called her?"

Griffin shook his head. "He was still a chicken; he called her secretary. But Elizabeth called back and personally accepted." He sat forward, elbows on his desk. "I've read the criticism of her in the newspapers—that she can be aloof—but that's not how she was here." It wasn't how Dana remembered her, either. "To us, she was the same old Elizabeth," Griffin continued. "Her speech was pointed and crisp. She was very poised and friendly. I got the impression she really enjoyed herself that day."

Dana looked past Griffin to a picture on the wall. She recognized her brother amid a pack of graduation-gown-clad men and women, the redbrick steeple buildings of the University of Washington in the background. When she looked back at Griffin, his eyes had narrowed. She knew he was seeing through her thinly veiled excuse for coming to his office. He was likely recalling their conversation by the pool at the reception following James's funeral.

"Why are you asking me this, Dana?"

The office door opened. Logan stuck his head in. "I need to get going. All set?"

Thankful for the intrusion, Dana stood. She shook Griffin's hand. "Thank you for your help."

"If there's anything that I can do . . ."

She shook her head. "I'm going to handle this. It's better this way," she said, hoping her tone would appease him. "I'll call you about the estate."

Logan waited in the hall. When she stepped out, Griffin followed her. "Dana?"

She turned.

"Is everything going to be all right?"

She nodded. "Yes, Brian. I'm going to see that it is."

LOGAN WALKED HER down three flights of stairs, holding her by the elbow as if to ease the pain he knew he'd cause by rushing her. When they stepped out the glass door, the pain stabbed at her side, making it difficult to catch her breath. She finally had to stop in the courtyard. "Why are we rushing?"

Logan let go of her elbow. "I'm sorry," he said. "Someone called the precinct with information on Laurence King's death. He wants to talk to me in confidence."

A light mist fell, and the wind blew her hair in her face. "Who is he?"

"He wouldn't leave a name."

"Did he say what it was about? Did he say what he knew?"

"No." Logan took her by the elbow again and helped her across Twelfth Street, where he had parked in front of a Starbucks. "He said he read about the killing in the newspaper and had information for the detective in charge of the investigation."

She stopped as he opened her car door. "Be careful, Mike."

He nodded, then gestured that he'd help her into the car. "He wants to meet at a restaurant downtown—a public place. I don't want to keep him waiting; he sounded squirrelly on the phone."

"It was her," she said, looking up at him. "It *was* Elizabeth Meyers."

"I heard your conversation from the hallway," he said, nodding. "But I also know we don't have a single witness who can verify that, and without one, we won't get very far, which is why this guy could be important." He closed her door and hurried to the driver's side, getting in.

"Where are you meeting him?"

"McCormick's Fish House on Fourth Avenue. He said he'd be there at noon." He looked at his watch. "And I still need to get you back to your mother's."

That meant driving her across the bridge to the east side of the lake, then driving back to Seattle. It was at least a half-an-hour detour. "I'll go with you," Dana said.

Logan shook his head. "This guy wants to talk to me alone."

"Then I'll wait in the car. I don't want my mother to see me like this just yet."

He shook his head. "I don't know how long this is going to take, and you need to rest. I think you feel worse than you're letting on." He looked to be considering their options, then said, "Hang on. I need to make some time here." He punched the accelerator. The Austin Healey shot down Twelfth Street and merged onto I-90, heading east, toward the bridge. The engine settled into a sweet hum.

"You're going the wrong way," she said, confused. "Downtown is the other way."

"We're not going downtown," he said. "I'm taking you someplace where you can rest."

40

∽

MICHAEL LOGAN EXPLAINED that his home sat atop Cougar Mountain in Issaquah, which had not escaped the massive development of homes, town homes, and shopping centers spreading farther and farther east of Seattle. Portions of the top of the mountain, however, had been designated a regional park and had not yet been stripped of dense foliage and old-growth trees. It remained home to an occasional but increasingly rare bobcat, cougar, and black bear. Radio towers were also atop the mountain, accessed by a gated dirt road on plots of land that Logan leased to the state. As the Austin Healey wound its way up the dirt and gravel road past the towers, Dana looked up at a three-story treated pine structure that rose from the ground, as inconspicuous as the huge trees surrounding it. The road circled around the back of the property. Logan drove around to the front. The house had been built around existing cedars and dogwoods. Huge cathedral windows rose to a pitched roof. Like

William Welles's home, it blended into the surrounding landscape and foliage. Tree stumps in the yard had been cored in the center and plugged with ceramic pots overflowing with flowers and vines.

Dana stepped from the car to a symphony of music. Large silver wind chimes hung from overhead tree branches, spinning and twirling in a light breeze. "Did you build those?" she asked.

Logan nodded. "Built it all."

She looked at the house, then back to him. "You built this?" It sounded more skeptical than she had intended.

He shrugged. "Be it ever so humble." He started for the front door. "I have to warn you that the inside is still a work in progress."

"It's incredible. Who designed it?"

"My wife." Logan walked across a wood bridge that crossed a creek and led to a large porch. He unlocked the front door, and Dana followed him inside to a slate-floor entry and river-rock wall. A waterfall cascaded into a pond of lily pads, plants, and koi fish. The entry led to a sunken living room with a rock fireplace that stretched twenty-five feet to the pitched ceiling. Timbered logs sprouted through the floor, intersecting with overhead wooden beams to form an elevated second floor. Footbridges spanned between the lofts. With the sweeping views of the surrounding landscape, it felt very much like being outside.

It's a tree house, Dana thought, recalling her comment to Logan as they had sat in her bedroom.

Perhaps recalling the same conversation, Logan said, "Sarah loved the outdoors. She loved to climb anything, really—rocks, trees. She said height gave a person a different perspective." He took Dana's coat and hung it in a closet near the front door.

"I can't believe anyone could design this," Dana said.

"It was part desire and part necessity," he said, walking back into the room. "The property belonged to her great-grandfather. The state of Washington tried to force a sale, but Sarah refused. She was concerned the state would just turn around and sell the land to the highest bidder. They hassled us over building permits and imposed regulations to prevent us from building anything that would disturb the land. I think they were pretty confident we wouldn't be able to build anything that complied, and figured we'd get frustrated and sell." Logan smiled. "They didn't know my wife."

"What does she do?" Dana asked, confused by Logan's prior statement that he was not married.

"She was an architect by education, but Sarah was really an artist." He pointed to the walls. "The paintings are also hers."

The walls were lined with abstract art. Dana stepped to one. "She did these?"

"Up until the day she died."

Dana turned from the painting.

"Sarah died five years ago."

"I'm sorry." She considered the paintings, then remembered the timing and started to ask the question before thinking better of it. "So she never..."

"Lived here?" Logan said. "No. No, she didn't. I started it after she died, and it's taken me five years to get this far. I haven't had the time to complete it, but I will. It's kept my mind occupied—helped me to forget when I needed that. Now it helps me to remember."

"I can't believe you built this. It's amazing."

"I contracted out some of the more difficult parts—it's next to impossible to get heavy equipment up here," he said, trying to sound humble. "We had to use some old building techniques to raise the platforms."

"It's spectacular."

"A labor of love, I guess you could say. I've become somewhat obsessed with construction details and paranoid about things like dry rot. So it's taking me longer than it should. But I feel an obligation to Sarah to get it perfect. It's the last thing she ever designed." He looked at his watch. "The kitchen's on the second level. Help yourself to whatever you can find in the fridge or cabinets. It's not much, I'm afraid." He stepped from the room.

"I'll be fine." Dana picked up a photograph from an end table. In it, Michael Logan knelt with his arm around a woman in a wheelchair, her head tilted awkwardly to the right, her mouth open, her arms and hands twisted and bent.

"That's Sarah," Logan said, walking back in.

Dana put the picture frame back on the table. "I'm sorry. I shouldn't have—"

He shook his head. "I invited you here, and that picture is on the table to be seen. Sarah died from complications from muscular dystrophy." He looked again at his watch. "You're sure you'll be all right?"

"I'll be fine. Go. You're going to be late."

"I'll call you later. And I'll have a patrol car sent over." He walked up the stairs to the entrance. "There's a guest bedroom, second loft on the right. Just be careful on some of the suspended walkways. I haven't had a chance to solder all the joints. Some are hanging on clips. They're safe to walk on, just don't jump around on them too much."

"I don't think I'll be doing any jumping." He smiled. "What I'd really like is a computer with Internet access."

"My office is over there." He pointed to a loft to the west. "Best view in the whole house. Try to get some rest, though; you've been going nonstop for a week."

"I'll have all my life to rest."

He nodded, resigned. "I'll call later." She walked him to the door. "You're not going to sleep, are you?" he asked. She smiled at him. "Lock the door behind me."

"I'll be fine, Mike. Who could find me all the way out here?"

41

⌒

McCORMICK'S FISH HOUSE, at the corner of Fourth Avenue and Columbia Street in downtown Seattle, was well-known. Within blocks of the King County Courthouse and the newly constructed City Hall, it had once been the Oakland Hotel. Built in 1827, it had a brick exterior and an interior decor that maintained a feeling from the past with dark wood booths, Tiffany lamps hanging from a bronze-plated inlaid ceiling, a white terrazzo floor, and hunter-green curtains hanging halfway up the windows facing the street. Logan told the maître d' he was meeting someone in the bar. The man directed him up three stairs to his left, where he found a traditional bar and an oyster bar. Logan sat on a stool at the corner of the traditional bar so he could watch the front door. On the wall above hung a sign counting down the number of days until next year's St. Patrick's Day. He declined a menu from the bartender, ordered a Coke, and watched the television above a huge stuffed salmon mounted on the wall.

After several minutes, Logan felt a tap on the shoulder. The man who stood behind him was heavy, the kind of weight acquired from eating and drinking well. His chin hung over the collar of his shirt, nearly obscuring the knot of his tie.

"Are you Detective Logan?"

Logan had not seen the man come in the front door and deduced that he had entered near the oyster bar. His head was enormous, even for his considerable girth. With a flat nose, prominent ears, and a receding hairline, he looked like a large sow in a suit.

"Yes," Logan said.

The man motioned to the restaurant. "I have a table at a booth in the back." Logan followed him through the restaurant, which was in full lunch swing. Waiters in long white aprons and black ties dodged one another, carrying plates of calamari and oysters. Logan detected the smell of butter and garlic. It made his mouth water. The man climbed stairs to an elevated seating area and slid into a booth. He picked up a drink that looked like Scotch and took a drink. The ice rattled in the glass—the man's hands were shaking. Logan hung his coat on a hook outside the booth and slid in the opposite side, watching as the man combed at imaginary hair on the front of his head, pressing down the few strands remaining. His scalp glistened with beads of perspiration. Logan didn't want to rush the man, but he had a feeling that nothing would get said unless he started.

"You indicated on your message that you might know Laurence King?"

The man shook his head. "No." He took another drink from the glass, finishing it and leaving the ice. "I didn't know the name until I read it in the paper." Again he paused. "I might know something about who killed him...maybe...I don't know."

Logan nodded, patient. "Why don't you tell me what you know?"

The man leaned across the table, lowering his head. "This has got to be in confidence. It has to be confidential. Anonymous. You know? I work over at the Federal Building as a clerk for an administrative judge."

"I understand," Logan said, making no promises.

The man sat back, his face flushed. "I'm married. I have a wife and three daughters. I'm a lector in the parish, and I'm on the PTA board at my kids' school," he added as if making a list. "I can't be a part of this. I can't testify or anything."

Again Logan did not commit. He now suspected he knew how the man had come into contact with Laurence King. "Just tell me what you know. Let's start with that."

The man seemed to gather himself. "I, um, I might have been there."

"Been where?" Logan asked, wanting the man to be definitive.

"At the motel—at the Emerald Inn."

Logan nodded. "You were with someone."

"It's sort of a...a thing I have for...well, I mean, my wife won't, you know." The man pointed under the table and made a face.

"Your wife won't give you a blow job?"

The man let out a burst of air. "No. It's more than that. We don't really have sexual relations anymore. She says it's something genetic—her mother was the same way. She's become paranoid about germs and things, you know, like

Howard Hughes got. Anyway...I heard about this bar off the highway where, you know, you can find a woman. And then you go to this motel."

"And you were there the night King was killed."

The man leaned forward, whispering. "I was in the room next door."

"All right, Mr. . . ." Logan tried to make it sound casual. He had deliberately waited to ask the man's name, not wanting to spook him, but the man's eyes widened in fear nonetheless.

"Do you need my name?"

"It would help if I had something to call you."

The man alternately bit at and licked his lower lip as if coveting the last morsel of food on someone else's plate. He sounded almost apologetic when he said his name. "It's Jack. Jack Ruby."

Logan chuckled. "You don't have to make up a name."

Ruby raised a hand and rolled his eyes. "I'm not making it up. That's my name. And please, no jokes. I've heard every one you could think of. If I had a dime for every time someone asked if I'm related to *the* Jack Ruby, I'd be rich."

"All right, I promise no jokes." Logan reached across the table, and the man gave his hand a perfunctory shake. "Just tell me what you saw and heard."

"Okay." Ruby took a breath as if preparing himself for an arduous task. "Like I said, I'm in the room next door, and I hear some things."

"Tell me what you heard."

"Well, not a lot. I mean..." He leaned forward again, blushing. "I like it when they talk—when they, you know, give me a little something for the effort."

Logan eased him along. "We all like a little encouragement."

Ruby rubbed a graying mustache above an upper lip too small for his face. Logan thought the man might have a heart attack right there in the booth. "Right. Encouragement. So I'm, well, you know, with this woman, and I hear...and then I hear the guy next door banging on the walls, telling us to keep it down. She tells me to ignore them, to do my thing, and she just keeps talking louder, you know, but I'm losing my concentration, and I can't...and then...then I hear what sounds like an argument."

"Did you hear what they were saying?"

"I could only hear one...one voice. He's saying he wants more money. He wants fifteen thousand dollars. I remember that. And then I hear him say...he says...'We didn't sign on for killing nobody.'"

Logan tried not to overreact. "You heard that? You're certain?"

Ruby put up a hand as if swearing on a witness stand. "I couldn't make that up, Detective Logan. And I'm thinking of getting the hell out of there, but the woman, you know, she just tells me to keep going and...well, I was right about to...you know...give her the Cheez Whiz when all of a sudden I hear two sounds like firecrackers going off. Bam. Bam."

Ruby's voice carried above the din of the restaurant. He caught himself and lowered farther in the seat. If the man could have blended into the upholstery, Logan was sure he would have. "Hell, I didn't know what to do. Everything just started happening. The woman's kicking and yelling for me to get off her. Then I hear a third pop, and it sounds like it's coming right through the wall. I guess I must've panicked, because next thing I know, I'm standing on the balcony in my socks, pulling up my pants and trying to zip my fly. And that's when I see him."

"Laurence King?"

Ruby lifted his gaze from the table. "No. Not King. This guy ... He's standing on the deck, and I'm staring at him face-to-face."

Now Logan leaned forward. "Face-to-face with who?"

Ruby looked up. "The guy," he said, more emphatic. "The killer. I mean ... I assume he was the killer. He had a gun in his hand."

Logan felt his pulse quicken. "Do you remember what he looked like?"

Ruby sat back and shook as if overcome by a chill. He wiped a green napkin across his perspiring forehead. "Yeah, I can describe him. I'll never forget it. It was night, but he was wearing sunglasses. I remember that. The kind that wrap around."

"What else besides the sunglasses?"

"He had short hair, not necessarily a crew cut, but short."

"What color?"

"Blond. Dirty-blond."

"How tall?"

"Six foot, maybe an inch more or less. Well built, stocky. He was in good shape, I think. He was wearing one of those bomber-type leather jackets—brown, you know, with the collar, and ... and he looks at me. I mean he stares me right in the face, you know, and I think I'm done for. That's it, right there. I'm going to get killed for sure because I've looked this guy right smack-dab in the face." Ruby leaned forward again, his voice straining and hushed as if he were gasping for air. "But you know what he does? He *smiles*." Ruby's eyes widened in amazement. "Can you believe that? The guy *smiles*. Then he puts a finger to his lips like it's our little secret, and he turns and walks away. Can you believe that? He just turns and walks away."

Jack Ruby had dodged a bullet. Unfortunately, that didn't get Logan any closer to finding the killer, and unless it did, all of this information was for naught. "You're lucky, Jack."

Ruby put up a hand, swearing on an invisible Bible. Then he put the hand to his heart. "You don't have to tell me. I thought maybe my name was an omen, you know, that maybe the guy was going to stick the gun in my gut and pull the trigger—like the real Jack Ruby did. But the good Lord was looking out for me that night. That was Jesus there who made the man turn and walk away, and he was telling me to go and sin no more. And I haven't. I've sworn off them for good. No more. Not even one. It was a sign, it was. A sign from God. I believe the Lord saved me and is telling me to do the right thing. That's why I'm here, to do the right thing. I'm doing the right thing in telling you, right?"

"You're doing the right thing. But what made you come forward now instead of when it happened?" Logan asked.

Ruby sat back and let his gaze roam the table before fixing it back on Logan. "Well, it's like I said. I was pretty scared, and well, having a family and all, but then... well... then I saw him again."

42

~

DANA STARTED WITH the most recent news articles and worked backward using a combination of different search engines that included the words "Meyers," "Senator," and "Elizabeth Adams." She had no trouble finding articles in the *Post-Intelligencer* and *Seattle Times* archives—the couple had become Seattle's darlings, and with Meyers's announcement that he intended to run for president, he had been in the news even more than usual. The public, it seemed, could not get enough of the attractive couple. Local and national papers printed an array of articles that ranged from Meyers's bold ideas on domestic economic policies and foreign affairs to the types of food he and his wife preferred. When the *Times* ran an article detailing the color schemes Elizabeth Meyers had chosen to decorate their home in the Highlands—an $18 million gated compound—there was a run on the wallpaper patterns and paint selections.

With long dark hair and an olive complexion, Elizabeth

Meyers contrasted sharply with her husband's beach-boy good looks. The articles described her as shy and demure in public, which also contrasted with his charismatic charm. It was no wonder she evoked memories in both appearance and demeanor to a young Jacqueline Kennedy, and the fact that she was just thirty-five encouraged the comparisons. Dana realized that Elizabeth, maybe even more than her husband, was the reason why the national publications had dubbed the campaign, "A Return to Camelot."

Dana wasn't sure what exactly she was searching for in the articles, but William Welles's description of the Elizabeth Meyers he had met continued to resonate. She suspected somewhere in the articles there was a clue to her brother's death that would lead to the man who had him killed. She made notes on a yellow legal pad, trying to find some connection, some common theme, but at the moment saw none. Saturday night Meyers and his wife would kick off his fund-raising campaign at a five-thousand-dollar-per-plate dinner at the Fairmont Olympic Hotel in downtown Seattle, but it had already been a busy week. He had campaigned in California, Oregon, and Arizona before returning to Seattle to dedicate a youth sports field that would bear his family's name. At each event, faithfully at his side, stood his wife.

The doorbell rang. It sounded like the outdoor wind chimes. Dana recalled that Logan had sent a police officer to watch the house. She walked across a suspended bridge—which shook like her office floor when Marvin Crocket roamed the hallways—and down the spiral staircase to the entryway. The waterfall cascaded into the pond, and she saw the flick of a red-orange tail of a carp. In the entry stood something much uglier and predatory.

43

JACK RUBY HAD perspired through his blue cotton dress shirt, and all the ice water in the pitcher on the table was not going to cool him down. He'd stained the collar, underarms, and sleeves. Like a leaky faucet, great globules of perspiration formed on his forehead as quickly as he wiped it with his handkerchief. Logan feared they'd have to wrap the overweight man in cold damp towels, to keep him hydrated, the way they wrapped whales that beached themselves.

It wasn't the temperature that was making Ruby sweat. The room in the Seattle Police Department's renovated downtown headquarters on Fifth Avenue was air-conditioned. It was the man's nerves. Ruby wanted to do the right thing. He just didn't want anyone to know he was doing the right thing. He apparently had convinced himself, or really wanted to believe that he could profess his sins and leave the booth as if stepping from a church confessional, completely absolved, free to go and sin no more, anonymous except in the eyes of God. Instead, he was sitting in a stiff wooden chair, fidgeting with a ball-point pen and sweating buckets.

Logan paced an area to Ruby's right, waiting while two uniformed officers argued about the various hookups between the television and the VCR. There was a lively discussion regarding the definition of the terms "input" and "output" and whether they referred to the cable to the VCR or the cable to the television. As the discussion lingered, Logan tried to calm Ruby with casual conversation, but he'd barely spoken a word since Logan slid from the booth at McCormick's and told Ruby they were taking a ride together. On one level, Logan felt sorry for the man. He didn't view Ruby as a hypocrite, as some might. He saw him as a God-fearing family man 95 percent of the time and a sinner the other 5 percent. It was the other 5 percent that usually got people in trouble. That was universal. The 5 percent was when people succumbed to human weakness or did something plain stupid. The 5 percent had put Jack Ruby in contact with a prostitute and the Emerald Inn. It should have gotten him killed. Unfortunately, in an investigation with little for Logan to hang his hat on, he couldn't pardon the man. Ruby was the stroke of luck he needed—what every investigation eventually needed. To Logan, Ruby had been in the right place at the right time, no less a gift from the same God whose benevolence Ruby now undoubtedly sat questioning.

A uniformed officer knocked on the door and handed Logan three VCR tapes. "These are the newscasts for the major networks the past three nights. For what it's worth, Giacoletti says he remembers the story this guy's talking about and thought it was on a couple nights ago.

Said he always watches CBS because they have the better newscasters. He thinks the story came on right before the sports."

Logan flipped through the tapes to the one marked CBS. "Great. Now all I need to do is find someone with an IQ high enough to figure out how to work the damn VCR."

DANA CONTEMPLATED RUNNING but fought against that instinct. She couldn't run—not with her ribs pounding a steady ache from no more physical effort than taking a breath. The man standing on Michael Logan's entry would catch her before she reached the living room. And running would only tip him off that Dana knew he was not Detective Daniel Holmes. Logan had also told her the man who'd killed Laurence King was an excellent shot. He'd likely pick Dana off before she made it to the stairs. Her one chance was to remain calm and to remember that she possessed the one thing the man wanted—the earring. He wouldn't kill her until he had it. And that gave Dana a chance.

"Ms. Hill, I'm Detective Holmes. We met Saturday at your brother's. The door was unlocked."

She did her best to force a smile. "Detective Holmes. Of course. I'm sorry. You surprised me. I was wondering how I recognized you."

He pointed to the bandage on her forehead. "You appear to have been hurt."

"Just a bump on the head from an accident."

"I'm sorry to hear that."

"What can I do for you?"

"Detective Logan asked that I stop by and make sure you're doing all right."

Dana looked past him to the dark blue American-made vehicle. "Yes, he indicated there would be an officer here at any moment. Thank you, but I'm fine. There's no need to trouble yourself."

"No trouble. I live out in this direction. I told Mike I'd be happy to come and get you."

"Get me?" She tried to disguise the tension in her voice.

"Mike would like you to come with me."

"Mike asked me to wait here."

The man shrugged. "Change of plans, I guess." He looked up at the sky. "You might want to bring a coat. The weather has turned. Forecast indicates a storm is moving in."

Dark clouds had spread across the sky like a pool of spilled ink. Dana stepped back from the entry toward the staircase. "All right. Just let me get my coat—"

The man stepped in. "Beautiful place Mike has here. It's really something to behold." He looked at Dana with hollow dark eyes. His grin brought the image of a jack-o'-lantern. "Oh, and Mike said something about bringing an earring with you. He said you'd know what he was talking about."

LOGAN HELD THE remote control, fast-forwarding through a story about a fire in Yellowstone National Park. Halfway through the first tape, Jack Ruby looked like a man with a heart condition waiting for a T-bone steak to hit the table—eager for the taste but nervous about what it could do to him. The tape hummed forward, the news-casters' stuttered movements making them look like people in an old newsreel.

Ruby finally spoke. "You understand why this could be so embarrassing. Something like this, well, it's bound to generate a lot of publicity, and my three girls—"

"Keep watching, Jack." Logan pointed to the television. "I'll do everything possible to protect your identity and your family."

"I'll be kicked off the PTA board for sure, and I could never show my face in church again." Ruby looked up at him like a bassett hound, jowls sagging, eyes forlorn.

"Look on the bright side. You could very well be dead. And if not this time, maybe the next. Prostitutes aren't the most upstanding citizens, and that motel has a history of violence." Ruby grimaced as if in pain. To have escaped with his life didn't appear to be much consolation to him. When the broadcast went to a commercial break, Logan handed Ruby the remote control. "If you see something familiar, pause it. I'm going to make a telephone call."

"Do you think this guy could really work for Senator Meyers?"

Logan pulled open the door and unsnapped his cell phone from his belt. "You sure about what you saw?"

Ruby nodded. "I'm sure. Like I said, I won't forget that face for as long as I live."

Logan pointed at the VCR. "You'll let me know." He turned to leave, already punching in the number to his home.

"That's it," Ruby shouted. His thick fingers fumbled with the keypad of the remote control. The tape continued to spin forward. "Dammit. I can't stop it."

Logan retrieved the remote and pressed the play button. The newscasters' movements slowed from cartoon-character speed to normal.

"Back it up," Ruby said, eyes fixed on the screen.

Logan hit rewind, and together they watched Robert Meyers walk backward up steps into a building. Then the television cut back to the news studio. Logan hit play, and Meyers walked back down the steps, his wife just behind him. The camera moved in for a close-up. Meyers waved with both hands over his head to a group of enthusiastic supporters carrying signs that read MEYERS FOR PRESIDENT.

"This is it," Ruby whispered. He slid to the edge of his chair. The back legs lifted off the linoleum, the front legs bearing the brunt of his weight. "Not yet. Not yet. There!" He lunged forward. The chair slipped out from under him, and he fell as if plunging down a slide, his backside landing hard on the floor. He teetered over, rolling to his knees. "That's him." He pointed at the screen, his finger touching the glass. "That's the guy."

DANA WALKED BACK up the stairs to the kitchen. "Let me get my purse," she said. "I'll just be a minute."

Her purse remained on the unfinished counter, the plywood covered with waterproof paper and chicken wire, the edges framed with metal strips that extended an inch above the counter. Logan had also left his tools there: tin snips, a hacksaw and hammer, and an assortment of screwdrivers, tile-cutting pliers, and a small crowbar.

Because the house was open, with high-pitched ceilings, Dana heard the man walking below her. She yelled over her shoulder, "Here it is." She picked up the purse. "Give me a moment to use the bathroom."

The telephone on the counter rang. When she answered it, Logan didn't bother to say hello. "We have him. I think we have him."

"No, I'm sorry. He's not home right now." Dana tried to maintain a flat, even tone despite her anxiety.

"What? Dana? The man I met, he's legitimate. He was in the motel the night Laurence King was killed. He can identify the kill—"

"No, but I would be happy to take a message for him." She looked over her shoulder.

Logan paused, but for only a second. "Dana? Are you all right? What's wrong?"

"Yes. I'm hoping he'll be home any minute."

"Someone is there," he said.

"Absolutely."

"Is it the same man who came to your brother's home?"

"Yes."

"Is the police officer there?" he asked quickly.

"No. I'm a friend of Detective Logan."

Now she heard the panic in his voice. "Can you get to my bedroom? I keep a gun in the nightstand. You have to flip off the safety."

"Maybe, but that could be difficult. A Detective Holmes is here, however. He's taking me to meet Mike. I could deliver—" Before she could finish, she heard a click.

Then the line went dead.

44

~

Do your best to stall. Do not get in a car with him. Dana?"

Logan looked at his phone. The call had ended. "Shit." He rushed back into the room where Ruby sat waiting to sign a sworn statement, and grabbed his coat from the back of a chair. "You're free to go."

"But—"

Logan rushed down the hallway, his pace quickening to a dead run, people getting out of his way. He pushed the speed dial on his phone as he slowed to take an interior stairwell to the underground garage. "Carole," he shouted into the phone. "Where's that patrol car you sent to my house? Why not? Have you heard from him?" Logan pushed through a heavy security door into the garage. "Then get ahold of the local police in Issaquah and the fire department. Tell them you have an emergency. I want any cars in the area, fire, ambulance, whatever you can get."

He paused to field her question. "My house! Send them to my house!"

DANA THREW HER purse into the refrigerator, the only place she could think to hide it, but as she looked around the kitchen, she was struck by a sudden, seemingly incomprehensible, and incongruous memory. In her mind, she saw William Welles sitting calmly in his rocking chair, fingering the tiny earring with his rough fingertips.

"Why design it at all?" Dana had asked him. *"Why would you create a piece like that, a piece that represents sorrow and pain?"*

"Because to not create it would have made me just as blind. To see the world and those who live in it is to see the good as well as the evil. We cannot see beauty if we do not see what is ugly. We cannot feel joy if we do not feel pain. We cannot smile if we cannot cry."

"But that wasn't the only reason, was it?" she had asked. *"That wall you spoke of. It was to protect her, wasn't it?"*

"Can you believe such a thing?"

She opened the refrigerator, removed the earring from her purse, and slid it in her bra. Then she reached back into her purse until she felt a cylindrical dispenser and shoved it beneath her bra on the other side. She closed the fridge and walked back to the staircase, peering over the railing. She saw no sign of the man. She slapped at the light switch, turning off the lights. With the dark clouds, the ambient lighting paled to a dusk gray. Every movement she made echoed up to the cathedral ceiling. The man would hear every step she took. She needed to get to the gun in Logan's bedroom, but his loft was on the other side of the house, across three bridges. And even if she was able to retrieve it, she had never fired a gun in her life. She had no idea what Logan had meant about a "safety." Besides, if the man had been listening to their conversation, he'd also know where she was going.

She started across the suspended bridge connecting the kitchen to the office loft, felt it vibrate, and was again struck by an unmistakable image. She closed her eyes, allowing herself to see it vividly. Then she opened them and turned back to reconsider the tools on the kitchen counter.

THERE WAS NO easy way to get home, not with a bridge to cross the lake and traffic on I-90 already heavy with the afternoon commute that wouldn't let up until Logan took the exit for Cougar Mountain. He drove with one hand on the wheel, weaving in and out of traffic. With his free hand, he continued to punch the recall button on his telephone. He asked Carole for an update on the local police and fire department's progress getting to his home.

"You have one fire truck on the way. No police."

"No police?" he nearly screamed into the phone. "Why the hell not?"

"Issaquah has an armed robbery in progress at a Bartell drugstore. The man is threatening to kill thirty hostages. All rescue and trained medical personnel are either there or on their way there."

He shut off the phone and dropped it on the passenger seat. The speedometer on the Austin Healey looked like a windshield wiper—accelerating one moment, downshifting and braking the next. He shot through the Mercer Island Tunnel, the yellow lights ticking past him at eye level. When the car emerged from the tunnel, Logan was still at least fifteen minutes away.

DANA STRUGGLED TO control her breathing. Waves of nausea swept over her. She went over her plan again while continuing to listen for sounds below. The lofts were interconnected in a circular manner. The man could come from only one of two directions, and it was her intent to limit him to the spiral staircase.

She picked up the remote control to the stereo and started back across the bridge. Eight feet long, it was suspended by spring-loaded clips resembling robotic clamps that gripped metal poles on each side. She aimed the remote at the stereo in Logan's den and pressed the power button. The front of the stereo burst to life in pulsating color. Guitars exploded from speakers throughout the house like the din of a shotgun blast echoing in a metal drum. An AC/DC CD had been loaded to play. As the singer's voice screeched throughout the house, Dana dropped the remote control in the sink. Then she gathered herself, exhaled, and started down the spiral staircase. The man appeared from the shadows at the base of the stairs. Dana turned and started back up, but her injuries slowed her to an awkward hobble, and her ribs ached with each sudden movement. The staircase shook below her; the man was climbing quickly. At the top step, she felt his hand grip her ankle. She held the railing and kicked at him with her other foot, managing to pull free. Stumbling forward, off balance, she fell against the unfinished counter. The metal strip dug into the bruised flesh over her ribs, and the pain took the last of the strength from her legs. She collapsed to her knees.

Just as quickly, the man was on her.

He turned her over, sitting on her, one hand on her throat, cutting off the flow of oxygen. The room spun. The images blurred. He leaned down, screaming over the clatter of the stereo, "Where's the earring?"

"Don't have it." She spit her words through clenched teeth. The pain made her more angry than scared. "Logan took it with him."

The man's eyes widened, indicating he hadn't considered that possibility. Then he pulled her to her feet and pressed the barrel of a gun against the bandage on her forehead. "The earring, or you die here."

LOGAN DOWNSHIFTED, TAKING the turns of Cougar Mountain Road at a ridiculous speed. Thunder rumbled and shook the mountain. Dark clouds had descended upon the top, swirling into a funnel cloud and turning the sky and woods dark. Then the clouds opened, releasing a torrent of water and driving wind. Logan fought the curves in the road, the tires of the Austin Healey struggling against centrifugal force. The cell phone on the passenger seat rang. Logan flipped it open. "Carole? Hang on."

He downshifted, slowing to make the turn onto the dirt road. The back tires spun in the loose gravel, the car nearly fishtailing out of control. Logan corrected and punched the gas, and the sports car shot forward around a blind turn. The red brake lights of the fire engine were suddenly windshield-high, flashing. Logan slammed on the brake pedal, the car skidding to a stop inches behind the truck.

"The fire truck cannot get up the road," Carole was yelling. "It can't make the turns. They say there is no place to turn around."

45

THE MAN SHOVED her against the refrigerator. Pain
shot through her. He tightened his grip around her
throat. With his other hand, he forced the barrel of the
gun against her forehead. "The earring, and I just might
let you live."

Rain battered the cathedral windows.

Dana grunted at the man through clenched teeth, "I
told you, Logan has it."

He jammed the side of her face against the refrigerator and pushed the gun in her cheek. She felt it pressing against her molars. "Then there's no reason to let you
live."

He pulled back the hammer on the gun and leaned
forward.

She resisted, stalling. He reached behind him, placed
the gun on the counter, and picked up the tin shears. Then
he grabbed her hand, tugging at her index finger, forc-
ing it open, and pinched it between the blades at the first

knuckle. Her skin tore, blood trickling down the back of her hand. She could feel the blade against the bone.

"No," she screamed, fear overcoming her judgment. "I hid it."

LOGAN JUMPED FROM the car, slipping in the mud as he ran to the cab of the fire truck. He leaped onto the running board, holding up his badge, and shouted at the driver over the rush of wind and rain, "Go forward! Go forward!"

The driver shook his head, yelling back at him. "Can't do it. It won't make it around that last turn. We've been trying for ten minutes. We need a smaller vehicle, but if this storm doesn't pass, nothing is going to get up here. Road will be too wet. I've never seen a cloud like that on this mountain."

Logan had, just once before, and the storm it brought had been monumental. He slapped the side of the fire engine in frustration. The narrow road did not allow the Austin Healey enough room to pass, and to back down the road and wait for the fire engine's slow descent would take too much time. Sheets of water poured down on him. He looked up at the steep hillside into which the road had been cut. He estimated it was fifteen to twenty-five feet of dense, steep terrain to the top. In this weather, it would be like climbing a slide in his socks. Lightning crackled overhead. Whether it brought the idea or not, Logan was struck by a thought.

"How high can you get those ladders on the back of the truck?" he asked.

THE EARRING, MS. HILL, or I'll take them off one knuckle at a time."

Blood dripped down her wrist. "All right. All right."

"Where is it?"

She looked down at her blouse, torn at the buttons. The man released her finger and dropped the snips. When he reached for her breast she covered her chest with her hands and burst at him in anger and rage, "Don't you touch me! Don't you even think about touching me!"

His body pressed hard against hers. "Oh, I've thought about it." His breath had a bitter, acrid smell. "I've thought about it a lot. I like the fight. I like the struggle." He licked at her cheek. Then he pulled back. "Get it."

Dana seethed and reached into her bra. AC/DC continued to shout at them. "Here." She depressed the button on the cylindrical tube, sending a stream of Mace into the man's eyes. He fell backward, growling, pawing at his face. Dana shoved him into the counter. She turned and started across the suspended bridge, using the railings on either side like crutches, each step bringing agony. It was all she could do to put one foot in front of the other. When she reached the opposite side she collapsed, her back against the wall, facing the bridge. The storm had pulled a black curtain across the cathedral windows, but in the darkness, she saw the man pulling himself to his feet, wiping at his eyes. Then he stumbled forward, hands in front of him, feeling his way blindly to the bridge.

"Come on," Dana said to herself. "Come on, you son of a bitch."

LOGAN STOOD ON the third rung from the top of the ladder as it rose. The ladder operator hugged the hill as close as he could, but because it sloped away, the top of the ladder was four to six feet from the ridge. Logan gestured to move the ladder closer. The man signaled back that it was as close as he could get it. Logan looked down. Lower portions of the ladder were already embedded in the dirt and rock. This was as high as the elevator would take him.

He took a breath, gripped the top rung with both hands, and cautiously stepped up, balancing like a swimmer on a platform, then leaped for the ridge. He landed just short of the top, gripped the roots of a bush with his hands to keep from plunging down the side, and kicked at the hillside in search of a toehold. It sent a small avalanche clattering on top of the fire engine. He pulled himself to the top, stumbled from his knees to his feet, and sprinted across the field toward the grove of trees surrounding his house. Though he was in good shape and worked out regularly, he could not control his breathing. He labored to catch his breath, adrenaline pushing him to an unbalanced speed. He swiped at branches, ducking and weaving between the trees, picking his footing where he could. He emerged from the grove twenty yards from the front of the house. The interior was dark. He saw no lights. Around him, the storm continued to overpower other sounds—the chimes in the trees were spinning and twirling mutely.

He shielded his eyes from the rain and saw a shadow inside the darkened panes of glass: someone standing on one of the suspended bridges.

∽

THE MAN STEPPED onto the bridge, gripping the railing, continuing to wipe his eyes.

"Come on," Dana whispered. She fought through the waves of nausea brought on by the pain. "Come on."

The man took several uncertain steps. Then he stopped. He looked back in the direction he'd come, and for a fleeting moment, Dana thought he would turn back. But then he stepped forward again. Halfway across, he stopped again and brought a hand to his temple, as if struck by a thought or a sudden intense headache. He turned to the right, craning to see over the edge of the railing. The image was as clear to her as the one she had seen while standing in Logan's kitchen, and as vivid as when she'd first seen the unfinished sculpture on William Welles's counter.

The man now gripped the railing with both hands, as if fighting vertigo that made his legs unsteady. He whipped his head from side to side in confusion, but his feet remained riveted in place, unable or unwilling to move. He looked across the bridge to where Dana sat. In the darkness, she saw the reflection in his eyes—no longer as dark as mining shafts. They had burst to life, reflecting the flickering red and orange of an unseen fire. He aimed the gun. Dana summoned what strength remained and pressed down on the raised end of the levered crowbar she had wedged between the clasp and the metal pole holding the bridge aloft.

The man teetered as if the bridge had swayed beneath his feet. The gun tumbled over the side. Lightning crackled, sending an electric blue pulse throughout the room. Thunder clattered and boomed.

The crowbar teetered on the block of wood stubbornly. Dana felt the strength in her arms waning. The man lurched forward, nearing the edge. She applied all her weight, her arms shaking. The crowbar gave way, the latch snapping like a tree limb, and the metal claws opened, releasing their grip.

"Go to hell," she said.

46

～

LOGAN FLUNG OPEN the front door, shouting her name, his voice suffocated by the din of the music and the rattle and pounding of the storm. He climbed the spiral staircase two steps at a time, saw blood on the kitchen floor, and stepped to the edge where the footbridge had once been but where there was now a twenty foot crevasse. On the other side, Dana sat slumped against the wall, unresponsive. He rushed around the house in the opposite direction, circumnavigating the bridges, feeling them bounce beneath his weight. He shut off the stereo, then knelt beside her. "Dana, are you okay? Can you hear me?"

Her eyes were blank and her skin cold to the touch. Fearing she was slipping into shock, he hurried to his room and pulled a quilt off the bed. Wrapping her in it, he carried her down the stairs. He laid her on the couch in the living room and started a fire in the fireplace. Then he hurried back to the kitchen and made a cup of tea, warming the water in the microwave as his mind continued to relive that moment when he had burst through the front door and saw the bridge give way. The man had fallen as if a trapdoor had opened beneath him, plunging feet first and landing on the glass table in an explosion of lightning, thunder, and shattering glass. Still alive, he had managed to lift himself to his knees, bloodied, and looked up as if in one final plea for mercy. The suspended bridge hanging above him swung precariously by one end. Then Logan watched its weight pull it from its remaining bracket and it fell like a slab of lead from the heavens, striking the man with an immense and hideous force.

The bell of the microwave pushed the vision from Logan's head. He removed the mug and added the bag of tea to the hot water as he made his way back down the stairs. He sat beside her on the couch and lifted the cup to her lips. She sipped it gently. Then she leaned sideways, bracing her head against his shoulder, and they sat in silence listening to the storm.

A POLICE CAR and Carole Nuchitelli's Land Rover were parked in the circular drive in front of Logan's house. The afternoon storm had passed, the dark clouds giving way to a persistent high gray and patches of blue. Logan stood at the front door, hearing birds and the chimes in the trees. The standoff at the Bartell drugstore had also kept away the reporters, and for that he was grateful. He was finishing his conversation with Nuchitelli and another detective from the North Precinct, James Fick, a former lineman at the University of Oregon who still maintained much of his playing-day build.

Logan said to Fick, "What went out over the radio? What does the press know?"

"Nothing, at the moment," Fick answered. "Everybody's dealing with the aftermath at Bartell's. They've had live coverage for three hours now. Any reporters not at the scene are at their desks trying to dig up information on the gunman and his hostages. You're all alone out here."

Logan nodded. "I need you to delay everything. I don't want anything reported in the newspapers. If any reporters call to question it, tell them there was a small fire, but the trucks never made it up because of the condition of the road. The storm extinguished the fire. Can we do that?"

Fick nodded. They had bagged the gunman's body and placed him in the back of Nuchitelli's Land Rover. Logan went on, "Nooch, bury the body in the reefer for a day or two until I can figure out what's going on here. If anyone, and I mean anyone, calls about it, play dumb. I don't know the full extent of what I'm dealing with yet."

Nuchitelli shrugged. "No real doubt what killed him anyway, is there? Who is he?"

"Trust me. This time you really do want him to remain anonymous." She smiled at him. "I won't forget it," he said.

Nuchitelli looked past him to where Dana sat on the couch, the comforter still wrapped around her. Then she and Fick left.

Logan shut the door behind them and walked back inside. He stood on the top step of the sunken living room with his hands in his pockets. Dana sat examining her bandaged hand.

"How's the finger?"

She looked up at him. "It's okay."

"How about the rest of you?"

"Better."

"Do you want some more tea?"

She shook her head. Then she looked at the photograph in the picture frame. "How long after you were married did you know?"

Logan stepped down. "About the muscular dystrophy? We knew in college. We were high school sweethearts. Sarah was diagnosed at eighteen. Some relatives on her mother's side apparently had it. She died at thirty-six. I'm grateful for those eighteen years."

"You knew she had the disease, but you married her anyway?"

The question came out of the blue but did not catch Logan totally off guard. He had been asked before. Even his parents had been against the wedding. They said he'd spend the best years of his life caring for an invalid. He sat in a chair across from Dana, elbows resting on his thighs. "I loved her."

"But you knew she would be crippled. That she was going to die."

He shrugged. "It didn't change how I felt about her. I didn't fall in love with her just because of how she looked, although to me she was the most beautiful woman in the world. I fell in love with her because of how she made me feel. That didn't change when she was confined to a wheelchair. She was still beautiful. She still made me feel special."

Dana looked up at the bridges. "You knew she couldn't have lived here, with the lofts and staircases and everything. She had to have known that, too."

He nodded. "I'm sure she did."

She took the quilt off. Her blouse was ripped and torn, her jeans spotted with blood. "If I keep this up, I'm not going to have any clothes left."

"You and Sarah are about the same size," he said. "There are some clothes left in the closet in the bedroom." Dana shook her head. He said, "Please. They've been in there for five years. Sarah was a very giving person. She would want you to get out of that blouse. A needle and thread is not going to salvage it." He started up the stairs. "I'm afraid it will have to be jeans and baggy shirts. Sarah wasn't much of a clotheshorse."

Dana smiled. "I think we would have gotten along just fine, your wife and I."

He stopped on the stairs and looked down at her. "I think you're right."

47

〜

T HE FLOOR-TO-CEILING bulletproof windows in
Robert Meyers's office offered a sweeping view of
the slate-gray waters of Puget Sound. The ferry from
Seattle to Victoria, British Columbia, skidded past Bainbridge Island like a water bug, leaving behind a V-shaped
wake amid several white triangles—sailboats flicking
back and forth. In the distance, a freighter carried stacks
of colorful cargo containers three stories tall south, in the
direction of the port of Seattle. The Olympic Mountains,
still sprinkled with winter snow, framed the horizon.

Seattle was no longer the hidden gem Meyers's great-
grandfather had discovered. Much to the expressed dis-
pleasure of natives, the rest of the country had discovered
the Emerald City. Weyerhaeuser and Boeing remained
significant players in the region and on the national stage.
Like grandfathers at the family reunion, they continued
to stand for hard work, persistence, and longevity. But
it had been the Internet and Microsoft, with Bill Gates's

and Paul Allen's billions, and the high-tech craze in general that made millionaires overnight and injected the populace with the entrepreneurial spirit that anything was possible. It had transformed Seattle like the gold rush of the 1840s had transformed California, bringing not just people in search of a quick fortune but an entire cottage industry of companies to support it. They came to the Pacific Northwest for the opportunity to get rich quick, then stayed for the affordable housing and the wholesome lifestyle that revolved around the outdoors.

The Internet, cell phones, and mobile e-mail had also made the world smaller. Where a person lived was no longer a primary factor in whether he could win a national election. A state far removed from the national political scene producing a president was no longer a pipe dream. Clinton came out of Arkansas, Jimmy Carter out of Georgia. Both were states that did not possess an avalanche of electoral votes. Robert Meyers sensed the time was ripe for a president from the Northwest. Two-term Republican president Charles Monroe would step down without much to show for his eight years in office, and the Republicans had been unable to drum up anyone to excite or even interest the American public. The powers in the Democratic Party had also been intent on marching out the same old tired names. They had implored Meyers to wait his turn, offering him positions of power and prestige in the Senate to appease him. They hinted that he was too young and too inexperienced. They said losing would tarnish him for future campaigns. Meyers, however, remained defiant. He had no intention of losing. He responded that Americans wanted an America that was once again bold and innovative, and the most recent polls, the results of which sat on his desk, suggested he was right. In the week since he had announced his candidacy, the percentage of Democrats indicating they would vote for him had jumped to 38 percent. He was confident that number would increase as his campaign reached full swing.

But he had always been confident, it was another quality his father had instilled. When he inherited the family compound, he added a steel and concrete structure connected to the house by a seventy-foot sandstone-covered colonnade that the newspapers referred to as the West Coast West Wing. It included his office, offices for seven assistants, secretarial stations, a conference room capable of seating fifty, a movie theater/media center, and a ballroom and dining room for entertaining nearly four hundred guests. Inside the complex, Meyers's and his wife's whereabouts were monitored from a control center in the basement that used a state-of-the-art security system to deploy a team of security personnel, most former Army Rangers or Navy SEALs. Getting accustomed to the Secret Service detail that, upon his election, would follow them the rest of their lives would not be a problem.

Casually dressed in a cashmere sweater, jeans, and penny loafers, Meyers sat at a desk hand-crafted from the timbers of a ship abandoned in arctic waters. When it was found by American whalers a century after it disappeared, attempts to raise the ship had been unsuccessful, but they had managed to salvage the wood. The desk and other ornate pieces in Meyers's office had been crafted from it.

Meyers looked up from the speech he would give to his supporters at the Fairmont Olympic Hotel Saturday night and reconfirmed the time by the clock on the mantel. He reached for the telephone and pressed a preprogrammed button. "Has Mr. Boutaire arrived yet?"

The shift leader of his security staff advised that Peter Boutaire had not reported in, and attempts to reach him on his secure cellular phone had also been unsuccessful.

It was not like Boutaire to be out of touch. "Send someone to check his apartment. When he arrives, have him report to me immediately."

Meyers hung up and returned his attention to the speech, but he found himself reading and rereading the opening sentence.

48

~

SHE TOOK A HOT shower, allowing the water and steam to soothe her aches and pains. She also relented and took one of her painkillers. It and the water helped to take the edge off the hurt. As she stepped from the shower, the bathroom mirror provided a full assessment of her newest bumps and bruises, cuts and scrapes. It wasn't pretty.

Dana slipped gently into the clothes Logan had provided for her. Sarah Logan had been an inch or two taller and maybe a few pounds heavier before her illness left her gaunt and weak. The extra inches made it easier for Dana to slip the pants and shirt over her assortment of bandages and bruises. With some difficulty, she rolled up the pants and pulled on socks and her own tennis shoes.

With the suspended bridge out, she had to walk around the perimeter of the house and enter the kitchen from the opposite side. Logan had his back to her; he was slicing fruit on a wooden block to accompany two turkey sandwiches and glasses of milk. He said, "I don't care if you're not hungry. The hospital released you to my care, and you are going to need—"

Dana was tying her hair in a ponytail when she realized Logan had stopped talking and was staring at her. "I'm sorry," she said, feeling uncomfortable in the clothes. "Maybe I should put on something else."

"No. No, it's okay." Logan put down the knife and wiped his hands on a white towel. "I just haven't seen those clothes in a while. It's time they were worn again. I've been planning to take them to Goodwill. Are you hungry?" He finished cutting the apple and scooped the slices into a bowl with slices of banana and orange.

"Starving."

"Good. Sit down. I'll fill you in on what I've found out."

She took a seat at the pine table. In front of her, Logan set one of the sandwiches, the bowl of fruit, and a glass of milk. He stood taking a bite of the second sandwich. "The man's name is Peter Boutaire. He was a marine, so his background check was relatively straightforward. He was forty-one, single, never married. Born and raised here in the Northwest. He and Meyers grew up together."

Dana stopped chewing.

"Boutaire joined the military shortly after dropping out of high school—a female student accused him of rape. The charges were eventually dropped, and the story died. Because the woman was underage, everything was sealed. Boutaire served in Desert Storm and Desert Fox and was part of a United States advance force in Yugoslavia. After the marines, he returned to Seattle and briefly joined the police force but didn't make it out of the academy. Meyers hired him to run his security staff. The man I met at McCormick's was in the motel the night Laurence

King was killed. Classic case of being in the wrong place doing the wrong thing at the wrong time, but he got a good look at Boutaire—one I don't think he'll ever forget. A few nights later, he was watching the news and just about had a coronary when he saw Boutaire standing in a crowd at Meyers's side. Let's just say it jump-started his conscience. He identified Boutaire from videotaped newscasts."

Dana shook her head. "What do we do now? Boutaire's dead."

"Yes, but we have a guy who will swear Boutaire killed King, and Boutaire is closely connected to Robert Meyers. That should rock Meyers's neat little world."

"I don't want to rock Robert Meyers's world. That's a false justice. I want him convicted for killing my brother."

Logan put down his sandwich. "I have an address for Boutaire—an apartment in Belltown. I tend to believe, given his relationship to Meyers, that he was acting alone and not part of a group of renegade security guards, but I don't know that. I've asked the medical examiner to keep the death quiet. It may give us some time to find out more before Meyers has a chance to cover Boutaire's tracks."

"Don't you need a warrant for that?" she asked.

He shrugged. "That would mean considerable paperwork and rousting a judge from bed to tell me I don't have enough probable cause." He took another bite of his sandwich. "Besides, we're just going to look. You feel up to taking a drive?"

"No. But if we wait until I do, the whole place will be as clean as the cabin in Roslyn."

"That's what I'm afraid of."

◦◦◦

Peter Boutaire's apartment was in a secure building on Second Street in Seattle's Belltown. Just north
of the financial district, Belltown had been cleaned up
considerably over the past five years. Developers had
built chic condominiums with views of Puget Sound,
new apartment complexes, and upscale restaurants. The
renovation had not, however, been able to remove all of
the rough elements. A few corner liquor stores and bars
remained. So did drug dealers and Seattle's many homeless, protected by a liberal King County Code that did not
include laws against vagrancy.

A guard sat at a security console in a white-tiled lobby
with potted ferns and a glass-bead chandelier. The guard
directed Logan and Dana to the manager, a thin, prema-
turely gray man who answered the door of his apartment
dressed in a purple University of Washington sweatshirt,
pajama bottoms, and slippers.

"Never had a bit of trouble out of him." The manager
spoke with a hint of a Louisiana accent as he led them
down a hall lit by candle wall sconces. "Is he in some
kind of trouble?"

Logan nodded to Dana. "His sister is worried about
him. He hasn't called in a couple of days. We just want to
take a look."

The manager turned to Dana as they stepped onto the
elevator. "I hope he's all right."

"What's an apartment here run?" Logan asked.

"Twelve hundred dollars and up, depending on the
view. The apartments on the top floors facing west go for
twenty-four hundred."

They stepped from the elevator onto the twelfth floor, to the apartment second on the left. The manager used a master key, and they walked into a sterile marbled hallway that led to a living room with a white carpet and little else. Furniture consisted of a straight-back couch and a table. There were no pictures on the walls or on the mantel over the fireplace. The built-in bookshelves were empty. There was no television or stereo. In the attached dining room, a gold-plated chandelier hung suspended over an empty space reserved for a table. The appeal of the apartment was clearly the view. Sliding glass doors opened onto a balcony that looked out over Elliott Bay and the lights of homes on Bainbridge Island.

Logan turned to the manager. "How long did you say he lived here?"

The man seemed equally perplexed by the meager furnishings. "He signed the lease about a year ago. I guess he wasn't one for a lot of possessions." He directed the comment to Dana.

In the kitchen, the white tile counters were spotless, the oak cabinets empty. Logan wasted little time there. He moved down a hallway to a bathroom on the left. A closed door at the end of the hall was locked with a deadbolt. None of the other doors had one.

The manager shook his head when Logan inquired about a key. "He must have put that on himself."

Logan stepped back, braced his back against the wall on the opposite side of the hallway, raised his leg, and smashed his shoe against the door. It took three kicks to knock it in. "Bill him for that," he told the manager.

"I'm going to have to," the manager said.

The room looked like a command center for a war. Multiple computer screens and keyboards were aligned on long folding tables. Beneath the tables were hard drives and a mass of computer cables, printers, fax machines, at least two shredders, a laminating machine, and other equipment whose immediate function Logan could not determine. He turned to Dana. "I'll bet this explains Detective Dan Holmes's credentials and scrambled telephone number."

Maps and photographs marked with a red grease pen cluttered the walls. On the desk were multiple telephones and a cache of driver's licenses, credit cards, and passports, each bearing Boutaire's photograph but with different names.

When the manager whistled, Logan led him back out the door and down the hall to the front door. "You need to keep this quiet."

"You think he was doing something illegal?"

"His sister thinks he was working for the government," Logan said.

"You mean like CIA or something."

"She doesn't know." Logan hoped to scare the man into keeping quiet. "But I would be extremely careful about what you say to anyone. In fact, don't say anything at all. It could put this man's life in jeopardy."

The manager raised his hands. "Hey, no problem. I don't want any part of something like this."

"I'll drop off the key when we're finished."

Logan closed the front door and stepped back inside the bedroom. Dana was sifting through a stack of manila files, reading the names printed on the tabs and thumbing through their contents. The names were easily recognizable—senior executives for prominent businesses throughout the United States. Dana recognized a wealth of private information on the executives, as well as what was ordinarily privileged financial information on their companies.

"I guess we now know how Robert Meyers did so well in the stock market when everyone else was tanking," Dana said.

Logan shook his head. "He doesn't leave anything to chance, does he? J. Edgar Hoover would have been proud."

Dana shuffled through the files. A chill ran through her. "Logan."

Logan looked over her shoulder. Inside were several photographs of Dana getting out of her car in front of Kim's Jewelers, at the airport parking lot, at her house in Montlake, and walking from the offices of Strong & Thurmond. Her heart skipped a beat when she saw a photograph of her carrying Molly from day care.

"Jesus, he has everything here: my addresses, telephone numbers, bank accounts . . . my parents' house." She flipped through the file and pulled out a sheet of paper. "This is Molly's day care. He has the whole schedule. My God, this is an authorization slip allowing him to pick her up."

Logan calmed her. "He isn't going to use it now, Dana. She's safe."

"But what if there are others?"

"We'll take that file with us." He bent down and searched the other files in the boxes on the floor, ready to be carried out at a moment's notice. "That's odd." He picked out one file. "Why would he have a file for Robert

Meyers?" Dana looked at it. "It's empty," he said, opening it.

She took it from him, studying it more closely. Unlike the others, it had yellowed with age. The print on the tab, handwritten in ink, had also faded. When she compared it with the print on the tab of the file bearing her name, the writing was also different. She compared it to the other files and confirmed the same result. She handed the file to Logan while showing him the file in her hand. "This is Boutaire's handwriting. That isn't."

Logan took both samples and considered them. "So where did Boutaire get this one?"

"And what was in it?"

They continued to rummage through the files but found nothing to tie Peter Boutaire to Marshall Cole, Laurence King, or her brother. Dana scanned a cork bulletin board on the wall above the table. Punch pins held various scraps of paper and newspaper articles. She stopped on a handwritten note, a name above an address in Redmond, Washington. Dr. Frank Pilgrim. She was certain she had seen the name somewhere but couldn't immediately pull it from her memory.

"Let's go," Logan said. "We can tie Boutaire to King's killing. That should be enough to get me a search warrant to come back. I'll have the DA go in and get a warrant tomorrow morning. Then I'll have the crime lab gather all this stuff, and we can take a closer look at it in my office."

"There's got to be something here. Something we're not seeing."

"Maybe with fresh eyes," Logan suggested. "It's been a long day."

They rode the elevator to the first floor and started down the hallway toward the manager's residence. As they approached, Logan heard voices coming from inside the apartment. The door was open. He held out a hand to keep Dana back and carefully peered around the corner. The manager stood talking to two men in suits. "Just about twenty minutes ago," he was saying.

Logan grabbed Dana by the arm and led her back down the hall to a metal door beneath an exit sign. He pushed it open, and they descended a stairwell.

SHE SAT IN the passenger seat, mulling over the name on the sheet of paper pinned to the corkboard in Boutaire's apartment, using all of her normal methods to spur her memory. She tried to picture a face with the name but saw none. Then she tried to retrace her steps to determine where she might have heard or seen the name. That didn't work, either.

"You were at the cancer center," Logan said while checking the rearview mirror. "It's probably none of my business, but I saw the sign on the side of the building in one of the photographs."

"I have cancer," Dana said.

Logan turned to her. "I'm sorry. Is it bad?"

She smiled at the comment. "Is it ever good?"

"I meant—"

"It's all right." She took a moment, realizing she hadn't discussed the subject with anyone. "I found a lump in my breast. I have to go in and get it cut out. Then they'll be able to give me a better diagnosis."

"You've been dealing with all of this *and* with that?"

"It's been a hell of a couple of weeks." She checked her watch. She'd missed Molly's bedtime. "I need to get home to see my little girl. I need something to remind me there are still wonderful things in this world."

49

~

LOGAN PARKED IN the driveway, the headlights illuminating the black-and-white patrol car parked conspicuously. He let the engine idle, got out and went around, then opened the passenger-side door to offer Dana his hand. Even with his help, getting out of the car was an effort for her. Her aches and pains had settled into an uncomfortable tightness, as if her joints had frozen. She grimaced as she stood. The rains that had fallen intermittently throughout the day had dissipated, and the gray cloak had rolled back to reveal a cloudless night sky pocked with stars. On the drive to her parents' home, she and Logan had considered their options, which weren't many.

"I could drive up to his house and knock on his door," Logan said, continuing their conversation. "Boutaire worked for him. It certainly gives me a reason to speak to Meyers and rattle his cage."

She shook her head. "You don't rattle a man like Robert Meyers. He'd have the word 'attorney' out of his mouth before you reached the front door. You have Boutaire connected to King and maybe to Cole, but we can't place the earring with Meyers. We have no evidence that the earring even belongs to Elizabeth Meyers. At least not anything that could be used in court. We also can't prove that James and Elizabeth Meyers were having an affair, which means we can't prove a motive. It's circumstantial. And that won't get us far enough. I'm not interested in convicting a dead man. I want Meyers. His wife is the key. We have to find a way to reach her."

"That's not going to be easy. If we're right, Meyers will have her under heavy lock and key. Besides, even if we could convince her that Meyers killed your brother, that doesn't mean she'll be able to do anything about it, especially now that your brother is gone."

Dana wrapped her arms around herself, feeling cold. "Then we'll have to find some other way."

"That's going to be tough if we can't get her alone."

"I know." They stood in an uncomfortable silence. "Thanks," she said. Then Dana turned and started down the walk.

HER MOTHER CAME across the carpeted living room to the foyer as Dana closed the front door. The female police officer sat on a blue leather ottoman, sipping a cup of tea. A silver tray of Danish butter cookies and the teapot were within reach on the walnut coffee table.

"Dana, dear God," her mother said. She had not seen Dana since her battering—first the car explosion, then Boutaire's attack. "Are you all right? What happened to you?"

"I'm okay, Mom. It looks worse than it is." Dana looked around the room. "Is Molly in bed?"

Her mother nodded. "She just fell asleep. What's happening? Why are the police here?"

"Let's sit down. I'm sorry I didn't get here sooner to explain things."

"It has to do with your brother, doesn't it?"

Dana took a deep breath. "I think so."

Her mother put her hand to her mouth, a move Dana knew from experience would precede tears. She grabbed her mother's hands. "It's going to be all right, Mom. I'm going to handle this. I'm sorry if you've been scared, and I'm sorry I haven't had more time to explain things. I couldn't do it over the telephone, but I can do it now. We need to talk about a lot of things."

Both women recognized from Dana's tone that it would not be a casual conversation or even one limited to James's death. It was a talk they both knew was long overdue. The silence between them had dug a chasm that had continued to expand, pushing them further and further apart. It was time to fill it in. Things were not discussed in the Hill household. Things were ignored, buried, made light of, but never seriously discussed.

"Can we just sit down and talk?" Dana asked.

The female officer stood and approached from the living room. "I need to call in. May I use the telephone in your kitchen?"

"It's on the wall," Kathy said and started for the kitchen. "I'll find it."

Kathy turned back to Dana, hesitated, then moved through the living room to the glass sunroom that had been added on. The room was awash in white wicker furniture and plants—tulips, ferns, and azaleas. In the center of the room, perched on a bar in his cage, stood Keeker, her mother's pink and white cockatoo. The bird squawked as they entered. Kathy picked up a package of sunflower seeds and pistachio nuts and filled the small plastic tray inside the cage to quiet him. Keeker hopped from his perch to the tray's edge and proceeded to crack the seeds, spilling the empty shells through the bars onto the bleached hardwood floor.

Her mother sat on the wicker couch. On a side table, beneath the tapered glow of a lamp, rested a needlepoint in progress, the needle piercing the fabric at a 45-degree angle. Her mother's reading glasses rested atop a romance novel. Dana slumped into the cushions of the chair. The descent caused a pain in her side that registered in a grimace.

Her mother started from her seat. "You *are* hurt. Let me call Jack Porter."

Dana raised a hand. "I'm fine."

Her mother sat back down. There was an extended pause. Then she looked past Dana into the darkened yard. "I used to love to sit here and watch you and James playing out there in those trees. Do you remember when your father built your tree fort?"

"He bought it, Mom. He didn't build it."

Kathy rubbed an age spot on the back of her right hand with her left thumb. "You even slept out there a few times."

Dana shook her head. "We almost slept out there. Every time it got dark, we'd find some excuse to come running back inside." She laughed. "That final stretch across the lawn to the back door was the most terrifying patch of earth in the world to a seven-year-old kid." She looked at her mother. "But you were always there for us, waiting with hot chocolate and cookies. You were always there." She fought back tears.

Her mother picked up the needlepoint and began to work the needle. The product was in its early stages and as yet undefined. "Your father thought he was getting a little girl in pink and lace, but that wasn't you. He got a tomboy."

"How long did you know about Dad?" There had been years to come up with a way to preface the question, but Dana never had thought of one. Now she just asked it.

The needle stopped. Her mother's gaze found another spot on the floor. A grim expression creased her face. She bit at her bottom lip, also a habit. Keeker stopped cracking seeds and squawked.

"I'm not a little girl anymore. I know about Dad."

"I know. And you've grown up to be so beautiful." She paused. Then she began to stitch again. "From the start. I knew from the start."

"What happened?"

Her mother took a breath and shrugged. "I suppose after the surgery, I was no longer attractive to him."

Dana felt tears well in her eyes. As she'd gotten older and pieced together what she could remember, she had suspected her father's affair started about the same time as her mother's mastectomy, but hearing her acknowledge it made it even more painful. "Did he say that to you?"

Her mother shook her head. "He never said anything. Your father wasn't a bad man, but... Well, a woman knows those things." She played with the wedding ring on her finger, twisting it. "He used to like to look at me, your father. He used to like to watch me get undressed. He said I had a great body. After the surgery . . . I don't want you to think poorly of your father."

"He's dead, Mom. And I already think poorly of him."

"Dana—"

"It's not my relationship with my father that concerns me anymore. He's gone. James is gone. You're all that I have left. We're all each other has left—you, me, and Molly." A strange feeling of sorrow and anger enveloped her and she started to cry. "Grant's cheating on me. Why didn't you ever say anything to Dad? Why did you let him get away with that, treat you that way?" She was asking herself the same questions.

When her mother spoke, it was with more stamina, the words direct and intended for her daughter, not herself. "I suppose at first I considered it my fault. I was deformed. I was missing a breast. I had a scar. Why would he want me? Why should any man want me? I felt like I was no longer a woman. I spent a lot of time feeling sorry for myself."

Dana shook her head. "Mom . . ."

"But I suspect you know why I did it."

"You did it for me and for James," Dana said, thinking of Molly, of why she had tolerated Grant for too long.

"I did it so that you and your brother would have a father who came home to you each night and who loved you. I wanted you to have a family. I didn't want you to be the kids at school whose parents were divorced."

The words stung. It was an answer Dana was not prepared to hear. It was easier to think that her mother had been weak and had simply succumbed to the infidelities. Dana detested the weakness she perceived in her mother because it scared her. It scared her to know she might also be that weak. Her marriage to Grant was over. She had known for some time, but she hadn't had the courage to walk away, and she felt weak because of it. Blaming that weakness on a genetic trait was easier than acknowledging her own failings.

"But what about you? What about your life?" The question was thirty years too late. Futile.

Her mother shrugged. "There was nothing I could do. I didn't have any education, and I didn't have any skills. There was no need. I was a doctor's daughter, and I married a man who would make a lot of money and who wanted to take care of me. Back then it was embarrassing for a man's wife to be working. People thought it meant he was incapable of supporting her. I was supposed to keep the house and cook the dinner, take care of you and James, and look as ravishing as possible for all of the office events and business dinners with important clients. At least I was good at that."

"You could have done something." It sounded bitter, not what Dana had intended. "There is so much more to you than that."

"What was I going to do? Divorce him and go back to school? How was I going to care for you and your brother? Your father was an attorney. I didn't stand a chance. And I had cancer. No one knew what the future was back then. What if I got sick again; then what? Was I scared? Yes, I was scared. Was I lonely and afraid? You bet. But I had you, and I had James, and you were the two things in my life I was determined to hold on to with every ounce of my power. You were not going to get hurt. I made certain of that. And you were never going to be in that situation.

When your father tried to talk you out of law school, I talked you into it."

Tears dripped down Dana's cheeks as she recalled her mother's encouragement. Kathy leaned forward across the table and grabbed Dana's hands. "You don't have to live my life. You are not me. You're strong. You have a good education, a good career. Don't settle for a bad husband. Don't settle for a bad marriage. It doesn't have to be that way for you and for Molly."

"I have cancer, Mom." Dana said the words as if they had been ripped from her body.

"Oh, Dana." Kathy went around the table and pulled her daughter to her, holding her head against her chest, caressing her hair gently, as she had done when Dana was a child. Keeker continued to squawk and to crack the shells in search of the soft seeds inside. Her mother took a handkerchief from her pants pocket and handed it to Dana, who had thought it odd that her mother always carried a handkerchief, but no longer. Kathy Hill had cried too many tears. It made Dana think of William Welles. It made her think of Elizabeth Meyers. They had so much in common. They all had so much in common.

"I'm afraid, Mom. I'm afraid for Molly if anything were to happen to me."

"Of course you are. That's what being a good mother is about—worrying about your children. Nothing is going to happen to you or to Molly. I won't let it. Neither would your brother. Why do you think he left his entire estate to you?"

Dana pulled back. "He did what?"

"Didn't Brian tell you?"

She had not gone back to meet with Brian Griffin. "No."

"James left his entire estate in a trust for you and Molly. He wanted you to have the same opportunity he had to start over and do whatever you want. So do I. Your father was not a lot of things, but he was one hell of a provider, and I've invested what he left prudently. I can give you your inheritance early. You'll be fine."

Dana sat back. "*You* invested."

Her mother smiled. "I may not be the smartest woman alive, but I am fiercely protective of my children and that little girl upstairs. And I would do anything for either of you. Anything."

Dana exhaled. She sat back and took a deep breath. "There are some things happening. Some things that could involve some very important people."

"Whatever I can do to help, I will. But first, go on up and look at your little girl and get some rest. You've been through so much. You're exhausted."

Dana stood, hugged her mother, and kissed her on the cheek. She continued to wipe away tears as she walked to the staircase. The mail sat opened on the hall table. On top was an invitation. Dana picked it up, read it, and felt a surge of adrenaline. She pulled the cell phone from her pocket, flipped it open, and dialed the number. It rang once before he answered.

"Mike? I know how to get to her."

50

SATURDAY EVENING, WHITE lights bathed the front of the Fairmont Olympic Hotel at Fourth and University in downtown Seattle. Built in 1924 and considered one of the finest hotels in Seattle, the Fairmont Olympic maintained much of the original brick, terra-cotta trim, and granite that made it look part southern mansion, part Italian monument. At the curb, beneath the white colonnade and arched Palladian windows, elegantly dressed men in tuxedos and women in long evening gowns exited a stream of limousines, Mercedes, and luxury SUVs making their way along the circular driveway and center island of manicured dwarf maple trees, boxwood hedges, and ferns. They handed their keys to young men dressed in dark gray wool topcoats and hats.

Dana watched the spectacle from the back of a taxi inching toward the front entrance. In the intervening two days, her body had recovered enough that she no longer needed the painkillers; the pain in her joints and muscles had become a numbed ache. Makeup helped to hide most of her facial bruises and long white gloves hid the scrapes and cuts on her arms and hands. Her mother had braided her hair into a weave, and she wore a white gown with a plunging neckline adorned with a diamond necklace. From the necklace dangled the large blue earring with the teardrop diamond.

As she waited to reach the designated drop-off point, Dana pulled out her cell phone and retrieved Michael Logan's number. Logan had initially been against the idea when Dana called to tell him she potentially had a way to get to Elizabeth Meyers, but his protest had been tempered by the acknowledgment that it was a good idea and they had no other immediate options.

"You said yourself there are only two people who can identify the earring, and one of them is dead. That leaves Elizabeth Meyers," she had told him.

Logan had remained skeptical. "*If* you can even get close enough to talk to her, and *if* she'll talk to you."

"I'll talk to her. I'm not going to sample the champagne and hors d'oeuvres."

"Let me escort you."

"Nothing will happen. It's a public function. Besides, there will be people there I know—friends of my mother and father. It would raise questions for me to walk in there with you. I have to do this alone. I have to find a way to get close to her without her feeling threatened. I can only do that by myself."

Sitting in the taxi, Dana contemplated what Logan had told her about his wife and the home Sarah had designed. Was it possible for a woman afflicted with a debilitating disease to know there was another person out there for her spouse to love? Could Sarah Logan have loved her husband so much that she knew there was another woman for him to spend his life with after she had passed—a woman who had grown up loving tree houses? A week ago Dana would have scoffed at such a suggestion. Now she was no longer certain.

One of the young men standing at the entrance pulled open her door and offered his hand. Dana stepped out. She felt the energy pulsating from the building as she stepped through the doors between the bronze cheetahs sitting at attention. The crowd was abuzz with anticipation. Dana handed the embossed white invitation addressed to her mother to a man wearing a tuxedo and a no-nonsense expression. The wire of a small earpiece disappeared beneath the collar of his coat. He motioned for Dana to put her purse on a belt to be scanned in an airport-type security machine, and directed her to move forward through a metal detector. She had read somewhere that while it had once been considered an insult to be subjected to such scrutiny, the wealthy establishment in Washington, D.C., had turned the inconvenience into a status symbol. The ultimate prestige of a function was now judged by the degree of security to which invitees were subjected. The dinner to kick off Robert Meyers's presidential campaign was apparently ranked very high on the prestige meter.

She retrieved her mother's black Gucci handbag from an equally grim-faced man on the other side of the machine and pressed forward with the line. She didn't know if the security detail was Robert Meyers's personal security, provided by the government now that Meyers was a candidate, or some combination of both. If the security detail was expecting her, they gave no indication.

The interior escalator rose to an expansive lobby of carved oak walls, white marbled floors, and long-leafed plants that made the room look as if it had sprang from an F. Scott Fitzgerald novel. Staircases descended from the second-story mezzanine on either end of the lobby, where guests stood on the balcony, glasses in hand, looking down on those continuing to arrive. Dana turned toward the wrought-iron staircase to the Spanish Ballroom. She had the sudden urge to look behind her, a feeling that someone had followed her, but she resisted anything that would make her stand out. At the top of the stairs, as she neared the tall mirrored doors leading to the ballroom, she felt a hand on her arm. Her heart skipped a beat, and she started.

"Dana."

Harry Block, her father's former law partner, stood with a statuesque, significantly younger woman who was holding his left arm. Dana surmised her to be Mrs. Harry Block III. It had been Block, a large contributor to the Democratic Party, who had sent the invitation to Kathy Hill. Block had apparently not been so embarrassed by his abandonment of Kathy after her husband's scandalous death that he couldn't solicit her for a five-thousand-dollar donation to the cause.

Dana recovered, smiling brightly. "Mr. Block, how are you?"

"No 'Mr. Block' anymore," he said. "Please, call me Harry." His eyes drifted to her plunging neckline and stopped on the blue stone. "Don't you look lovely," he said, speaking directly to her cleavage. "I didn't take you for a Democrat. I was thrilled when your mother called to tell me you would be coming. I haven't spoken to her in so long." Block paused. His expression changed. "I was so very sorry to hear about your brother, and even sorrier that I couldn't attend his funeral to offer my personal condolences. Have there been any developments in the investigation?"

"Nothing yet," Dana said. She held up the invitation. "Thank you for facilitating this. I know my RSVP was last-minute. It was very kind of you."

"I'm happy to accommodate you." Block spied someone out of the corner of his eye. "I look forward to chatting with you later," he said, taking another look at her cleavage before departing.

Dana looked up to find that while talking with Block the line had moved forward. She had reached the main doors to the ballroom and recognized what was akin to a receiving line at a wedding. At the front of that line stood Robert Meyers.

She stopped. This was not what she had expected; she had hoped to mingle freely through the crowd until she spotted an opportunity to speak with Elizabeth Adams in private. But Meyers was not about to pass up the personal touch—the chance to shake a hand and make everyone in the room feel important enough to contribute financially to his campaign. If he recognized Dana's name and knew she was in the room, it could make him ever more diligent about his wife's whereabouts. She considered making an excuse to step out of line, then told herself to remain calm. Stepping out of line would make her look even more conspicuous.

The couple in front of her handed their invitation to a man standing to Robert Meyers's immediate right. The man reviewed the name on the card, deftly turned his head, and whispered the name in Meyers's ear. Meyers greeted the couple without missing a beat. He took each hand in his customary two-handed grip, smiling warmly and looking them directly in the eye as he thanked them for coming. Then he removed his right hand and placed it on the man's back to shuffle them down the line to his wife, who stood at his side.

Elizabeth Meyers wore a white sequined gown, in sharp contrast to the deep rich color of her hair, which had been pulled back in a clip to reveal the lobes of both ears, each adorned with a teardrop-shaped diamond earring.

"Ma'am?" The man on Meyers's right extended his hand, waiting for Dana's invitation.

She handed him the card, and he turned and whispered her name in Robert Meyers's ear. His expression did not change, but his robotic movements seemed to hesitate, if only for an instant—a glitch in the circuitry. Then he turned toward her. Dana raised her gloved left hand and pulled her silk wrap together to cover the earring dangling from her necklace. She held out her right hand.

Meyers took it with charm and grace. "How do you do, Ms. Hill? Thank you for being here tonight and for your support."

Dana smiled, though inside she felt repulsed at the touch of Meyers's hand. "It's a pleasure to be here, Senator Meyers."

The couple in front of her lingered. Elizabeth Meyers laughed out loud, a full, husky chuckle. Meyers looked to Dana's left. "Tell me how so beautiful a woman can be unescorted."

Dana smiled again. "The flu, I'm afraid."

"I'm sorry to hear that, and even more thankful you

would come. Please enjoy yourself tonight. I hope this is the start of four years of change."

Meyers released his right hand and turned to Elizabeth. Dana felt his hand on her back. It made her skin crawl. Elizabeth was still laughing when she turned to acknowledge Dana. The smile did not diminish. Her eyes showed no sign of recognition, even when her husband introduced her.

Dana continued to work through what had happened. Could William Welles have somehow been wrong? No. They'd sent someone to kill him. He'd designed the earring for Meyers. When Robert Meyers turned to greet the couple behind her, Dana lowered her left hand, revealing the earring.

"Hello, Elizabeth." The informal tone found its mark.

"Good evening, do I—"

Dana gently fingered the earring on the chain. "Those are lovely earrings."

Elizabeth's eyes drifted to Dana's neck. The smile vanished, replaced by an uncertain grin.

Dana went on. "William Welles was a remarkable artist. I understand they're one of a kind."

Elizabeth's expression froze. In her peripheral vision, Dana saw the sweep of Robert Meyers's right hand, an indication that he had finished greeting the couple behind her and was prepared to pass them to his wife. Dana turned. "James was my brother," she said softly. Then she stepped down the line.

AN ELEVATED ORCHESTRA of tuxedo-clad men and women from the Seattle Symphony played under soft white lights, the harmonic sound mixing with the drone and hum of voices. Tables and chairs draped in white linen with gold trim surrounded a parquet dance floor. Overhead hung a fishing net filled with hundreds of black and white balloons and a shower of confetti to be released at some predetermined moment. Men and women in white coats glided among the guests, carrying trays of champagne glasses and hors d'oeuvres. The lighting in the room from the glass-bead Spanish chandeliers was muted, giving the candles on the tables a chance to glow. The room had been squeezed tight, every seat another five thousand dollars toward the Democratic effort to elect a president. At the front of the room stretched an ornately decorated, elevated table for the senator and his wife and a few privileged guests. Only a podium and microphone in the middle disrupted the elegance.

Dana mingled with the crowd, recognizing faces she'd seen in the newspaper, in magazines, and on television and movie screens. She sipped champagne and found a corner of the room near a potted fern not far from the receiving line where she could study Elizabeth. Elizabeth seemed out of step, like a dance partner uncertain of the next move. Her smile no longer looked radiant. It appeared hesitant and forced. Her eyes had lost focus and occasionally wandered, searching the crowd. Robert Meyers must have noticed that his wife was out of step. In between heavy hitters, he turned his head and whispered something in her ear. She nodded once, almost imperceptibly, then continued with a more polished routine. But it didn't last.

Dana continued to ponder the situation. Judging from the look of astonishment on Elizabeth Meyers's face when

Dana revealed the earring, she had no idea that she'd lost it. That meant one of the earrings she wore was a forgery. Somehow Meyers had learned that his wife had left the earrings at her brother's home, and Boutaire had sent King and Cole to retrieve them. When they failed, Meyers must have had an earring quickly crafted to conceal the absence of the mate while waiting for Boutaire to recover the original. Everything was being orchestrated to eliminate suspicion that her brother's death had been anything other than a brutal act during the commission of a robbery.

After another thirty minutes, the receiving line split apart, and the doors to the room closed. The orchestra stopped playing. Two men dressed in medieval costumes—red and white skirts with black stockings and hats with plumage—stepped forward, raised two long horns, and greeted the guests with a short blast. Dinner was served. Dana located table twenty-nine and found her assigned seat. Harry Block had treated her well. Her table was in the center of the room, not far from the elevated dignitaries. Though each table seated ten, and Dana was unescorted, her table was full. A handsome man with a dark complexion pulled out her chair and introduced himself as Leonard Berdini, a director of films for National Geographic.

With the guests seated, the conductor raised a baton, and the orchestra broke into what sounded very much like the President's March. The crowd stood in unison, applauding as the doors once again opened. Robert and Elizabeth Meyers emerged, waving and smiling like a newlywed couple at their reception. The applause continued long after the guests of honor had found their places, and increased each time a dignitary attempted to quiet the throng. Finally, Robert Meyers stepped to the podium amid the wave of adulation.

"Your dinner is going to get cold," he said, "though your reception warms my heart." A minister blessed the food, and the sound of voices again mixed with the clinking of silverware and glasses. Throughout dinner, Berdini's eyes frequently found Dana's neckline, as if he were considering it for one of his films. He told her of his most recent venture in South America, filming in Brazil. Dana provided polite interest but focused much of her attention on Elizabeth. It was clear Elizabeth was doing the same thing, listening politely to the dignitary to her left while searching the tables.

Dinner was salmon and filet mignon, potatoes, and green beans. As waiters cleared the plates and brought chocolate mousse and coffee, the same dignitary who had opened the evening stood again to robustly introduce "the next Democratic candidate for president of the United States, Robert Meyers."

The crowd again stood and burst into applause as Meyers stepped to the podium and basked in the spotlight. When he raised his hands, the applause increased. He looked to the table of dignitaries with a sheepish "What can I do?" grin and shrugged. After another minute, the crowd regained composure and settled back into their seats.

"I take it from your response that you enjoyed the meal. I told you that you would."

The audience laughed.

"Tonight we begin the first step together toward what we all hope will be four years of change." Everyone stood and applauded, then stayed standing throughout the remainder of Meyers's thirty-five-minute speech. Dana paid little attention to his words; her focus remained on Elizabeth. When he had finished, Meyers stepped back from the podium, took his wife by the hand, and led her to the dance floor. The conductor initiated a waltz. After several minutes, others joined them. When the song ended, Meyers moved in the direction of a large group. This would not be a night for dancing. Meyers would not waste an opportunity to speak to as many guests as possible. The flow of guests and well-wishers soon separated Meyers from his wife. This was Dana's chance, perhaps her only one.

She worked her way toward the front of the circle of guests surrounding Elizabeth. As she emerged from the pack, Elizabeth made eye contact with her, politely ended a conversation, and turned toward her, but not before she scanned the room, presumably to locate her husband. "Dana," she said softly.

"You remember me."

"Yes, of course."

"It was only one Thanksgiving dinner many years ago. Is your memory that good?" Elizabeth just stared at her. "I'd be flattered to think you remembered me from that one dinner, but I think we both know that's not the case."

Elizabeth looked down at the earring attached to the chain and unconsciously fingered each earlobe.

Dana lowered her voice. "I found it in my brother's home beneath his bed. William Welles told me the rest. Then someone killed him."

Dana watched as Elizabeth processed the information—James's death, Dana's knowledge of William Welles, the fact that she was wearing one of the earrings. It couldn't have come as a total surprise; Elizabeth must have at least suspected that James Hill's death was not a random murder. Yet her blank stare indicated she either had not considered the possibility or had not wanted to.

"My God," she said softly.

"There you are."

Elizabeth's head snapped as if on a string. Robert Meyers had appeared at his wife's side.

51

~

T HE TAXI DROPPED her at the front entrance to the Columbia Center, the black monolith that pierced Seattle's skyline like the Washington Monument did three thousand miles across the country. Dana walked across a vast marbled atrium of multiple elevator banks and escalators that serviced the building's seventy-six floors and rode an elevator to the top. She stepped off into a private club where her father had been one of the charter members.

The black marble floor and walls were bathed in a soft blue light. It took a moment for Dana's eyes to adjust. Three black men sat illuminated in a jaundiced glow, cradling instruments. A saxophone wailed a soulful tune. Two well-dressed couples leaned in to each other, swaying on a tiny dance floor. Candles burned on tables along perimeter windows that afforded a 360-degree overlook of Seattle and Puget Sound, stretching north from the West Point Lighthouse and south to the Duwamish Waterway.

He stood at the bar, a glass in hand. The look on his face when he saw her—profound relief—told her he had been watching the door, worried. Michael Logan's chest heaved. He smiled softly, an almost sheepish grin, then he greeted her halfway across the floor. They stood like a couple deciding whether or not to dance. Logan led her to an open table along the west wall, pulled out her chair, and sat across from her, ignoring the view. A waitress appeared at the table. Logan looked to Dana.

"Scotch and water. Heavy on the Scotch," she said.

Logan nodded. "Make it two."

For a moment they did not speak, choosing to stare at the flickering flame on the table. Then Logan asked, "Are you okay?"

Dana smiled. Of all the things Detective Michael Logan could have asked her—whether she had spoken to Elizabeth, and whether Elizabeth would identify the earring, being foremost among them—he had chosen to ask her the one question that mattered most to her.

"I'm fine. Thanks for asking," Dana said. Logan sat back, considering her like a portrait on the wall of a museum. "What?" she asked, embarrassed, though she knew what his eyes were doing.

"I don't know. Nothing, I guess. Actually . . . you look very beautiful, if it's okay for me to say so."

"It is." She smiled. "And thank you . . . again."

"So, how did it go?"

She exhaled a deep breath. "Just like Cinderella at the ball."

"You spoke to her?"

"Briefly."

"And?"

"She remembered me. Once she got past the foreign surroundings and the makeup and the dress, she knew who I was. I don't think it was from one Thanksgiving dinner nearly twenty years ago."

"What did she say?"

"She didn't have to say anything; I could see it in her eyes. I sought her out later in the evening."

"Did you ask her about the earring?"

Dana nodded. "She recognized it, and she recognized William Welles's name. I think it caused her heart to skip a beat or two."

"How so?"

"She was wearing two earrings."

Logan considered this. "Meyers must have had one made."

"I think so. Based on her reaction when she saw it, I don't think she knew one was missing. But how could he know when she didn't?"

Logan shook his head. "I don't know. But I doubt there's much he doesn't know. If he suspected her infidelity, he likely was having her watched. Boutaire could have noticed she wasn't wearing the earrings when she left your brother's home, and confirmed it later. That could have been the impetus to get into his home."

"Why wouldn't Boutaire do it himself?"

"Too risky. If anything went wrong, it would have been a direct link to Meyers. He needed King and Cole as a buffer."

The waitress set their drinks on coasters on the black slate table. For the next thirty minutes, Dana recounted the details of her evening. She told Logan how, in the middle of their conversation, Robert Meyers had appeared as if out of nowhere, and Dana had managed to step back into the crowd, disappearing just as quickly.

"It took a lot of courage to do what you did tonight," Logan said.

She shrugged off the compliment. "We didn't have a lot of options. We took the one we thought was best."

"That's why it took guts. I'm serious, Dana. Sometimes you find yourself in a situation, and you just react. Instinct takes over. If you're fortunate enough not to get yourself killed, they call you a hero. What you did tonight took a lot more courage, because you had time to consider and understand the danger, but you did it anyway."

"My brother is dead. Robert Meyers had him killed. I can't accept that. I won't accept that."

"I know. I'm just telling you that you should be proud. Most women—" He caught himself. "Hell, most men would have folded their tent a long time ago, given what you've been through. Your brother would be proud."

"That sounds like a concession speech."

He sat back and looked out the window.

"Mike?"

He turned back to her. "I don't want to throw cold water on this, but I'm not sure this puts us any closer to getting Meyers. It's sort of like O. J. Simpson and the shoes—you remember? He denied owning a pair like the kind that left an imprint in his wife's blood on the sidewalk. Then they found photographs of him wearing the same shoes, and everyone thought that was it. Still, it wasn't enough—far from it."

Dana folded her hands on the table. "She knows now, Mike. She knows what happened to James. She knows what her husband is. We've never had any control over whether she would be willing to do anything about it. But we had to give her the opportunity. The next step is hers. If she doesn't take it . . . well . . . We have an earring, a dead member of Meyers's security staff, and a lot of circumstantial evidence. No prosecutor would touch this with a ten-foot pole."

"What do you want to do?"

"Let's give her some time," Dana said. If my brother loved her, there has to be some innate good in her. We have to assume she loved him. Now she knows."

They sat in silence. Dana watched the young couples dancing on the parquet floor. The glow of the alcohol replaced the edginess of the adrenaline, and she felt a desire she hadn't felt in some time. She wanted to hold someone. She wanted to be held. She wanted to love and to feel loved. As Logan reached for his drink, she let the wrap drop from her shoulders, leaned forward, and touched his hand. Logan kept his head down, his eyes on the candle. She pulled back her hand and sat back, wrapping the shawl around her shoulders.

"I'm sorry. I shouldn't have done that."

Logan shook his head and looked up at her. "Your husband called."

"Grant?" she asked, puzzled.

"He called your mother. I got worried and called her to see if she'd heard from you. Grant's home; he's waiting for you at your house. Your mother didn't want you to be surprised."

52

HER HANDS SHOOK. She dropped the screw-on clasp. It bounced from the walnut dressing table, lost in the carpet. Elizabeth Meyers set the earring down next to its match and turned to the curtained windows of her private dressing room. On clear days, sunlight bathed the wedge-shaped room, and she would sit for hours watching the sailboats on Puget Sound's slate-gray waters, dreaming of the freedom. Tonight the drapes had been pulled closed. The room felt smaller because of it.

She turned from the windows, absently massaging her earlobes as she considered her reflection in the antique oval freestanding mirror. She hardly recognized the woman she saw. Her hair was darker than natural, nearly black. Though she preferred to wear it down, it rarely fell free from the clip that pulled it off of her face. Her blue eyes, once radiant, had dulled. Her nose and cheekbones were the product of a plastic surgeon's knife, though she had considered them fine the way God had made them.

When she wasn't in public, her broad shoulders—muscled from years of swimming in the ocean off La Jolla, California—slumped, and her chest became concave from the weight. A tear seeped from the corner of her eye and rolled down her cheek, dropping onto the table next to the earrings.

She lowered her eyes. The blue stones no longer sparkled without the glitter of light. She recalled William Welles telling her when they met that diamonds reflected light in a prism of colors, but that it was a false light, an illusion caused by refraction. True light, Welles had said, came from within. "Without it, even earrings as beautiful as these will look like ordinary pieces of glass." She thought she had understood him. She hadn't. Now she did.

She raised her head and stared at the reflection in the mirror.

"You appeared deep in thought," Robert Meyers said. "I didn't want to disturb you. Is everything all right?"

"Just tired," she whispered.

He walked past her through the ten-foot-high double doors to the master bedroom. There was a separate entrance, but he often came through her dressing room. He turned on the gas. Flames erupted in the fireplace. He considered a collection of CDs neatly arranged in an ornate armoire once owned by John F. Kennedy. Meyers had purchased it at a Sotheby's auction.

"Two point two million dollars." He slid a CD from its slot, opened the plastic case, and fed it into the machine. The beat of drums and cymbals mixed with the hum of violins, flutes, and horns. She did not recognize the arrangement, a mix of opera and raw street music. Tribal. "That's the initial estimate. Not bad for a night's work."

He turned up the volume and closed the hand-carved cabinet doors. "It's a good start. It will get the campaign headed in the right direction. A few more nights like this, and there will be nothing I can't do."

He stood, the back of his head juxtaposed with a framed portrait of her hanging on the blue-and-gray-striped wallpaper. But for her portrait, a full-body painting, the dark colors and heavy pieces of Victorian furniture were distinctly masculine. Meyers slid off his tuxedo jacket and carefully placed it on the arm of a standing clothes rack. Staff would take it to be dry-cleaned and pressed. He pulled the bow tie free and undid the top button of his shirt, the collar spreading open.

She stood from the dressing table and walked into the room, keeping the canopied bed between them. She felt the pain deep within, but now it mixed with another emotion. Anger built, giving her a strength she had not felt in years. "Did you do it?" she asked.

Meyers paused before removing the black onyx cuff links and the buttons of his tuxedo shirt. He returned each to its slot in a mahogany box. "You seemed distant tonight, out of sorts. We can't have that."

She hated herself. She hated what she had become. "Did you do it?" she asked again.

He slipped out of his shirt. The muscles of his shoulders, well-defined striations, quivered beneath his skin. "If we are going to do this, we need to give it our all from here forward. The difficult states will be out east. Richardson will be painted as a sharp contrast to my Northwest background. They'll make him out to be an eastern gentleman and me a cowboy. That's all right, though. It worked for Ronnie, didn't it?"

She returned to her dressing room and looked down at the earrings.

"Of course, Richardson is not a great speaker; he's stiff as a board. I'll seek every opportunity to debate him."

She rolled over the first earring. The interconnected "W"'s were etched on the gold clasp. Her heart pounded in rhythm to the beat of the drums from the stereo speakers. She closed her eyes, rolled over the second earring.

"The contrast between the two of us, our significant difference in age and hair coloring, will be symbolic of the differences in our political and economic philosophy and appeal."

She opened her eyes. The gold clasp was unmarked. Her stomach gave way, dropping like a free-falling elevator. Her knees buckled. She reached for the edge of the dresser, holding herself upright.

"I'll continue to promote youth, vitality, and change. It will make him appear to be an old man, stuck in the mud of special interest, partisan—"

His voice became a hollow echo. She struggled to swallow. The room spun around her, and she thought she might get sick. Then her stomach returned, the elevator catching on the cable and jerking to a stop. An intense pain spread across her chest and down her limbs. The veins in her forearms, still well defined from hitting countless tennis balls in her youth, bulged beneath her skin, and her knuckles on the dresser turned white. Intense hatred boiled in the pit of her stomach, inching upward until it burned the back of her throat. The fear she had felt for so long dissipated. In its place, rage.

"You bastard." She slammed her fist on the table.

He stood in the doorway, suspenders dangling at his

sides. "It is important that you participate in this campaign, Elizabeth." He spoke without emotion. "I'd win without you, but the American public has taken a particular fancy to you. The polls indicate you could become the most recognizable first lady since Jacqueline Kennedy, but we both knew that comparison would be inevitable, didn't we?"

"You killed him."

His mouth pinched. His eyes hardened. He returned to the bedroom, sitting on the canopied bed to slide off his shoes and black socks.

She followed him. The words came from between clenched teeth. "I want to hear you say it."

He stood slowly. "Do not question me."

She took two steps forward, each word spoken deliberately. "I . . . want . . . you . . . to . . ."

"Do not question me!" He spun, lunging at her like a snake striking, suddenly and without warning. His hand gripped her face, pinching her mouth. He spoke in a sadistic hiss. "Don't you ever question me." He shoved her across the carpet, nearly lifting her from the floor. The back of her head hit hard against the wall. An aurora of lights danced before her eyes. His hand dug into the flesh of her cheek and forced her head sideways. He leaned closer. She felt his breath on her neck. Spittle sprayed from between his teeth. "What I do is my business. You don't question it. You don't ask for answers. You don't get them. You don't offer advice. You don't give opinions. What you do is exactly what I tell you to do."

He turned her face toward him, his eyes wide, like those of a spooked horse. His lips pulled back in a demonic snarl. "You want to know? You want me to tell you?"

She struggled to swallow. His hand raised her chin, stretching the muscles of her neck. She thought her jaw would snap. She had seen him like this before, when his pores seeped with anger and brought a feral, inhuman smell. His voice deepened and became a rough, low growl. So many times she had feared it would be the occasion when his anger peaked and he could not control the force of his blows. Living with a full staff of servants had not tempered his anger or lessened the ferocity of his fists. He had only learned to lower his voice, increase the volume of the stereo, wrap his hands before striking her. Only the level of his deception had changed.

"Your boyfriend? You want to know what happened to your boyfriend?" Meyers started to laugh. "He died. There was a robbery. He walked in on them and they beat him to death, just like the newspapers said."

His hand caressed her jawline. She pushed from the wall. He thrust a knee between her legs and pressed against her. "They said his head split open like a piece of fruit. They said he felt every blow." His fingers traced the lines of her throat and neck and along the rim of her cleavage. "Thirteen blows," he whispered. His hand found its way beneath her dress, his fingers digging into her skin. His knee forced her to her toes. Her neck craned. She let out a feeble whimper and hated herself for it.

"Did you think I was going to give you up so easily, Elizabeth? Did you think I would allow you to humiliate me after all I've done for you? Is this the thanks I get?" He kissed her throat and chest, openmouthed, warm wet kisses. He lingered over her flesh like an animal licking the salt from the skin of something it had killed. She felt his erection.

"I will be the most powerful man in the world. There won't be anything I cannot do or have done. Did you think I would allow you to keep that from me? Did you think I would allow my wife to be a whore? Was it the sex? Do you not get enough here in your own bedroom?" He ripped the white evening gown from her body and struck her across the mouth. The force of the blow knocked her sideways, upsetting a lamp on the nightstand. He grabbed her by the shoulders and backhanded her, her body spinning onto the bed. Before she could cry out, his free hand returned quickly to her throat. He wedged a knee between her legs, spreading them as he struggled with the clasp of his pants.

"Is that what this deceit and deception is about? Sex? Because I can surely remedy that." She closed her eyes. "Open them," he growled. His grip on her throat tightened, cutting off her flow of air. "I want you to see exactly how easily I can do it." He lunged on top of her, smothering her. She felt his hands tearing at her panties, ripping at them, then his skin against hers. His tongue and lips smothered her breasts. His teeth clenched her nipple. Pain shot through her, but the hand gripping her throat prevented her from screaming. He bit her about the shoulders and neck and forced his way inside her, raw and dry. He pulled her to the edge of the bed, standing, back arched, each thrust more violent. His head tilted upward, and she saw the image of an animal baying at the moon. Then he lowered his gaze, staring at her in odd, contorted angles—the head of a cobra flexing and writhing above her, his eyes pools of darkness. She struggled for a breath. Her lungs burned. Her vision blurred, the aurora of black spots and unfocused images returning.

His rhythm increased with the primal beating of drums. Strange sounds came from his throat, like water gurgling in a pipe drain and the gasps of a man stricken with emphysema. The flames in the fireplace reflected in his eyes, dancing blades of red, orange, and yellow. His tongue darted, hissing. The aurora spread, the dark spots melting together in one dark mass. Then the image faded, leaving darkness and the hollow echo of his moaning as the drums beat to a furtive and violent climax.

53

THE BLUE BMW sat parked in the driveway, the only indication that Grant was home. The porch light, activated by a timer, cast a tapered glow beneath the small portico, but the eight windows that faced the street—four on the ground floor and four on the second story—were dark. Logan pulled the Austin Healey to the curb. Dana did not immediately get out. She stared at the house. Strange, given that she owned it, but she could not recall seeing it from this angle. She had always driven down the driveway and parked under the carport. They had spent a small fortune remodeling the interior with fresh coats of paint, bright drapes, and refinished hardwood floors, but the house had never felt like home. It had the neat, refurbished appearance of houses in magazine photographs—stale and stiff, without depth or warmth.

Dana pushed open the car door and stepped onto the sidewalk, wrapping the white shawl around her shoulders, listening until the sports car's engine became a distant, faint hum. She went through the front gate, walked down the brick path outlined by English boxwood hedges, and looked up at the darkened windows of her bedroom. While a part of her hoped Grant was already asleep, another could not bear the thought of climbing into the same bed next to him for even one more night. She'd sleep in Molly's room. She pulled a key from her handbag, took a deep breath that brought a dull ache to her side, and opened the front door. The ambient light of a streetlamp seeped through the shuttered windows in the living room, leaving stripes on the floor. She held the door handle to keep the lock from clicking as she carefully closed the door. Then she slipped off her high heels, holding them by the straps, and started up the stairs.

"I'm in here."

She stopped on the second step. The voice sounded foreign. "Grant?"

"In the living room."

She stepped down and peered into the darkness. "Grant?"

"Here."

She found the switch beneath the lamp shade on the end table and turned it on. It emitted a soft glow. Grant sat in a wingback chair, staring into the empty fireplace. When he moved, it was to raise the glass in his hand.

"Why are you home? Why are you sitting in the dark?" she asked.

He finished what remained in his glass, reached for the bottle partially obscured by the legs of the chair, and poured the glass half full. If he had noticed the disruption in the house, he did not say. Dana sat near the window. The fifteen feet between them felt like a buffer zone for doomed peace negotiations. Grant looked up long enough to consider her attire through bloodshot and glassy eyes. "Where have you been?" he asked.

"The firm anniversary party." She was reasonably certain he wouldn't recall that the yearly event was held each October, not April. He detested going, for reasons he had not expressed, but which she had come to understand on her own. He felt inferior to the attorneys who worked with her. She knew he would not pursue the matter now with questions she could not truthfully answer. She didn't want to lie, not anymore, not to him and not to herself.

"Why are you home? I thought the trial would go at least another two weeks."

"So did I." He sounded and looked like he had a bad cold. His eyes were red and puffy.

"What happened?"

He cleared his throat, taking several moments before he spoke to the fireplace. "We presented our case, just as I imagined we would. We put the witnesses on one after the other, smoothly, without any glitches." His words slurred, but he maintained control of his vocabulary. "It went perfectly. They hardly objected. When they did, it was half-hearted. I thought they would throw in the towel, come to us with a settlement package approaching the hundred and fifty million we sought, and it would be over." He raised the glass and took another drink.

"Don't you think you've had enough?"

"Oh, no." He laughed, though it was pained. "I'm just getting started."

Dana wrapped the shawl more tightly around her. She could not keep her legs from shaking. "What happened?"

"After we rested, the judge excused the jury and told

us to reconvene in the morning. There was something in his tone of voice, something I picked up on that sounded like he didn't expect things to take very long." He laughed again and looked up at an oil painting mounted above the mantel, two horses charging, wild-eyed, whatever chased them left to the imagination. "I remember looking over at Bill Nelson and smiling. At dinner that night, we discussed whether the judge intended his comment as a warning to the defense to settle the case, or if he expected them to put up very little defense. We were counting the money." His voice choked. He cleared it with another gulp of the drink, grimaced, and refilled the glass.

"The next morning they stood and presented a motion for a directed verdict. I had to suppress a smile, though I gave them credit for having the balls to bring it. And then the judge said...he said... 'I thought you might.'" Grant paused, as if hearing the words echo in his head over and over again. "'I thought you might. I thought you might.'"

He continued to stare into the fireplace. "Their motion was premised on an argument that we had failed to establish a legally binding contract. They argued that because the defective component parts were manufactured by an entity independent of the limited partnership, we had failed to establish that Nelson Industries had standing to bring the action." He stood, stumbled, then regained his balance and raised a finger in the air, she assumed to impersonate the lawyer making the argument. "And furthermore, Your Honor, any subsequent attempt by the proper entity would now be barred as beyond the statute of limitations and without exception or relation back to the original complaint." He turned, finally looking at her, and raised the glass in a mock toast. "In other words, yours truly had fucked up big-time by filing the lawsuit in the wrong name, and they had waited until the statute ran out to mention it. It actually expired a week before trial, but they decided that rather than rush to court and expose my error, they would wait to embarrass me in front of my client, my managing partner, the judge, jury, and God Himself." He shouted the end of the sentence like a Baptist minister before a Sunday-morning congregation, then he broke down in a strange cackle of laughter and tears.

Dana stared at her hands, folded in her lap. She felt sad for him, but try as she might, she also could not dismiss some satisfaction, and she hated herself for it. She did not want to take any solace in Grant's failure. She knew he was hurting, and no matter what they had become, they had shared ten years of their lives together and would always share a child. She had once cared for him. "Is it correctable? Wouldn't it relate back to the filing of the original complaint? What about excusable neglect?" she asked.

He laughed and bent forward at the waist, as if bowing. "Oh, that's where it gets really good. The fucking judge took great pleasure in announcing his ruling. He took great pains to note this was a matter that could have been corrected by a more *diligent* attorney. 'A lack of diligence, however, is not grounds to accommodate a motion to amend the lawsuit to add a new defendant and have it relate back to the original filing date,' " he said, in a voice that apparently mimicked the judge.

"He didn't say that."

"Oh, yes, he did. He said exactly that. Which pretty much rules out any basis for an appeal. He also said that his father once told him…" Grant paused as if to remember the words exactly. "'Arrogance leads to ignorance, because it colors one's perception.'"

"He didn't."

A tear rolled down Grant's cheek. "Bergman has assembled the partnership to brace for the inevitable malpractice suit. Nelson Industries will seek to recover the hundred-and-fifty-million loss, and if that doesn't make a shareholder's ass pucker, I'm not sure what would."

"The insurance will never cover it."

"No, it won't." He tilted the bottle to refill the glass. "Which is why Nelson Industries will go after the personal assets of each of the individual equity partners. How happy do you think they're going to be when they're told they're likely to lose all of their accumulated wealth to cover for my fuckup?" He laughed once more, a sad prolonged cry. When he had finished, he looked up at her, a hand covering his mouth. "And that...badee-badee-badee...is all, folks." He spread his arms, glass in one hand, bottle in the other as if to say, How do you like me now?

"I'm unemployed. Bergman will have a security guard meet me at the front entrance to the building at ten tomorrow morning. I have twenty minutes to gather my things and leave. Any files or papers I take will be reviewed by my paralegal to distinguish between my personal and professional papers. They've locked me out of my computer and confiscated my laptop. In other words, I'm on a fucking island. Not that it would matter, because after the story is printed in the local papers, no law firm in the country will touch me." His voice grew cold and angry. "They're giving me twenty minutes, after nine years of sweat and labor." He seemed to miss his own point entirely. "'Twenty fucking minutes."

"It could have happened to anyone," she said. "If Nelson Industries gave you the wrong partnership information—"

He threw the glass at the fireplace, where it shattered. "That's the best fucking part. I have memoranda throughout the file confirming my research of the appropriate entities and my unwavering confidence in the positive outcome of the litigation. Nelson baited me into it by repeatedly asking for my evaluation of the file and holding out the golden carrot of doing their legal work if we won. He set me up. I was a fucking clay pigeon. He put his company in a can't-lose position. If they won the lawsuit and rang the bell, he had his money. If they lost, he had his pigeon. The company lawyers are hand-delivering the lawsuit tomorrow. They already had it drafted." He took a long drink from the bottle. "He is a fucking crook. This has been a scam from the start."

"You did your best." Her words sounded hopeless. "No one worked harder on a file than you—"

"Bullshit." Alcohol spewed from his mouth. "How could I have done my best? How could I even concentrate when I have you calling me all the time about picking up Molly, taking her to school, or some other asinine request?"

The words stuck in her chest like a dull knife, piercing the skin but inflicting little pain. There was little pain left to suffer. He blamed her for his failure. In ten years, he had never given her an ounce of credit for his successes, but now she would shoulder the blame for his failure. He wobbled on his feet, weaving, and waved a hand in the air. "I told you that I needed more time. I told you that my cases weren't like your little nickel-and-dime mom-and-pop clients. This is fucking war. This is a jungle—a battle of wills and strength and stamina. You don't understand that. You've never understood that."

"I understand." She stood from the couch and pulled the shawl around her shoulders. "I understand better than you think."

He approached her. She could smell the alcohol on his breath, and perspiration. "Do you, Dana? Do you really? Because I don't think you do."

This was not how she had envisioned the inevitable confrontation, but he had chosen the battlefield. Her eyes met his. "Maybe you would have had more time if you hadn't been out screwing your paralegal, Grant."

He stumbled backward as if the words had pushed him off balance. He looked stunned. Then he started to laugh. "What? I get through telling you that my life is ruined, and you say something like that to me? That's just like you—just like you not to support me."

It was not something she had intended or wanted to do; she had no desire to kick him when he was down. But this was his war. "Nelson Industries might have ruined your professional career, but you ruined your own personal life."

He shook his head, defiant. "How about a little support here, Dana? How about a little *fucking* support? I dragged your ass through law school—if it weren't for me, you wouldn't be standing here right now."

"No. Let's get that straight also. You didn't drag my ass through law school. I dragged you through; you just made it seem the other way. And I'd be standing with or without you."

He jabbed his finger at her. "I've supported you. I bought this house and all this shit." His hand swept across the mantel, knocking a porcelain clock and two vases to the floor.

She didn't care. "How long?" she asked.

He shook his head and resumed stabbing a finger at her. "You're crazy. You know that? You're *fucking* crazy."

"Am I, Grant? Am I really crazy? After ten years, can't you even be honest with me about it? Or do you have to take me for such a fool? Because that's what I've been—a fool. Or maybe you're right. Maybe I was crazy. But I'm not crazy anymore."

He put the bottle on the table and seemed to momentarily compose himself. "Dana—"

She raised a hand. "Don't disrespect me by lying about it."

He lowered his head, staring at the red Persian rug. Then his shoulders heaved and shook, and he slumped to his knees, sobbing. His body shook as if stricken by a gust of chilled wind. A part of her still wanted to cradle his head in her lap, to tell him that everything would be all right. But she knew it wouldn't be. She wasn't the same person she had been, and she never would be again. James's death had changed her. It had not weakened her, as she had feared it would. It had strengthened her. It had given her a resolve to change her circumstances, to take a chance, as James had, to live her life as she chose. She started out of the room.

Grant looked up from the floor. "Where are you going?"

"I'll be at my mother's."

"Don't leave me, Dana. Please don't leave me," he pleaded. "I need you tonight."

She turned at the doorway. "I'm sorry. I wish I could help you, but I have nothing left to give. What I had, you took from me. There's nothing left. I'm empty. I've been empty for a long time; I just didn't know it. I thought everyone felt hollow inside. I thought it was just a part of life. Now I know it's not."

He screamed as she walked across the marble floor to the front entry. "You're a runner, Dana. You've always been a runner. You never confront anything."

She stopped and faced him. "You're right. I was a runner. But I'm not anymore." She pulled open the door.

"It won't be that easy. You can't just walk out on me. I deserve more than that. You owe me more than that. I'll . . . I'll take Molly. So help me, I'll take Molly," he said, and the words punched the final hole in her paper heart.

She took the keys off the table, closed the door behind her, and started across the lawn to his BMW. The moist blades of grass felt cool and damp between her toes, and she felt lighter than she could recall having felt in years.

54

~

ROBERT MEYERS EXITED the bathroom, cinching his white bathrobe around his waist. He brushed his hair back off his forehead, placed the brush on the hand-carved mantel, and picked up a widemouthed glass, sipping a liqueur, warming near the gas-burning fire that cast flickering shadows about the darkened room.

"The water is wonderful." He ran a hand through his hair and considered the lines of his face in an ornate gold-leafed wall mirror. "You should take a shower or bath. It might help to soothe your nerves."

She sat against the headboard with her legs bent beneath her, clutching the cotton sheets and blankets to her chin like a child afraid of monsters under the bed. A dull ache masked the deeper penetrating pains between her legs and along her throat. The corner of her mouth felt puffy and tender to the touch. It hurt to swallow. But it was the dull ache on which she focused—an ache that emanated from the depths of her soul and trickled from her body like the water draining from the bathtub in the other room, slow and constant. He would continue to drain her of her will to live, and it would be a slow, painful process. She looked up at the canopied bedpost but doubted it would support the weight of her hanging body. The blown-glass chandelier in the ceiling was old, and the walls were plaster. It would pull from its housing. She had no access to a gun, and prescription medications would never be provided. Knives were unreliable. She was a prisoner, fame and celebrity the bars of a cage she could not escape. She couldn't even allow herself to die to his words or to his touch. He wouldn't allow it. He would continue to force himself upon her and to force her on the public. He needed her to complete the picture he had carefully crafted and which an American public, in desperate need of hope and leadership, would cling to—the modern-day Camelot.

Meyers sat on the edge of the bed, speaking to her like a parent to a child. "I've rung the kitchen and asked for a late-night snack. Would you care to join me?"

His words remained a hollow echo somewhere outside the place she had chosen to go. He reached over and brushed strands of hair from her face, then leaned forward and kissed her gently on the mouth. She fought the urge to pull away, fearing it would only set him off again. His anger tended to linger—sometimes for days, just below the surface, capable of erupting with minimal provocation.

"You see how much I love you? How hard I'm willing to fight to keep you? I won't let anyone or anything come between us. I love you too much to allow that to happen. What you did was wrong, but I've handled it. Now everything can be as before, as I've planned. I forgive you. I forgive you because I am a big enough man to do so. I understand that what you did is partly my fault. You lack discipline. We need to change that. I know now that you wanted me to catch you, that you were seeking attention, questioning my love." He stood and reached for her hand. "Come down and get something to eat with me."

She did not move.

He took a deep breath. "All right, I'll bring something back for you. You need to keep up your strength. Then we'll talk about a new schedule for you. I'll want to keep a closer eye on you." He smiled. "You expected that, though, didn't you?" He kissed her on top of her head. "Of course you did." He started out the door, stopped. "You smell. Take a warm bath and put on something nice. Wear the perfume I gave you for your birthday . . . and the earrings. I love to watch them sparkle when we make love. We'll make love as soon as I get back," he said, and the dull ache inside of her exploded.

55

DANA HEARD HER mother's footsteps descend the staircase, the familiar creaks of wood and the pad of slippers on the marbled entry. The door to the kitchen swung open, but if her mother was surprised to find Dana sitting in the dark, she did not say so. Kathy paused just long enough to touch Dana's shoulder. Then she retrieved the teakettle from the stove and filled it at the kitchen sink. Dana recalled reading in one of her parenting books that mothers never stop being mothers, even after their children have grown, and that children never stop being children. They left home for school, got married, started families of their own, but the minute they stepped back into the family home, they reverted to childhood, expecting to be fed, sheltered, consoled.

Kathy yawned, shut off the water, and placed the kettle on the front burner. The blue-fingered flames engulfed it until she adjusted the fire. Then she pulled two mugs from a cabinet and placed them on the slate counter, rummaging through an old cookie jar for two bags of tea. Dana traced an imaginary line on the kitchen table. Her mother knew Grant had called, and she likely knew they'd had the inevitable confrontation. But still Kathy remained silent, and Dana now realized it was because it was not her mother's battle or her place to give advice. It was her place to console, and to listen when Dana felt up to discussing it. Dana had mistaken another of her mother's strengths—silence—as a weakness.

Kathy came over from the slate counter to the kitchen table with a plate of Danish butter cookies sprinkled with sugar specks, slid out a chair, and nibbled on a cookie. Kathy remained an attractive woman, a few pounds heavier and a lot less primped to order than when she was the wife of a prominent attorney, but her skin remained unblemished by age, and her blue eyes were as clear and bright as a young woman's.

"My biggest concern is Molly," Dana said, continuing to trace the imaginary line. "I don't want to hurt her. I don't want Grant to hurt her."

"You won't hurt her. You're a good mother. You'll put Molly's interests before any anger you feel for him."

"Then how come I feel like I failed?"

Her mother shook her head. "There is a very big difference between being a good mother and being a good wife. They aren't mutually exclusive, but they also are not the same. And you didn't fail at either. The marriage failed. It failed for any number of reasons, but none you can blame yourself for solely. It takes two people to make a marriage work. You can't make it work on your own, no matter how hard you try. And you did try, Dana. But that doesn't reflect upon your abilities as a mother. You'll do what's best for you and for Molly. You won't be able to help yourself. You love her too much not to."

"How long did you know?"

"That Grant wasn't right for you? The first day I met him."

"Really?"

"I suppose that's why Grant and I never got along. A mother never thinks anyone is good enough for her son or her daughter, but I *knew* he wasn't good enough for you. He didn't love you. He loved the thought of you. You fit into his idea of what life was supposed to be—a nice house, nice car, nice furniture. You were a part of the facade, part of the landscape he had painted in his mind. I know. I was part of the same landscape."

"Why didn't you ever say anything?"

Kathy shrugged. "Would you have listened? There was nothing to say; I wasn't the one marrying him. It was my place to hope I was wrong and to wish the very best for you."

"But you knew it wouldn't work out."

Her mother took a deep breath. "If I had told you I didn't like him, it would have only made you want him more. The hardest part of being a parent is allowing our children to fail. At some point they become adults, and you have to let them make their own choices, make their own mistakes, suffer their own consequences, as painful as that is to endure. When you told me you were pregnant, I was overcome with both joy and sorrow for you."

"What do I tell Molly?"

"The truth. Be honest with her. The marriage didn't work. You'll know what's best to tell her. That instinct will take over, and it will be stronger than any desire you may have to punish Grant."

"I think he's been punished enough."

"This is the only advice I'm going to offer: He won't be your husband any longer, but he will always be Molly's father. No matter how many times he disappoints her, she will always love him. She's entitled to a father, and he is entitled to his daughter. I just don't know whether he's up to it."

"He says he'll take her from me."

Her mother laughed softly. "Let him. She'd be home in twenty-four hours."

Dana smiled. "I know."

"You can't be a father for him." The kettle on the stove hummed a low whistle. Her mother stood and kissed her on top of the head before going over to the stove to pour the tea.

Then the telephone rang, shattering the silence.

56

◆

ROBERT MEYERS FINISHED the crumbs of his slice of freshly baked apple pie and washed them down with a gulp of cold milk. "The best," he said, setting the glass on the table.

Carmen Dupree stood in the stainless-steel kitchen waiting to take his plate and glass. She wore her black overcoat over her uniform and white tennis shoes. She had been prepared to leave earlier, just before Robert Meyers rang the kitchen and advised that he wanted a slice of pie. That required her to wait. Meyers demanded that she serve him, then remain to clean up.

Meyers sat back against the blue floral fabric. "It's your best apple pie yet, Carmen."

She smiled, closed-mouthed, and hoped his relaxed posture was not an invitation to continue their conversation. After thirty years of supporting her weight in awkward positions cleaning other people's homes, Carmen's arthritic ankles and feet ached after a full day. The doctor said there was little they could do for her. She wanted to go home and soak them in hot water and Epsom salts.

Meyers patted his stomach. "I think I'll have to step up my workout regimen. Nobody wants a fat president." Carmen took the plate and glass, hopeful it would signal an end to their evening. The fact that she continued to wear her coat hadn't. "You don't seem yourself tonight, Carmen. You seem anxious. In fact, you've seemed anxious for some time. Why is that?"

Carmen walked the plate and glass to the counter. "Just tired, Mr. Meyers. Been a long day, and I'm not getting any younger. And my boys are in trouble again. Seems if one isn't in trouble, another is. Mothers are anxious when they have sons."

"I suppose." Meyers stood and adjusted his bathrobe. "But I'm looking forward to more years of long days. Would you like to work in the White House?"

She smiled. "No, sir, don't suppose I would. I'm home here. Happy to stay here."

He laughed. "Of course you are. That's why you keep secrets from me."

She dropped the plate in the sink, but it did not shatter. She picked it up, rinsing it. "All women have secrets, Mr. Meyers. Nothing new about that."

"I'll bet all the tea in China still wouldn't persuade you to divulge your family's recipe for that apple pie, though, would it?"

Carmen shook her head. "No, sir. Couldn't be doing that."

Meyers shook his finger at her playfully. "You have me over a barrel. You found a path to my stomach, and now I'm an apple-pie junkie, just like my father. I'll keep trying, though. I'm a persistent man, and I'm going to figure out all of the flavors and spices in there. I can't go to the White House without it."

Carmen put her hands in the front pocket of her overcoat and produced two black gloves. "Good night, Mr. Meyers."

He nodded to her. "Good night, Carmen."

MEYERS STARTED UP the main staircase, stopping to consider his recently finished portrait. It was a good likeness of him. He'd decided to smile, believing it reflected his youth and vitality. Modern presidents were getting younger, a trend that reflected the demands of the job. The days started early and finished late. That was all right by him. He didn't need much sleep. If he caught four hours of uninterrupted sleep a night, he considered it fortuitous. The pressures of the day required his strict attention, which was what had upset him about Elizabeth's recent transgressions. She knew the demands upon him. She had known when they married. He had made it very clear that politics was his calling, his destiny.

A security agent stood at the top of the staircase. The sight of the man reminded him that Boutaire still had not reported in. That was not good. Dana Hill was bold. Too bold. She had come to Robert Meyers's party, walked right in, and shaken his hand. Meyers gave her credit for guts but little for brains. Maybe it no longer mattered. Elizabeth now knew the truth, and there was nothing anyone could do about it. He had planned it well. James Hill was dead. So were the two men Boutaire had sent to rob him. Dana Hill had an earring. She could keep it, for all he cared. Still, he didn't like the woman. She clearly did not know her place. In that regard, Boutaire had failed. He should have killed her, but it was not too late to put Dana Hill in her place. Meyers had that kind of power.

Meyers walked the carpeted hall, wondering what it would be like to stroll the halls of the White House in his slippers and bathrobe. He wouldn't feel the least bit self-conscious. It would be his home, after all. He could dress however he damn well pleased in his own home. He had read somewhere that Lyndon Johnson held meetings with staff while sitting on the toilet. The press and biographers said it reflected Johnson's megalomaniac personality, his need to degrade those who worked for him. Meyers knew otherwise. Johnson didn't have enough time in the day to take a crap in peace, and staff needed to be reminded that they were not on par with the president of the United States. It helped keep them in line. For similar reasons, Meyers insisted on a fresh-baked apple pie each day, whether he ate a slice or not. The rest of the country could eat day-old pie. Not a future president.

Tonight Carmen's pie had hit the spot. The warmth from his contented stomach spread to his groin with the thought that Elizabeth awaited him, smelling of flowers and wearing the white lace nightgown an assistant had purchased. He smiled. His wife remained a beautiful woman. He had done all right for himself. She'd always had suitors, but he'd been the one to bag her. He quickened his stride. Making love to her remained an enjoyable task. In college, he'd considered her youth and vitality an attri-bute, but keeping her under control had been hard work. She acted out to test his love and sought to be punished to affirm that he still loved her. Now she could have no doubt. She had made a mistake, a terrible mistake, but he truly had forgiven her. What were his options? Divorce? Under the circumstances, it was out of the question.

Meyers walked into the parlor and started toward the closed double doors leading to the bedroom. Light crept out from beneath them onto the carpet. She had waited up, as he'd requested. He pushed open the door to the low hum of music. The lighting from the candle wall sconces cast a soft glow across the bed, also as he preferred. But the bed was empty. The sheets lay in a crumpled pile in the center. He walked to the bathroom door, about to knock, when he heard the slow trickle of water. His wife preferred to fill the tub to shoulder level and allow a continuous flow of hot water to soothe her as she soaked, sometimes for an hour. He looked at his watch. It was already late. Still, he decided not to rush her. He contemplated calling the staff to change the sheets on the bed but instead pulled them tight to the corners and tucked in the sides. He fluffed the pillows and put them at the head of the bed. Then he took a seat on the sofa near the window, picked up a copy of *Newsweek*, and slipped on a pair of reading glasses.

After ten minutes, he tossed the magazine on the teak table, stood, and looked about the room. He was growing tired, and his interest had begun to wane. He picked up the telephone, a direct line to the security office in the compound.

"Who am I speaking with?"

"This is Garth Schlemlein, Senator."

"Has Peter Boutairc checked in yet?"

"No, Senator, he has not."

Meyers rubbed his chin. It had been over forty-eight hours

since he'd heard from Boutaire. It was not uncommon for the man to disappear for stretches of time only to surface with the task accomplished, but Meyers did not think this was one of those times. "I asked that his apartment be considered. Has that been done?"

"It was done, Senator. The manager said he had not seen Mr. Boutaire in quite some time. His unit was nearly empty."

Meyers took a deep breath.

"He also said Boutaire's sister and a police detective had been to the apartment earlier in the evening. Our men missed them by—"

"His sister?"

"Yes, sir."

"He doesn't—" Meyers caught himself.

"Sir?"

Meyers's focus shifted to the closed bathroom door. "Keep trying to reach him. Have him report to me as soon as he arrives. I don't care what time of day or night." He hung up, went over to the bathroom door, and knocked. "Elizabeth?" There was no answer. He pressed an ear to the door. "Elizabeth?" He heard only the trickle of water. He jiggled the brass handle. The door was locked. "Elizabeth!"

He walked to the dresser and reached for the key to the lock but did not feel it. He stood on his toes and swept his hands over the top. The key was not there. She'd taken it. He banged on the door. "Elizabeth!"

Moisture seeped through the soles of his wool slippers. He stepped back and saw the discoloration of the carpet near the door. "Elizabeth, open this door. Elizabeth!"

He smashed a shoulder into the wood, but the heavy

door did not give. He hit it several more times, growing angry, calling out her name. He picked up the phone on the nightstand by the bed, yelling, "Get somebody in here. Now."

Within seconds, the compound was in a flurry. Two security agents burst into Meyers's bedroom. Meyers pointed to the door. "Bust it down."

The agents looked about the room, perplexed. "Do you want to get—"

"Bust it down, goddamn it."

The bigger of the two agents moved quickly to the door and tried the handle.

"It's locked, you fool," Meyers growled.

The man hit the door hard with his shoulder. It did not budge. He stood back, used a swinging motion to propel his weight forward, and crashed his shoe against the handle. Again the thick oak shook but did not give. A second kick had similar effect.

"No good."

"Get something," Meyers shouted to the second agent.

Minutes later, with Meyers alternately pacing the room and banging on the door and calling his wife's name, the agents reappeared, one carrying a sledgehammer.

"Go," Meyers said when the man hesitated.

The agent swung the hammer at the door handle. The door frame cracked. A second blow splintered it. The third blow exploded the door inward. The bathroom emitted a blast of hot, humid air. Meyers shoved the agents to the side and rushed in, fanning the steam. The mirrors dripped with condensation. Water overflowed the bathtub's beveled marble rim, an inch deep on the tile floor.

∽

MEYERS RUSHED DOWN the hall, the two agents trailing behind. A clearly perplexed third agent stood outside the closed door to Elizabeth's study. "She asked not to be disturbed," he said.

Meyers shoved him aside and tried the door. Locked. "When did she go in there?" Meyers asked.

"About thirty minutes ago, sir."

Meyers knocked on the door. "Elizabeth, open the door."

There was no answer.

Meyers knocked more forcefully and raised his voice. "Open the damn door." He stepped back and motioned to the agent holding the sledgehammer. "Break it in," he instructed.

The agent swung the hammer, repeating the process until the door burst open. Like the bathroom, the room was empty. Meyers spun to the agent who had stood outside the door. "Where the hell is she?"

"I don't—"

"Did you see her leave?"

"No, sir, the door never opened."

"And you never left?"

The guard shook his head. "No, sir, I asked Mrs. Meyers what she was doing up so late. She said she couldn't sleep and was going to be working late and wanted absolutely no interruptions. She asked me to stand guard outside her door."

Meyers ran a hand across his face and closed his eyes. "Then what the hell did she do, pull a fucking Houdini?"

The agent did not respond.

"Tell me," Meyers yelled. "I'm asking a question. How did she get out?" He stared into the empty room. It was the question that had perplexed him most about her affair with James Hill. How did she get out of the compound? Based on Peter Boutaire's investigation, Elizabeth had left the compound when Meyers was traveling. Her meetings with James Hill had transpired at a mountain retreat and once or twice at his home in Green Lake. The pair had even stopped once at a roadside motel, like two high school students unable to control their raging hormones. Meyers had no doubt that once off the compound grounds, disguised in a wig or other attire, his wife could disappear into the everyday masses. Those who might recognize her would dismiss her as a look-alike. But Boutaire had never figured out how Elizabeth managed to get off the compound grounds.

"There is another exit," the agent said.

Meyers turned. "What?"

"Another exit from the study." The agent pointed. "The wall is a doorway, sir, just under Mrs. Meyer's portrait."

Meyers considered the man for a moment. The windowless room had been intended as a room for servants, so as not to disturb the family's privacy, but Elizabeth had chosen it for her study. Her preference for it over other, more suitable rooms had always perplexed him. Below her portrait on the red silk wall, he found a recessed handle within the woodwork. He pressed it and pushed open the wall to a bleak staircase.

"I thought you knew," the agent said.

"Of course I knew," Meyers hissed. But he had not. Even as a child, he had never mingled with the staff. He descended the staircase to a door, opened it, and emerged at the back of the pantry. The door was concealed on the opposite side by shelving stocked with food items. Meyers walked into the kitchen, where, moments before, he had sat eating apple pie. The servants' locker room was to his immediate right, as was the servants' entrance to and from the kitchen.

"Call the front gate. I want to know if she leaves the grounds." Meyers spoke to the agents through clenched teeth. His chest heaved in a single gasp of air. She was such a child. Such a goddamned child.

"Mrs. Meyers's car is still here, Senator," the agent reported. "No one has left except the maid."

"Search the upstairs. Be sure she's not in one of the other rooms."

The two agents went back up the stairs. Meyers started from the kitchen, then stopped. In the sink, unwashed, was his nearly empty glass of milk and crumb-specked plate. It was not like Carmen to leave the plates out, unclean. She would not have done so unless she had been in a hurry. He pressed the crumbs with his finger, then turned back to reconsider the hidden stairway.

"Son of a bitch."

57

❧

She stood at the windows, looking out into the garden patio, a silhouette in the silver glow of the moonlight through the glass panes. She could have been a ghost. Thick black hair cascaded to a tip between her shoulder blades, nearly undistinguishable against the black leather jacket that extended to the back of her thighs. Tall and slender, she wore dark jeans and flat leather shoes.

As Dana stepped into the room, the shadow at the window did not turn.

"James loved this view." Elizabeth spoke to the glass panes. "In the spring, when the tulips bloomed and the cherry trees blossomed, he liked to sit here at night with the lights off and watch the way the moonlight reflected on the petals. We sat on the couch and let the minutes tick by. Even when our time together was limited, he refused to rush. There was never a sense of urgency. He said it was something he had to relearn after practicing law. He said law had taught him to count the minutes but not to appreciate them."

The movers had not yet removed the furniture or throw rugs, but the African masks and tapestries no longer adorned the walls. The room felt empty without them. Fallow ground.

Elizabeth turned. The light reflected on her moistened cheek. "Your brother learned to appreciate the minutes, Dana. He really loved his life."

Without the jewelry and designer suits, Elizabeth looked even younger than forty. She could have been any of the mothers Dana saw rushing to pick up their children from day care. It made Dana think of Michael Logan's astonished reaction when she'd told him that James and Elizabeth had had an affair. Logan saw the wife of a billionaire senator, the wife of a potential president. He did not see the eighteen-year-old college freshman Dana's brother had fallen in love with.

"I wondered why he faced the couch toward the window," Dana said. "The brother I knew would have watched *SportsCenter*."

Elizabeth hung her head and started to cry. "I'm so sorry. This is my fault," she said, her voice fading. "It's all my fault."

Dana went to her, now drawn by a common bond— two women who had met only briefly years before but who would forever be linked by tragedy and sorrow. She wrapped her arms around Elizabeth's shoulders, holding her, letting her cry. "What happened here was not your fault. It was not your doing."

Elizabeth stepped back and pressed her palms against her eyes, wiping the tears from her cheeks. Dana had mistaken the discolored welt near her right eye as mascara, but she now saw the ugly markings on her neck as well.

Her lip was swollen. Dana thought of William Welles's description of Elizabeth being a prisoner.

"It is," Elizabeth said. "I never should have pursued it. I never should have put James in harm's way. I knew it couldn't work out. I knew it but—" Her breath caught.

Dana realized that she and Elizabeth were also similar in that neither had yet had time to grieve for a man they loved, and as much as Dana had loved her brother, she had loved him as a sister. Elizabeth had clearly loved him as a soul mate. She had a right to know what had happened to James. "They found him behind the couch," Dana said. "The two men who killed him are both dead. We think a security agent who worked for your husband hired them, then killed them."

"Peter Boutaire." Elizabeth spoke the name as if uttering a profanity. "He and Robert grew up together. He is a terrible man; he has no conscience."

"He won't be bothering anyone anymore, either."

Elizabeth's chest heaved, as if in relief.

"One of the men was found with cash in his pockets. We think they were paid to break in and given a list of things to get, the earrings obviously foremost on the list. Somehow your husband knew you had left them here. When James surprised them, they must have dropped one and didn't have time to retrieve it. I found it under the bed. How could that have happened?"

Elizabeth stood shaking her head. "I usually put all my jewelry in my purse, but that night... That was our last night together. We didn't take much time to talk or to undress. I put them on the windowsill above his bed, behind the blinds. I left in the middle of the night, not wanting to wake him. I was so upset, I wasn't thinking about anything except that I would never see him again. I must have assumed I put them in my purse, which I normally did. The next time I needed them, they weren't in my dresser. I panicked, but I found both in my purse. Robert must have put the match there along with the earring they found." Elizabeth used both hands to wipe the tears freely flowing down her cheeks. "I'm not sure how he found out, but there was little I could do without him knowing. Boutaire likely followed me, realized I wasn't wearing the earrings, and later determined I didn't have them." She found her way to a simple upholstered chair and slumped into it. "I suspected something when I heard the news, but I didn't want to believe..." The words stopped in her throat. "Oh God, it hurt. It hurt so bad to know he was gone and I couldn't tell anyone or let anyone know. I wanted to go to the funeral, but I couldn't. I've been so blind. I've been so afraid."

Dana sat on the black leather couch. "How long has it been like this?"

"When hasn't it been like this?" Elizabeth thought for a moment. "Robert was always so in control. I liked it when I was eighteen years old and a long way from home; it gave me a sense of comfort to have someone take care of me. I didn't have to do anything. He bought me clothes because he said he liked to and his family could afford it. He told me which perfume to wear, how to cut my hair, everything. When you're eighteen, it can be intoxicating to have someone care so much about you. I'm not going to lie to you, Dana. I had never been around so much money. Everything was taken care of. All I had to do was get up in the morning." Elizabeth shook her head. "At the end of my freshman year, I stayed the summer because Robert said he wanted me near him. He rented an apartment for me in the University District so I wouldn't have to work. He said I should relax. He even developed a schedule for me. He said it would make me more disciplined." She smiled at a recollection. "James came to my apartment, took one look at the schedule on the wall, and burst out laughing. He asked me if I had lost my mind. I was too embarrassed to tell him Robert had made it. James took a black marker and wrote 'Gone Fishing' across it. Then he said we were going to the Kingdome to see a baseball game because I'd never seen one before." She laughed. "I was so excited. I changed into cutoff jeans, a tank top, and sandals." The smile faded from her face. "Robert hated those clothes. He said they made me look cheap." She bent forward and clasped her hands against her stomach as if fighting a stomachache. "James's car started to overheat, and I remember thinking how disappointed I would be if we didn't make it, but he told me we'd walk if we had to. He said no life was complete without seeing a baseball game in person. He was right, too. I ate everything I wasn't supposed to, and James taught me how to boo and whistle between my fingers and yell at the umpires. After the game, we went to one of the local bars near the stadium and had a few more beers." She turned her attention back to the patio garden. "On the drive home, I had this haunting feeling, like when I was a kid and we'd have to leave Lake Tahoe at the end of the summer. I knew it couldn't last forever, but just the same, I wanted it to."

"So what happened when you got home?" Dana asked, knowing that Elizabeth was building toward something.

"Robert was waiting at the apartment. That was the first time he hit me." She felt the corner of her lip with her fingertips. "He said he'd spent all afternoon and evening trying to find me. He held the schedule in front of me like a report card and yelled, 'Is this supposed to be funny? Is this the thanks I get for trying to help you?' He said what good was a schedule if it wasn't followed. He said I didn't appreciate all of the things he'd done for me."

She turned to Dana. "I knew what he did was wrong, but it all seemed so surreal to me. He kept saying how much he loved me and not to spoil what we could have together. I didn't know what to do. My mother and father adored him, or at least the thought of him, and I didn't think it would be this bad. I thought he just lost his temper. Two weeks later, he had a ring and asked me to marry him at the end of the summer. I was supposed to finish college in Massachusetts. But I never did."

Dana sat listening to the hum of the refrigerator. A pipe in the walls creaked.

"Isn't it every little girl's fantasy to marry a prince and live happily ever after?" Elizabeth asked. "I remember when the stories first broke about Princess Diana's depression and bulimia. Part of me refused to believe it. She was a *princess*. And how could it go on? Where were her parents? Where were her friends? How could we not know such a public figure had such a horrible life?" She let the question hang in the stillness of the room.

"We do it for a lot of reasons," Dana said. "We do it because we're young and naive and we think things will change for the better. We do it for our parents and friends. Then we do it for our children because we don't want them to grow up in a broken home. But in the end, we come to realize that things aren't going to change. Our parents and friends aren't the ones who have to live with him, and it's our children who suffer the most."

Elizabeth shifted uncomfortably.

"But we're the only ones who can change it, Elizabeth. We're the only ones who can make it different. The question is whether you are prepared to do so."

58

~

CARMEN DUPREE LIVED in a predominantly black
neighborhood in Seattle's Central District. It was
a tough neighborhood, like the neighborhood in Balti-
more where she had been raised. It was hard living. People scratched out an existence whatever way they could.
Good people lived there—honest, God-fearing people
who never got any recognition because the drug dealers and thugs got all the news. Carmen worked hard. It
was in her blood. Her mother had been a maid for fifty
years and her grandmother before that. The Duprees were
descended from slaves and took no shame in it. Cleaning homes was an honest living. It put food on the table
and clothes on her four son's backs. But the legacy of the
Dupree women had always been their recipe for apple pie,
a recipe passed from generation to generation, starting at
a South Carolina plantation where her ancestors picked
cotton. It was passed by word of mouth along with the
rest of the family history. The secret ingredients would

not be found on even the smallest scrap of paper. They would also likely die with Carmen. The good Lord had not blessed her with a daughter, and her sons showed only an interest in eating the pie, not in baking it. It was a shame. Apple pie had gotten her a job working for one of the richest families in Washington. She had been hired to clean the house and bake apple pie. Then, when Robert Meyers III was born, she took to caring for him along with doing the cleaning. But the child was different from his father; he had a mean streak, and she sensed a propensity for evil in him. It didn't help that they spoiled him, made him think he could do as he pleased, then allowed him to do just that. Carmen had swatted his behind once, after finding him torturing a cat with matches. He had lied and said she made up the story, and he was convincing enough that his parents chose to believe him. He had that ability to lie and look like he was telling you the honest truth. A born politician. They told Carmen to never again lay a hand on him, and they demanded that she apologize. She would have told them all to kindly depart this world for Hades, but she had four babies of her own to feed and no husband to help pay the bills. So she had swallowed her pride and apologized. From that moment on, Robert Meyers had done as he pleased.

She parked her Impala along the dimly lit street. She had switched to working nights to avoid Meyers as much as possible, mostly cleaning and tending to things in the kitchen. It was how she had come to know Elizabeth. The poor woman stalked the hallways at night like a ghost in a haunted mansion, and it didn't take a Ph.D. to know why. A woman who'd rather walk the halls alone than share her husband's bed had a bad marriage. Her heart was heavy, like her husband's hand. Carmen had taken to bringing her a slice of pie in her study at night, and their meetings had become conversations and their conversations a friendship. Elizabeth became the daughter Carmen never bore. They talked on about every subject a mother and daughter could—children, men, sex, cooking. It took some time before Elizabeth confided in her about the beatings. Such things were not unfamiliar to Carmen. Her husband had hit her, too, once. Then she woke him from a dead sleep with a cooking knife pressed to his throat and made it clear that he would never hit her again if he hoped to ever have another untroubled night's sleep. He never did. He left.

Carmen crossed the street in the sporadic light of burned-out streetlamps, some of which had been broken for nearly a year. Despite the late hour, young men stood in the concrete park across from the apartment complex, their talk loud and animated. Carmen detected the sweet aroma of marijuana, but the young men never bothered her. She knew their mothers, and she was not adverse to giving each of them a tongue lashing if they disrespected her.

When Elizabeth Meyers came to her the first time, Carmen never hesitated. It wasn't any of her business what the young woman chose to do or not do, or who she chose to do it with. All Carmen knew was that it had brought a sad soul to life, and for her, that was worth the risk. Everyone was entitled to a bit of happiness in life. Her mother liked to say that life was a blink of an eye. There were no second chances. Carmen knew it.

As she reached the door to her low-income town home, Carmen heard the sound of car engines revving and tires squealing. She watched the cars turn the corner onto her street and approach the concrete playground at high speed. The young men scattered like a flock of birds taken to flight. Visits from the police were frequent. But the men who emerged from the cars and rushed across the park and through the chain-link fence were dressed in suits. They were not policemen. Carmen had expected them at some point. She never flinched.

Lights came on in the windows of the other homes. The faces in the windows would look out, wondering if this time it would be their brother or father who would be taken to jail. But the faces in the windows did not look down upon a young black man surrounded by white police officers. This time they saw Carmen staring at the outstretched barrels of weapons in the hands of four white men wearing dark suits—men Carmen knew but who stood yelling at her just the same to get down on the ground and keep her hands where they could see them.

"Gentlemen," Carmen said, crossing her arms, "I have no intention of getting on that cold ground. And if you intend to shoot me, then do it here in front of God and everyone else. As for my job, you can tell Mr. Meyers I've never liked him much, and I'd as soon see him in hell than to continue working for him." She started for her door, then turned back to the men. "Oh, and tell him he can make his own damn pie."

59

I KNEW THE MOMENT I saw him that day at the law school." Elizabeth Meyers sat in the chair near the window. "Just seeing James again brought a smile to my face and a joy I hadn't felt in a long time. He was still so full of life. After the conference, I made an excuse to call him. Like I said, a part of me knew it couldn't work, but I wanted to talk to him. He always took my calls, so I suspected he felt the same. Ten-minute conversations became an hour. An hour became two hours. I began to worry about the phone bills and the repeating number. I'm sure Robert had the calls screened. Then, during one conversation, James and I discussed meeting. Robert was traveling to D.C. quite a bit, and I'm sure he never suspected I would dare do anything like that. It was his arrogance that gave me the opportunity."

"But how could you get out of the compound without people seeing you? I've read that it has a state-of-the-art security system and that he employs his own private security force."

"Initially, I had my driver take me to the school. No one knew James worked there. I told them it was to visit a college girlfriend. When that became suspicious, I began locking myself in my office and used a stairwell to get to the servants' locker room. A dear friend drove me out under a pile of coats in the back of her car. I kept a wig and sunglasses and a coat in a locker there. I also had access to the maids' uniforms. She picked me up in the morning, and I made my way back."

Dana looked at her in amazement.

Elizabeth started to cry again. "I would have held on to the bottom of the car to see him. We both knew it couldn't last, but we couldn't stand the pain of not seeing each other, and I began to hope that maybe, somehow...I don't know. It was naive, but some days it was the only reason I could even get out of bed in the morning. James gave me hope. Then he said he would find a way."

"How did your husband find out?"

"When it became apparent that Robert would seek the presidency, Boutaire became more prevalent. That was never a good thing. I suspected he had become suspicious. So I told James I couldn't see him anymore. We agreed to meet one last time to say good-bye. I dressed up for him that evening and wore the earrings. We had a candlelight dinner near these windows and held each other. Leaving was the hardest thing I've ever done. But you have to understand, there was nothing he or I could do. There's nothing I can do now."

"So then why are you here now? Why did you ask to see me tonight?"

Elizabeth looked as though she hadn't considered the question, or the answer was obvious. "Because I thought you deserved an explanation. That's why you came to the Fairmont, wasn't it? Because you wanted to know what happened?"

Dana shook her head. "I already knew what happened. I came to the hotel because I need your help."

Elizabeth looked genuinely puzzled. "My help?"

"I want your husband to pay for killing my brother."

Elizabeth shook her head. "You can't get him. No one can. No one has ever been able to get him."

"You're wrong. I can get him, and I will. But I need you to state that the earrings are yours, that the one I found in my brother's house is yours, and that the two of you were having an affair. That gives Meyers the motivation to kill James. It ties him to Boutaire and to the deaths of the two men who killed James."

Elizabeth shook her head. "I can't do that."

Dana closed the space between them. "Yes, you can. You can do it for James, and you can do it for yourself. James was going to do it for you. The day he died, he called me and said he had a problem he wanted to talk to me about. He was going to find a way to save you. I don't care how powerful your husband is. He killed James, and I want him. That's my motivation. You have to motivate yourself."

"I can't—"

Dana's voice rose. "Then he will continue to abuse—"

"Dana, I'm pregnant"

Dana took a step backward. "What?"

Elizabeth turned to the window, silent for a moment. Then she turned back to Dana. "I'm pregnant. I didn't think it was possible, but I am. I don't care about myself anymore, but Robert would never let me take his child, and I won't leave my son or daughter to that man. I won't do it."

Dana sat down in the chair, utterly defeated. She felt the onset of a headache. "You think you're doing your child a favor, but you're not. I used to think the same thing. Raising your child in an abusive home, in an unhappy marriage, is not protecting your child. It's..." She was struck by a thought. "What did you mean, you didn't think it possible?"

"I've never been able to conceive. We tried for years. Nothing worked. The doctors had no explanation for it."

"How far are you? How many months?"

"Just about seven weeks," Elizabeth said. "I'd been feeling nauseated, and I thought it was the flu.... What are you doing?"

Dana had taken out her cell phone. "I need to make a phone call."

60

THE MEDICAL CLINIC in Redmond wouldn't open until eight-thirty A.M. Logan had rushed to get there for nothing. He and Dana sat parked outside the two-story redbrick building, sipping coffee. Dana rested an elbow out the window and considered an ugly slate-gray morning dampened by a light mist. She had slept little, but she was not tired. Her adrenaline was pumping so hard it was difficult to sit in the car, waiting. If she was right, they had a real shot to take down Robert Meyers.

Logan had met her and Elizabeth Meyers at James's home. They had driven to the Hill home on Lake Washington. Dana gave Elizabeth her room, and though Elizabeth professed to be incapable of sleeping, it was like watching a weary traveler making it home to a comfortable bed. She was asleep minutes after her head touched the pillow. Logan beefed up security with two additional uniformed officers, one in the front and one in the back, in addition to an officer inside.

The sound of a car entering the parking lot diverted Dana's attention. A cherry-red Jeep pulled into a reserved space near the glass entrance to the building. That was a good sign. So was the license plate: KIDDOC. A tall woman with shoulder-length hair emerged, paused to consider Logan's car, then unlocked the door to the building and disappeared inside. Dana pulled out the scrap of paper and looked again at the name written on it. She wasn't sure what had triggered her memory, but when she'd gotten back to her home, she'd found the story she recalled reading on the Internet and confirmed the name.

During the next few minutes, two more cars arrived, and two more women followed the same routine.

Dana pushed open the car door, stepped out, and pulled her sweater on as they approached the building. The glass doors remained locked. Logan knocked with a key on the glass, a metallic ting. No one came to the door. He knocked again, this time with more force. The woman who had exited the Jeep appeared in the hall, looking annoyed and slightly anxious. When Logan held up his badge, her eyes narrowed and her brow furrowed. She unlocked the door and opened it only enough to talk. "Can I help you?"

"Sorry to bother you before you've opened. I'm Detective Michael Logan. We'd like to ask you a few questions."

"What's this about?"

"Dr. Frank Pilgrim," Logan said.

The woman shook her head, perplexed. "I don't understand."

"Just a few questions," Logan said, and the woman stepped back from the door with a bewildered look. Dana followed Logan into a lobby of miniature chairs and tables with a box of well-worn toys in the corner.

"I noticed your license plate," Dana said. "You're a doctor here at the clinic?"

"Yes."

"Did you know Frank Pilgrim very well?"

The woman laughed in a burst. Nerves. "I should think so. He was my father. I'm Dr. Emily Pilgrim."

"I'm sorry about your father," Dana said.

"Then you know he's dead."

"I read his obituary in the paper."

"Did you know my father?"

"No, I didn't," Dana said.

"I don't understand. What is it you want? I'm afraid this is a bit disconcerting."

"I'm sorry to trouble you. I don't mean to cause you any grief, but where was your father when he died?" Logan asked.

Emily Pilgrim shrugged and closed her eyes. "Where he has been most nights for the past forty-eight years. In his office, doing paperwork."

"How did your father die?" Logan asked.

"He had a heart attack."

"Was your father in good health? Did he have any health problems that you know of?"

"No. He was seventy-eight years old, but fit enough to run the Seattle marathon again this year."

Logan smiled. "That's quite an accomplishment at any age."

"My father refused to accept any suggestion that he could no longer do the things he did as a young man. So, health problems? No. Why do you ask?"

"So I take it that his death caught you by surprise, given his overall good health."

She gave a resigned shrug. "We were surprised, but good health doesn't always mean a good heart."

"I understand. This is a pediatric clinic?"

"Yes."

"And your father was also a pediatrician?"

"For forty-eight years."

"Was he retired?"

"No. I bought the practice from him eight years ago, hoping he would retire, but he wouldn't have it. He was supposed to work another two years, then he was going to retire so he and my mother could..." She choked back tears. Dana handed her a tissue from a box on the receptionist's counter. Pilgrim wiped a tear from her cheek and rubbed the Kleenex beneath her nose.

"Were you here with your father the night he died?" Dana asked.

Pilgrim shook her head and crumpled the tissue in her hand. "Why are you asking me these things? What is it you want to know?"

Dana decided to simply ask the question. "We understand from his obituary that your father was Robert Meyers's doctor."

Pilgrim stopped wiping her nose. She looked from Dana to the detective. "Not for many years, but yes, he treated all of the Meyers's children, Bob Meyers included. He also treated Bob's father." She turned to a table filled with sympathy cards and chose one. "He sent us a card, after my father died. And he telephoned my mother. It meant a lot to her."

"I don't imagine his medical file would still be here in this building?" Dana asked.

"Whose medical file?"

"Robert Meyers's."

Pilgrim shook her head. "One would think that, but as I said, my father wasn't very receptive to suggestions or to change. When I bought the practice, I tried to modernize it, but he resisted, right down to insisting that all of his files remain in his office, whether they were active or closed. We had to wire the office around him."

Dana felt a growing sense of optimism and tried to keep Pilgrim disarmed. "My father thought of his computer as a large paperweight."

"So you would expect that file to be somewhere in your father's office?" Logan asked.

Pilgrim shrugged. "Yes, I suppose so, but—"

"Could we check?" Dana asked.

Pilgrim rocked back on her heels. She shook her head. "Not without some authority."

"We're not asking to read the file or for you to tell us what's in it," Dana said. "We just want to know if it's here."

Pilgrim crossed her arms. "May I ask why? This is really disturbing."

Dana spoke politely. "Dr. Pilgrim, I'm sure these questions are coming out of the blue, and I'm very sorry to bring up your father's death. I recently lost a brother myself. But a full explanation at this point would be long and convoluted. Before we take up that much of your time, could we first check to see if the file is even here?" Pilgrim took a deep breath and closed her eyes. Dana feared she was becoming reticent. She asked, "Would you recognize your father's handwriting?"

Pilgrim opened her eyes. "Absolutely."

Dana pulled the empty manila file from her briefcase, the one they had taken from Peter Boutaire's apartment.

She handed it to Pilgrim, who considered the name written on the tab in faded blue ink, then opened it and asked, "Where did you get this?"

"Do you recognize it?" Dana asked.

"Yes. It's one of my father's files."

"That's his handwriting at the top?" Logan asked.

"I'm certain of it." Pilgrim opened the file and pointed as she spoke. "Do you see these markings here inside the cover? Those are my father's doodles. He was a doodler. You couldn't leave anything of importance near the telephone or he would scribble all over it. You'll find these markings in all his files." She shook her head. "Where did you get it? Where is the rest of it?"

Dana said, "Could you check and see if your father has a file here for Robert Meyers?"

"That *is* his file. At least that's his folder."

"Could we check? We won't disturb anything," Dana said.

Pilgrim considered them for another moment. Then she sighed. "Come with me."

She led them to an office at the back of the complex, talking as they walked. "My father's office is as cluttered as a museum, and I haven't had the time or the courage to try and clean it out. I don't think I will for some time." She pushed open the door.

"Is this where you found your father?" Logan asked, stepping in.

"Yes. I found him here, on the floor. My mother called and said he hadn't come home yet." She looked down at a commercial-grade blue carpet with flecks of color. "He appeared to be reaching across his desk for the telephone, trying to call for help, I suppose, when he collapsed."

Logan stood at the desk with his back to them and looked over his shoulder at the bank of green filing cabinets with a small television on top. "What time did you find him?"

"My mother called me around eleven. She spoke to him earlier that evening, and Dad said he was on his way home. They had a routine. They spoke at ten sharp. Dad was home by ten-thirty. When he didn't walk in the door, my mother started to worry. When she couldn't reach him at the office, she called me."

"So you found him?"

"Yes."

"How long do you estimate your father had been dead?"

"Probably an hour. Maybe an hour and a half."

"What would your father have been doing at ten at night?" Logan asked.

"As I said, sitting at his desk, doing his paperwork and listening to the television, if the Mariners were on."

"Could we look for that file?"

Pilgrim walked to the file cabinets and considered the letters on the white cards in the slots on the front. She found the drawer indicating the closed files for patients with last names beginning with the initial "M" and pulled open the drawer. She was about to thumb through the files, then stopped. One of the files had been pulled out and placed at an angle, as was her father's custom. Emily Pilgrim looked at the name on the file in the drawer, then considered the file in her hand. She straightened and turned around. "I think you better tell me what you're doing here."

THIRTY MINUTES LATER, Emily Pilgrim sat with her elbows propped on the desk in her office, a fist pressed against her lips. Behind her, framed diplomas and family portraits lined the wall. Her father looked like an elderly Burt Lancaster—a polished gentleman with watery blue eyes and thinning snow-white hair.

"And this man had my father's file?" Pilgrim asked.

"Yes." Dana knew she and Logan had given Pilgrim a lot to consider. Now it was simply a matter of whether she believed them or not.

"I don't suppose you had an autopsy done on your father?" Logan asked.

She shrugged. "There was no reason to. And now... Well, he was cremated. Why? Why would someone take Robert Meyers's file? Why would someone want my father dead? It doesn't make any sense. My father devoted his life to helping children. He had no enemies, none."

"I don't think it had to do with your father, Dr. Pilgrim," Dana said. "I think it had to do with something that was in this file—something that your father would have known. Whatever it was, it appears to have been destroyed."

Pilgrim looked up at them from across the desk, her look of confusion replaced by one of intrigue. "Would you excuse me for a second?" She pressed the intercom button on her telephone. "Michelle, can you come in here?"

A moment later, there was a knock on the door, and a petite brunette stuck her head in. Pilgrim introduced her to Dana and Logan, explaining that Michelle was in charge of updating the office computer system and inputting the file information.

"How far did you get scanning my father's files into the system?"

"I'm sorry, Dr. Pilgrim, I got tied up with the bills this month. The computer double-billed everything, for some reason, and I had to hand-correct each one," Michelle answered. Pilgrim rubbed the back of her neck in frustration. "I'm sorry. I can continue it this morning."

Pilgrim stopped rubbing her neck and looked up. "Continue?"

61

His fingers formed a small steeple, his rage reflected in the white tips where he pressed the fingers together, cutting off the circulation. Meyers waited in his private study, the voice inside his head anything but quiet. The fucking black woman had refused to utter a single word about where she had taken Elizabeth, and despite what Meyers had wanted to do to her, he knew his hands were tied. Carmen Dupree had, in essence, told him to go fuck himself. That was gratitude for you.

Now he was in a real predicament. He had been careful; no one on the staff knew of Elizabeth's infidelities except Peter Boutaire. When Elizabeth disappeared, he told his security staff that his wife had been acting strange, that he feared the pressure of a public life was beginning to overwhelm her, and that he was concerned she could be suicidal. He told them to quietly find her. He didn't want any information leaked to local authorities or to the press. That was over twenty-four hours ago.

He interlocked his fingers, his thumbs rotating.

She disobeyed you. Deliberately disrespected you. Humiliated you.

He closed his eyes. His hands shook. He had tried everything he could to make her grow up. Hadn't he fulfilled his promises to her? Didn't he teach her everything she needed to know? Didn't he give her everything a woman could ever want? He stood, unable to keep from pacing, hands clenched at his sides. Didn't he have enough pressures? Didn't he have enough responsibilities? He had a fucking campaign to run, and instead, he had a dozen of his security team hunting the city for his own wife? *His wife! His fucking wife!* And he'd be damned if he would give her up. He'd be damned if he would let her waste everything he had done, all of his hard work and effort. He'd be damned if he would let another man enjoy the fruits of his labor.

Someone knocked on his door. Meyers stopped pacing. "Come in." An agent stepped into the room. "She's here, Senator. Mrs. Meyers is here. "

Meyers took a deep breath. "Where did you find her?" His voice quivered.

"We didn't, Senator. She came back on her own. She walked through the front gate a few minutes ago."

Meyers stared at a painting of Elizabeth hanging over the fireplace. Of course she had. Where else could she go? What else could she do? She had undoubtedly wandered aimlessly, taking a hotel room until realizing what her life would become without him. She had to return. He supposed she could have killed herself, one final effort to embarrass him, but he knew she wouldn't. Not when she was with child.

"Send her in." Meyers turned from the agent and headed back to his chair.

"Sir?"

Meyers looked back at the agent, perturbed. "I said send her in."

The agent cleared his throat. "Mrs. Meyers is in your office, sir. She said she would wait for you—"

Meyers tilted his head as if he had not heard.

"She said she'd wait for you there."

He felt the dull ache at his temples penetrate the back of his eyes like two serrated daggers. "Leave," he said.

WHEN THE DOOR to the office opened, Elizabeth did not move. The grandfather clock in the corner of the room chimed as if to announce Robert Meyers's arrival. He paused in the doorway at the sight of her sitting in the captain's chair. His chair. She knew that he had positioned it directly in front of his desk to face two mustard-yellow couches separated by a glass coffee table. It was the same type of chair and setup John F. Kennedy had used in his Oval Office.

Meyers closed the door behind him and walked calmly to the river-rock fireplace. "What we must determine, Elizabeth, is a measured response." He spoke to the plate-glass windows. "What we must determine is an appropriate form of punishment. I understand that you are testing me—testing the limits of my patience and tolerance. I understand that you are seeking my attention, that you want me to punish you." He stopped and turned to her. "What will that punishment be?"

"My life," she said softly.

He shot forward, knocking the vase of freshly cut flowers from the glass coffee table and gripping both sides of the chair. His face contorted within inches of hers, but he spoke barely above a whisper. "Don't think I haven't considered that very thought.

"Just like you killed James Hill."

He smiled. "Yes, just like I killed James Hill."

"The difference, Robert, is you can't kill someone who's already dead."

He laughed, softly at first, with a shake of his head, but it grew in intensity until he collapsed on one of the couches. He put his head in his hands and rubbed at his face. "Do you know how ridiculous you sound, how fucking melodramatic? Am I supposed to feel sorry for you?" He stood again and looked around the room, his arms sweeping. "You're in one of the grandest homes ever built, with a staff at your beck and call."

"You built a prison and employed guards to watch me."

"Really? You've traveled to nearly every country in the world, met the most famous people alive, worn the most expensive clothes, and eaten the most exquisite food." He gripped the arms of the chair again, shaking it, shouting, "I've given you more than even you could have possibly dreamed. What would you have preferred? Did you want the beat-up home in Green Lake with the view of the back of a building? Was that my competition—an underpaid law professor at a second-rate law school?"

"James Hill was a better man than you'll ever be," she said.

He started laughing again. "This has got to end. This demented and tormented way of thinking must come to an end."

"I'm glad you agree, Senator."

Meyers's gaze remained on his wife. Slowly, he removed his hands from the chair and stood upright, a thin, almost imperceptible grin creasing his lips, as if he were enjoying this. "Is she what this is about?" he asked his wife. He waved his hand in the air. "This whole charade of insisting that I meet you here in my office, you sitting in my chair like a defiant brat?" He turned and held out his hands. "Welcome, Ms. Hill. I don't believe I invited you, but please make yourself at home. Don't let the surroundings intimidate you."

Dana stood just inside the door that led to Meyers's private bathroom. "I'm not intimidated by the surroundings or by you."

Meyers walked toward her. "Good." He spread out his arms. "Well, here I am. If your presence is supposed to have made a statement, I'm afraid I missed it."

"I'm not surprised; I doubt you've ever seen anything clearly."

"And you're going to be the one to enlighten me, is that it?" Meyers walked behind his desk, pulled out the highback leather chair, and sat, offering Dana a seat with an upraised palm. "Please, by all means tell me what I have been missing."

Dana stepped forward. "The question is not whether you had my brother killed or even how you did it. You did. The question was always the evidence needed to convict you. How could I link a United States senator and presidential candidate to two petty thieves who killed a law professor in the middle of a botched robbery? Peter Boutaire got us close, but not close enough. He might have helped if he were still alive, but even alive, I doubt he would have said anything."

Meyers nodded. "May he rest in peace. He was a dedicated public servant and a sick son of a bitch."

Dana pulled the earring from her jacket pocket and held it so that it dangled from the end of the chain.

Meyers smiled. "Ah, yes. The precious jewel. I've thought of it often, since the moment I saw it perched so elegantly between your breasts. I must admit, I found it a bit erotic. Elizabeth, remind me to get you something similarly suitable. You see, Ms. Hill, since the moment I opened the little care package brought to me, I've been considering the problem of the missing earring. It was Mr. Boutaire who initially noticed that Elizabeth had left your brother's home that morning without them, and that the earrings could very well tie me to your brother's death. Still, when King and Cole failed to deliver both, I decided to disregard it. I speculated that they had pawned it and that it would disappear forever. But then you took your trip to the jeweler and to the Hawaiian Islands, and I had to conclude you indeed had it. So I had it replaced with an identical, if less expensive, duplicate."

Meyers reached into his desk drawer and pulled out the matching earring. "The thing about a pair of earrings is that they're not much good unless you have them both. One without the other isn't a pair. It's just an earring." He put the earring on the desk pad and pulled his chair forward. "You can still admire it, of course, but it isn't quite the same, is it?"

In one swift motion, Meyers reached for the bronze bust of a buffalo on the corner of his desk, stood, and smashed the blue and diamond jewels, continuing his assault until he was breathing heavily through his nostrils. Strands of hair fell across his face. He flung the buffalo across the room, hitting a bookshelf and toppling ornamental plates.

"Worthless," he said, out of breath, swallowing hard. Then, just as abruptly as he had stood, he smoothed his hair back with his palms and sat back down.

Dana stepped forward and placed the other earring on the desk. "I agree. One without the other is no evidence at all. What I needed was evidence you couldn't destroy, something that could exist on its own."

She pulled a folded sheet of paper from the front pocket of her shirt. Meyers's gaze grew more intense as she unfolded it. "One of the problems with being a public figure is the public scrutiny accorded such a person. A public figure can't engage in the anonymous types of activities that others routinely engage in. Even the most minor ailments can be blown out of proportion." She dropped the sheet of paper on the desk. "A childhood illness like the German measles is just a childhood illness. When, however, it leaves a man sterile, without sufficient sperm production such that, even in this technologically advanced age, it is *impossible* for that man to conceive, that information can become a valuable piece of evidence, don't you think?"

Meyers stared at the sheet of paper, then reached forward and picked it up.

"For someone with ambitions of someday being president, it takes on even greater significance when the wife of that man somehow *does* become pregnant. How, Senator, does something like this happen? And how does that man react—a man who knows he's sterile—when he learns that his wife is bearing the child of another man? What does he do? He'd prefer that she get an abortion, but there are several problems with that scenario, a lack of privacy being preeminent among them, as I just mentioned. Where would she go? How could it be done quietly, discreetly, especially now, with a campaign and all the comparisons to John Kennedy? If the religious right found out, his election campaign would be over before it started. And why would she do it? How could he convince her? She has no idea he's sterile. He's blamed her for his lack of progeny. The doctors tell her there is nothing wrong with her, but he has convinced her otherwise. So if he insists on an abortion, she will suspect immediately that he knows the child is not, that it cannot be, his. And that would reveal that he knew of her affair, which is the very reason why he needed to make the duplicate earring. If she has both earrings, she will not suspect that she's left behind evidence to alert him and given him a reason to kill her lover. So, no, abortion is not a good option."

Elizabeth, who had sat like a jury listening to a lawyer give a closing argument, stood and faced her husband. She reached beneath her blouse and pulled out the tape recorder and wire that led to the tiny microphone hidden behind a button of her leather jacket. "It's over, Robert."

"At a preordained time today, fax machines throughout this city will start sending two documents to every major news network and newspaper in the country," Dana said. "The first document will be a copy of your medical records—the one you had Peter Boutaire kill Frank Pilgrim to retrieve. The second will be bloodwork that proves, conclusively, that the child your wife is carrying is not yours but the son of James Andrew Hill, who was murdered in his Green Lake home."

The door to the office opened. Detective Michael Logan stepped in with several uniformed officers.

"After that," Dana said, "the Seattle Police Department will issue a statement that you are charged with conspiracy to commit murder and two counts of murder in the first degree."

Meyers stood and came out from behind the desk, his voice more a plea than defiance. "Elizabeth, I did this for you. Don't you see? I did this because I love you. You'll be ridiculed and humiliated; your son will be a bastard. Think of what the press will write. Think of how they will treat you."

"I already have," she said. "And I can't think of anything they could do that would be worse than how you've treated me all these years."

Logan and the uniformed officers neared the desk, handcuffs in hand. Dana watched the blood vacate Robert Meyers's face. His blue eyes seemed to turn black. "Elizabeth!" Dana screamed. But it was too late. Meyers's right arm moved quickly, locking across his wife's throat. His left hand pressed the barrel of a gun against her forehead. Logan and the officers froze.

"I can't let you do this, Elizabeth." Meyers spoke into his wife's ear. "We were meant to be together. I can't let you go like this. You know that, don't you?"

"Don't do this, Senator," Logan implored. "Put the weapon down and let her go."

Meyers pulled his wife toward the exit with his face buried in the flow of her hair. "We're supposed to be together, Elizabeth. That's why you came back tonight. That's why you're here, to be with me, forever."

Dana looked to Logan. This was not what she had foreseen.

She thought of William Welles, and her heart swelled with the guilt that, blinded by her thirst for justice, she had been irresponsible, and it had resulted in his death. She couldn't bear to think that Elizabeth Meyers would face the same fate.

"I came back," Elizabeth said, her voice strangled but still strong, "because I wanted to see the expression on your face when I told you to go to hell."

She stepped down hard on his foot and at the same time whipped her head backward, smashing the bridge of his nose. Meyers stumbled, blood flowing down his face, but the gun still in hand. Logan and the officers pulled their weapons. He repeatedly exhorted Meyers to drop the gun. Meyers twisted his neck, the vertebrae popping and cracking, and looked at them as if just noticing them for the first time. Then he smiled, raised the gun, and pulled the trigger.

62

❦

THE NEWS OF Robert Meyers's suicide exploded across the state and the nation, erupting on the afternoon newscasts and spreading quickly to the front page of special editions of the *Times* and the *Post-Intelligencer*. Television stations interrupted scheduled broadcasts. It became the lead news story on CNN, MSNBC, and the other national news networks—national coverage of the grandest proportion. No coverage was too much. No story was too small. Camera crews and news reporters camped outside the locked gate to the Highlands. Helicopters broadcast shots of the Meyers family compound until police helicopters patrolled the skies.

Washingtonians watched the news in stunned silence. In downtown eating establishments and bars, from the Pike Place Market to Pioneer Square, televisions were tuned to news of the event. Patrons mumbled in low-level disbelief. Those old enough to remember said it was like the day John F. Kennedy died. Those younger likened it to the day the space shuttle *Columbia* exploded or to 9/11, events that would forever change the world. Everyone would remember exactly where he or she had been when ABC News correspondent Bill Donovan broke the story that presidential candidate Robert Samuel Meyers was dead. A helpless feeling caused most to simply stare dumbfounded at the television, considering in silence what had actually happened and what the ramifications would be.

Footage showed Meyers being rushed by ambulance to Northwest Hospital, but it was a formality. He had been pronounced dead at the scene. The news hung over Seattle like the persistent gray, an event that transcended race, gender, and social status. People who would never again speak with one another were suddenly bonded by a familiar topic. They said it was more than the death of a man. It was the death of another generation's dreams and hopes. It left them feeling hollow and, unlike the assassination of John Kennedy, without anyone at which to direct their anger. There was no Lee Harvey Oswald to vilify. They could only stand in shock and disbelief, asking why. The question started as an almost imperceptible murmur, but by the end of the day, it had grown to a chorus of millions. At a candlelight vigil held outside the gates, everyone wanted to know what had happened. It didn't make any sense. When no clear answers emerged, the public began to speculate, as only Americans could, and rumors spread quickly that there was more to the suicide than was being revealed.

For two weeks, Elizabeth Meyers healed in seclusion, unseen and unheard from except at the formal affairs— funeral and burial. Then one afternoon she appeared unexpectedly on the front lawn of the family compound to address the press. Dressed in black, standing behind a throng of microphones affixed to a podium, she stoically announced to the American public that she was a fraud. She told them she and her husband had had marital difficulties, that Robert Meyers had been verbally and physically abusive, and despite the conception of their first child, she had recently informed her husband of her intention to end their marriage. She said Meyers had become despondent and irrational and that his behavior had caused her to flee the compound two nights before he took his own life. She returned after he called to plead that she meet with him and talk things over.

Meyers's security staff and house servants would confirm those details. They spoke of a man in a heightened emotional state, agitated and irrational. They reported that he had sent several of his security staff out in search of his wife, demanding that they bring her home. Others would come forward to report having overheard violent clashes between the couple. From there, the rumors spread like the tributaries of a river, and it would be quite some time before Washington and Hollywood had its fill of the story. Dozens of people would become wealthy writing accounts of life in the Meyers compound.

Elizabeth Meyers apologized to the nation for what she termed a deceptive public persona and said she had chosen to reveal the truth because she had a duty to be a role model, as her husband had repeatedly demanded. She said she hoped her own public acknowledgment would help women similarly situated to find the courage to change their lives, and she said she would use her abilities and wealth to influence government agencies to help them.

Her news conference was both hailed and assailed. Some questioned her motivation to cleanse her soul and ruin the image of the fair-haired young senator with the charming smile. Like those people who continued to cling to their perception of Kennedy's Camelot despite the stories of his infidelity, they did not want their perception shattered by reality. They wanted to believe in the man who had so confidently vowed to lead the nation on a course of change. They didn't want to see cracks in their leaders or believe that the men they elevated to bronze busts and marble statues were really just men with all the same flaws and weaknesses. They didn't want to know that Robert Meyers, stripped of his outer garments, was an abusive husband. They wanted the fairy tale. They wanted the storybook ending. They wanted a return to Camelot.

Those were not the people to whom Elizabeth Meyers addressed her comments. She spoke instead to the verbally and physically abused women, and to them she became a modern-day Joan of Arc. She brought attention to a problem that had been far too long ignored, a problem that the O. J. Simpson fiasco had only exacerbated, and that had left so many similarly situated women feeling hollow and empty.

As for Dana's quest for justice, she and Elizabeth decided that any announcement of Meyers's involvement in James's murder would only serve to ruin the lives of those left behind—most notably Elizabeth and James's unborn child. It would be a selfish act that James would not have wanted.

The day after her press conference, Elizabeth Meyers left the compound. Staff within the compound walls would later report that she left nearly everything behind, taking only one small suitcase. Her clothes, perfumes, strands of pearls, diamonds, and other jewelry were given to a cook named Carmen Dupree. Elizabeth returned to southern California, not far from the small beach town where she had been raised. She implored the press to allow her to raise her child in peace.

Dana Hill had left the compound through the servants' entrance in the trunk of Michael Logan's car. She thought it fitting. She returned to her mother's home and stayed several days. It was while standing in the kitchen, making a cup of tea, that she heard the news on the radio about Elizabeth Meyers's plane landing at the airport in La Jolla. Dana wondered if the woman would ever find peace, or if she would, tragically, end up like Jacqueline Onassis and Princess Diana.

The following morning, Dana faced the inevitable task of cleaning out her office. As she filled boxes, she felt the floor outside her door tremor but made no effort to reach for the telephone. She no longer cared when the door burst open and Marvin Crocket stepped inside. His face was flushed red, a sinister smile on his lips. "Two weeks without any calls to check in? It's over. I have the support—"

In the midst of his tirade, Crocket had apparently missed the boxes and the empty shelves. When it finally occurred to him what he was witnessing, he reacted as if somehow being cheated out of the pleasure of firing her. His eyes widened, and the smile disappeared. "What the hell are you doing?"

Dana pulled a diploma off the wall and slid it into the box. "I'm leaving."

"You're quitting?"

Dana smiled. "You were always a quick learner. Nothing escapes your trained legal eye."

"You can't quit. Where will you go? If you think I'm going to let you take a single scrap of paper out of here, a single client, think again."

Dana turned to him. "Marvin, you are a pompous ass. For three years, you've been trying to fire me. Now you're trying to keep me? Without the specter of employment, do you think there is any chance that you could intimidate me?" She stepped from behind her desk and approached him. He eyed her with caution. His feet, anchored by male ego, refused to budge, but his upper body leaned away from her. "I have a job, a good job with a strong salary, stock options, and flexible work hours. They've even agreed to my suggestion that they include a day care at the facility for employees. I can take my daughter there and see her during the day as much as I choose."

Crocket scoffed, "You're dreaming. Those places don't exist."

"Don't they? Why don't you call Don Burnside and ask him if that place exists?"

"Corrugate Industries?" Crocket said with alarm. "You wouldn't dare."

"I didn't have to. Don called me. He loved my presentation, and truth be told, I think he likes my blue eyes. I begin next week as in-house counsel. Linda will be coming with me."

Crocket's bottom jaw hung near his chest.

Dana went on. "Look at the positives. You got rid of us both, which is what you wanted. And I won't be taking any of the firm's files. I will, however, be in need of outside counsel to assist with litigation and business matters.

I can't possibly handle the legal issues confronting what has grown to a multimillion-dollar business on my own. Send me your résumé. I'll consider it."

She winked at him, then went back behind her desk and picked up a letter opener. "Now, if you don't mind," she said, turning to him, "I need to finish clearing out my office, and I would appreciate it if you would knock before you barge in here."

Epilogue

༄

W HAT SHE NOTICED was how easily her blouse buttoned. Putting the small glass bead into the stitched hole required little effort at all. Dana held up her hand and examined it. No shakes. Not the slightest movement. They had performed another mammogram, this time with a small wire inserted into her breast to identify the exact location of the cancerous bump. The surgeon would remove the bump in the morning. It had hurt like hell, but Dana felt at peace.

Her mother sat across the room in a chair, holding Molly in her lap. Her outward composure required a great deal more effort. When she wasn't entertaining Molly with a book, Kathy's lips moved, silently praying. Occasionally, she looked up at Dana and smiled, but not a word was spoken between them.

Dana finished buttoning her shirt, tucked it into her blue jeans, and sat next to her mother, holding her hand. There was nothing left but the waiting. After two weeks, she had overcome her feeling that Robert Meyers had cheated her—that his death had been a false justice, without the satisfaction of finding him responsible for her brother's death. She had wanted him punished like any other American. Like Martha Stewart's trial and the trial of the Enron executives, it would have proved once and for all that a justice system designed by the people and for the people actually worked for all the people. But that had been a selfish desire, and she had realized it in that horrifying moment when she thought Meyers would kill Elizabeth Meyers.

There had been no blood tests performed on Elizabeth Meyers or her unborn child. There had not been time. Dana had bluffed, knowing from her years as a lawyer that the threat of such information, taken in context with Meyers's childhood medical records, would be sufficient to convince him there was enough evidence to convict him.

The door to the room opened. Her mother squeezed her hand. Dr. Bridgett Neal came in holding a mammogram in each hand, studying them intently. Neal walked in silence to the small counter at the back of the room, turned on the viewer on the wall, and snapped the two images in place. She stepped back and pondered the X-rays, one arm folded across her chest, the other arm bent, finger tips at her lips. Dana and her mother stood. Kathy put Molly on the blue plastic chair with a copy of Dr. Seuss's *Green Eggs and Ham*.

Dr. Neal took a deep breath and shook her head.

Kathy, no longer able to control her instincts, shouted out her questions. "What is it? How bad is it?"

Dr. Neal turned to the two women. "They can't find it."

Kathy's voice rose with alarm. "Can't find it? What do you mean?"

Dana squeezed her mother's hand. "Mom, calm down."

"They can't find the lump," Neal said. "And neither can I."

The pain of having her breast flattened between the two plates of glass with a needle and wire inserted through it remained fresh in Dana's mind. "Don't tell me I have to go through that again."

"No. No. The technicians are confident they have all the X-rays they need. They have every possible angle."

"Then why can't they find it?" Dana asked.

Neal shrugged. "Because the lump is no longer there."

Kathy put both hands to her mouth.

"What do you mean, not there?" Dana asked.

"It's gone. It's completely gone." Neal's face contorted in a pained expression. "It's possible, I suppose, that it was some type of cyst and, when punctured, over time, shrank, but…"

As Bridgett Neal defined in medical possibilities what could have happened to the cancerous lump in Dana's breast, Dana heard a different voice, the voice of a troll-like English gentleman. She felt William Welles's hand on her arm and heard him whisper in her ear as he handed her the bag of tea: *Drink it every day with sugar until it is gone.*

Dana had finished the bag that morning. She and her mother each had a cup. She had assumed Welles had meant to drink the tea until it was gone, but she now understood that wasn't what he had meant at all.

Neal continued, "I have to tell you, however, that I have never seen this before. In fifteen years of practice, I have never seen a lump just disappear. Nor have I misdiagnosed a cyst. Dana?"

"Hmm?"

"I know this must be a shock to you. I can't explain it, I'm sorry."

Dana smiled. "Don't be. I'm not."

"I feel badly that I put you through this. I don't know what could have happened."

"Some things in life can't be explained, Dr. Neal. It's why we still have miracles."

Neal shook her head. "As much as I would like to believe you, I have to caution you not to get too carried away with this. I'm sure there is a diagnostic explanation, and I will continue to review your records and the prior images. In the interim, I am recommending that you have a mammogram every four months for the next year, and every six months thereafter."

Dana smiled. "Then I'll see you in four months." She walked to where Molly sat.

"Green eggs and ham," Molly said, showing her the book.

Dana picked up the little girl and hugged her, then turned to her mother. "Let's go home."

As Dana emerged from the Cancer Care Center, she saw the green sports car parked at the curb beneath a no-parking sign. Only a cop could get away with that. Detective Michael Logan leaned against the Austin Healey holding a huge bouquet of red roses, smiling.

Kathy reached over and took Molly, setting the little girl down and holding her hand. "Go," she said to Dana.

"Are you sure?"

"Go. Carmen will watch her." At Elizabeth Meyers's

request, Kathy had hired Carmen Dupree, who would not leave her beloved Seattle for Los Angeles, professing that the smog would kill her. But living on the lake, she said, was something she could get used to. The pay was room and board. In return, Carmen baked apple pies and cared for Molly like her own. She told Dana she would teach the little girl the secret ingredients of her pies.

"I have to get ready for tonight. Dr. Porter has asked me to the symphony," Kathy said, smiling.

Dana hugged her mother, then knelt and kissed her daughter. "I'll be back later, honey. We have to help Grandma get ready for her big date."

"Grandmas don't have dates," Molly said.

"Yours does," Dana said. "Make sure you feed Freud and Leonardo. Just one can each this time. They're getting too fat."

The little girl stood holding her grandmother's hand. Dana hugged her mother again, then turned to the car. When she reached Logan, she was unable to keep from grinning. "My divorce isn't final yet."

Logan handed her the roses. "I know."

"Grant is going to make this difficult."

"I know."

"I have a child."

"I know."

Dana laughed. "And one hell of a lot of baggage."

Logan turned and opened the car door for her. "I know."

As she lowered to get into the car, Dana heard her mother calling and turned to see Molly running down the sidewalk toward them, the little girl's short legs pumping furiously, Kathy in pursuit. Dana turned to Logan.

"Bring her," he said.

"Are you sure?"

"Absolutely. What little girl wouldn't love a tree house?"

Dana loaded Molly into the Austin Healey, sharing the seat with her. As they sped off, Molly looked up at the sky in amazement. "Mommy, we're flying. Just like the birds."

Dana laughed and cradled her tightly. "You're breaking the law, Detective."

Logan looked over at her. "Yeah, how's that?"

"No child seat." She looked at the back, which didn't exist. "No seat, period."

He shrugged. "I've been meaning to get a bigger car. Perhaps you could help me pick it out, Molly?"

The little girl smiled. "Can I have an ice cream?"

Logan looked at his watch. "After lunch. You don't want to spoil your appetite."

Dana smiled. Was there anything not to like about him?

As they sped across the I-90 bridge, Molly squealed with delight. "Look at the boats."

Dana looked at Logan. "She's having fun."

"How about you? Are you having fun?"

She nodded. "More than I've had in a long time."

They took the exit for Cougar Mountain and started up the hill. Molly kept her head tilted to the sky, partially obscured by the tips of trees and overhanging branches.

"What is that?" Logan asked the question as they made the final turn to the front of the house.

Dana lowered her gaze and saw the metal sculpture at the entrance to Michael Logan's home, the same sculpture that had stood outside the entrance to William Welles's home. Logan parked the car, and the three of them got out and walked around it.

"What the heck is it?" Logan asked.

As she circled it, Dana watched the strips of metal bending and twisting, melding together as they had done that day on the mountain above Maui. Before she could answer, Molly spoke.

"They're dolphins, Mommy."

And Dana saw them. Two adult dolphins, their bodies entwined around each other, and a third, smaller dolphin below them. "Yes, they are," Dana said. "That's exactly what they are."

Acknowledgments

∽

ON A WARM AND SUNNY Sunday morning in July 1992, while I lay in bed reading the sports section, my telephone rang. It was my sister Susie. My sister's role, as a doctor, in my large family has since become medical guardian and bearer of bad news. But fifteen years ago my family had experienced little such news and I remained blissfully oblivious to the possibility.

"I have bad news," Sue said that morning. "Mom has cancer."

To illustrate my naïveté, my first question was "Is it bad?"

Cancer, I have come to learn, is never good.

The doctors had found a lump in my mother, Patty's, breast during a routine examination. She had undergone a mammogram and a needle biopsy with the expectation that it was a cyst. A full biopsy proved that expectation wrong. The doctors gave my mother two choices—a lumpectomy or mastectomy. At sixty, with a handicapped son still living at home whose future my mother worries about daily, she chose the mastectomy. Her treatment would include chemotherapy. The oncologist added, unsolicited, "And yes, you will lose your hair."

For the next eight months my mother underwent Friday-afternoon chemotherapy treatments. She would sleep and fight sickness over the weekend, then get up Monday morning and go to her office as a CPA. A self-proclaimed "tough old Irish lady," she missed just one day at the office and refused to let any of her ten children see her suffer. Every phone call I made resulted in the same report. "I'm fine," she'd say. "I'm fine." Eventually, she would be.

In 1996 she had breast reconstruction surgery. She did it not so much for herself, but for her four daughters. My eldest sister, Aileen, had several breast lump scares. My mother wanted her daughters to know that cancer did not have to be a death sentence, or leave them deformed.

Eight years later we would all learn an ugly truth about the nondiscriminating, heartless disease.

In December 2003, just before a family cruise, my cousin Russ's wife, Lynn Dugoni, just forty years old and the mother of two grade-school-age boys, Eric and Paul, felt a lump under her left arm. The lump was malignant. The diagnosis was small-cell carcinoma. Lynn had the lump removed in February, and the day after her forty-first birthday an oncologist prescribed a rigorous twice a week, four-month chemotherapy treatment. On August 24 Lynn had a mastectomy and her lymph nodes removed. Four days after her surgery, Lynn got out of bed and traveled to San Francisco to participate in a gala celebration for my uncle Art. I saw her there, had breakfast with her the next morning. She looked to me as she always did—beautiful and optimistic and full of life. I gave her holy water I had brought back from a pilgrimage to Lourdes, France, with my handicapped brother. I fully expected I would see Lynn again.

Lynn's lymph nodes tested positive for cancer. She underwent a second round of chemotherapy. By Christmas she regained strength and started to recoup. She and Russ and the boys vacationed in Lake Tahoe. Lynn complained of back pain. New Year's Day the pain became so extreme she could not get out of bed. On January 3 she was admitted to the hospital. Her cancer had spread.

Over the course of the next three weeks my cousins Mary and Diane and my own sisters provided my family in Seattle with daily updates on Lynn's condition. I sent her Saint Catherine's medal—The Miracle Medal, a gift I had received while in Lourdes. But Lynn's body was too weak, her blood count too low, to receive further treatment. The doctors sent her home.

Lynn left for heaven January 28, 2005, at 10:30 p.m. Russ and his two sons buried her February 2—two days before his fiftieth birthday.

I continue to believe in miracles. I've come to learn there is no miracle for cancer. My father, Bill, the best man you'll ever meet, now battles melanoma. Lifelong friend Barbara Martin fought and survived breast cancer. Other friends have called to deliver the same bad news my sister delivered fifteen years ago.

There is no cure—yet. Perhaps someday there will be. A donation has been made to the Susan G. Komen Breast Cancer Foundation in the names of Patricia and Lynn Dugoni. I encourage all to do the same.

As always, there are many to thank—Northwest Publishing consultant and good friend Jennifer McCord always looks after me. The Jane Rotrosen Agency—Don Cleary and Jane Rotrosen and the gang—make it a team effort, and my agent, Meg Ruley, continues to amaze me with her boundless optimism, energy, and wonderful sense of humor. You make it fun. To the talented people at the Hachette/Warner Book Group—Publisher Jamie Raab and my editor, Colin Fox, who've made me feel at home. To the copyediting team that makes me look smart, to Ann Twomey, who continues to design interesting covers, to Rebecca Oliver for ensuring my work is read in numerous foreign countries, and to everyone in publicity, particularly Lisa Sciambra, I am appreciative and thankful.

Here in Seattle, to all the boys in the Sacred Heart men's group—good friends who have prayed faithfully for my family members, and who stand by with beers and cigars ready to celebrate my accomplishments. To all at Schiffrin, Olson, Schlemlein, Hopkins and Goetz, who help keep the lights on. And to my own wife and children, who have been with me each step of this journey. May God bless you all and keep you safe.